POETRY

LONDON

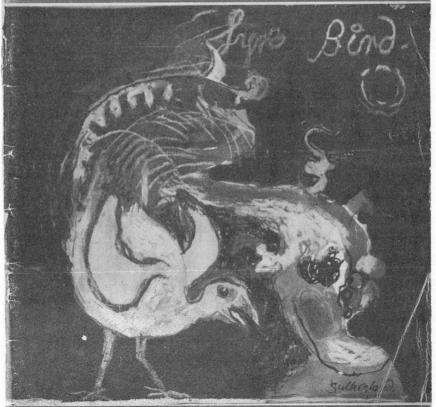

NUMBER NINE PL **TWO SHILLINGS NET**

NICHOLSON & WATSON

Tambimuttu

Tambimuttu

Bridge between Two Worlds

Edited and with a Preface by
JANE WILLIAMS

INTRODUCTION by
ROBIN WATERFIELD

Consultant Editor KATHLEEN RAINE

Peter Owen · London

ISBN 0 7206 0718 3

This edition is limited to 1000 copies

PETER OWEN PUBLISHERS
73 Kenway Road London SW5 0RE

First published in Great Britain 1989
This collection © Jane Williams 1989

Printed in Great Britain by St Edmundsbury Press Limited, Bury St Edmunds, Suffolk.

Acknowledgements

First of all my thanks go to Robin Waterfield, whose idea it was to produce a Festschrift in memory of Tambimuttu, for his advice and encouragement on various trips I made to Oxford to consult him as I gathered in all the material over a considerable period of time. I am grateful to Sebastian Barker, who at strategic times has somehow never failed intuitively to know precisely what to say at the right time to help me. But most of all I am indebted to Kathleen Raine, who has staunchly supported me through so many difficulties and crises during the past few years as slowly the book has come together, and, when at times I felt daunted and like giving up, encouraged me to keep going.

I am grateful to Lord Moyne, the Henry Moore Foundation and Jack Barker for making it possible to include colour plates through financial help, and to Bill Tokeshi, an old friend of Tambimutti's in New York, for financial help in the early stages.

Finally, this book would not exist if it were not for Tambimuttu's very wide circle of loyal friends, so many of whom, either as contributors to the book or as well-wishers, have given help and encouragement in different ways, especially Bettina Shaw-Lawrence, Bob Kingdom, Mel Gooding, my Indian Arts Council friends Balraj Khanna, Maria Souza and Bhavani Torpy in London, and Rakshat Puri in New Delhi. I should like to mention many more, but such a list would be too long to include here. I know they all join me in offering this gift of friendship and tribute to Tambimuttu and his life's work.

J.W.

'The Coming to Birth of the Spirit' by Dr Ananda K. Coomaraswamy was first published in *D. R. Bhandarkar Volume*, edited by B. C. Law, Indian Research Institute, Calcutta, 1940, and contained extensive notes which it has not been possible to include in the present volume. It is reprinted with the kind permission of Dr Rama P. Coomaraswamy.

'Poets under the Bed' by Lawrence Durrell originally appeared as an obituary in *The Sunday Times*, 26 June 1983. It is reprinted by permission of Times Newspapers Ltd.

'On a Ledge' by Bryan Guinness was first published in *The Irish Times* in 1980, under the title 'The Finger-tips'.

Nicholas Moore's poem 'Dreamscape' is printed by permission of Peter Riley. 'Tambi the Knife' was written by Nicholas Moore specially for this book.

The extract from 'Dig a Grave and Let Us Bury Our Mother' by Elizabeth Smart first appeared in her book *In the Meantime*, published by Denis Deneau, Toronto, 1984. Her poem 'What Is Art? Said Doubting Tim' first appeared in *Eleven Poems*, published by Owen Kirton, 1982. Both these contributions are reprinted by permission of Sebastian Barker.

'Fitzrovia' by Tambimuttu appeared in its original form in the February 1975 issue of *Harpers & Queen*. Tambimuttu's poem 'For Katharine (*Kamala*) Bennett and All True *Sadhakas*' first appeared in *Festschrift for KFB*, edited by Tambimuttu and published by the Lyrebird Press, 1972.

The checklist of Editions Poetry London and Poetry London 1939–1951 publications, compiled by Alan Smith, was originally published in *ABMR* (*Antiquarian Book Monthly Review*), April/May 1979. The photograph of Tambimuttu reproduced at the front of this section is by Hugh Miles.

Peter Owen Limited gratefully acknowledge the assistance of the Arts Council of Great Britain in the publication of this book.

The publishers also wish to acknowledge with thanks contributions made by Mr Jack Barker, the Henry Moore Foundation and Lord Moyne towards the cost of reproducing illustrations.

Preface

> 'Every man has poetry within him. Poetry is the awareness
> of the mind to the universe. It embraces everything in the
> world.... It is a universal force and like God it can never be
> *discovered*, although it will always be present directing
> thought.... Poetry is a descent to the roots of life.' –
> Tambimuttu, *Poetry*, No. 1 (February 1939)

With these words, taken from his First Letter and at the age of only
twenty-three, Tambimuttu launched *Poetry London*. The first number
of the magazine, which included poets such as Dylan Thomas,
Stephen Spender, Herbert Read, George Barker, Gavin Ewart,
Lawrence Durrell and others, created more than a stir in the literary
scene of the time. I quote from Dylan Thomas: 'I congratulate you a
lot on the handsomest "intelligent" poetry magazine I know of, and
on the courage of your unfashionable introduction.... *You've* shown,
in your introduction, how much you believe in the good of poetry and
the mischief of cliques, rackets, scandal schools, menagerie menages,
amateur classes of novitiate plagiarists, etc. More subscribers and
power to you.' John Gawsworth: 'Such a platform for free speech as
Poetry is extremely desirable at the present time. It has begun a needed
service which I hope will achieve a far-reaching influence.' And
Lawrence Durrell: 'The real excellence of *Poetry* lies in the fact that you
have created a forum capable of accommodating every kind of poet
writing today; and in doing so you have given the lie to those poetical
axe-grinders, theorists and critical fish-slices who have imagined that
poetry is really a manner, and that no one without that manner can
possibly be a poet.'

Tambimuttu was born on 15 August 1915 into an aristocratic
family of distinguished scholars with a long tradition in the arts. The
great Jesuit lexicographer, Gnana Prakasar, whose image at one time
appeared on German stamps, was his uncle, as was the famous

Indologist, Dr Ananda K. Coomaraswamy. A meticulous family tree traces the family back to the kings of Jaffna, north Sri Lanka, in the thirteenth century. Tambimuttu was brought up a Roman Catholic and was educated mainly in English, with an emphasis on English literature and history. From an early age and despite the discouragement and disapproval of his English teachers, he sought out the ancient history of his homeland and his Hindu roots, with which he identified for the rest of his life, although he never actually rejected the heart of his Christian faith. In an autobiographical piece 'Swami Rock, Raga Rock', printed here, he gives us a truly evocative account of those formative years.

By the age of twenty-one Tambimuttu had already published three volumes of poetry, having set the type himself for printing at the press of his grandfather, from which he had developed a love of fine typesetting. He also ran a theatre for the village, in which his own operas in verse were performed, and composed a whole jazz musical, all in English.

It was Robin Waterfield, who, when Tambimuttu died in June 1983, suggested immediately that the most fitting tribute to Tambimuttu would be to prepare a Festschrift in his honour, in the tradition of the celebratory books Tambimuttu prepared for others, such as T. S. Eliot, Marianne Moore and his partner and co-founder of the Lyrebird Press, Katharine Falley Bennett. Yet while I have called freely on the advice of Robin Waterfield and Kathleen Raine, among many others, the book has evolved in an organic way far beyond its original concept into a substantial portrait of Tambimuttu. Within these pages, through the many sidelights on his complex personality, I believe something of the essence of Tambimuttu emerges – as best expressed in his own writings, which I am especially happy to include in this book – that deeper part which he kept quietly to himself. As Betty Relle says: 'Tambi never talked to me in a deeper way about his work, and when "off-duty" he played very much on the outside. But when I come to think about it there was a tremendous depth to him.' This is expressed, or sometimes merely hinted at, by many contributors. Their views are of course subjective and I do not agree with all of them; but I have made no attempt to exclude references to Tambi's weaknesses or faults, since they help give us a composite picture of him.

The pieces in this book fall mainly into the four main phases of Tambimuttu's life: his childhood in Sri Lanka; the *Poetry London* of the war years and just after, leading up to about 1949; Tambimuttu's life in America from 1952 to the late sixties; and his return to England about 1970 until his death in 1983, with special reference to his very successful trip to India the previous year. Tambimuttu's own writings will be found at the beginning and end of the book. The war years of *Poetry London* magazine and Editions Poetry London is the period which is most substantially represented, as this was the time when Tambimuttu established himself and with which many of his friends identify him. Of equal importance are the other phases of his life, through which we can trace, by means of his own writings and those of his friends and colleagues, the development of his character and his philosophical thinking.

This is particularly true of America. Tambimuttu's second wife, Safia, whom he had married in India, describes their life together on arrival in New York in 1952, where they soon became a celebrated couple with a wide range of friends. Tambi was invited to guest lecture and give talks at academic and literary institutions as widespread as Mount Allison University in Canada, Brown University in Connecticut and New York University. It was a time when Tambimuttu settled down to writing his autobiographical short stories, several of which appeared in American magazines like *The New Yorker*, a whole book of them having been commissioned by a leading American publisher. Before long, however, he was distracted from this work by an irresistible urge to start his magazine again – this time under the title *Poetry London/New York* – notwithstanding the financial stress it would induce. It was to result in the break-up of his marriage to Safia.

There followed another marriage, to Esta, who has also contributed to the present volume, during which Tambimuttu's only daughter Shakuntala was born. They were hard times for Tambi and Esta, and after the breakdown of this marriage there followed a period during which Tambimuttu stayed at Timothy Leary's LSD centre at Millbrook. While writing this Preface I came upon a sheet of paper in Tambimuttu's own handwriting, written at Shakespeare & Co. in Paris, which was obviously a part of his memoirs, never completed. It describes how, when he was on his way back from a visit to Rammurti Mishra's Hindu ashram at Monroe near New York and had dropped in at Millbrook, he was waylaid and, to his surprise, was immediately voted Vice-President of the centre! The role he played there at their invitation, as their 'guru' conducting meditations, was one he took seriously and with which the Hindu in him closely identified. Timothy Leary's piece in this book tells of their special friendship and his love and respect for Tambi.

It was typical of Tambimuttu that, despite the changing fortunes of life in North America, he never relinquished his publishing activities. Towards the end of his stay in the United States, Tambimuttu lived in Cambridge, Massachusetts. It was while he was there that he wrote his exquisite 'Gita Sarasvati', certainly my favourite of all his writings, which contains the core of his philosophy. In 1968 he was invited to apply for the post of running the Poetry Room at Harvard, and had been told that it was as good as in his pocket. Among his many supporters was Dwight MacDonald, who hoped for 'a whole new school of Cambridge poets to poke their heads up under his ministrations', and Allen Ginsberg even wrote to Tambimuttu, 'care of Harvard'. However, in the end Tambi did not get the appointment.

In 1960 Edith Sitwell had written to him: 'We need you in London. The bosh purporting to be verse, and matter about poetry gets worse every day, and needs some corrective influence. I wish to goodness you would come back!' Yet it was a stroke of fate that caused him eventually to settle down again in London around 1970 after at least eighteen years in the United States. He had intended to come to London on a business trip to sell his memoirs, but instead he made plans to launch the Lyrebird Press with his American partner, Katharine Falley Bennett. Paving the way for this venture came the complete reprint by Frank Cass of *Poetry London* magazine in five volumes, which is still available.

It was in 1972, just before the Lyrebird Press launching, that I met Tambimuttu. The small flat-cum-office in Cornwall Gardens, South Kensington, was a flurry of activity, as he worked with his very efficient assistant, Rosie Hunter, and his typographer/designer, Charles Blackburn. Day and night a steady stream of well-known writers, artists, poets and personal friends came and went. When Tambimuttu was in the throes of intense creative activity he would sometimes work almost obsessively with little regard for his physical health. His magnetism was impossible to resist and I, like so many others before me, would find myself assisting him and turning my hand to things I never thought I would or could do. He had a special gift of being able to draw out the latent qualities and creative talents in others, with personal friends as well as writers and artists. He was prone to occasional alarming outbursts of terrible temper, and while I was drawn to the spirituality in him to which I have referred, I found him a little frightening at first, too. However, I soon came to appreciate his basic gentleness. I recall that after having 'sacked' me as a temporary shorthand typist when I first met him because I could not understand his dictation, I was told by 'Blackie' to knock on his door and say goodbye before I left. 'He's a very gentle person, really,' said Blackie. I did so, gingerly, and Tambi opened the door. I wished him the best of luck with the Lyrebird Press, at which his brown eyes softened. He was clearly touched. He gave one of his typical little laughs, told me to come in, and searched out a press cutting for me and signed it. He then asked me to come for a drink with him and Blackie and that's how my friendship with him started. But despite all the excitement and activity, I sensed a profound loneliness and a sadness in Tambi I felt powerless to reach.

Almost inevitably, the financial crisis came, as a result of emotional stress and the lack of vital managerial organization in London. But with Tambimuttu there was always, whatever the odds, something happening. There was the wonderful de-luxe edition of *India Love Poems*, illustrated by John Piper, which sold at £250 a copy (£450 with an original Piper painting), produced by David Frost's Paradine Publications, a copy of which was presented personally to the Queen by David Frost; the writing of the 'Fitzrovia' piece for *Harper's & Queen*, reprinted in this book, which was to form the first part of his memoirs, linked with Anne Barr's visits; and meetings with Lawrence Durrell, full of encouragement for Tambi's plans to relaunch *Poetry London*.

October 1979 saw the launching of *Poetry London/Apple Magazine* No. 1, the 'Apple' section coming from a plan Tambimuttu had originally made with the Beatles in New York before they changed managers. He was assisted by the late Dhiren Bhagat, still then at Oxford and later to become New Delhi correspondent for *The Observer* and *Spectator*, as well as Sebastian Barker and myself. Shortly afterwards, the October Gallery, with their community atmosphere of co-operation which Tambimuttu loved, lent him an office, where he hoped to edit the new series of *Poetry London*. There followed the preparation of a special book to mark the wedding of Lady Diana Spencer to Prince Charles. Unfortunately it was never published, since the promised funds did not materialize.

There was one further issue of *Poetry London/Apple Magazine* in 1982. It is a pity it did not carry Tambimuttu's last editorial, which was never completed. In that same year Tambimuttu embarked on a trip to India, accompanied by his only daughter Shakuntala, to seek material for an Indian number of *Poetry London/Apple Magazine*. It was a visit which meant a great deal to him, and he was welcomed there with open arms and to a blaze of publicity. He was guest of honour at the Gandhi Peace Foundation, where he gave a talk, was featured on television and in the press, and entertained by goverment ministers and leading figures in the arts. And he had a private audience with Mrs Ghandi, who gave him money to travel through India. It was while he was on this trip that Tambimuttu laid plans for the establishment of the Indian Arts Council – with a committee in New Delhi consisting of various top figures in the arts and government, and later, in May 1983, a committee in London – whose purpose was to establish a bridge for the increase of cross-cultural understanding between the great tradition of art and culture of the Indian subcontinent and the West. Tragically, after the first two inaugural meetings, which were supported by Sri Varadarajan and S. N. Chakraborti of the Indian High Commission, by Tambimuttu's friend Caroline Hamblett as Acting Secretary, and many leading figures representing the art and culture of the Indian subcontinent in London, as well as personal friends, Tambimuttu had a fall in his office. A few days later he died in hospital of a heart attack. It is significant, and very typical of him, that on the night before he died he dictated from his hospital bed several letters to Bhavani Torpy from the Sri Chinmoy Group, having just heard that the Indian High Commissioner at the time, Dr Seyid Muhammad, had agreed to become a Patron along with Yehudi Menuhin and Lord Harewood. The IAC now has its permanent premises in Marchmont Street, Bloomsbury, incidentally one of the first streets in London where Tambimuttu lived when he arrived in England in 1938.

My last full evening with Tambimuttu had been at the Bharatiya Vidya Bhavan in West Kensington, where we watched a play by the Indian spiritual teacher, poet and painter Sri Chinmoy, called *The Son*, which was about the life of Christ as seen from an Indian perspective. It is described below by Bhavani Torpy.

Tambimuttu once said to me: 'I am the quiet stream. I leave my works by the wayside like flowers for other people to find.' For Tambimuttu, being an Oriental, there were no boundaries between the 'spiritual' and 'temporal' and no one has described this so well in the pages following as Kathleen Raine. The unity at the heart of all religions is a feature of Hindu philosophy, and this is expressed in the early part of Tambimuttu's very beautiful 'Gita Sarasvati'. It was therefore quite fitting that after his death there was both a Roman Catholic funeral and also a Hindu ceremony, although, not knowing of his Roman Catholic upbringing, most of his friends identified with the Hindu ceremony held by the Registrar of the Bharatiya Vidya

Bhavan, Sri Mathoor Krishnamurti. He spoke of their affection for Tambi, and how they had come to respect him and appreciate his special qualities in the frustratingly short time they knew him. It was also significant that when his friend John Sharkey, writer on Celtic mythology, heard Tambi had died, he immediately made his way to a Samye Ling Tibetan monastery to keep vigil.

I am proud to include, as a special tribute to Tambimuttu, an important article by Dr Ananda K. Coomaraswamy on the subject 'The Coming to Birth of the Spirit' and, appropriately, Dr Coomaraswamy refers to various sacred writings, including Christian ones. His piece has not previously appeared in the West.

There are some sixty contributors to this volume, and there could easily have been sixty more – or even 240! It would be impossible to make such a collection fully representative. But there are contributions by many who played an important part in Tambimuttu's life: from Miriam de Saram, one of Tambi's oldest friends from his youth in Sri Lanka, to his assistant during the Nicholson & Watson Editions Poetry London days, Nicholas Moore, and, I am glad to say, two ex-secretaries – Betty Relle (previously Betty Jesse), who later became Production Manager for Nicholson & Watson, and Helen Irwin (previously Helen Scott). I should also like to mention especially Tambi's great friend, the late Anthony Dickins, co-founder of *Poetry London* with Tambi and General Editor of the first two issues. Tambimuttu's first wife, Jacqueline Stanley, mentioned with affection by several of the contributors, died while he was in the United States, but there are contributions from Tambimuttu's second wife, Safia Tambimuttu, and his third wife, Esta Busi. There is also a contribution from Bettina Shaw-Lawrence, the artist, representing the Shaw-Lawrences, whom Tambimuttu regarded as his 'English family'.

I should have liked to have had more contributions from the United States and India. I think these areas are under-represented and do not give a balanced picture, for which I have tried to compensate a little. Some contributions have had to be omitted for various reasons, such as limitations of space, but it is a triumph that we have been able to include so many.

For me Tambimuttu's greatest quality was that he never lost faith with his vision, and never compromised it. His first editorial in *Poetry London* No. 1 should of course be read in full for a proper understanding of his philosophy. He was generous and kind, but in search for that divine spark of creative imagination, in various media of the arts, he would accept nothing less than what he was looking for

– no matter who they were or whatever the stakes. I remember the occasion when considerable private funding was in the balance for the revival of *Poetry London/Apple Magazine*. There were, I was told, four people in the room: Tambi, a rich new acquaintance with his friend who could influence him, and their mutual friend and helper. The atmosphere was very tense. The friend with the 'influence', a rather proud and conceited young man, decided to present Tambi with his poetry. There was a heavy pause. Then, slowly, Tambi looked up, and remarked bluntly: 'You don't know how to write poetry.' The 'mutual friend' lay flat on the floor of the office, waiting for the walls to fall in! If the poems had been good, Tambi would have said so. They weren't – and the money didn't come!

The one thing Tambi could not stand, and which provoked great anger in him, was phoniness of any kind, or hypocrisy, and I have seen him lash out at people when he felt they were not being true to themselves or their art. He was a mirror to falsity of any kind – unbearable to some whose defence was to be patronizing, slighting, or to those who refused to take him seriously or were simply jealous of him.

Tambimuttu understood the Eastern notion of the 'Impersonal'. For many of us, the concept can be frightening, so attached are we to the 'individual' identity. He expressed it himself in these words: 'I am not a person: I am a mood, a weather, an accent of the mind.' He was a great spirit: a man with a vision, who lived it through to the end.

Jane Williams

Contents

Illustrations

In the text

The endpapers show covers of some early editions of *Poetry London*. Nos. 7, 11 and 12 are reproduced by permission of the Henry Moore Foundation; No. 9 is reproduced by permission of Kathleen Sutherland.

Nos. 7 and 12 use the same drawing by Henry Moore. The lettering and feathers on No. 7 are red, with touches of green; on No. 12 the colours are blue and chalk white.

Introduction

Let us celebrate a miracle: here it all is in print at last, and nobly produced and illustrated as its inspirer would have wished. And only six years after his death, a delay which he would have countenanced and not have felt excessive. I cannot quite overcome, and no doubt some of the contributors will feel the same, a sense of amazement that it has actually reached this stage of completeness. Most of the contributors will probably have long forgotten what they wrote, one at least has died, and all will commend the tenacity of Jane Williams – helped by me in the early stages – who must surely have been inspired by the spirit of Tambi, that relentless searcher for perfection.

Tambimuttu was truly a man of two worlds, and what is rare, articulate and relevant in all he wrote about both of them. Descended from the kings of Jaffna in Ceylon and heir to centuries of Hindu culture, he nevertheless was educated in English and brought up as a Catholic. Consequently he conceived a genuine love for and under-standing of Western literature, especially poetry. He was an inspired editor and his magazine *Poetry London* was influential in releasing English poetry from its middle-class, academic, narrow confines and allowing the free wind of inspiration to blow through the fusty rooms where poets had hitherto congregated. His list of contributors was virtually a catalogue of all the most innovative poets from Dylan Thomas onwards.

Tambi was also, as are all Hindus, deeply imbued with a mystical sense of the reality behind the passing show of life and literature. He saw poetry as a means of reaching this deeper reality, and his own contributions to this book are perhaps its most important part.

What struck me when I renewed my aquaintance with Tambi in 1973 after my return from sixteen years in Iran, was how utterly and essentially Hindu he was. How good it is to have not only his own writings but those of his wife and some of his Indian and Ceylonese friends; more lively, more direct, more illuminating perhaps than

21

some of the Western contributors. For let us all admit it, we Westerners were perpetually puzzled by Tambi. There was a dimension we could guess at but could not share. That dimension can only be described as 'spiritual', that all-embracing medium in which the Hindu lives, however worldly and secular and unreligious he or she may be, and nevertheless treats as absolutely natural and as essential for them as the air they breathe. So much so that it hardly ever surfaces in conversation, and yet is an invisible attribute which separates the possessors from their secularized, materialistic, aspiritual friends in the West. For most of his friends this attribute of Tambi's was only guessed at, or at best half understood. His own writings, printed here, give us a new insight both into the confusing mixture of East and West in Tambi's education and early years in Ceylon, and into the way in which all this remained a surface influence which left untouched the deep centuries-old Hindu inheritance which was the mainstay of Tambi's life.

Tambi's American and European friends saw him as a cultural phenomenon, strange to them, a Tamil with a love for English literature and a driving energy, at least in his early years, to revive the art of English poetry and release it from the seeming sterility and provinciality of the Auden years. It is significant, I think, that Tambi did not have much success in the United States where, for half a century, they had experienced the effects of cultural influences from all over the world and where maybe Tambi seemed no more than the latest of a long line of gurus, shamans and avant-garde entrepreneurs who rise and fall continuously on the American scene. England and wartime were the ideal confined place and time for Tambi to be and to do what he set out to do.

But perhaps when the spiritual history of the West is written he will be seen as one more example of the counter-attack of Hinduism against the spiritual and cultural imperialism of the Empire builders and their attendant missionaries. To us Christians, for whom the sacred and secular are firmly held apart, the idea of a spiritual man who spent a lot of his life in pubs, drunk or semi-drunk, and was unashamedly promiscuous, is ludicrous. There is no doubt that Tambi would have rejected any such designation as guru or holy man, for it is the essence of the spirituality to which Tambi was heir that, as I have said, it is part of the very fabric of its possessor's life; an attitude of mind and an instinctive guide to practice and behaviour rather than any set religious beliefs backed by doctrine and dogma which define and exclude all those who don't share them. This inclusiveness which is typical of Hinduism worked itself out in Tambi as a belief in everything and everyone. The last example I recall was a grant given to Tambi from somewhere, for editorial expenses, which he handed on to the window-cleaner of his flat to encourage him to write poetry; and I recall a Royal Literary Fund grant, most of which was spent on a lunch for Myfanwy Piper and her husband John.

Tambi in all essentials was to the Western, logical, rational, analytical mind, incomprehensible – he had just to be accepted, lived with, argued with, rejected in exasperation for a while, but subsequently found to be just as friendly and affectionate and forgiving as he ever had been. He may have borne grudges; he certainly didn't like some people; but he was enormously tolerant of himself, of his friends and, I sincerely believe, of his enemies and those who couldn't stand his inchoate life-style and irresponsible obstinacy in search of his ideal.

RIP seems the least appropriate wish for this restless spirit who is, I have little doubt, pursuing newer and still wider dreams of perfection in whatever realm he now finds himself.

Robin Waterfield

Sketch of Tambimuttu by Feliks Topolski. 50 × 32 cm, charcoal heightened with white, about 1972. (Original in Tambimuttu estate)

Tambimuttu

My Country, My Village

When I was young, the flame-tree and the jasmin
Gilded my youthful eyes with tenderness
For natural things – the lotus-pond and the palmyra:
The ring-dove tore the air with natural passion;
At Atchuvely, my Northern home, all else
Seemed unimportant beside a bassia star.

The carrion eagle atop the rambling lanes
Wheeled in the pastel sky, and a big owl
Dozed in a tree beside the tethered cow;
The goat coughed among the pecking hens
Of which I owned two, three; and morning's haul
Of eggs belonged to me, they said, for supper.

I had a goat too, a cow and Lakshmi,
Gentle, big-eyed mongrel of a dog;
And when she died I did not feel like supper –
And there was Aachi, wrinkled kind old Aachi.
At six, she told us stories about a frog
In a well: food slipped down like sweetened milk and guava.

Around our house the mango shoots were pink.
The big bassia dropped its blossom like snow.
The pomegranate spun its exciting wheel
Against the dropcloth of palmyra mink,
Between the oleander's and trumpet-lily's show
Pencil of grey areca nut, was wire of steel.

I was four or five, and grandfather, the poet,
In turban of gold and coat of black was a prince
Who was kind to us; he flicked the coiled whip,
And off we went down limestone white roads

25

Fringed with lantana eyes; from prints
He cut us paper dolls, with a clever snip.

Remember evenings in the theatre, his plays
Like Kalidasa's full of dance and song;
(My father once taking the leading role,
Great-uncle Thambar dancing with a painted face,
Agile as Nijinsky); his poems, a gong,
Stung me to listen to the metrics' whirl.

All this was home, and we were self-contained.
Our fields provided grain, tobacco, shallots,
Garlic, pepper, bay-leaves, ginger, saffron,
Yams, greens, herbs, fruits, famed
For delicacy and flavour. The seas filled with pots
And nets, rang in the whole sea's kingdom.

This was long ago. And there was home
Beside the Eastern harbour full of ships,
And pretty shells on the deserted lunar beach;
Goatsfoot underfoot, and a lyric poem
In the screw-pine smell. The harbour lips
Enclosed a town beyond the railroad's reach.

There was peace in Trincomalee too:
With leopard, deer and buffalo I roamed
The jungle paths with Elizam and my brothers;
And beyond were the dead cities, the clue
To ancient hubbub, now becalmed –
All the mighty dead Anuradhapuras.

Colombo. Ah, Colombo. Excrescence of Trade,
Competition, Endeavour – the pattern did not hold;
Chaos of many patterns, amorphous –
The island's harlot, and Empire's accolade
In those days; still you were home, a mould
That shaped me in the Western swirl and rush.

Colombo was home indeed. The silver lights
Etched the night's dark with fauns and delicate shapes,
The streets magical by the half-light;
And when the moon dispelled the grey nights,
Silver palms stood by elfin capes,
Proud and feminine in their lissom flight.

All this we loved, my friends, Noel, Rowan,
Tissa (a young school of friends);
All this was heaven, until we grew
And learnt the dog bit, the moon was ruin,
The gilt wore off, and all that magic lends
Is a false perspective, with the chocolate-box view.

And there was Nuwara Eliya, the new-found escape
With a trout stream in the well-kept park;
Upcot, Haputale, Maskeliya knew few rivals,
But, alas, the concrete base and rubber crêpe
Brought my village, all villages to mind, from far dark.
Self-contained, these knew no rivals.

So on this festive day, with bells and bunting,
I am wondering whether the hectic pace
Will give the peace and plenty that we seek;
Whether the brash plane and limousine affronting
Shiva in the wooden cart can grace,
Or start a new tear, on the ancient cheek.

Whether it's better to adorn the top or bottom,
To increase the village round, and soul's girth,
Or roundly add to world's hue and cry –
The bazaar's cheating, and the traffic's hum;
But, this is my island, this my native earth
That bore me gently from a woman's sigh.

Her eye a blackbird among the tumbling bushes,
Her lashes, the black silk of a deep night,
Her body the pure long scarf of Laxapana,
Lights of an ocean liner in her tresses,
Black tresses, filled with dark and light;
Cry, O cry, *Namo, Namo Matha.**

* Glory to thy Name, O Mother (Ceylon national song).

Tambimuttu

Swami Rock, Raga Rock

Swami Rock, which played a part in the shaping of my life, and my family's, was a wonder to me before I ever read of the other wonders of the world in the books at the Catholic school, in Trincomalee, where I was educated until I was seven. Admittedly the Franco-Ceylon atmosphere of the small school was exotic. The bearded priests, in white cassocks and dangling black sashes, which alternated with magenta, were French, with one Ceylonese and one Indian – Fr Bonnel, with white, tobacco-stained beard, stretching well below his navel, dispensing beautifully grained wooden kazoos from France (the sounding diaphragm was purple paper, of special manufacture, and there were whole orchestras of kazoos in France); Fr Dupont, from an industrialist family that manufactured textiles and candy, and his memorable present of a heraldic standard of silk for the school, woven in one of the family's factories, and, for the boys, chocolate with liqueur and brandy centres; handsome Fr Gregory, the Brahmin from India, later Prefect of Sports and Discipline, in my college in Colombo, first cousin to my favourite nun, Sister Dolores. But Swami Rock was more fulvous and fulsome, more exciting. Its bare-chested priests, wearing the sacred triple thread, chanting into the wind's throat, on top of the high cliff, and showering flowers into the shuddering sea, were echoes from millennia ago when one of the six great linga, or phallus, temples, sacred to India and Lord Shiva, stood on this spot.

Ceylonese history was not taught at school (we were cramming for the external examination of the Universities of Cambridge and London), and what history I was taught by my family, or learnt from the gossip and folk-tales of our own people, was scoffed at. Ours was only myth and legend, uncorroborated by scholarship and the archaeological finesse of Europe. Even the pioneer work of our own historians, my uncle S. Gnana Prakasar, for instance, exerted an influence only when he based his judgements on Portuguese, Dutch or British sources. Whatever our historians had gathered from Ceylon and Indian records was not history, since we claimed for ours an impossible antiquity.

28

Swami Rock, which had fired my imagination as a boy, was a case in point, along with many others, including statements in my grandfather's biography (at least I had treasured the photos – the two great-grandfathers I had never seen, the other two I had known and loved, especially the Hindu-orientated one) and points about my family's history which I had learnt from the lips of our ayahs as they fed me. Dinner-time was story-time out of sheer necessity, to keep our minds off the gestatory exercises, and it was confusing to me during my long school years that I had not seen any of the historical tales we had heard in print. They constituted 'embarrassing knowledge', making me uneasy and apprehensive of my own family.

It is only since Independence that there have been many interesting and probing articles about some of them in *The Ceylon Daily News* and *The Times of Ceylon*. It was only as recently as May 1967, for instance, that the latter journal sent me a scholarly version of one of my favourite dinner-time stories, the story about one of my ancestors, Pootha Tambi, descendant of Pararajasingham VIII, King of Jaffna. It was a stirring story for us children, involving the building of a fort on the romantic and magical island of Hammanhiel between India and Ceylon, a beautiful lady, his wife, who had sent a slipper back to a would-be lover (the worst form of insult) and the enraged man betraying Pootha Tambi's intended uprising to the Dutch governor with a forged letter. Pootha Tambi was convicted and executed on that evidence. The dramatic ending involved a herd of stampeding elephants. When the would-be lover was being led in chains through the jungle for trial in Colombo, he and his guards were killed by a herd of stampeding elephants, seemingly, but probably brought there for the deed by Pootha Tambi's supporters. Elephants were traditional executioners in Ceylon. But in those days, this bit of history was only myth and legend, along with Swami Rock, and it gave me the split personality very early in life which was characteristic of Ceylonese and Indians in colonial times.

Swami Rock, as I remember, is a giant, roughly spherical boulder, about eighteen feet across, with a pillar of the same granitic rock inserted in its middle, silhouetted starkly against pink and golden dawn skies, or those of brazen and burning sunsets, the skies of Sarasvati, the Goddess of Night. It had this simple, majestic and elemental setting, since it was built at the very edge of the cliff.

The monsoon tempests (Ceylon has two monsoons, unlike India) literally screamed past and the waves roared way, way down below, nearly at the centre of the earth where the Sunken Temple of Shiva now lay. The Portuguese, who had given similar treatment to my family in the sixteenth century, had vandalized it in their Christian zeal, hurling it into the sea, and using portions of it for the bastions and walls of what is now Fort Frederick, with Swami Rock within it. This, too, was only a Ceylonese legend, a silly story, and search as I might, and O how eagerly and often I did that as a boy, I never found a fragment of the magnificent carved granite pillars: only the smooth, accurate, sturdy and lasting architecture of the walls and bastions. I had also seen it in the Portuguese-Dutch-British forts in other parts of the island (they had settled in that order on the same sites, the French having been driven off) which only further drove home to me in strange, bewildering fashion the reality of European history versus our own, and the strength and vigour of European feats – even of foods, I believed, since I was told the eating of rice is debilitating and the eating of wheat strengthening. It is necessary to eat much meat to build strong muscle and plenty of fish to nourish the cells of the brain as the great seafaring nations did. The amount of fish and meat Europeans consumed at one sitting was impressive. We did not eat that much meat and fish, or so I had thought at the time, which further made me hesitant, embarrassed and even apologetic for our customs, manners, ceremonies, beliefs, even not eating fresh Scotch salmon which our 'elocution' teacher had extravagantly praised, our lack of history, the feeling stretching back to the years before I was seven, the creeping mist over the bright film of childhood.

Fort Frederick, to the north of our hibiscus-covered Dutch house with its great brick Dutch ovens and, to the south of it, Fort Ostenberg, high on the hill overlooking the third largest natural harbour in the world, large enough to float the entire British fleet, were the symbols of my boyhood predicament at Trincomalee. As I lay at night in that thick-walled and then walled-in-again house with the thick, curved tiles of terracotta that ran down its head like jazzed-up rivers of rufous hair (the one dominating note over that part of Trincomalee, as ever, the thunder of the waves of Eastern Bay in my ears), time and again Fort Frederick and Swami Rock bore into my vision, and I eagerly anticipated the next Sunday when I would be able to grub for some slight and precious evidence that the Sunken Temple bells still rang in that sea, and had once really existed.

We played games most evenings, or merely strolled on the lunar-shaped white beach of Eastern Bay. It was on Sundays that my brothers and I, and my Hindu friend Suppiah when he visited us, made the longer trek to the Fort and to Swami Rock. Although we were a very close family, who worked and played together, to the extent of publishing rival weeklies with interweaving threads of interests and comment, I don't know to this day whether my brothers shared my thoughts on Swami Rock and Fort Frederick. The subject, being Hindu, was *verboten*, perhaps, and that was another mandala of furious clarity in my confusion. I had been brought up to be proud of my family's Hindu heritage which had been besieged in 1505 and a few years later captured by the Portuguese. My ancestor and his five brothers, as children, were taken to Goa in India to be educated in the Catholic tradition before their return to Ceylon. I was told that St Francis Xavier's correspondence about him is preserved in Lisbon, but I have never gone into the matter, seen any reference to it, or bothered about it since my departure from Ceylon thirty years ago.

To have shared my secret thoughts on Swami Rock with my brothers may have puzzled them and made our life unreal, since we were taught the falsity of Hinduism and distrust of things Hindu at school, and they may not have thought as much as I did of the dualism at home, of accedence and philanthropic contribution to Christianity, counterpointed with our Hindu mode of life, Hindu customs and close affinity with our Hindu relatives. I was told my paternal grandfather had Hinduized the Catholic Church at my birthplace, Atchuvely, in several ways, introducing Hindu drummers and shenai players in ceremonials, for instance. To discuss these matters with them would have disturbed the spontaneity and flow of our young lives. And maybe, on the one hand, I never did discuss Swami Rock with them in order to preserve a flickering source of wonder and, on the other, elicit information from my Hindu friend, Suppiah, to fan it to a revelation.

A quarter-mile of red gravel road fringed with *Bombax malabaricum*, flamboyante and rain trees, past cottages, led us to the beach. At the road's end was a bathing club for Europeans from which, we were told, one member drowned each year. Opposite it, almost on the beach itself, was the low, squat Trincomalee Library with me as its only non-adult member. It had trellis-work of wood painted grey for the upper walls, and it was a marvellous experience to be inside with the sea breeze spanking through and the sun shining on the incandescent pages of books. The eyes of open windows at the back of the library stared at the wooden-hulled schooner of my friend Major Graham, riding at anchor, her belly full of foreign marvels. It was his houseboat where he lived year after year with his man, Murugesu, who often rowed me over in the ship's dinghy to borrow books from the Major's library. He had many books by G.A. Henty, of the *Kitchener in Khartoum* and *With Clive in India* sort, books on pirates and great explorers and had, surprising as it may seem, since he was a Briton (perhaps he was a rebellious Scot!), presented a set of Horatio Alger to the Boy Scouts' sanctum at school, all of which I hungrily devoured.

He had arrived in Trincomalee after the First World War and was mostly seen ashore in the mornings, when he attended mass to sit next to the Duke or King of Saxony, a somewhat mysterious figure who was in exile somewhere around Trincomalee. At this distance in time the warm and affectionate figure of the Major is very vague except that he was blond and tall and wore white shorts, shirt and yachting cap, was stiff and straight, reticent, and had the peculiarity of never walking back to his seat after Communion. With his eyes riveted on the officiating priest and chalice that contained the host, and palms pressed together in the Hindu custom of greeting, he backed his way to his seat, accurately and neatly, in a kind of naval strut which I have seen only at State funerals. He had arrived in his schooner at Trincomalee after the First World War to stay, except for one last journey in her to Scotland from which he did not return. He died on his journey back to Ceylon, somewhere around Suez, and I grieved for him and his individualist dream which, inchoately, the instinctive animal within me had perceived, even at my tender age. The vacancy left in my life by his death, even to this day, is something inexplicable. Was it the first death in a journey of one's own? Murugesu presented us with the Major's cavalryman's sword, with which we played until it disappeared in yet another mystery which is so typical of childhood.

The Trincomalee Library was to our right as we entered the beach, beyond it Government Agent's Hill and, to the left, in the distance, Fort Frederick. In the centre was the open sea, which stretched in a wide swathe to the South Pole without ever touching land, except Ceylon's. Once I was startled to see a long British cruiser, HMS *Effingham* or HMS *Emerald*, racing full steam ahead against a clear afternoon sky with her funnels belching the blackest clouds I have ever seen, keeping in mind all the incendiarism I had watched in war-torn London. She was firing all her guns, it seemed, and I could see six to eight great powerful flashes at a time ... broadsides. It was impressive and awesome. I knew every ship of Britain's East Indies Squadron when Trincomalee, not Singapore, was its base. That is, all except for HMS *Rapidol*, which was the ugly duckling of the fleet. She was the tanker which fuelled the fleet before the great oil tanks in the jungles of China Bay were built by Mr Dickens (descendant of Charles Dickens and friend of my father), and she was painted a ghastly grey.

The Boy Scouts and Cubs of the famed 1st Trincomalee Troop to which I belonged (as far as I know there was only one in Trincomalee) were often invited to the various ships of the fleet for tea and refreshments and we were shown the ship's innards and the working of the smaller guns as sailors polished the great big ones fore and aft. How the metal gleamed over extraordinarily well-scrubbed decks! I loved the ice-cream. Our troop had won the King's Medal for the island for five years in succession, which meant we kept the silver cup, and I don't imagine there was any dark brainwashing and colonial plot involved in presenting it to the Boy Scouts of this great naval base.

Admiral Thesiger often asked us to tea by the old banyan tree by Admiralty House. My brother once fell down from its smooth branches and was carried stunned into the house by the Admiral, who managed to revive him. In return for the Navy's courtesies, which included invitations to soccer matches and boxing tournaments, we staged an annual play and variety entertainment for the Admiral and the fleet in which I took part and I once, voluntarily, repeated my ridiculous performance of singing 'Felix the Cat' on board ship in return for some favour. As for the sailors, I made friends with three of them – Harry Frampton, Freeman and Gibbs of HMS *Enterprise*. My elder brother and I had met them one day walking along the harbour's edge, which is free of buildings along its entire front except for two jetties and a single 'boutique', the term used in Ceylon for a small café. As we strolled, we swung bunches of palmyra *kilangu* which fascinated the sailors.

'What is that you are eating?' Harry Frampton, the leader of the trio, asked, pointing to the *kilangus*, each of which was about a foot long and more than an inch in diameter at the base.

My elder brother and I explained that they were the boiled germinated plumules, or sprouts, of the palmyra palm. We peeled off the brown fibrous husks of the taper-shaped, wax-coloured sprouts, split them in halves and broke off sections for them. Harry Frampton's face expanded in a smile as he savoured the smooth, nutty flavour and texture, and that seemed to seal our friendship. We visited them a couple of times on board the *Emerald*, where we entertained each other as best we could. Ever since then, over the years and from several cities of the world, I have often thought of getting in touch with the friends of my boyhood through the British Admiralty but, alas, I have not yet done so. I liked the flow of their names and I feel all three of them exist somewhere and remember us and the strange *kilangus* they once ate on the sunny shores of Ceylon.

My outgoing nature was attracted to the 'otherness' of the British and their way of life, their assurance, their sense of power, the delicate tints of a woman's lamp-lit arms, face and hair glimpsed through an open door or window or on the lawn in the well-groomed and lush tropical garden at dinner with a lampshade of delicate colour glowing over the dinner-table in that languorous, easy, quiet and yet pregnant atmosphere which is typical of nights in Ceylon.

As we entered the perfumed beach of Dutch Bay, heavy with screwpine smell and, underfoot, the thick bilobed leaved goatsfoot with indigo and white-trumpeted flowers for a soft carpet or pet-rabbit feed, my thoughts would bell high on the right over G.A.'s Hill. The cool, old, white-pillared, one-storey building on it was surrounded by beds of flaming canna, and the most venerable banyan tree in Trincomalee with its multiple trunks, silent as a cathedral nave, stood brooding in front of it.

It was my ambition to become government agent one day and occupy that house and many were the excursions we made towards it, along a dangerous path on the sheer seaward side of the hill's armless shoulder, which had a fascinating, tiny trickle of water falling into a rock cup, and then on to a modest cave filled with subsided rock which was my reference-point for the others in story-books. But opposite it, more insistent than the puffball fantasies of G.A.'s Hill and the intriguing exterior spit and polish and orderliness of a foreign mode of life, more personal and powerful than the headlong cruiser with her winking guns, was the ancient thrusting of the tongue of land into the waters of Narayana, the Lord of the Waters, the flow and ebb of the expanding and contracting universe, creation and destruction, the cosmic rhythm of which the ancient temple of the Linga of Shiva was the symbol. The symbol (in the Hindu tradition in which construction and locale are inseparable and the particular but an undifferentiated part of all progressively larger units: man, man-god, god-creative energy, creative energy-substratum of creative energy, which is undifferentiated and without beginning, middle or end) was not the temple alone, but the whole terrain itself, as implied in the name Thiru-konar-malai, Anglicized to Trincomalee, the port for which the notorious great iron ship of England, the largest ship in the world of those days, was built. *Thiru* means sacred, *konar,* Shiva, and *malai* hilly place, from which names like Malaya, Malabar and Trincomalee are derived. The terrain of the Sacred Hill of Shiva was the symbol, now reduced to a boulder representing the yoni of the goddess, pierced by the granite pillar, the lingam of Shiva, the yīng-yang in its more obvious representation. The lingam, planted in its square, leaf-shaped and other pedestal yonis, was placed in the sanctum sanctorum of Shiva temples which are in the majority in India. Sometimes a simple mound of earth, an upright oval pebble or a stalagmite in the icy caves of the Himalayas, as at Badrinath, sufficed for worshippers. Although this was not the original lingam of the Temple, Brahmin priests had very cleverly preserved the meaning of the terrain in the colossal symbol of Swami Rock, fooling the European puritanism, ignorant of its meaning, which had ordered the naked arms and torsos of the Kathakali (story-telling) dancers of Malabar covered in red flannel, and attempted to do the same with the naked breasts of our Rodiya girls in Ratnapura Province. (The story goes that the king's mischievous chef had served him roast monkey. The infuriated king had ordered him and his descendants thrust down a few social scales to the Rodiya caste whose people should henceforth forbear to wear clothes above their waists, which to my mind is a blessing, not a punishment in the tropics.) All this information was not, of course, available to me during my years in Trincomalee, which were charged with the irrelevancy of Christianity to my own life, and that of my family, my intense involvement with the mystery of Swami Rock, and the search for some evidence, however slight, that Thirukonarmalai Temple was not a figment of our anti-colonial, defensive or aggressive minds.

It is impossible for me to describe the perfect high that a Hindu temple with its site, its rituals and atmosphere gives me: the total involvement with all one's senses engaged, liberating, exhilarating, like a plate of very hot rice and curry (Ceylon has the hottest curries in the world), savoured with sweat pricking and flowing from the hair roots and forehead, psychedelic, round flavoured and universalizing in its intent and being ... all individual flavours and feelings lost in a oneness, the long note in which all the flavours persist in an indescribable but deeply felt unity. The self, ego, lost in the universal flow of hot energy, one hundred per cent energy, through the yoga of taste. Harmony with one's surroundings. The perfect high. For instance, I remember my first visit to Mahabalipuram in South India. (The poet Louis MacNeice rushing at me in the Stag's Head pub in London after his first tour for the BBC in India: 'Ah Tambi, South India.... You must go to South India ... Mahabalipuram!') The temples chiselled out of solid rock, pillars, rooms, deities, attendants and beasts, lamp-holders; the landscaped water by the temples and the fierce sea wind driving across like a sound boom from a gigantic high flyer with a hundred jets. The façades of the temples eroded by the invisible, blown sand, the features of the many cows surrounding one of them sand-blasted into blobs of Henry Moore heads. Out at sea the sunken temples, and nearer shore, bobbing out of the water, eroded shrines and other works of granite laced by the million-eyed foam, winking in the afternoon sun. It was from this great port that Indian ships had sailed with Buddhism, Hinduism, merchandise and settlers to Malaya, Burma, Indonesia, China and farther. I was curry-high again and at Swami Rock, with that howling wind of home blowing monolithic through me as if through a tunnel: the Hindu symbols pat, pat, pot, vivid in front of me like blood cells, with the static of memory roaring in the energy circuits. Which I heard again on the high eyrie at Thirukalukunram, reminiscent of the Rock, as the eagle swooped down to the constructed pond on top of the eyrie at sunset every evening to be fed by the Brahmins as part of the temple's ritual, surrounded by a glut of temples on the plain, courtyard within courtyard with highly ornamented *gopurams* or pyramidical towers growing out of the earth among the geometric palmyra palms; and again at ancient Conjeevaram (Kanchi) among the thatched cottages, near Madras, with water-cooled courtyards and jasmine which transported me to Atchuvely, my birthplace, and the Northern Province of Ceylon. Even though nowadays I have resolved the mystery of the Rock, the old wonder and uncertainty persist whenever I think of it, part of the ringing dawn of childhood which the mind is unwilling to discount or forget.

The bone-stark, low, T-shaped school building at Trincomalee, across the road from our house, was fleshed in cassia and casuarina trees, and two unnamed trees of small height with pale-green leaves growing together which were its prominent sweet navel. The boys nervously plucked at it constantly, and ate the pale-green leaves with questioning looks. They tasted leafy and sweet. Occupying the bottom third of the foot of the T, and adjoining the Boy Scout sanctum, was the vernacular school where the language of instruction was Tamil. The rest of it with English for the medium (we were fined one cent if we talked Tamil) had the lower classes from standards one to five on either side of the long hall, with the school certificate and the metriculation classes occupying the wings. A long aisle led to the principal's desk, the memory of which still fills me with foreboding.

If I dreaded the aisle leading to the principal's desk down which many a boy was summoned to be reprimanded, I dreaded the maths teacher even more. I was not too good at arithmetic. And it seemed ominous to me that it was in his class I once fell and broke my arm. He had a youthful, clear-skinned face, pendant like a waterfall, with a black moustache adorning extraordinarily sensual lips, and his long shapely limbs were encased in a flowing white verti, which is five yards of cloth wrapped round the waist like a sari. Whenever he wished to punish a boy, he asked him to hold out a palm and then rapped it with the edge of a foot-rule. I had often been his victim and, as far as I remember, he was the only teacher who was such a disciplinarian.

He made me feel very uncomfortable with his large, black, moist eyes, his coaxing, insinuating speech and the moist look of his mouth. There was something subterranean and pleading about him which terrified me. I had often felt that he wished to take me aside to have a private conversation and he had time and again suggested a visit to his house which I took pains to avoid or sneak past quickly.

As for the boys, we were a motley lot. Some wore shoes and boots and other sandals. The Moors, who are Muhammadans, wore colourful sarongs, which are known in America as Madras prints, with red fez and black tassel for headgear, while the Tamil Hindus preferred their 'national costume' which is the long verti, with or without a thin ornamental border of vermilion and yellow which matched the pottu or caste-mark of sandalwood paste and vermilion on their foreheads. The boys from families which had to traffic with or work for the British (politicians and some business men excluded) dressed like the British in shirt, shorts and tie. These woollen-socked and heavy-booted boys considered themselves the 'in' people, a feeling that I myself have experienced, which accentuated the split nature of my personality oscillating between the European and non-European. I felt exhilarated and proud when my grandfather, dressed in black coat, turban of scarlet and gold and foam of white verti playing over *Arabian Nights*' shoes, took us out riding in the phaeton. He flicked the coiled whip and we bowled down the roads of Atchuvely which were limestone white when I was a boy, built of the limestone rock of the peninsula, crushed by the wheels of the bullock-carts. My father and some members of the family dressed similarly on ceremonial occasions and holidays, while others stuck stubbornly to their vertis and kurtaus (long Indian shirts).

The feelings of division, hostility, confusion, superiority and inferiority, and so on, evoked by clothes alone, would be unfamiliar to a more homogeneously dressed people like the British or American, though there was a humdrum snobbism about them in the England I knew which was, however, free of the several implications intended by us. In Ceylon or India, the dress and the way it is worn indicates race, religion, sect, profession, caste and marital state. People wore Hindu or non-Hindu clothes in public and these too were apt to be changed abruptly. The most dramatic exhibition of the phenomenon happens daily on the Colombo–Talaimanaar Express. The passengers who board the night train *en masse* in Colombo, and are tightly packed in the compartments, are Tamils, mostly in European dress, on their way to the Jaffna peninsula. They are the most conservative and yet progressive people in Ceylon, Jaffna Tamils, Jaffnese, who consider themselves distinct from the Indian Tamils of Ceylon.

By daybreak the jungle has given way to the coral plains and salt estuaries of the North with groves of coconut and palmyra, and the passengers have been transmogrified overnight, effecting a sartorial and personality change. The starched, constricting suits and shoes intended for the jungles or a cold climate have disappeared in an avalanche of silk vertis, kurtaus, and sandals, and limp bracelets of cleverly interlinked gold, flat as a watch-band, dangle gracefully from wrists, the affectation of the dandies. Cigarettes have been routed by the concerted assault of the northern-grown Jaffna cheroot, which is named after the Tamil word *churutu* – something rolled. The acrid fumes released have quickened and excited conversation, the former bilingualism drowned with the sole use of Tamil, the voices deafening and singsong in the manner of farmers and villagers, deliberately raised as a protest to present affronts to their individuality and sense of nationalism, with others trying to steer a sheepish middle course.

I felt the same stress and strain in my class at school. The obviously middle-course boys were Sethukavaler, son of a government official in the *kaccheri* (town hall), and Brito, whose family lived in Fort Frederick in a small house on top of soaring steps and a hillock which intrigued me. Every stone and shard in Fort Frederick had an esoteric meaning for me and, from its age, I imagined the house was built by the Portuguese and may therefore have incorporated parts of the fabric of Thirukonarmalai Temple. The other two boys who stood out in my class were Hindu Suppiah and the Moor, Mohammed, with the fez and tassel and sarong, whose father owned a general store in the bazaar and meat and fish market section of Trincomalee. I often wandered there in the evenings fascinated by the brightly lit one-room shops of silks, chiffons, organdies, saris of gold and silver, a cascade of colour as the shopkeepers unrolled and heaped them for display on the floor. The scent of the new cloths was freshening and heady like the sachets of blotting-paper some companies sent out.

Suppiah lived by the modern Hindu Temple, some distance beyond the bazaar, in what was the Hindu quarter, the quarter of mysteries, and invariably wore a pottu of sandalwood with a spot of vermilion in its centre, in the middle of his forehead. One Saturday I paid him a visit on my own, an unusual mission for me, since it was so far away. Like Swami Rock, and the houses of my Hindu relatives, his place had an aura of 'otherness' which fired my imagination. I expected to find some sign, some great, healing revelation there – perhaps in the pergola of jasmine that led to the front door, which had the characteristic Hindu garland of mango leaves strung across it; perhaps in the side-room inside the house, the worship- and meditation-room, where an oil lamp burned in front of a framed oleograph of Ganesha, the jolly, big-bellied son of Lord Shiva, the Supreme God. He is the most popular god in India and Ceylon who is invoked before journeys and any sort of undertaking. Two multi-wicked brass lamps which were not in use stood on the floor on their tall pedestals flanking a polished *chembu* or engraved brass pot filled with a bouquet of yellow and vermilion flowers from the garden, ringed with spears of mango leaves. This puja or worship-room was dark like the innermost sanctum of Hindu temples, evoking the same sensations of the primeval and the secret, the centre of the earth with its brooding silence, as I imagined it at the time, the cave.

Suppiah was delighted to see me. 'Did the temple really exist?' I could not help asking him. He believed it had, and that it now lay at the bottom of the ocean floor.

To complete the 'otherness' of the afternoon, Suppiah's mother sent the servant out to buy some Bengal-gram (*ulunthu*) doughnuts made fat with hot water and curds for tea, a delicacy of Brahmin teashops. Since we never had them at home (they are seldom made at home, I didn't know at the time) and a Hindu cousin of my father's also served these when we visited him, I've always associated them with Hindu households. Suppiah's house had ancient roots, undisturbed by the fortunes of the nation. In his mango grove lurked shadowy beings of the past. He could tell me much I wished to know.

After this visit, Suppiah came to our house frequently at weekends and joined us on our treks to Swami Rock and the miniature spring and the cave by Government Agent's Hill. We called at Admiralty House (the son of the caretaker was in our class) and Fort Ostenberg, to visit the other boys and girls who had previously been at school with us in the Catholic Convent School and were looking forward to 'higher' education in England. (At age five it was considered too dangerous for the boys to mix with girls – I was already playing hide-and-seek in the hibiscus bushes with an English girl from Fort Ostenberg – and so we were transferred to one of the all-male schools.) We wandered through the salt estuaries and their banks thick with salty portulaca, and through the Royal Navy's rifle-range into the thick jungle, where we opened our picnic baskets. It was one of my first close friendships.

Suppiah and I were soon roaming together all over the town's esplanade, which stretched from near our house to the bazaar and Fort Frederick. It was ringed with tulip trees whose dry fruits made excellent spinning-tops. We watched the soccer games, the Royal Navy versus Trincomalee, our school versus the rest, and the sailors drilling in the broiling sun. Once we saw one of the sailors fall down dead with sunstroke. We thus became involved and we attended his funeral.

We roamed over the grounds of the Trincomalee Club and the Rest House looking for fragments of the sunken temple. We looked in the grounds of the Catholic Convent adjoining the esplanade. A large boulder stood there under a temple tree (*Plumeria acutifolia*) on which I used to sit and listen to the breakers, the crisp sea breeze carving my face. It must have come from the rocky site of the temple, and search as I might for an ancient inscription, all it showed were the incisions and scribblings made on it by the children. We stood in a semicircle round it for our singing lessons and the words of the songs I learnt, mixed with the sea breeze, still hum in my ears.

> Poor Mary is a-weeping, is a-weeping, is a-weeping,
> Poor Mary is a-weeping by the side of the sea.
> I'm weeping for my true love, my true love, my true love,
> I'm weeping for my true love by the side of the sea.

Another focus of our search was at the base of the towering and venerable rain tree by the cool Rest House, since shrines for worship are sometimes built at the base of such trees, besides the bo, banyan and neem. What we found were iridescent beetles which we kept alive in matchboxes, with rain-tree leaves, to no purpose. The most intriguing spot was the manhole cover on the seaward fringe of the esplanade. Rumour said it was the exit from a secret tunnel from the Fort. Workmen had once entered it and discovered colonies of snakes.

One Sunday, Suppiah and my brothers were at one of our favourite pastimes, jumping down to the beach from the sea wall that buttressed the road and entrance to the Fort, when he gave me a tiny bronze statuette of Ganesha, the big-bellied, elephant-faced god.

'I thought you might like to have it. My grandmother gave it to me long ago,' he said.

The image was passed from hand to hand and Suppiah told us the story of how Shiva's son came by his elephant head. His wife was so proud of his beauty when he was born that she asked the evil planet, Saturn, to admire him.

'Don't show him to me,' warned the planet. 'You know I destroy everything I look at.'

But the proud mother, wife of Shiva, the Supreme God, wouldn't listen. 'Look!' she said, unveiling the child's head, and it was instantly consumed.

The distraught mother bore his limp body to Lord Shiva.

'Go into the jungle,' Shiva ordered his attendants. 'Hurry! Bring me the head of the first animal you meet.'

The first animal they found was a baby elephant. They cut its head off and hurried back with it, and Shiva attached it to his son's body. That is how the much-loved and jolly Indian god, with the elephant's small eyes, happens to be elephant-headed.

Suppiah's gift was indeed a treasure. It was the first time I had had the image of a Hindu god all to myself and I did not look for fragments of Hindu sculpture in the walls of the Fort that day, or in the rusting gun emplacements and ruined houses, and the jungly patches within the Fort. I had a piece of sculpture that was all my own, and it was burning a hole in the pocket of my shorts.

The sky was a blaze of colour that evening at Swami Rock as the officiating priest at the farthermost end of the dangerous crag first purified himself with water poured from a delicate brass lota. He seemed as ancient as the earth, and the granite in the ocean below, with a sinuous string of large rastrakuta seeds round his neck. More and more worshippers arrived, as scantily clad as he, bearing libations of water or milk in brown earthenware chatties, and offerings of coconuts, coconut flowers, jasmine, oleander, betel leaves, money, bunches of bananas, rice. Surya, the Sun God, was closing his opaline eyes, bathing Trincomalee with his flood of blessing. The priest spoke to him in the ancient tongue, the people responding. It seemed the earth rumbled and the stars came out to watch. Chanting more fervently, he poured water and milk on the colossal lingam and then cast the people's gifts into the waters of Narayana from the giddy heights, the fruits of the earth unto the Giver, for Narayana (Vishnu) and Brahma of the Aryan Brahmins are but Shiva (Goodness), the most ancient pre-Aryan god of the Indians, as is graphically incised on the stone lingams of Ceylon. He kindled Agni, the God of Fire, on the rock, and held aloft a burning brand as the people threw up their arms heavenward. The sun's eyes were closed and the priest covered the earth with gossamer incense from the brass censer he swung high over his head, binding everything present, and not present, into a close unity. Incense. The love-in of universals at Swami Rock.

Then he descended from the crag and with the ashes of Agni made the sign of Shiva on each worshipper's forehead. And I had a feeling that at least a part of the puja (holy mass) was intended for the god in my pocket. I was not far wrong since, as I learnt in later years, sculptures of Shiva and his wife Parvati, in the temples, often included his sons Ganesh and Subramanya, the God of War, in one sweeping concept.

I was proud of my possession when I got home and put him on display to my parents, who smiled indulgently.

'I must take you to Manipay Hindu Temple. My grandfather was a trustee,' my father said. I was pleased, but the dualism of my family, always impenetrable, was, as usual, perplexing to me.

But I owned Ganesha for one day only. I had him in my school satchel on my desk. Unfortunately for Ganesha and me, it was during the period of the maths teacher. As he passed down the rows of desks, foot-rule in hand, peering at our work papers and making us highly nervous, he spotted Ganesha.

'What is this?' he roared, snatching him up. The whites of his moist eyes, which were usually red, through over-indulgence in arrack, I thought, and demons had red eyes, looked fearsome as they rolled in their sockets. Seized by powerful emotions, his eyes sparked more fiercely than usual. 'I am confiscating this,' he shouted, 'and I'll report you to the principal.'

I waited apprehensively for the note I would have to take up the long aisle to the principal, the Ceylonese priest Fr Marian, to be reprimanded, which was an ordeal that troubled me for days, and then remained as a threat and menace. He was the fountainhead of authority and virtue and that ineffable goodness, touchstone of my own, which had once forced me late at night to steal to his room and make a clean breast of having lied to the drama director.

During rehearsals for our annual play, there was a part where I had to guffaw in an acceptable British manner. My production was put down by the director who gave us his own version, which sounded as weird to me. He guffawed, and I guffawed, and the performance was so ridiculous and embarrassing, just guffawing into the empty air with nothing to follow, that I fell silent when it came to the speaking part. I pretended illness and went home, to be troubled by my conscience all evening. Then, when it was very dark, I stole to the rectory to make a clean breast of it to Fr Marian, to confess I had not really been ill at all, an incident I still don't like to think about, since the experience was so painful and unreal.

And now Suppiah and other friends shot sympathetic glances at me as I sat tensed for another confrontation with him. And I was filled with hatred for the maths teacher.

Fortunately, the bell for the interval between study periods rang, and the note to the principal was never written. But I had lost Ganesha and felt troubled as I lay in bed that night, listening to the thunder of the waves in Eastern Bay.

I wondered what the maths teacher had done with Ganesha, and my resentment against him mounted up rather alarmingly. It was his custom to draw us round in an arc, of prey, in front of his desk, for exercising us in 'mental arithmetic', a procedure fraught with tension and apprehension which numbed my brain, and made me even more hopeless at figures.

'Subtract 813 from 1,350. What is the square root of 25?' He fired his questions at us, and swung his heavy foot-rule whenever he felt a boy was too dense.

And that was how the curtain fell on my schooldays at Trincomalee. The 'mental arithmetic' session had been too hectic and confusing that morning, and it ended up with the teacher belabouring me with the foot-rule. I tore it from him, snapped it across my knee and threw it on the floor. Then I marched up the aisle to Fr Marian's desk and blurted out angrily, 'That man . . . has beaten me. I am never coming back to your school again!'

I walked home and explained to my father why I could not go back to school again. 'You don't have to go back to school,' he said simply when he returned from his visit to the principal, rather flushed, and I was grateful. He had seen my point of view, and I was proud of him. In fact, from that day on, none of us went back to school. My elder brother caught a train for Colombo within a few days to stay with my maternal uncle and attend the premier Catholic college in the island, and we were to follow him. I think my father had decided his children were now old enough to receive 'higher' education, after our incubation periods in Singapore, Kuala Lumpur and Trincomalee. His own idyllic days in Trincomalee were over. I visited Suppiah and my other friends and my favourite, Sister Dolores, at the Catholic Convent. (She was so very beautiful and kind that I visited her on Saturday mornings when no other children attended school. I liked being with her, and she went out of her way, in those days, to keep me busy in the playroom. There was a close attachment between us – I made a special trip to Trinco years later to visit her – and not even the rude shock of seeing her, in her *déshabillé*, with a shaved head, daunted me.) Though looking forward to the metropolis, I was sad at leaving Trincomalee and all my boyhood associations. Sea-blown Swami Rock is their nostalgic symbol and it has haunted me ever since.

Throughout the years in England, India and New York, I did not succeed in solving the mystery of the Rock (I recently discovered that certain writers mean the whole area of Fort Frederick when they use the term) although, on occasion, I took out an annual subscription to a Ceylon newspaper, and read every book, annual and article on Ceylon I could lay my hands on.

Then, one day, I had a great surprise. As I was walking down West 8th Street in Manhattan, I spotted a book on Ceylon remaindered for one dollar in Marboro's shop window. Its title, *Skin-Diving in Ceylon*, made me immediately think of Swami Rock. I staked my one dollar, and while flicking through the pages of the book in a café to study the fine photographs, there, incredibly, right in front of me, was the evidence I had so eagerly searched for as a boy. It was only a fragment of the great temple – an ornamental capital and part of the column – that the Brahmins had worshipped with flowers and the gifts of the earth, but, as with some of the stories I had heard as a boy, here was proof of the legend of the temple under the sea, tumbled down there by the Portuguese, 'and the thread of truth in our own versions of history. I felt excited and heady. Yet another lacuna in one of my double selves had been filled up, a process which works in either direction bolstering either man, and is continuous.

Some time later, I was also stirred to learn of the discovery of one of the icons of worship that the Sunken Temple's priests had spirited away. Workmen, on the esplanade by Fort Frederick, had dug up a great bronze statue of Shiva's consort, Parvati, which is on permanent exhibit in Colombo Museum today. According to our fifth-century poet, Varotheiyan, the temple had been built by a Tamil king from the Coromandel coast in the year 512 of the Kali, or fourth and final, age of the present cycle of evolution and dissolution of our universe, or 2588 BC. The Revd James Cartman in his 1957 book *Hinduism in Ceylon* comments on this: 'The date 2588 BC is most doubtful, but the reference to the famous temple is genuine. This famous temple, known as the temple of a thousand columns, once stood 400 feet above sea-level upon the Swami Rock which is situated in Fort Frederick. This Rock, about which many strange legends are told, has long been a place of pilgrimage.' I also learnt from the Revd Carter's book that two stones from the original fabric of the temple are to be seen on either side of the main entrance to the Fort. On them are carved the twin fish emblem of an Indian king who invaded Ceylon in recent times and claims to have planted his flag in Trincomalee. These two happenings relieved me of one of the nagging doubts involving the genuineness and validity of my Ceylonese heritage.

As for our not eating enough meat, and rice being debilitating, I had satisfactorily solved the problem for myself while still at school. The most celebrated dinner of the Dutch in Indonesia (now transported to gourmet restaurants in Amsterdam) was *rijstaffel*, or rice table, which is rice with several curries, curry being a misnomer, since grilled sausages, or bacon or meat, cut bite-size, would also be curries for us. It was *rijstaffel*, sanctified by a foreign name, that sustained us in Ceylon, according to tastes and needs created by our climate, and the Dutch did not err in their preference. I remembered that at my grandmother's house, in Atchuvely, we had the inevitable thirty-six dishes to choose from on Sundays. Some of them were only relishes of the shrimp and egg-plant, fish *blachang*, or mango chutney sort, but there was no lack in the variety of cooked meats, seafood, fruits, flowers, vegetables, and grains of all kinds.

Impressed with this discovery, I once wrote an article for *The Ceylon Observer*, whereupon a lady of Dutch descent wrote to say she had had more than a hundred dishes to cope with when she was a little girl. I think her name was Van Dort, and she was well over a hundred years old. It was compliment enough for our cuisine which is as subtle and potent, in every way, for our climate, as Indian music.

As for my double self, in today's world of raga rock and yoga, flowers and incense, and flower power, it would be reasonable to assume that they have merged. I cannot say so since, in many a situation, I find a Western echo in an Eastern setting attractive. I am content to be double, at least nowadays, since I've actually always wanted to be the sound in the holy Brahmin's conch.

THE GLASS TOWER

BY

NICHOLAS MOORE

DRAWINGS
BY
LUCIAN FREUD

P L

Cover design by Lucian Freud for *The Glass Tower* by Nicholas Moore, Editions Poetry London, 1945. (This and the drawings on pages 64 and 72 are in the private collection of James Kirkman Ltd, London.)

Robin Skelton

The Book

For Tambimuttu

First a photograph
of the author smiling,

then the words, the pages
and pages of words,

the words indenting the paper
ever so slightly

and carrying colons and commas
and semicolons

along with them in their flow
like river-borne leaves

fallen from some madrona
leaning over

hurrying, scurrying water,
then one empty

page revealing the weave
of the paper, white

as earth before the thaw
that set the river

running. End or beginning?
Close the book.

Observe the photograph
of the author smiling.

Diana Gardner

Tambimuttu and *Poetry London*

Late in 1938 my brother Paul and I met Tambi through a young poet, Robert Bruce, who told us that together with Anthony Dickins, freshly returned from India, Tambi was to produce a completely new type of poetry magazine: new format, new attitudes. The first number would carry established contemporary poets, but later ones were to be an open sounding-board for a new kind of poetry which had not then been heard. He was totally confident that this would happen, along with other developments. He came to London when the literary scene – the content and production of books – was in some ways stereotyped. Tambi's view was inspired and original, also exotic because of his background: that of a highly placed Tamil family in Ceylon.

We met in a small room – it might have been in Grafton Street – which, like most rooms all over London at that time, had cream-coloured walls and cream-coloured paintwork. It had almost no furniture, but on a bare table and covering the floor was paper of every description: books, pamphlets, newspaper cuttings, letters, manuscripts – and half-consumed cups of tea: Tambimuttu was in the act of creating the first number of *Poetry London*!

He was wonderfully enthusiastic and welcoming. Then in his early twenties, on that day he was wearing a dark suit and open-necked white shirt, I seem to remember, and his long, loose, silky mane of black shining hair kept falling around his sallow, slightly bony face, and had to be swung back with a jerk. His great, thoughtful eyes were brilliant and shining and nearly black. He was a very sensitive young man with a sweet smile. You realized at once that he was carried away by his vision of his new poetry magazine and his belief in poetry as one of the great emotional expressions of mankind, if not the greatest. Anthony Dickins, also in his early twenties, kept in the background, saying little but unquestionably dedicated to Tambi's vision.

Tambi was looking for small, fine drawings or woodcuts to accompany certain poems. This, too, was one of his firmly held ideas, also new at the time when illustrations mostly followed literal translations of the text. He believed that illustrations needed to convey the feeling or *sense* of a poem, and could be of an apparently totally unrelated subject or design. He believed that all the arts are interchangeable; an emotion could be expressed in poetry, painting or music. In the late thirties this seemed to have been lost sight of. I had three small wood-engraving blocks which Tambi said he could use, together with a fine, small photograph of a beech tree by Edwin Smith. After the first number of *PL* came out, in February of the following year, and the printers had not been paid, they generously let me have these blocks back, which they had been holding along with other 'effects'! I remember going with Tambi to collect them, and witnessed how his gentle courtesy softened their determination not to let anything go just then! He also had an assurance which seemed to come from his belief that he was an important living representative of poetry.

The first number was now out, with its striking cover design on cream-coloured paper, quarto size. The word 'Poetry' was a free flourish in scarlet; the contributors' names in flowing copperplate, and centred, a black, vigorous shape: Hector Whistler's rendering of Tambi's flowing hair. The number contained work by Stephen Spender, George Barker, Dylan Thomas, Lawrence Durrell and many other important young poets. It sold at a shilling!

We spent many evenings with Tambi and Anthony and their friends, discussing over cups of tea the situation which was growing ominously in the world. Hitler was beginning to shout over the loudspeakers. When Tambi came to make a statement, he would say, 'Let me consult my navel' and, after looking for some time at his diaphragm, would then express his point of view, clearly and with conviction.

In that year, 1939, my brother and I went to the United States on a special New York World Fair trip, by sea, and Paul went as representative for *Poetry London*. Tambi gave him letters of introduction and the names of bookshops to visit. One was the Gotham Bookmart in Greenwich Village. Everyone he spoke with was impressed by the unusual poetry magazine from London, and it could be assured of a market if delivery were regular! In those days it was inexpensive to mail journals to the United States.

Later, after the war broke out and a story of mine called 'The Landgirl' was published in *Horizon*, Tambi used to say, whenever we met in London, 'Ah, the landgirl', and enthusiastically put his arms right round me! At that time I was living in the country and, compared with the pale Londoners who were then facing black-outs and bombs, must have glowed with health! Just after the war ended and Tambi had his own publishing house in Manchester Square, he wrote saying that he would like to print a volume of my short stories – if I had enough. I went to see him – he was working in a large, elegant room with Georgian windows – and he said: 'I have never read any of your stories, but I am certain that I want to publish them!' I have always felt this to be one of the greatest honours I have ever received, to be chosen in this way by Tambi! And wonderfully fortunate that all the books on Tambi's first list (it included work by Kathleen Raine, Anaïs Nin, and the first novel by Vladimir Nabokov to be published in England – *The Real Life of Sebastian Knight*) were carried through into publication and out into the world of reviewers and booksellers by the immensely businesslike drive of Editions Poetry London's secretary, Helen Scott, who, on her marriage to John Irwin, curator of the Indian section of the V & A, had an entire small volume of poetry printed in her honour, and written by Tambi's poets.

In my view the debt to Tambi for his dynamic influence on the content and format of British books has never been wholly appreciated. His ideas were seminal and triggered off so many of the new lines which seemed to burst out after the war. Until that time, jackets were pleasing but based generally on the use of elegant type-face. Almost no books of serious literary value had illustrated covers. Tambi used brilliant artists for his cover illustrations, both of *Poetry London* and his books. Henry Moore had designed several covers for *Poetry London*, and some of his Underground shelter drawings had appeared first in *PL*. Graham Sutherland also contributed. If you walked through a bookshop after Tambi started publishing, your eye would catch a 'new look' – brighter, more interesting. Other publishers soon followed these ideas.

I remember thinking on meeting Tambi then that he did not look robust or well. Wartime city living may have debilitated him; his skin was yellowish, and he looked thin, and he seemed to lack his original gaiety and enthusiasm. Later, he went back to Ceylon. When I next saw him, he was travelling through London on his way to America to start a new poetry journal there. (*Poetry London* had been taken over by Richard March, but, without Tambi's spirit, it had folded.) This time he was accompanied by a sweet young wife from India. Kathleen Raine gave a party for him at her house in Paultons Square, Chelsea. Tambi wore a dazzling white suit, cut in the Eastern style: high-buttoned collar and stove-pipe trousers. With his long black hair, brown skin and dark, shining eyes, he was wonderfully impressive and happy. This time he looked filled out, radiant and glowing. That evening there seemed to be an atmosphere of a special, brilliant welcome: the sense that a prince of poetry was calling in on a journey across the world.

The next time I saw Tambi was many years later, again in London. He was walking down the steps at Gloucester Road Underground station in the rush-hour crowd. He was once more thin-looking, contracted by the London winter. He wore a sand-coloured raincoat, and he seemed to be all of that colour. But his face, though thinner, held the same sweetness. About two months later his exquisite large volume, *India Love Poems*, translated and planned by him, and illustrated by John Piper – it sold at £400 per copy – was on display in the window of Spinks.

The year before Tambi died, he again invited me to submit work – this time drawings and an excerpt from one of my stories which had appeared in the original volume, for inclusion in another fine book he was planning, to celebrate the marriage of the Prince of Wales to Lady Diana Spencer. He was working now on the top floor of an old Church of England school building in Old Gloucester Street, WC1, which was reached by an outside iron staircase. Once more he was surrounded by paper of every kind – for the creation of that magnificent book which was, however, not to be. He was working as hard as his health allowed; he even contemplated sleeping on a kind of makeshift bed in a small gallery high up in the room, in order to get the outline copy of the book to Buckingham Palace on time. Despite the confusion of paper and books and film, he knew exactly where every detail lay.

I can see him now, as I came away. He was sitting at his paper-strewn desk, his once shining black hair now, of course, grey and thinner. His trench coat hung nearby on a coat-stand. He looked over and smiled slowly, his expression gentle and tired. Tragically, we have been robbed of the wonderful book which was then in his mind, and which would have been another valuable offering to literary and artistic London.

Russell McKinnon-Croft

Der Erl-König

A Personal Memory of Meary James Tambimuttu

September. The war barely declared. A party – paean or dirge? – some of each, perhaps – swinging fully in my shared Charlotte Street flat. Bottled beer raised and lowered, to and fro; voices in syncopation, also rising and falling, mostly rising. Guests, invited or uninvited, announced or self-announced; several waving contributory quart bottles. Decibels now mounting inexorably. A gramophone in the hazy background playing an elegiac obbligato of 'Smoke Gets in Your Eyes' with whimsical appositeness. I top up a few sporadic glasses, offer French bread open sandwiches, pass the time of evening with Francis and Pat, Hetta and Charles.

Suddenly in front of me: an apparition. No less! Thin, flailing arms ending in dark slim hands, one pinioning a cigarette, the other batoning with a half-full pint glass. A sunburst of a smile; dark rock-pool eyes, shining with spontaneous, exuberant joy; dark ascetic (O! artless fraud) face mantled by puma-black mane.

'Hello, Russell! Thank you for asking me to your party.'

I hadn't – except by proxy, he had come with other people – but I *would* have done if this hadn't been our first meeting.

'My name is Tambi. Are you a poet?'

I said I had dashed off a poem or two between one woman and the next, or some such flippant idiocy.

He pealed with unrestrained laughter.

Next morning, Sunday, not very early, the doorbell extracted me none too willingly from my illicit bed. He was there on the doormat. The same transcendent smile, eyes more hooded in the greyish morning light, fingers still trailing a cigarette.

'Can you come to lunch with me, Russell?'

I glanced automatically over my shoulder; he became aware of my hunched dressing-gown and bare legs and feet. 'Ah, you like girls? I like girls very much. I can see they like you too.'

I glanced back again to where a smiling, tousled head now peered round the bedroom door.

'We must be friends!'

We took it from there.

I gave him lunch at a rather seedy restaurant farther up Charlotte Street, which he liked because they gave you a good overflowing plate for about one and ninepence. We talked: poetry, girls, Ceylon, T.S. Eliot, girls, Trincomalee, poetry; himself, sex, various modern poets, arrived and coming, girls. The hours passed.

The war's exigences dissolved our assorted bachelor ménage. Improbably I moved into a room above Tambi in a rather slummy house we found in Whitfield Street. A few doors away was Marie Stopes's clinic. The smell of new bread still wafted up from pavement gratings in Charlotte Street. Autumn spread its beautiful melancholy over Soho.

To Tambi's door strode relays of poets bearing gifts of verse. The unused chamber-pot beneath Tambi's bed became a modern Palgrave. Tambi would sit up in bed – his favourite, cherished throne – and leaf through them, periodically exclaiming at something that took his enthusiasm: a passage, a line, a metaphor, a felicitous simile; sometimes a whole short poem; and as like as not, when I was in, he would patter precipitately upstairs and read bits aloud to me: voice vibrant, eyes alight, long sinuous fingers describing parabolas in space. Thus *Poetry London* came to its climax.

The winter advanced and we sat and listened to Chopin nocturnes on my aged portable wind-up; and drank beer and coffee and put our arms round girls. With Finland's invasion, it was Sibelius. We sat in the cheap back stalls of local cinemas showing the marvellous thirties' French films and in even cheaper seats while Sir Henry Wood conducted the old Queen's Hall's last concerts. Through Tchaikovsky's 'Pathétique' Tambi, blissful in oblivion of his staid surroundings, beat ecstatic time and stood up once or twice to do so.

In the unreal claustrophobia of the 'phoney war' we lived out our counterpoint to the humbug and sterility of leaflet raids, Ministry announcements, empty war news bulletins; groping our way in the black-out from the Fitzroy to the Wheatsheaf, the Black Horse, the Wellington and back, through one anaesthetizing party to another; played music, read and talked poetry, ate in odd little restaurants and cafés where the rationed food grew steadily more wan. When spring came, Tambi and I forded Tottenham Court Road and so moved from Soho to Bloomsbury. I shared a flat with Charles Archer (later killed tragically in the Merchant Navy) in Great Ormond Street; Tambi settled into Marchmont Street with Jackie, his English rose (first) wife. Our hub was now the Lamb in Lamb's Conduit Street and the rather weird world of *Horizon*. I scrounged bits of cash here and there for the somewhat tenuous finances of *Poetry London*, once managing to dun Eddie Marsh in his flamboyant Gray's Inn chambers. Tambi appraised and selected unerringly, edited, rhapsodized, expounded. We both proof-read, talked, drank beer regularly; synthesized ourselves in the miraculous organic chemistry of poetry.

In the autumn of 1940, as the Blitz began, I took a house in Chelsea. Tambi came to a room round the corner in Oakley Gardens. The chamber-pot retired gracefully in favour of a rather grubby cardboard box. At various times we both managed to prevent Dylan Thomas from stealing our shirts, though not from drinking my beer. Tambi now had a dark suit, tailored and sober. It covered his spare frame well enough and, with a long blue Melton overcoat, another recent acquisition, cushioned his thinness from that damnable winter. But neither really suited him (no pun intended). An encrusted turban and long white dhobied robes would have done much more just tribute to his slim, warm, remote dignity. Once he enticed me into eating a Ceylon curry in a Tottenham Court Road Indian restaurant next to Mr Mendelssohn-Barthholdy's (great nephew of Felix) dust-encrusted Aladdin's cave 'antique' shop. 'In Ceylon, Russell, we have the hottest, the most delicious curries in the world.' My gut reaction has never been the same since.

The time came for me to forsake my wartime ministerial secondment and, at my urgent request, to return to uniform. I got married again. Then I went off to war in greater earnest in the Mediterranean. So that it was the beginning of 1945 before I saw Tambi again. No real change, thank God. The suit a little more worn, because continuously worn. The seraphic smile, the curling, expressive fingers, the transcendental talk. 'Everyone is a poet, Russell.' He gurgled at my multicoloured medal ribbons: an aesthetic gesture, merely. Otherwise, the war – happily – might never have been.

Yet before long I became embroiled once more in it; in northern Europe, Belgium, Holland, finally Germany. Tambi, now under the wing of John Roberts and Nicholson and Watson, soldiered on in London in a worthier cause. When I had leaves, we closeted ourselves in familiar pub bars with pints and friendship. He ate a little more regularly now and had an agreed beer allowance. A small strewn room in the publishing house was technically his office, but the real one was the saloon bar of various 'locals', where court was also held. It warmed me to know that he was now materially 'looked after' on a stable base.

The poetic adrenalin could flow without distraction.

Then suddenly it seemed both the war and its aftermath were over and we slid uncertainly into peace. Most of us were not ready for it, mentally or emotionally. To Tambi it had been a proper irrelevance. Life was about quite other things; transcendental things, poetry inspired, poetry flooded. Transcendental; it was still a favoured word with him; with me, too. And he loved words and arrangements of words, rose to them if used as vessels of pure deep feeling, of 'things felt in the blood and felt along the heart'. For Tambi not only the world, in its grosser aspects, was 'too much with us', but perhaps even more destructively, man's niggling, over-analytical mind, always probing, always breaking up, forever intellectually nit-picking; never, it seemed, blending, moulding, making the right, the sublime poetic syntheses of living and being which were there: around, above, under and inside, if only they were recognized, accepted joyfully, transmuted into poems which themselves would forever be a joy and a spur to men.

We settled, he and I, into a sedater, less intensely lived post-war companionship; I with a young family and a fresh career to carve; he to make peace – as far as he could or would – with the constraints of publishing 'admin'. We enjoyed many fond times together; until he translated himself to America and I to the country, when the grip on our sociability loosened. But never broke, nor the friendship itself. That was something that would go on in our hearts and minds without cessation, if our bodies should never meet again. Which at last, at one far-flung point they never did. And now ... and now ... bodies are a frailer medium for friendship.

He was a philosopher, a dreamer, a balmy companion, a man suffused with the spirit, the essence of poetry and poems. He was both an elf and a prince, and altogether lovable. I loved him. Now I mourn him.

David Wright

Winter Verses for Tambimuttu

What, in a letter to the dead,
Is better than to say what is?
Dear Tambi, as I write the snow
Wheels slowly down, and will not stay;
And I am lost for words to say
This January afternoon.

Here is the view from my window:
Dark branches draw a skeleton
Tree against the fail of day,
And under, Eden's waters run
In stillness to the Irish sea.
They falter only at the ford

To etch a line of white across
Their moving motionless surface
As dark as the denuded boughs
That frame a glimmer in the west:
The sun that is about to die,
To burn tomorrow in the east.

I turn the leaves of memory
To see you, prince of Rathbone Place,
In black-out years, defying with
Magnanimous and careless spirit
A boring war, and holding court
In fly-blown pubs for useless art.

You kept a spark alive, I think,
In that dead time, as dead as this
Midwinter landscape I look at,
Where, though the summer leaves be lost,
The living sap's in branch and root,
In ambush for a certain spring.

Nicholas Moore

Tambi the Knife

When I first met Tambi he was living in a tiny flat in Marchmont Street with his blonde wife Jackie – a tiny kitchen and an iron bed. There wasn't room to swing a cat! Nor was there room for a Red under the bed, for it was typically chock-a-block with manuscripts, mostly of unhopefuls – and manuscripts in those days had not yet become the objects of suspicion and subversion they seem to have become today. They were ignored; except by their precious authors. And Tambi, who put them under his bed! There was nowhere else to put them.

I don't quite know when this could have been, I am very bad at dates – probably early in 1939. Nor can I remember the occasion. It was unlike me to go visiting people, as I was rather shy and tended to stay aloof from literary people, if not to shun them like mad. Though I had had my own magazine since 1938, my partner, John Goodland, who was really more interested in finding a *Weltansschauung* than in literature, did most of the contacting of people, whether in person or by letter, though I wrote a few letters. These were mostly to people I had already been put in contact with like George Fraser, who had been my senior (and exemplar) when I was a bejan at St Andrew's University (even then he was an incredibly scholarly and learned critic and poet with a begrudgingly lucid and mellifluous style), and Lawrence Durrell and Henry Miller, with whom another school acquaintance had put me in touch. Kay Boyle I believe I may have written to off my own bat. They were the ones whose help and suggestions and contributions from themselves and their friends really enabled me to start my magazine with the kind of standard I wanted. It may have been through this that I met Tambi, for Durrell at least of these was also very helpful in supporting the beginnings of Tambi's own magazine, too. Or it may have been (as so many later) that I was in search of my precious manuscript which had laid too long under that bed. (I remember from later the many infuriated visits from Kathleen Raine, who would storm at him. After bowing meekly before this wrath, and when she had stormed out of the room like a tigress, he would lift his head a little wearily and say to me with a grin

57

– and rueful really was the word for the expression on his face – 'Isn't she sweet?') But in spite of this, he wasn't really as chaotic as he was made out to be. It was the times that were chaotic and the conditions that surrounded him, rather than he.

Unfortunately, at the time Tambi died, my diabetic sight had become so bad that I had given up taking the papers and heard of it only through my correspondence about Cambridge literary life: it took me a long time to get copies of any and it was too late for me to say my piece, but I didn't and don't go along with very much of what they said. It is true that I have been more or less *hors de combat* since 1969, but when I saw Tambi at a poetry reading in 1969, where I was performing as part of Tony Rudolf's Menarderie, he seemed much the same, happy among his group of adherents, who included Audrey Beecham, as charming – and unchaotic – as ever. It was a curious event if only because it was not I, with my groggy leg, distinct queasiness and nervousness of public appearance whose chair collapsed under him, but one of the other, more assured readers, poor man. I was gratified to see many of my old friends there including Charles Fox, the jazz critic, and Ernst Sigler who had been my friend in the days when I worked for Charles Wrey Gardiner at the Grey Walls Press. It was the last time I saw Tambi.

But he still wrote to me. I remember that when the Cass edition of the complete *PL* came out and was given a full-page rather disparaging and misleading review in *The Times Literary Supplement*, and I managed to get them to print an almost equally long letter that set at least some of the facts right, he wrote: 'You are the only one who had the decency to reply.' I remember also the still boyish enthusiasm with which he wrote to me of the incipient launching of his new *Poetry London/Apple Magazine*: 'I have found a wonderful new backer.' And I remember too how he actually sent a taxi for me to take me to one of his launching parties. Unfortunately, I was still too unwell to get in it myself but I sent the taxi man back with a *Sempervivum* named after him (it is registered with the Sempervivum Society, 'M.J. Tambimuttu'), which I had bred. He was delighted, though later I'm afraid it died. But he was an enthusiast and very single-minded in pursuit of his aims. He was also very generous and gave of himself to others perhaps too freely for his own good, having an innocent, almost naïve trust that the good faith and generosity of others would be as great as his own. And these are qualities that he kept even during the most dire moments of distress and poverty and nervous breakdown that he went through. The sending of a taxi for me like that was typical of the kind of extravagant gestures he would make towards his friends. And many of those he had, especially among artists.

Early on, I seem to remember also meeting him in a pub; I don't think someone took me there to meet him, but that Tambi took me there to meet some of his friends. I recall Tony Dickins expounding the virtues of the magazine with great gusto in his guise of advertising manager, and I think Roy Campbell, who was later a frequent visitor to the office at Manchester Square, because Tambi was intending to publish his translation of St John of the Cross. However that may be, when I did meet Tambi, we took to each other at once.

In 1941 I had started publishing some pamphlets in Cambridge. The first one came out as an Epsilon pamphlet, but the other four came out as *PL* pamphlets. They were by George Scurfield, G.S. Fraser, Anne Ridler and myself. One of them had an illustration by Cecil Collins on the cover, the others had beautifully designed typographical covers by A.D. Nightall of Diemer and Reynolds. Tambi had agreed to take them on under his imprint because I was no business man and he had distribution facilities that I did not. He also had in mind even then the publishing business which he was to develop later on when he could find the backing, and then or soon after he promised me the job of his assistant when he did: a promise he duly kept when he was established. The *Antiquarian Book Monthly Review*, April/May 1979, contains a good account by Alan Smith carefully researched from all available sources of the history of *PL* from 1939 to 1951.*

It seems perhaps slightly to over-emphasize my influence in getting the jazz books published – Tambi was keen on this in his own right – and under-emphasize my influence on the other prose books: that was what Tambi got me there for. I was also there to sort out and return, or occasionally pass on to Tambi, those hosts of manuscripts that would otherwise have reclined for ever under various beds and thus prevent the hordes of angry young women and stern young men coming and shaking their fists at him too frequently. It worked very well. If the poet had any kind of reputation anywhere, or if he did seem to have any talent, he would usually get a polite note with his rejection, or even a letter.

The books I reported on and we discussed where necessary. But we usually agreed on most things. I can think of only one book on which I gave a totally adverse report which he nevertheless published, and of

---

* This is reproduced in facsimile at the end of the present volume.

that it was not the idea I objected to, though the title was pretentious, but the fact that I simply didn't think the contents were good enough. There were some people whose work he liked and knew I didn't and, of course, those he wouldn't give me to read. We simply agreed to differ. That was one of the nice things about Tambi. There was no untold pressure to agree with him when one didn't, so it was easy to work for him and say what one thought. That was maybe why he wanted me there because he tended to be surrounded by sycophants, of whom it could be said you couldn't tell what they were thinking, nor why. The magazine, once the manuscripts had passed, or occasionally circumvented, the first line of defence – me! – he edited entirely himself, as he did the art books and supervision of the details of production. For the early books he employed Berthold Wolpe as typographer. While I was there he had a typographer on his staff: first Michael Swan, who had worked under Wolpe at Faber's and was something of a literary man, too, a Somerset Maugham enthusiast; later Gavin Ewart. He was also much and very intelligently helped by Helen Scott (later Irwin), who assisted him most ably through the chaos.

Now we come to the chaos again. I didn't go a-roving in Fitzrovia, where Tambi made such a good job of a bad job. Some of the myths and misconceptions about the forties which have been repeated *ad nauseam* were set about by people who were on the fringes of the Fitzroving crowds and looked on in awe or envy. Others were set about by those who avoided the scene themselves and therefore knew nothing about it, either at first or second hand. Still others were gleaned by those who read works like Maclaren-Ross's posthumous memoirs; and misunderstood them.

On one of the few occasions I did rove, I remember Julian Maclaren-Ross sitting in the Wheatsheaf, elegant in a seersucker suit, smoking his cigarettes through a long elegant holder and casting a cynical and ironic eye on the proceedings around him. Although he was a nice man and a very good short-story writer, one had the uncomfortable feeling that one was being observed. As indeed one was. With accuracy, but not with malice. But what he was observing was the scene before him; and hearing perhaps some of the conversation – he was good at naturalistic dialogue and at describing the quirks and oddities of people's behaviour. But he was not observing as a social historian or a journalist. All this was grist to his mill as a short-story writer. It was stuff he could use and shape to the demands of his stories based on factual observation, perhaps, but not fact – fiction.

Writers of fiction then did not, as is the habit today, especially among journalists turned writers, do research – with the emphasis on the American *ree* – and then write their fiction against a background of what they took to be solid fact. Fiction, after all, is still fiction anyway. It is really the Personal Heresy all over again. Writers may use real facts, real people, aspects of themselves, but they are putting them into fiction and thereby changing them. They may express more real truth than facts. For facts are nothing in themselves. They need interpretation – and that is where fancy may run riot. Everyone knows that two witnesses seldom see the same thing. Journalists claim to report facts, though they often distort them for political reasons or to make a good story, yet still claim they are true. A writer of fiction may use facts but he writes a story round them which he doesn't claim to be true but which he hopes may express a better, deeper or more interesting truth than do the facts by themselves. I can't think of a better example of the difference between journalists (ephemeral writing) and real writing (of more permanent value) than Kay Boyle's anthology of very short stories, *365 Days*, in which a selection of writers are asked to write a fictional story about some news event for every day of the year. It puts a human perspective on the events.

The forties were not a good time for poets. They were a good time for hangers-on, for literary gossips, for mediocrities, for people who wished to gawp at the great or the would-be great or the play actors. They were good for the kind of people who hoped to see Dylan Thomas crawling round the tables pretending to be a dog begging for pennies, or Roy Campbell taking hold of Stephen Spender by the seat of his pants and having a fight with him. It was a gossip-writer's or literary hanger-on's paradise. But for the serious writer it was a hell. That Tambi had to live in this milieu was his misfortune, but he made the best of it. And his resilience and insouciance made at least his part of the scene a relatively merry one; and of course he had some good friends among his drinking companions. But it was a milieu that gave Dylan Thomas a dual personality and forced him to spend time writing promised kitsch for the BBC rather than getting on with his poems. It was a milieu in which the seeds of mediocrity which afflict us now were sown. Tambi, however, was not mediocre. He cut through this mediocrity like a knife. Most of his well-known friends were not mediocre and he stuck to his purposes through all the trials and tribulations that beset him and managed to achieve some of them against all the odds. The chaos that surrounded him came mostly from the difficulties of the times and from his own impecuniosity: he had the perpetually bothering task of finding backers, getting them to let him have the free hand he wanted and then getting them to get on with the job to his standards. That he wouldn't compromise except on inessentials seemed to me a good quality. Even when he did of necessity have to compromise on these he was reluctant and always felt rather shamefaced about it. I think probably his greatest achievement and, I suppose, his first love, was the production of the illustrated books of poetry illustrated tangentially, so to speak, not literally: Kathleen Raine's *Stone and Flower* by Barbara Hepworth; David Gascoyne's *Poems 1937–1942* by Graham Sutherland; and my *The Glass Tower* by Lucian Freud; and there was a cover and nice drawings by Franciszka Themerson for Ronald Bottrall's *The Palisades of Fear*.

There would have been more of these illustrated books of poetry, possibly by the same authors and others, if Tambi's plans had not been stopped by circumstances. He would have liked to do Durrell and Anne Ridler similarly, but both were already contracted to Faber. Eliot, the director most concerned with poetry at Faber's, was something of a father-figure to Tambi (in the most agreeable sense of the term); he had given him both moral and practical support at the lowest ebb of his fortunes and Tambi was always on his best behaviour when he visited Eliot. I remember his putting on his best suit and asking me if his hair was neat and his tie straight, like a schoolboy going for an interview, and with the same nervousness, when he went to see Eliot. Eliot gave him full-hearted support in his projects. They would not poach from each other. But there were authors we would try to get if their publishers didn't want them. We thought we might, for instance, publish Robert Penn Warren's poems if Eyre and Spottiswoode, who published his novels, didn't want them. But they did, and I remember we got a very agreeable little note from Graham Greene saying, 'You are a good loser.'

Tambi used to keep all his most interesting correspondence and press cuttings, but these all disappeared at some point – God knows where. Of course there are excerpts from some of the reviews in the catalogue which I compiled, but though it was a fairly luxurious affair there wasn't room for much and anyway it was the letters that were the real loss.

Maclaren-Ross, in an amusing but factually inaccurate piece about Tambi, mentions a lunch we had with him. He speculates as to why I was there, and suggests that perhaps it was in order to pay the bill, for I was then working for the Grey Walls Press and he knew that, but not of course that I was promised to Tambi for the future. I was actually there for moral support. I was doing the *PL Book of Modern American Short Stories* for Tambi and he asked me if there were any young English short-story writers I thought good, and I said 'Maclaren-Ross'. I pointed out that he already had a perfectly good publisher, but Tambi still thought it worthwhile to try to get him on his list. I told him it was hopeless. And it was.

We couldn't always get all the people we wanted, and of course other projects never came off because the firm was cut short in mid-career. Some of 'our' books strangely appeared soon afterwards from closely allied firms – the Jankel Adler and Alfred Wallis art books from Nicholson and Watson, for instance, and the Panassie jazz book from Weidenfeld and Nicolson. I negotiated with Wallace Stevens for a selected poems, as I was already friendly with him, but his American publisher Knopf wouldn't sanction it. He had something against Tambi, I don't know what. Later Stevens wrote to me, 'You have taken a bad beating.'

Then, in the prose, though we published what we could of Henry Miller, we couldn't publish his most famous book because of the so-called obscene passages. (Michael Neal, who is still publishing in his magazine *Stroker* in Paris posthumous letters of Miller's tells me that right to the end he never found a regular major publisher.)

There was also *Lolita*. We had published Nabokov's *The Real Life of Sebastian Knight* and so we were offered it. We had a lot of discussion about it but we turned it down, mainly on the grounds that we didn't think it was as well written as *Sebastian Knight*. In spite of the haunting character of Lolita herself and the subject-matter, the book seemed to me to be written in an almost woman's magazine novelettish style. In hindsight, perhaps that was intentional irony on Nabokov's part. But at the time we didn't like that and didn't think it was good enough to risk the future and probable banning or confiscation it would at that time have caused. What effect it would have had on the fortunes of PL, I don't know, but I still think our literary judgement was probably right, unless he revised it later; I read it only in manuscript. But when it did come out, it made Nabokov's fame and fortune and, one hopes, encouraged people to read his better and more important books.

Perhaps I should make a reference too to 'the little prince', the 'mystic guru' and the 'intuitive editor', since these seem to have appeared important to the obituarists. None was very apparent in the practical life of the office or in our personal friendship. Some were more than anything gambits to persuade backers that he was a genius, which, perforce, he had to do. It was true that he said he could judge whether a poet was any good at sight, so to speak, with a first glance at their first manuscript. But I don't think there is anything very special about that or anything different from the way other editors work. On the whole, I think Tambi was more conscientious than most. One of the reasons for the piles under the bed was that when he did read them, he really did read them. And quite contrary to the opinion that he was a charlatan or a fake, he relied far less on 'received opinion' than most editors or publishers, many of whom in my opinion had practically no taste of their own but put an ear to the ground and relied almost entirely on what they thought other people thought good. And far from acting 'the little prince', 'the superior genius' or 'the abstruse mystic', he had very wide and balanced interests and was really an innovator in many directions that are taken for granted now, but were not then, some of which have become perverted by time, as things often are. But his interest was in popular culture as much as in high culture and he was one of the first to seek an interaction between all the different arts and different cultures (taken for granted now and perhaps overplayed, but practically non-existent then).

You can always fault anybody in detail. Everybody makes mistakes. But I don't think you can fault Tambi in tenacity of purpose, worthiness of purpose, nor in what he actually achieved in difficult times and always against the odds. And as well as that, he had a fine sense of fun. Though sometimes a bit touchy about his *amour propre*, he had a sense of purpose and a sense of humour. The chaos lay all around. But given half a chance he would come and cut through it like a knife to attain – with his lyrebird beside him, like some god from one of those ancient Indian legends – yet one more of his long-sought objectives.

Nicholas Moore

Dreamscape

For M.J. Tambimuttu

I expected this reprehensible building
　　　　　Of glass to come shattering down
At Time's bidding,
　　　　　To the wolf's howl.

I had seen the gleam and glint
　　　　　Of it in the wood
As the sun came over the hill
　　　　　And struck it with blues,

Golds and reds, and I said,
　　　　　'It is a monument
In the pines, and tells
　　　　　Of the shine of sense

Among the darkness of living,
　　　　　A cool tomb
That will not wither
　　　　　As the trees in the wood

Or be culled
　　　　　By time's axe
For the woodman's hut
　　　　　Or the fetishist objects one has.

It is indestructible
　　　　　As the imagination
Before the eructations
　　　　　Of visible hatreds.'

Yet I had expected
　　　　　Time to damage
What one erects
　　　　　In youth, there being no bridge,

And age to look upon a hollow
　　　　Emptiness of air
Where once the tower had shown
　　　　Its reflected shapes.

But we live in a glass country
　　　　Among the bones
We knew once
　　　　For their virtuous glow.

Old habits
　　　　Die hard,
And Humanity lives
　　　　Behind its bars.

Kathleen Raine

London did not appreciate Tambimuttu; by this I mean that although many loved Tambi, and others took unscrupulous advantage of him, while others again, who made a point of knowing only the 'right' people, wouldn't have wanted to be known to know Tambi at all, we did not understand who, essentially, he was. There are no nations so culturally provincial as those whose expansionist economics foster in them the illusion of cultural superiority. America is, and England was in this respect unaware even of being unaware of other values enshrined in other cultures. The situation of 'subject races' was in the case of the Indian subcontinent (Tambi was a Ceylonese Tamil) aggravated by the willingness of the Indians themselves to accept the claim of the British Raj that the latter is the superior culture. Did not Macaulay decree for India Western education on the grounds that any Indian literature equal to that of the British could be written on a postcard?

Tambi was of course born and educated under the Raj; his family was Catholic, one brother a Jesuit, another principal of a college in Ceylon. English was for him, as for many Westernized Indians, his first language. He was childlike in his eagerness to conquer the literary world of London – which he did; and the title 'Prince of Fitzrovia' scornfully bestowed (the Fitzroy is a pub in Soho) he sported with joyful pride.

Yet Tambi *was* a prince, and how deeply Indian I came to appreciate only after visiting India myself. He was, for many years, a most beautiful human being, and carried his ragged attire, long hair and nicotine-stained fingers with a childlike innocence of the kind of social rules that might have looked upon them askance. He really was a prince of Bohemia, or rather a prince *in* Bohemia, coming as he did from a Tamil royal house. His background was also learned: 'My uncle is the greatest aesthetician of this century,' he once told me – the name of A.K. Coomaraswamy (friend of Yeats, later curator of the Oriental Department of the Boston Museum of Art, where his superb collection of Northern Indian miniatures remains) meant little to me at the time, and nothing at all to most of those for whom Tambi bought drinks in the Fitzroy Tavern (they hoping he would also publish their poems). But of course Tambi was perfectly right, and my own debt to Coomaraswamy is, since I grew up in these matters, incalculable. He, on the level of his great erudition and expertise, has brought to the West what Tambi also in his degree brought to the London of the war and post-war years, a different scale of values.

To return to that provincial London duck-pond that imagined itself the great world. The current fashions, whether for left-wing political verse (the Oxford poets), for the 'scientific' criticism and its resulting poetry (the positivists of Cambridge under the sway of Russell and Wittgenstein, the Cavendish Lab, and, more immediately, of I.A. Richards and William Empson) or surrealism (there was a small overflow of the surrealist movement of France and Belgium) had one thing in common: Marxism, logical positivism and surrealism were all secular movements and, with the partial exception of some surrealists, took 'reality' to be what post-Cartesian science had told us it was. All these were, explicitly or implicitly, atheist ideologies of a generation in which the majority had never given serious thought to the spiritual nature of man, of which truly imaginative poetry is the expression.

Of course the greatest poets living at that time were remote from that duck-pond: W.B. Yeats in Ireland, Vernon Watkins resolutely living in Wales, Edwin Muir rooted in Scotland, David Jones scarcely emerging from his room in Harrow. Dylan Thomas was an exception, he too being a frequenter of the Fitzroy, and I wonder if we know who *he* was, either. Stories about Tambi and Dylan Thomas usually concerned some drunken incident in a pub; fewer understood the springs from which their poetry flowed.

Chaos, to be sure, suited Tambi very well; princes need no social ambitions, and there is a tradition in the subcontinent of leaving home and kingdom with a begging-bowl. Tambi's begging-bowl, filled from time to time by people in high places (his friends tended to be as often as not members of the Indian or the English aristocracy – and Tambi treated all men alike as if they too were princes), was a cornucopia generously poured out on the just and the unjust alike, as long as they were poets. Between penury and princely magnanimity *Poetry London* came into existence, a beautiful production, visually and in other ways. Somehow among all the dross Tambi picked out the gold of pure imagination; a quality unregarded in that time and place, but Tambi discerned the imaginatively authentic as naturally as an animal selects its proper food. As an editor he had no programme, no party to support; he chose by the direct perception of that living radiance which is the sole mark of genius. One touch of imagination was for Tambi worth more than all the acquired artifice of talent. He saw right through pretences: 'Mr Eliot is really a wild man, like me,' I remember him saying with that warm, happy laugh of his; and the grave Mr Eliot had a warm spot for Tambi; he too recognized the authentic.

In what way was Tambi Indian? I have since asked myself. What is that other culture which he brought – perhaps unawares, for he was under the spell of the West – to the judgement of ours? I have an Indian friend whose culture-shock in England was severe: 'In India,' she explained, 'everything has inner dimensions. Here there is only the outside.' She felt more at home in Ireland in that respect. Tambi had those inner dimensions. *Sat-chit-ananda*, being-consciousness-bliss, is at the heart of Indian spirituality, and that spirituality extends from the lingam of Siva to the world-renouncing of the Lord Buddha (and indeed Siva is himself the supreme ascetic also, in another aspect). There is no break between the sensual and the aesthetic. The touchstone is life, not concept. Where Christian theology has lost itself in a mass of abstractions, India makes living experience the test: the *guru* is not one who gives lessons in philosophy but in a refinement of consciousness itself. To Tambi, wine, women and song (dance too, on occasion he would dance like Siva Nataraja himself) were not vices but the ecstasy of life. He had no sense of guilt whatsoever in the moralistic Western sense, although he did on many occasions have a headache or hangover.

Although his father was a Catholic, Tambi preferred his Hindu uncles and aunts and cousins, and the Hindu festivals (where he ate, against the injunction of his parents, 'food offered to idols'), and his own finest poem is his 'Gita Sarasvati', Hindu goddess of the arts. As to all the isms of the time (positivism, existentialism, structuralism, surrealism, or for that matter Marxism and Thomism) no ism had for Tambi any significance whatsoever, and the idea of attempting to write, or to judge a work, according to any formula extraneous to the work itself was simply not a way of thinking he could have conceived. For him a work of art was a blossom on the deathless tree of life.

At the Hindu memorial service for Tambi which I attended in London, as I looked at the enlarged photograph of Tambi's beautiful eloquent face, wreathed in marigolds, with the many bunches of flowers, and incense, with the rhythms of Indian music transposing the disused church hall of the Bhavan Centre, somehow to the banks of the Jumna, I felt that the great river of Indian civilization which had brought him was carrying Tambi away from us, who had thought we knew him. I felt his reproach to me, who have for so much of my life abandoned the *sat-chit-ananda* of poetry for the sterilities of criticism and scholarship. That, it seemed, was Tambi's loving parting message; that most Indian genius of the pure spirit of ecstasy at the heart of life was what we recognized and responded to in him, and what he discerned and evoked in those poets he gathered round him in a magic circle, not of the Fitzroy where the drunks thought they knew him, but of *Poetry London* whose English title was belied by Tambi's symbol of pure ecstasy, the lyrebird, theme on which so many artists designed variations for its cover. 'I love ecstasy,' Tambi once said to me; not heavy English beer, but *amrita*, drink of the gods of India, was the sacred draught of Tambi's genius.

Kathleen Raine

Time-lag

Remembering my long-ago friend Tambi

Words spoken long ago, unheard, unheeded then,
Voices of friends unprized in time's day-to-day,
Only now in this long-after where I am
I have received messages from the long gone
Whose past is in my present always.

And before lifetime memories
Those spacious regions of the mind,
A once familiar land that opens in this room
That immemorial imagined city
Where deathless words were spoken,
Heard here and now, a world away.

Drawn to our times and places, who can say
What law of that remembered country we obey,
Those friends who come and go, knowing no more than we
What purposes join hands and hearts
From the ends of the earth, from the beginning of time.

No truth of the living,
Spoken or unspoken, can cease to be,
And will, on some predestined day
Be understood, as I from beyond years
Have overheard the wisdom that circles the world for ever
Speaking immortal words in loved familiar voices.

Patricia Ledward

A Few Recollections of Tambimuttu

How about Tambimuttu? The dauntless Tambi?

We all had countless stories to tell. Some of my stories I would never tell a soul. But I remember this blazing young poet from Ceylon in many guises during those years when he regenerated English poetry. His passion overcame all obstacles. He disregarded the physical necessities of life: yet food, clothing, shelter, money to pay the printers; they all materialized. Poetry was his goddess.

He and I walked the black streets one rainy November night. Rain dripped from his hair, his nose, his sleeves; he coughed incessantly. A passing car lit up the trees in Leicester Square and he said, 'In the summer, dear, we must come and sit together beneath these trees. It would be such fun.' A few soaking blocks farther on, another inspiration seized him. 'I know a stall in Sloane Square where I've always wanted to go and eat pies. Let's go there now. It has a little awning to keep the rain off. Let's go there now and eat pies. It would be such fun.'

Another time we sat together at a table. His hair fell into his eyes; he twisted his fingers together until they cracked. He began to recite:

> 'Take of me what is not my own
> My love, my beauty and my poem
> The pain is mine and mine alone. . . .'

'Kathleen Raine is so good,' he said, 'so good. I'm fighting to achieve stillness in myself. Then I shall be able to produce something good. T.S. Eliot says I'm going to be a great poet. I could have cried when he said that. He's so kind. He's like a father to me. Sometimes I suffer dreadfully. You have no idea how I live. Such loneliness. No home, no one to belong to. But I have to go through all this. I have to suffer life so as to understand life. One day perhaps all the people in the world will be chanting my poems. Perhaps one day I shall be a saint.'

We stood by the ticket-machines in Piccadilly tube station. He was telling me extraordinary happenings from his extraordinary life. I said, 'You've had a lot of luck.'

'Not luck. I don't believe in luck.' He was almost angry. 'I have a vision, a *vision*. I follow where the vision beckons.'

Passers-by stared at him curiously, this gaunt young man with the burning eyes.

'You see, I am not a man. I am a spirit. I am everyone. I am everywhere.'

At that moment he did, indeed, look more like a spirit than a physical being.

We dined together at the Café Royal where we all used to meet from time to time when we weren't meeting in the pubs made famous by Dylan Thomas or Maclaren-Ross. Or perhaps we were dining with somebody else, because Tambi seldom had money for any food other than pies in Sloane Square or from similar all-night stalls.

He was saying, 'You English are funny people. You can't bear too much truth, too much nakedness. You have to wrap your feelings up in Cellophane. I feel so much older than any of you. You lovely English people! I love you all so much. You'll be much poorer after the war. But you'll be happier.'

Then again a mood of anguish clutched him. 'I have nothing, I tell you, nothing. I have no home, no child, no place where I belong.' He crashed his fist down on the table. 'You don't know what it's like.' He took me by the shoulders and shook me. 'You, the evening before you go away into the Forces, promise you'll come out with me. Then, at least, I shall possess the thought that you chose *me* to spend your last evening with.'

Joan Wyndham-Shirarg

The following poem of Tambi's was written to me when I was in Cambridge after a rather sad little happening at the Hog in the Pound. Tambi was propounding to me his usual plans – that we should get married and have lots of little coffee-coloured children. I was, as usual, resisting. Then Tambi suddenly dashed out to Oxford Street, returning with a very small ring (purchased, I think, at Woolworth's) set with lots of brightly sparkling fake opals, which he pressed on my finger amid cheers and toasts.

Retiring to the loo in embarrassment I made the mistake of washing my hands, only to find my ring was now a skeleton – all the little stones had come out and been washed down the drain!

Such was my shame and embarrassment I didn't dare return, but slipped out the back way and took the next train to Cambridge. Soon after, I received this rather touching poem.

Letter to J.W.

Sprawling in my bed on Sunday morning
I am wondering why I'm still alone,
While my charming friends are at Cambridge and Doncaster,
Why is it I'm always on my own;
But I accept it as the awful warning
This is all, this is all there is to love's fiesta.

How is it that all my friends arrange it
On the LMS flying to home and wife,
Their baggage bursting with wonderful things to eat,
With F.L.s, chocolate and their suits that fit;
But I'm a simpleton, cannot fix my life
To bring me these nice happinesses and treats.

I've always loved the tied-up, wonderful object
And the hidden fire behind the screen.
I've loved the girls, Swansdown and Black Amber
And lost all hope, half-way through the project.
No, Joan dear, I'm not what I seem,
(I also love the Cambrian dales in November.)

73

While you are dreaming by the quiet Cam
And the dappled willows lightly kiss your eyes,
I am a prisoner with my lonely task
Worrying like Prince Hamlet who I am.
I plan as usual, but the golden prize
Is still, alas, beyond my sensual grasp.

You walk about in green lanes, protected
From the beer-stains and the toothy traffic.
You talk with Chopin in secluded spots
And in the crowded Carib feel elated;
While nightly I with dust and ashes maffick
By the fireside, you are patching Chris's coats.

You are, my dear, I see more temperate and calm
Like the Provençal sun and limpid air;
The vineyards full of palpitating fruit
And the weathered arches of Avignon.
Your dreams full fair and golden like your hair
And gentle as the warm lights twinkling there.

Not too reckless when you go to the greyhounds
And not too hasty when you choose a man.
With level eyes and heart you take the fences
Like Golden Miller, easily, in the jumps;
And I think you've narrowed all your fancies
Underneath the mind's glittering lenses.

Your life is run with Thomas Cook precision;
Work from seven to six and then you rest.
On Friday you will go to the Sadler's Wells
And grace the Gargoyle with your vivid presence;
And then on Saturday you'll pack your best
And off you'll go to hear the Cambridge bells.

But then, my dear, my friends are all like that,
They all are happy and I wish them well.
They have their shining cars and planes at Heathrow
To fly their noble dreams to Rome and back;
And if the weather wished them any ill
They'll no doubt find their fun and games in Soho.

But I was always moody, aimless, pointless.
I never seem to understand the set-up.

I am, perhaps, the thunder-carrying cloud
Or brittle wool-pack, and really couldn't care less.
My home has been the solid London pub
For eight long years, beloved.

I spent the first years of the war in Holborn
Eating bacon and chips and spam and chips
In the Coffee An'; or rice and curry
At that Indian place where I first took you, darling.
But then, that was before the place was hit
By the ghastly famine in rice, and Jerry.

But now, at last, the splendid rain is falling,
And the hungry earth is spoiled with kisses.
The bird of sleep has fallen on my eye
With its raven breast and duskier wings;
And I, no longer, have my rambling wishes,
The singing rain has nested in my eye.

O bless the summer of this forgotten country,
And praise the offerings of tangle, corn and fern.
In every well, dear, there is a reflection,
In every tangled heart a shaft for entry.
I send you all my love; and fair return
For me, a modest share of your perfection.

Tambi

Betty Relle

It was in late 1942 or early 1943, when I was working at the Foreign Office, that I first met Tambi. The rendezvous was the famous meeting-place for much of artistic and literary London, the Swiss Pub in Soho. I seem to remember that Mulk Raj Anand was among the group.

Tambi immediately impressed me with his charm and enthusiasm; there was something very sympathetic and childlike in his approach to life and people. He believed in giving everyone a chance regardless of their status or fame, so he attracted the widest possible range of collaborators from Henry Moore, whose *Shelter Sketchbook* Tambi published, to people like myself without any training or experience.

During the course of the evening Tambi suddenly asked me to become his secretary. The fact that I knew no shorthand and couldn't type did not seem to worry him in the least. I was interviewed by John Roberts, the shrewd and amiable business manager of Nicholson and Watson, the parent company of Editions Poetry London. He warned me that Tambi did not usually keep his secretaries very long and that it would be no use coming to him for help if I found life with Tambi difficult. This in fact proved to be the case; Tambi made so many good-natured advances to me in the office that Nicholas Moore, who was also working there, had to put up his umbrella to keep him at bay. After a while I got fed up and said I was leaving.

It so happened that to amuse myself I had done a design for a letterpress jacket for *The Poems of Hölderlin* which Michael Hamburger had translated. When I finally went to John Roberts and told him I wanted to leave, he opened a drawer in his desk and pulled out the Hölderlin book jacket and asked if I had done it. When I said I had, he said it was very good and would I like to take charge of production for Nicholson and Watson. On my demurring that I knew nothing about typography, he said, 'Well you can learn, can't you?' And on my supposing that I could, he gave me the job and so I got my start. In this position I found myself acting as liaison between frustrated authors who couldn't get an answer out of Tambi, and Tambi himself. So the stock answer to many people's frustration was 'Go and see Betty Jesse', and up to a point this worked.

John Roberts, who was acting on behalf of a firm of printers with a large paper allocation and nothing to print, had a lot of vision and had done the same with Tambi as he had with me. On the strength of an early number of *PL* he had responded to Tambi's request for financial support in much the same way as he did later with me. John knew how to handle Tambi and with a printing background he appreciated Tambi's insistence on high standards of typography and production.

People were drawn to Tambi because they sensed in him a special understanding of their creativity. A poet or an artist needs to be 'fed', and once one little thing is published you can then branch out. It happened to so many people through Tambi and he seemed to give

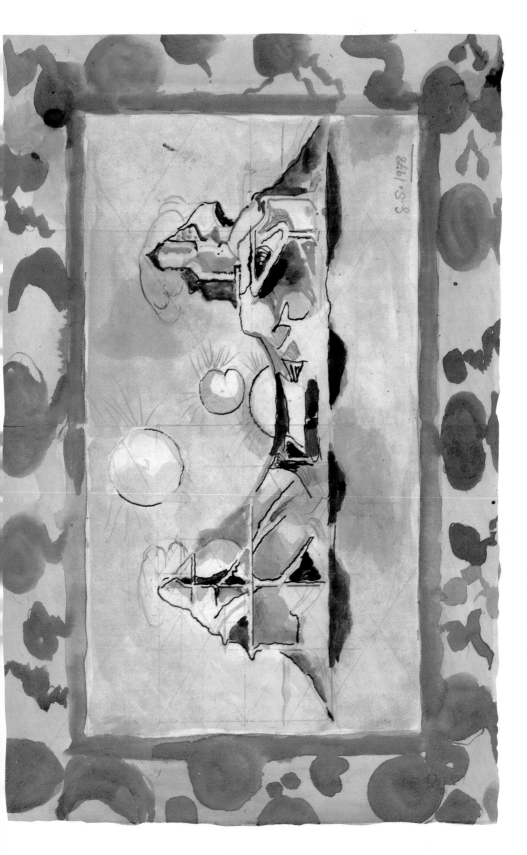

Untitled, John Piper. 39 × 27 cm, ink, chalk and gouache on paper, 1986. The artist made this painting especially for the present volume.

Overleaf: Illustration to David Gascoyne's poem 'Mountains' (page 119) by Graham Sutherland. 24.5 × 37 cm, ink, watercolour and gouache on paper, 1978. This is one of a set of four illustrations by Sutherland of Gascoyne's poems, painted especially for Tambimuttu for use in *Poetry London* magazine. (The illustration to Gascoyne's 'Inferno' was published in *Poetry London/Apple Magazine* No. 1, October 1979.)

Lyrebirds by Ceri Richards. *Above*: 26 × 20 cm; *left*: 25 × 18.5 cm, ink and gouache on paper, 1943. Two of a series of 'sketchdesigns for a cover design' contained in a sketchbook, 26 × 20 cm. (Reproduced by permission of Mel Gooding)

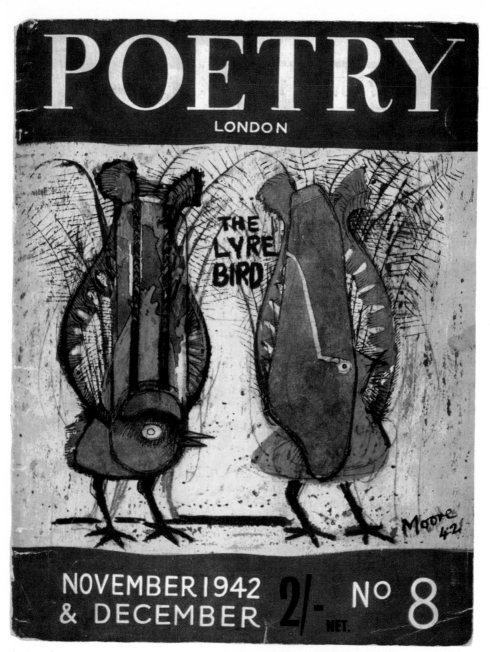

Cover of *Poetry London* No. 8, November/December 1942, with lyrebird design by Henry Moore. (Reproduced by permission of the Henry Moore Foundation)

them this gift – and it *is* a gift. Tambi was able to see beyond what most people did, as with Dylan Thomas. He was a modern visionary – an outmoded word, but it applies to Tambi. Tambi would go to see T.S. Eliot occasionally (he used to call him 'Uncle Tom'). He respected Eliot and was always quoting him, and I think Eliot recognized the person Tambi was.

Tambi never talked to me in a deeper way about his work, and when 'off-duty' he played very much on the outside. But when I think about it there was a tremendous depth to him which I wasn't lucky enough to plumb, because ours was not really that kind of relationship. This was a secret side of Tambi which didn't really impinge on me. We all went round in droves and it was all fun – drinking and laughing and Tambi playing the fool. We used to go to Julian Trevelyan's house down by the river where we would stay during the bombing. There would be quite a few of us there. Tambi would strip naked and run through the rooms just like a little boy. He was to have Helen Scott, his next secretary, bathing him, and she used to run through whipping him with a towel, and it was all fun. It should be remembered that this was the war and we all felt lucky to be alive – there was bombing every day – and so life took on a completely different meaning. We wanted a laugh and a joke. We also used to visit the Shaw-Lawrences at Richmond. Muriel Shaw-Lawrence was a great friend of Tambi's and very kind to him, and there were many parties there.

I did notice Tambi's underlying loneliness and I remember how he used to remind me he was a prince, and I used to wonder why he became conscious of this. But I realized that, coming from Sri Lanka at such a time to literary London, which was full of snobbery, he needed to draw others to him to give him confidence, and very good he was at it, too. I remember Tambi's first wife, Jackie, a pretty blonde with a gentle personality and sweet nature, who was diabetic. Tambi was broken-hearted when eventually they separated.

Tambi very much enriched my life; the six or seven years I worked with him were some of the most stimulating times I have ever had, full of interest, amusement, humanity – but sometimes maddening! For instance, I remember the time when Tambi hadn't got a coat, because he didn't really think about his own comforts. One day John Roberts said, 'Here's some money, Betty. Take Tambi out and buy him a coat.' The weather was freezing cold (in 1947, I think). Do you think I could buy him a coat? No! He wanted some porcelain or glass. I said, 'For God's sake, Tambi, we're supposed to buy you a coat.' We never got him a coat. He wouldn't have it. He had no sense of money whatsoever. That was his one big weakness and the reason that people got fed up with him. He didn't spend money on himself, except when he was wining and dining people. He certainly loved helping people; if you needed any help of any kind you could always go to Tambi and he would do what he could. He also loved bringing people together, not only through their writing or art, such as the great poets, writers and artists he brought together in collaboration for *Poetry London* or the Editions Poetry London books; but many personal relationships were formed through Tambi, and of this he was always proud.

During and just after the war, Tambi seemed to have the world in his hand and everybody on his side. Thanks to John Roberts who backed him loyally, he achieved a wonderful seven years of publishing. After the war things changed and money was much tighter.

Tambi brought home to me the fact that always in my inner heart I believed that there might be somebody, somewhere, who thought the same way as I did about freedom and generosity of spirit; and in a curious kind of way, why I was one of his fans was because he gave me back faith in human nature. It is simple generosity of spirit which is to me so valuable, and Tambi had this in abundance. I think a lot of other people were aware of Tambi's special qualities, and of his great flair and intuition, and his open-handed generosity persuaded many people to work for him for very small rewards. His success made some people jealous.

Tambi had the tremendous gift of being able to get right down to people's psyche immediately and bring out the child in them, because he was a child himself. I have never met anyone like this since, and I don't suppose I shall ever again, and that's the greatest compliment I can pay him.

Michael Hamburger

For Tambi

In 1942, when I was eighteen, Tambimuttu accepted my Hölderlin translations for his Editions Poetry London. They had already been considered and, I believed, accepted by another publisher, who changed his mind; and T.S. Eliot at Faber and Faber had also read them, but could not see his way to publishing such a book in wartime. (More than ten years later, Eliot was to quote a passage from the rambling Introduction to that first book of mine, in his Goethe lecture of 1954.) The book, *The Poems of Hölderlin*, duly appeared in 1943, in time for the centenary of Hölderlin's death – thanks to a happy conjunction of Tambi's enthusiasm with the efficiency of Nicholson and Watson, who had taken over the practical side of his publishing affairs. After a glaring misprint on the first page – 'greatful' for 'grateful' – even the printers' devils were not more in evidence than in many subsequent books of mine. By the time it appeared, I was doing intensive training as an infantryman in Kent, and could no longer obtain progress reports from Tambi at the Soho pub – the Swiss in Old Compton Street – at which we had first met and continued to meet almost nightly whenever I was in London. The timing had become acute not only because of the centenary, of which I had been quite unaware when I began to translate Hölderlin at school, but because that first prospective publisher had commissioned a rival translation, so that a race had started between the two firms, over a German poet known only to a handful of English speakers at the time, in the middle of a war against Germany.

In my book of 'intermittent memoirs', *A Mug's Game*, I told the story of my being marched into my company commander's office, expecting some reprimand or punishment, and ordered to 'represent the Regiment', the Royal West Kent, at a Hölderlin reading and talk I had been invited to give at the Poetry Society, but refused on the grounds that I was otherwise engaged, as a soldier – though really because I was too shy to appear in public. This officer's command was as characteristic of a vanished era as the circumstance that my juvenile book was reviewed in *Punch*, amongst other periodicals – and more seriously, more magnanimously, than I could now expect any work of

79

mine to be reviewed anywhere in Britain. I can't recall with certainty whether Tambi was present at this launching of the book, but suppose he was. The occasion was such an ordeal for me – many years were to pass before I could bring myself to read in public – that I hid in the audience while friends read my scripts.

Because the Army granted me a wholly unforeseen spell of leisure in 1944, when I was stationed in the Shetlands, where military routine was in abeyance, I was able to offer Tambi another translation, *20 Prose Poems of Baudelaire*, published by Editions Poetry London in 1946. Before the first book had sold out, Tambi had not only broken with Nicholson and Watson but left the country. Some three decades later, and back in England, he astonished me by asking me to let him reissue that first book. He seemed not to know that I had completely recast and enlarged my Hölderlin for a book published in England and America in 1952, produced a Penguin paperback with prose versions in 1961, and added many more verse translations for my *Hölderlin: Poems and Fragments* of 1967 (enlarged yet again for the edition of 1980). Tambi was on bad terms with time. That was his distinction and his affliction.

Although my association with him had continued sporadically throughout those decades, for me, too, Tambi remained bound up with that first phase, with the magnanimity, muddle and unworldliness of that vanished era. On brief leaves I would return to Soho, most memorably for a celebration of VE day with Tambi and other Soho friends; and after my demobilization and return to England in 1947, I still went to the Soho pubs, though Dylan Thomas was no longer a regular at the Swiss, and not only the haunts, but the company, had changed. From the early years I remember only one visit to Tambi at his home, where I met his frist wife Jacqueline, and several visits to his office in Manchester Square, where my later sister-in-law, Elizabeth File, was to work for Nicholson and Watson.

I think it must have been in 1952, at a party given for him and his second wife, Safia Tyabjee, by Kathleen Raine, on their way to New York from India, that I saw Tambi again after our Soho meetings. In the later 1950s I contributed a poem and a book review to his *Poetry London–New York*. In 1958 he published an American edition of my book of poems, *The Dual Site*. (Only one poem of mine, very soon condemned and never reprinted, had appeared in his original *PL* magazine.) One day in the later 1960s, I set out on a search for Tambi in New York, mainly in Greenwich Village, walking from street to street, temporary home to temporary home, in sweltering heat, finally tracking him down in a restaurant where we had a meal together before he went off to his temporary lodgings of the moment. Because that meeting had nothing to do with publishing business, it was a true celebration of the continuity. In 1968 I received a series of desperate letters from Tambi. He was at Cambridge, Massachusetts, trying to write a book on Tantra and a book of memoirs, which he wanted me to get serialized in *The Sunday Times*, to earn him the 'pot of money' which Lawrence Durrell had told him the serialization would bring in. 'Marsha phoned me from New York to say you could arrange for me to write my memoirs in *The Sunday Times*. Could you?' I had to tell him that I could not, having no connection whatever with that or any other Sunday newspaper. Meanwhile, 'Telephone and gas will be cut off next week unless I pay, and the rent is due on the first,' he wrote on 25 June. His papers and books were scattered among three different refuges. He was also waiting for an appointment at Harvard that cannot have materialized, since he returned to England that year.

Other parties followed, other homes and offices, other patrons, other publishing schemes that always tended to begin with a bang and end with a whimper. Tambi came to our London house but did not get on with another old Soho friend, Tom Good. I went to his Kensington home and we talked mainly of old times. In 1972 my son Richard was called in for the frantic last-minute preparations for Tambi's *Festschrift for Katharine Falley Bennett*, assembled overnight in a burst of activity as typical of Tambi as his long periods of illness, despondency and idleness. My contribution was a scrap of verse jotted down on a transatlantic flight.

After we moved to Suffolk in 1976 I saw little more of Tambi, though we met again by chance at one of the Cambridge Poetry Festivals. His invitation to the launching of his *Poetry London/Apple Magazine* party in 1979 reached me after the event, and I did not contribute to the last resuscitation of his old imprint. The next invitation was that to South London for his wake and funeral. It was only at his open coffin that I learnt about his Roman Catholic baptism, his brothers in London and his daughter in America. Tambi had rarely been explicit about his background or relationships. Direct, inquisitive questions were apt to be deflected by a cryptic chuckle and a muttering of jocular red herrings. In the early years he had called himself Meary James (or John Meary, I understood at one time), in later years, Thurairajah. To his friends he was always Tambi, a person one did not wish or need to place against any particular background – a queer and unique fish swimming against the current, against time.

Since by now I have translated very nearly all the poems of Hölderlin that appeal to me, it was hard to find one left untranslated; and a new Hölderlin version seemed the right pointer to our association, a closing of the circle. It happened that I found a little poem I must have overlooked in all my successive translating bouts. Probably written in 1800, at a time when Hölderlin had already turned to his visionary, prophetic 'hymns' and fragments of 'hymns' in Pindaric or free verse, it was one of the last of his classicizing odes and elegies. Although only thirty years old in 1800, he had come to the end of his personal hopes and ambitions. Another five or six years remained before his total change of personality, the death-in-life of his so-called madness; but the 'arc' of his first life, his spring and summer, had run its course. What was left was the life-in-death of these elegiac lines.

Strangely enough, this little poem says what I feel, but have been unable to write, about the many old friends I have lost in recent years – so many of them that one commemoration has jostled, clashed with the next. That made it more appropriate still than the mere authorship or its connection with Tambi and my first book.

Friedrich Hölderlin

The Departed

Translated from the German by Michael Hamburger,
in memory of Tambimuttu

With my own kind I lived and could grow for a day that was fleeting,
   One by one they depart, gone from me into their sleep.
Yet you sleepers within me are wakeful, and in my related
   Soul an image of each, fugitive, lingers and rests.
And more living there you live on where the God-given spirit's
   Joy rejuvenates all, all who have aged, and the dead.

Bryan Guinness

On a Ledge

Le silence éternel de ces espaces infinies m'effraie.
                                        Pascal

Caught from oblivion on a ledge
We've made the world our trysting-place
And watch earth's marvels grow to mask the edge
While the sequence of the seasons
Beats the drum of endurance
The long slow tocsin of time.

And to that pulse
Who feels the most the onrush of the year
The Young Ones when it surges with the first force
Or the Old
Across the swirling orchestra
Of springs that are no more?

But we at least have never seen
Such silver in a hedge
Such gold as on the furze that crowns the hill,
Such glory spout in water as it falls. . . .

Yet all's been seen, all's been felt
All's been sung before
And Time there is no more:

Yet Time there must be more
For Time will still rotate, revolve
On spiralled turn
Towards no end. . . .

By chance in Time
Can I have stood
Under another sun
To see the selfsame rose,
One petal less or more,
Since all's been seen before?
Been felt, been sung before?

Or shall I touch your fingertips?
This once, and never more?

Anne Ridler

Wentworth Place, Keats Grove

The setting Sun will always set me to rights.

Keats, to Benjamin Bailey

Keats fancied that the nightingale was happy
Because it sang. So beautiful his garden,
Behind the gate that shuts the present out
With all its greed and grimy noise,
I fall into a like mistake: to think
Because there are such depths of peace and greenness,
Greenness and peace, because the mulberry
Invites with laden arms supported like the prophet,
Because the chestnut candles glimmer crimson,
That heartache could not flourish among these flowers,
Nor anguish resist the whisper of the leaves.

Angry for him, blessing his gift, I accuse
The paradise that could not save him,
Sickness and grief that sunsets could not heal.

Helen Irwin

Tambi

It is of no great consequence, what I have to tell, but Tambi would have liked it. Forty-three years is a long while. It was May or June 1945, the year after D-Day, when I went for an interview to 26

Manchester Square for the post of secretary to *Poetry London*. Re-entering in my mind that familiar scene, trying to recapture images of the past, I find myself wondering why the name 'Tambimuttu' suddenly evokes for me a flower – an iris: not one of the slender, spiky kind, but a purple giant of the old-fashioned type called 'bearded', with velvet petals laid back and three petal-like stigmas at the centre. Why, indeed? I remember a whole bank of these in childhood – especially the scent. This is of no consequence, so casually I take down the *Oxford Dictionary of Gardening* (1956), Volume II, CO–JA. I am still peripatetic around my subject. Now there is no way of knowing when this volume was last used, or by whom; yet the back flap is folded conveniently into IRIS. Before me lies a perfect diagram of the flower itself, in monochrome. (Colour I shall return to.) And the form? Yes, of course! The lyrebird.

In May 1945 a small advertisement had appeared on the back page of *The New Statesman and Nation*. It was headed 'Progressive Publisher' and gave a box number. Progress, in those days, meant freedom and breadth of vision; it meant rebuilding, with a proper intelligence. We who had survived the Forces (largely by letter-writing), who had discussed articles, poems and short stories in monthly journals such as *Horizon* and *New Writing* and had feasted critically on each slim volume of poetry as it appeared, were attuned to the very word. We were more or less marked by experience; we needed our deeper values. That is where Tambi with his editing of the magazine *Poetry London* came in. His precision and creativity encapsulated our need.

The publisher of the box number might have been one of several or somebody quite new. I took a chance and answered the advert. I was not yet demobilized, though hostilities in Europe were all but over. I had spent a doleful two years in the War Office (issuing wireless equipment). This had followed a longer spell of nursing in an army hospital as a Red Cross VAD. It was the sixth year of war. I was twenty and a ballet dancer when it all began.

The house at 26 Manchester Square (now No. 4) had a large, carpeted landing on the first floor, at the top of curved stairs. Here was a switchboard and friendly young telephonist. She directed me to the second floor, where Editions Poetry London occupied the front room. (Weidenfeld and Nicolson were in a smaller office behind.) The *PL* room looked north across the square to where the Wallace Collection could be seen through trees. As I entered the room, bright afternoon sunlight was flooding in diagonally. It lit a marble mantelpiece and a clutter of memorabilia: large invitation cards; small snapshots; shells and a piece of driftwood silvered by tide. Tambimuttu's desk was, just then, in a strip of shadow between sash-windows and facing the door. He came to the centre of the room, holding out his hand. He looked slim and prosperous in a brown corduroy jacket (borrowed, I later learned) and a beige shirt. Tambi always wore a tie – a dark blue one of Indian silk, perhaps.

His weight never altered. Grey trousers just balanced on hip-bones, and when he moved about the room, making rhetorical statements or proclaiming bits of poetry, he would hitch them up, tightening the long end of a leather belt with a slick gesture.

'Won't you have a cigarette?' he said immediately, proffering a packet of twenty Player's Navy Cut.

The courteous gesture and the deep, melodious voice with its long vowel sound ('Woon't') triggered an identical memory of exactly two years earlier. Then I had met Tambi for the first time, having gone to Craven House, Kingsway (the address of the magazine), to find him in a long, narrow upstairs room teeming with books and letters. It was dark there, in contrast with the lovely May morning. I had just received a War Office telegram saying that my husband, R. Brian Scott, had been killed in North Africa. I wanted to know which poems of his Tambi still had and what was happening to them.

Tambi's response was simple, practical and exactly right! I liked the tone of his voice. Just as now, he had offered me a cigarette (everyone smoked in those days). We had met casually once or twice since, at crowded poetry gatherings. Each time he would come up to me with great kindness: 'I'm going to publish your husband's poems in *PL*,' he would say. Nothing happened. Meanwhile, I had withdrawn into myself.

At Manchester Square now, two years on, I noticed that Tambi's slim, brown, double-jointed fingers turned back like flower petals as he struck the match. They were stained by a pen of purple ink (the iris!). Every other sentence of his was punctuated with 'y'know'. It gave a confiding air of unconventionality, until one became used to it. Tambi conducted the interview in a relaxed and friendly manner, but with perfect adequacy. Betty Jesse was there to help him. She had come up from Nicholson and Watson, on the first floor. Theirs was the publishing house; they paid all the bills. This was good for Tambi and *PL*; but it tied him, increasingly, to an inferior printer who was on the board. Tambi asked whether I did shorthand. 'Very convenient, y'know,' he said solemnly; so I didn't tell him how I hated shorthand for its massacre of the English language! (Typing was all right – that was like piano playing.) Instead, I told him my 'speeds', lately acquired through a Pitman's course.

He began to move about the room, selecting objects to show me. There was a large, natural flint, for instance, holed like a sculpture, a present from Henry Moore. Moore's lyrebird drawings were familiar to me from Nos 7 and 8 of *Poetry London*. Tambi fetched books he was proud of: Kathleen Raine's first book of poems, *Stone and Flower*, with drawings by Barbara Hepworth (1943); Nicholas Moore's *The Glass Tower*, with drawings by Lucian Freud (1944) and David Gascoyne's *Poems 1937–1942*, sublimely illustrated by Graham Sutherland.

We were still living in a restricted world, largely cut off from the Continent of Europe, but broadened by the many cultured refugees for whom Great Britain was now 'home'. A small international stream found its way continuously through London: poets and painters, those returning from the Forces; also journalists, diplomats and lecturers on leave from foreign missions. All these appeared to pass through the *PL* office, or were sooner or later introduced to the Hog in the Pound. Tambi brought people together, within a bond of art and friendship, by dint of his own natural ego. It was by this same unitary instinct, refined, that he gave London publishing a new frame.

There was a childlike vanity about him which was most disarming. I must have noticed it on that first afternoon in Manchester Square as he showed me the treasures of *PL*. It was the 'child' in him that touched one's maternalism (he was five or six years older than I), and this brought a tolerance of his unremitting ego. I never went to bed with Tambi. It would have been unthinkable: like incest, rather.

The Gascoyne volume was really the apotheosis of Tambimuttu's early book publishing. It continued to make its mark at exhibitions and book fairs. Graham Sutherland's cover design (jacket and binding the same) was in orange, grey and black. The front cover showed stylized mountain peaks, rigid like large teeth of a saw, pierced and riveted by a pencil (which was at once a penis and a feathered arrow). Beyond the peaks, scimitar-like black flames rose out of an orange fire of dawn or sunset; there was a dotting of black rocks upon grey, as in the Pembrokeshire landscapes. The back cover had one huge white orb of sun or moon. Three gigantic dragonflies were passing swiftly across it, from right to left, each with its orange fire-cloud. The dragonflies had large, fishlike eyes and seemed to emanate from a world in process of being born. In the bottom left corner a primitive white crab (having emerged from dark waters) waited, its claws extended towards the light.

Lachrymae

Slow are the years of light :
                    and more immense
Than the imagination. And the years return
Until the Unity is filled. And heavy are
The lengths of Time with the slow weight of tears.
Since Thou didst weep, on a remote hill-side
Beneath the olive-trees, fires of unnumbered stars
Have burnt the years away, until we see them now :
Since Thou didst weep, as many tears
Have flowed like hourglass sand.
Thy tears were all.
And when our secret face
Is blind because of the mysterious
Surging of tears wrung by our most profound
Presentiment of evil in man's fate, our cruellest wounds
Become Thy stigmata. They are Thy tears which fall.

These lines are part of *Miserere*, the first of five sections which make
the book, each with a Sutherland drawing introducing it. The poems
are as powerful now as ever.

In June 1945, when I quietly demobilized myself to join Editions
Poetry London, Tambimuttu had just returned from a holiday in the
Scilly Isles. He was to talk about this for many months: tales of his
exploits and love-making on idyllic shores; small boats between
islands; friendships, drinking – in particular, a wild, impromptu dance
in moonlight to Stravinsky's *Rite of Spring*. (Anyone knowing Tambi
will get the drift.) Whenever friends from Cornwall – Dr John Wells
(painter of abstracts), Sven Berlin or W.S. Graham, for instance –
appeared in the *PL* office, key memories for Tambi would be revived.
He did not weave myths about himself, he lived them – in his usual
sensual and pragmatic way.

Nicholas Moore (who, like me, would be aged twenty-seven, come
November) was the son of G.E. Moore, the Cambridge philosopher.
He already had two or three complete volumes of poetry to his credit.
As well as being the mainstay of the *PL* office – reading all new
manuscript poems as they came in – he was an authority on the
American short story and on jazz. Nicholas worked away quietly at his
desk, wearing his Cambridge scepticism with a mixture of pride and
disaffection. He was invariably good humoured, even among the
dramas of each day and when Tambi was at his most provocative!

Nicholas was at work in the morning before anyone else arrived. At 3.30 p.m. exactly he would leave the office for his train to Cambridge, where he lived with his wife Priscilla and their little daughter. Sometimes Nick would bring flowers from his garden. One morning he arrived with a large bunch of Darwin tulips, cool and long-stemmed. These I put in a tall vase on my desk. It must have been the anniversary of my coming to *PL*.

As an editor, Tambi had judgement, instinct, panache. That day-of-the-tulips he was in a bad mood after lunch. Nicholas had been arguing, perhaps too logically, about some piece of writing. Suddenly Tambi grasped the large bunch by the neck. Lifting it clean out of the vase, he scathed the stems repeatedly against the corner of the desk. I went cold. Nobody made any comment, deliberately. In the unusual silence we went on working, until a bluff blow on the door signalled the entry of teacups. Today it was the young telephonist's turn: 'Ow! What's all this?' she exclaimed in vigorous Cockney as her high heels scuffed the slivers of green stem lying all about the carpet. 'Coo, what a mess!' I managed not to laugh as solemnly she placed the cup on my desk and our eyes met. Tambi seemed engrossed in his work. He did not even look up. The girl, missing his usual banter, withdrew with a pout. Silence again, until Nicholas prepared to leave for Liverpool Street and his train. Methodically he put some manuscript into his case, and then collected his loose umbrella which, though a conventional black, looked suitably faded and 'academic'. From the door he gave an amiable 'goodbye', laced with a sharp witticism.

Next morning Tambi arrived soon after eleven o'clock, as usual, and was his engaging and outgoing self. He opened personal letters and read us liberal portions with obvious pleasure. 'This little girl, Nicholas, I think she's in love with me. What do you think, Helen?' and so on and so forth. He would stand by the mantelpiece, letter in hand, chin lifted in a warm, toothy smile ('Gat-toothed,' Chaucer calls it). It was impossible to concentrate!

About this time Gavin Ewart came to *PL*, to learn the production side. Michael Swan had left to join another publisher, I think, taking with him his essay on Henry James (published by Longmans, Green in 1950). Gavin, just out of the Army, had been a contributor to the magazine's first number of February 1939, with a poem entitled 'Ambivalence'. More followed. My impression was of a quiet, steadfast character – nice, but a little dull! Or do I mean conventional? Who could have guessed that his quirky genius would lead him to future fame as he sat bent in determination over his desk, one lock of black hair falling forward, the only renegade from an officer's neat haircut? His sallies of a more surgical humour passed unnoticed in the general conversation as, patiently, he tried to master the typography and layout of a title-page. Individual, and only more or less happy, like the rest of us, he fitted well into the pattern of *PL*.

Young Lucian Freud was a frequent visitor to the office. We did not believe him when he said that he had set fire to Cedric Morris's art school at Dedham. Lucian would disappear into the green bathroom (there was a door in the corner, behind my desk) and be gone for so long that we forgot about him, until somebody noticed that the door was shut. (Tambi *never* shut the door.) I remember Lucian emerging, after an hour or more, with studied coolness, quite effective. 'What have you been doing, Lucian?' Tambi would inquire with a friendly, avuncular smile. 'Thinking,' said Lucian, coldly. He was an awful poseur! Said he had been lying in an empty green bath. He probably had.

Tambi seemed to go on wearing the same shirt until some kind friend made him a gift of another, a good one, perhaps from his own wardrobe. Tambi never smelled noxious (unwashed), as did many a poet and painter I knew! Partly, I think, it was the light-brown Indian skin, which is smoother and finer than the white kind – less 'porous'. (There was not the same colour complex then as today. What might be called the old Commonwealth spirit of human brotherhood needed no comment. It was just intelligent; a matter of course.) Perhaps the fact that Tambi ate so little and drank so much contributed to this modest body odour – pints and pints of bitter beer! When we had complained of a shirt's 'pong' for a day or two, and its disposal was deemed necessary, we persuaded him to take a bath. In the middle of the morning I would scrub his back. Such was the din – the shouts, the howls and splashings of water – that you could have expected help to rush up from below. Like a schoolboy, Tambi made the most of it, calling through the open door: 'Nick, Gavin! She's raping me!' To which, after a bit of banter, they replied that they rather doubted it.

Between me and the green bathroom and in the kneehole of my desk were large brown paper parcels containing halftone blocks which awaited their final stages: Sven Berlin's *Alfred Wallis* (published January 1949); *Jankel Adler*; *Ben Nicholson*, to be published in conjunction with Peter Gregory of Lund Humphries; and more. The immovability of these copper blocks depressed me by the lack of progress. From time to time that nice man from the block-maker would enter the room through the much-frequented corner door.

Patiently one would once more compare 'progressives' with their precious originals, explaining that there was too much red or yellow, not enough blue. But the main trouble, I suspect, was finance.

Ben Nicholson's appearance in the office was a pleasure. He would come in the morning off the early train, from St Ives, bringing a freshness of sea and jugs by open windows! I sold him my bicycle (a good one), which had belonged to my late husband. I rode it to work one morning – from Chelsea to Manchester Square, across the park – with difficulty because of gears and crossbar, holding in one hand a full, red skirt, such as I wore then. I think Ben gave me £3 for the bike, which was about what you would expect. I remember he rode off looking small and adept, like a charming pixie in his navy-blue beret, waving goodbye.

An important package of colour blocks under my desk, in 1945, were those belonging to the *Shelter Sketchbook* of Henry Moore. Of all the visitors to *PL*, Moore was the most welcome. He had a quiet kind of omniscience, as if the working of stone and wood made simple words more real. He had a good effect on us all, I think; particularly on Tambi, who much respected him. It is a pity that the end product, a small book of eighty plates (no text), was badly bound in a loose and inadequate spine. This was through no fault of Tambi's.

There was an easy chair beside the marble fireplace. Here, special friends or VIPs would sit, having got beyond the centre of the room with its encircling desks. Here, Philip Toynbee, slightly boozed, would while away the afternoons. Here, Edith Sitwell sat enthroned.

I was on my own in the office when the switchboard rang to say that the lady had a lunch appointment with Tambi and was on her way up. This was easily my most terrifying moment. Other entrances – that of Stephen Spender, whose poetry I rated highly and whose 1942 paperback, *Life and the Poet*, had been both a fillip and consolation in my barrack-room days, nursing, or (later on at *PL*) of the flamboyant entrance of Roy Campbell complete with sombrero and his devoted wife, Mary (Catholics, they supported Franco, which was shocking), or of the latter-day Wyndham Lewis, returned from America to his 'Rotting Hill', near-blind, and wearing a long, smart, overcoat, navy-blue like a stockbroker (an elderly man with short 'fascist' hair) – all these were mundane compared with the entrance of Miss Sitwell.

I went out on to the landing. There on the stairs was a tall figure approaching, very upright. She was wearing a narrow black taffeta dress, ground-length and swathed with black frills. Pink topped, with long pink gloves, she was ascending the last flight as if borne upward on a wave. How could I mask the fact that Edith Sitwell was *not* in Tambi's diary, that he had already gone to the pub? How regale her fittingly when I really didn't like her poetry (*Façade* was a different thing altogether)? Now, if it had been the tiny, intelligent Stevie Smith.... I escorted her to *the chair*, which itself was ordinary, and made some conversation. She sat straight, looking like Queen Elizabeth I, in a pink cartwheel hat.

But Tambi remembered and came back, charmingly apologetic, and was of course forgiven.

Unlike most of us, with Tambi there was no division between the PR man and his real self. People remarked that Tambi had virtually no private life – he talked about it so openly. But he was loyal to his friends and disliked any form of meanness.

One morning, not sunny but with a cold, white light in the room – others will know the date better than I – Elizabeth Smart appeared. She was damp and smiling gently, blue-eyed with straight golden hair tied back, and a red 'coldy' nose. A little baby, quite new, was in her arms – Sebastian. He was damp, too, and needed changing. She stood in the centre of the room while three of us looked up from our desks, wondering if this was something special or just typically *PL*. She handed Tambi a note from George Barker which read something like '& this is my angel.... Take care of her for me.'

'The angel' remained standing in the centre of the room looking helpless, unsophisticated, untroubled. Tambi was very sweet to her. The little baby was a month old, I guess, with a neat, well-shaped head and very short foxy hair. Tambi was intrigued. 'Have you ever seen one so small, Helen?' he kept saying. I said I hadn't (but was not envious). Elizabeth's slim form, her round, pink nose and thin hair lent 'devoutness' to her posture. She had no clean napkin for Sebastian and stood in the centre of the room, talking in her quiet drawl, while infant faeces were escaping through her fingers. Tambi commented good-humouredly on the smell (of which we were all aware). 'Oh, don't you like it?' she said, slightly piqued, 'I think it's delicious when they are breast-fed.' This was new for *PL*, where abortions, perhaps, were a topic more common.

It was all but impossible to get on with one's work when Tambi was present; one had to be a permanent 'ear', with ever-ready comment. He never sat long at his desk. I see him standing, characteristically, his back to the mantelpiece, manuscript in hand, proclaiming in his beautiful voice lines from a poem or, from the same station, talking sex, happily and overtly as Tambi did, to the point of boredom! Or else he would prowl to and fro like an animal, dictating a letter. To any author who wrote in, anxious about the progress of his book, there was one answer: I was told to send an immediate telegram inviting him to lunch.

In cold weather Tambi mooched to the Hog in a blue tweed overcoat, with his head bent forward, collar turned up and his hair breaking over it in 'rats' tails'. A sad sight! Despite woollen gloves (a Christmas present), his hands would be deep in the pockets of his flapping coat. I never heard him complain of the cold.

Trimming Tambi's hair was easy because, though straight, it curled at the ends. It was very thick to handle, in texture not unlike my own, which was a throw-back to a Bengali great-great-grandmother. Quickly a circle of black ringlets would appear on the floor. This was just one of those diversions of the *PL* office which might confront the unsuspecting visitor. Tambi thrived on attention!

This was the environment of those twenty-one months or so during which I was secretary to Editions Poetry London. That head of hair, by Hector Whistler, depicted on the cover of the magazine numbers 1 and 2 of February and April 1939, is a stylized version of Tambi's, as I recall it.

The Hog in the Pound had a sympathetic landlord in George Watling. The building was on the corner of South Molton Street and Oxford Street, where now is Ratner's, the jewellers. Tambi made of it an important lunchtime meeting-place for literary London. All of us drank bitter beer – ordinary bitter, in glass pint mugs, with handles – for war involves us all, even the non-combatant, and the unravelling, like the rebuilding, is slow. It would have been considered a deviation from the ethics of *PL* (and Tambi and *PL* were one) if a newcomer asked for spirits, and I have seen a bumptious neophyte, who drank mild instead of bitter, relegated to the background as 'not one of us'. Perhaps there was another reason! Tambi was kind. You were free to be yourself, but there must be no splinter movements.

When the pub closed at 2.30 p.m., Tambi and a smaller party of three or four made their way to the Victory Café, not far up on the left-hand side of Marylebone Lane. (London was full of 'Victory Cafés' during the war.) It was a modest place. Once again, Tambi was friendly towards the good man who owned it and who must have been quite amazed, at first, by the uninhibited nature of the conversation. It was late for lunch and we were usually the only ones there. We ate sausages and mash or spaghetti Bolognese, with extra grated cheese, and for Tambi, chillies, washed down with the ubiquitous cup o' tea, pale symbol of fortitude and hopefulness.

With the afternoon thus eroded, we returned to Manchester Square, where Nicholas would just be preparing to leave for his train.

I liked the warmth with which Tambi greeted old friends. When he smiled spontaneously, his rather outward-slanting white teeth gave to the upper lip a charming 'frill'. New friends, too: Pablo Neruda (who interested me because of Garcia Lorca), introducing himself to Tambi, was most warmly received.

Some of Tambi's oldest friends I knew only by report. 'Larry Durrell – my blood-brother, y'know!' Tambi would say (celebrating a memory) as I gave him a letter from Greece or Rome. Reminiscences would follow.

Tambi loved to receive visitors from Ceylon (as it was still called). A Sinhalese lady, wife of a chief government minister, came to London with her plump, young, nubile daughter. The lady was friendly to us all and no doubt a good chaperone. She gave me a beautiful sari of deep-blue silk, with the Benares gold border. I was shown how to pleat it the Ceylonese way *in front of the left hip*, which is more elegant, I think, than the Indian fashion. I wore it on certain occasions, loving the colour, but I did not have the figure for a sari, really, being too athletic and slim-hipped. (It is better to be 'round'.)

So many came through that door in the far corner: Alan Ross, for instance. I visualize him with neat, black hair and a small 'imperial' beard – a sailor on leave from active service. Equally individual, in Fair Isle beret and trailing a different environment, came Diana Gardner – by train from Lewes, Sussex. She had come up from Rodmell, on the west bank of the River Ouse, where dwelt the Woolfs, Leonard and Virginia – she had drowned herself four years before. Kingsley Martin (editor of *The New Statesman and Nation*) and Dorothy Woodman lived farther up the hill on to the Downs. Diana was secretary to the local Allotments Association (her 'war work', as she said); Leonard Woolf was chairman. He was one of the founders of the thriving 'Dig for Victory' campaign, I think.

Tambi had printed three of Diana's engravings in the first number of the magazine – two of the subjects being the sea at Newhaven (the River Ouse estuary) and the third, the Helston River, Cornwall. But it was as a writer that she now came to inquire about the progress of her short stories, *Halfway Down the Cliff* (published in 1946, with a jacket by Michael Swan). The setting of her title story was Beachy Head (with an odd denouement). Diana's entrance brought back to me memories of that bare downland area where I had lived from early teens into the Battle of Britain period (1940–1).

Some other friends to come through that door were Tom Scott (with his Lallans), whom I liked especially, and the 'Army journalists' returning from Cairo: Anthony Schooling, with a wonderful nose and country-rectory background, and George Fraser of liberal erudition and Aberdonian burr. Sometimes Paddy Fraser came too.

By the summer of 1946 there was the Glaswegian poet, W.S. Graham – rarely seen in London, being too poor to afford the train fare from St Ives. His *Second Poems*, published by *PL* in 1945, had seemed to me the best thing since Dylan Thomas. Sydney Graham peopled the Cornish peninsula with his tongue, took Benzedrine (the artists' current pep pill), got drunk often, fell off a roof and bust his knee, sang songs in pubs with Nessie Dunsmuir.

There was Sven Berlin (ex-bombardier from the Normandy invasion), up from St Ives for his first London exhibition of paintings and drawings at the Lefevre Gallery, Bond Street (an exhibition shared with Keith Baynes and Quentin Bell). This happened in September 1946. All of us went to the private view and I bought my first picture for £5. It was a small, 'visionary' Cornish seascape – oil on panel – effulgent with colour: two fishing-boats moored under a black moon. Sven was a writer as well as painter and, later, a sculptor (I liked his drawings particularly). The text of his *Alfred Wallis* book, referred to earlier, was said to have been written largely in NAAFI canteens.

It was the fashion to knock intellect in those days (as a reaction to Audenesque poetry of the thirties), to see intellect and emotion as antithetical. I could never understand this! To me, emotion and intellect shared the same depths, fed by what Coleridge calls 'the living educts of the imagination'. Sven and Tambi were both denigrators of 'intellect'. 'Poetry is the awareness of the mind to the universe. It embraces everything in the world,' Tambi had stated in his credo, in the first number of the magazine. Fine, but then this follows: 'The instant man starts to write, he ceases to live. Before he began he had the universe in him, but the very moment he put pen to paper he went into a tiny coil of intellectualization and became only partially alive.' This attitude held sway in the *PL* of my day and made things uncomfortable! It seemed to me so 'negative' to say that the moment of awareness, which brought with it the impulse to write a poem, had no natural continuity in the intellect nor warmth of recognition afterwards, in the emotional life. Useless to challenge, though. I should only be condemned as 'intellectual', whereas it was *oneness* that I was about.

The legend of the evening pub-crawl, known as 'Fitzrovia', has its inaccuracies. But the title is beautifully correct. Soho was the venue. Tambi and one or two companions would leave the *PL* office before 6 p.m. for the Hog in the Pound, Oxford Street. This was the first stage. Only occasionally would the whole evening be spent there: perhaps when Tambi had invited some elder along, such as Roy Campbell. Usually the party, conflated, would make its way easterly down Oxford Street – now spacious and empty in contrast with the great midday – and turn north, at last, into Rathbone Place, spreading out across the road in conversation. You didn't have to frequent Soho for long to realize that drinking-time on the left side of this street ended half an hour earlier than on the right. The necessary change-over could be dramatic, as on one particular occasion when a small flood of people had issued from the Fitzroy Tavern into the dark little square. It swept towards the Wheatsheaf on the opposite side of the street, a hundred yards down, narrowing to the entrance like sheep into a pen. But something was wrong. I was behind, with Tambi and Brita de Mare. People began circling back, seemingly unable to gain entrance. Somewhere in the middle an angry voice opined that the door was locked, *half an hour early* (limp cries of 'Shame'). The night was totally dark.

Suddenly, over the heads, a streak of light was seen. The inner door opened a little. We were on the move! Still it appeared that an obstruction was filling the porch. Edging by with difficulty, I turned my head as light came fitfully through that inner door and saw Dylan Thomas necking imperviously in the entrance. As usual, he was fairly drunk, the unknown face of a girl looked over his shoulder in alarm at the sudden invasion. I just had time for an impression of short, curly-blonde hair and a 'country' face of wild-rose complexion (different from us London dwellers) – a face which, at that moment, was deep pink, and hot and dewy with embarrassment. Only recently, forty years on, was the identity of this 'unknown girl' discovered. Quite by chance, in conversation with her, I found she is my friend of three decades: my old friend, Mary Wedd, then Mary Harris!

Tambi, despite his fine sensitivity, did not understand the need for solitude sometimes. His loyalty to his friends was strong. Individual moves *away* were to him a breaking of faith. By autumn 1946 I felt it was time to get on with my own life again, and decided to read for an

English degree at Birkbeck College, University of London. Lectures were in the evening; during the day I would continue to work for *PL*. But Tambi didn't like it! There were innuendoes, more frequent as the afternoon wore on; snide remarks about 'people' who 'thought they were' this or that!

Initially I did five subjects and was able to choose Ancient Greek, which I had longed for, instead of Latin, ever since adolescence, when I began reading the plays with Professor Gilbert Murray's introductions. But to placate Tambi was important, so I continued to do the evening pub-crawl *once a week* to keep the peace!

Oh those wet, beery tables where friends would make room for me, and soon a new pint would be set down among the cigarette-ash! Conversation was boring, really, like an electrocardiograph – a level of sympathetic listening (on my part), interspersed with *bon mots*. I dare say one always hoped for the sharing of ideas that had once been the loveliest part of life. At a certain stage of the evening, while Tambi was lording it at the bar, I would be on the alert for any change of tone. Tambi could be *difficult*, but if drinker and landlord turned nasty against him, at once one went maternal, and two or three of us would carefully unite to shepherd him out. Seldom did the shadow of knuckles persist into the street. (Yet it must have been on one such occasion that Tambi lost a front tooth.) Then food would be sought in some ghastly basement smelling of frying. It is significant of such places that at the hint of 'trouble', all cutlery would be swept from dirty table-cloth to floor.

Only once do I remember feeling completely relaxed. Tambi would take us, late in the evening, to the Caribbean Club off Piccadilly Circus, behind the Regent Palace Hotel where, whether or not his membership was paid up, he managed to talk our party in. I remember the delight of excellent rhythm, dancing here with Sven who, before the war, was a professional dancer like myself.

Tambi, when he danced, gave solo performances, short and arbitrary. It began always in the same way, a strong stance in a wide, second-position *plié*. From here he would execute little jumps, in the same place, to a heavy beat reminiscent of the dance-drama *Kathakali*. I believe this to be from Kerala, South India. (Is there a Sri Lankan form he might have learnt from Miriam Peiris?) It is a warlike dance, story-telling from the Epics, and is accompanied by facial expressions, fierce and introverted. Instead of the blinking eyes, however, fiery-pink (seeds in corners), Tambi's eyes would be tight shut – with a heavy frown! His individualistic performance, brief though it was,

was all the more remarkable since, in the London of those days, ballroom dancing consisted entirely of close couples. Even in the sensuous *tango* one never lost physical touch.

And it is to touch that I return. His poetic integrity, that *awareness of touch* (as manifest in the early numbers of *PL*), is for me the nub of Tambi's genius. I have written of his influence, at that time, in *Blackwood's Magazine* (September 1980). It was the same innate sense that made him pick up a pen – even a quill – to redesign a book jacket, with verve. Or when, for instance, he took up the dummy of *Poésie (1939–45)* with translations that I had been getting in over many months and, first using Indian ink which he speckled and splurged over the white jacket, then a dripping red pen for the title, he created a design so exactly right as to leave one jubilant. The fine lettering of the cover of the catalogue of March 1948 was also his.

Thus I come back to the hands, pale brown, slim-fingered and to that bottle of Stephen's 'violet' ink! Tambi used an ordinary wooden penholder and broad relief nib. Three supple fingertips, pressed closely together, guided it as he signed his name and added little serifs with thoughtful concentration.

R.M. Nadal

Tambimuttu, Lorca, Roy Campbell

The Failure of a Big Project

November 1944; King's College, London. Tambimuttu again comes to tea to continue chatting about Lorca. At that time Tambi was one of the few people who saw in the work of the Spanish poet something more than the exotic of the *Gipsy Ballads* or of the rural trilogy so suddenly enhanced by the tragic death of the poet. We both believed that Lorca would become and remain world famous because the constitutive elements of many of his poems and plays were universal. And I reminded Tambi of the two short poems which, some few years later, a Chinese poet would quote to me as the only European poems he knew of which, translated into his own language, sounded Chinese:

Hunter

High pine grove!
Four doves in the air.
Four doves
Fly and circle.
They carry wounded
their four shadows.
Low pine grove!
Four doves lie on the ground.

They Cut Three Trees

They were three
(Day came with its axes).
They were two
(Low-flying silver wings).
It was one.
It was none.
(The water became naked).

After a short silence Tambi, almost whispering, said, 'If I find a real good poet-translator, and if you accept acting as general editor, I will publish the complete works of Lorca in English.'

I had almost forgotten that afternoon when, a few months later, Tambi introduced me to Roy Campbell, 'the ideal poet for *our project*'. No doubt, on paper, Tambi was right. The colourful, adventurous South African poet knew and loved Spain, its language, literature and customs. He fought on Franco's side during the Civil War and was wounded; but he condemned the brutal repressions of the dictator after victory. Roy fought bulls in Spain and gained the 'Silver Picador Jacket' in Madrid's bullring. Roy had translated St John of the Cross; Roy admired Lorca. So the three of us started the preliminary work at once: Tambi was to seek financial help, Roy to read all the Lorca available at that time, I to secure from Lorca's mother the exclusive copyright for the English translations.

As soon as everything was arranged, Roy began to pass on to me his first translations of the *Gipsy Ballads*. I immediately foresaw dangers ahead. Roy insisted, against all advice to the contrary, in translating the eight-syllable lines of the Spanish *romance* into traditional English ballad form while at the same time keeping the same number of lines in English as in Spanish. This inevitably resulted in the need to add to or gloss over Lorca's shorter lines. Here are three small examples. (The literal translation, almost word for word, of the original, is followed by Roy's rendering.)

From the ballad 'Preciosa and the Wind'

Lorca: Girl, let me raise
Your dress to look at you.

Campbell: Allow me, girl, to raise your skirts
And let me see you plain and clear.

From 'Saint Gabriel'

Lorca: When he lowers his head
Over his chest of jasper.

Campbell: When to his jasper breast he stoops
His forehead in that pensive way.

From 'The Death of Antonio El Camborio'

Lorca: He bit on their boots
bites of wild boar.

Campbell: He bit the boots that kicked his ribs
With slashes of a tusky boar.

I warned Tambi and Roy that the latter was 'Campbellizing' Lorca too much and that, unless this was corrected, I would find it impossible to accept them as real translations, however good they might be as English poems. Here is one typical answer from Roy:

> My Dear Rafael
> Here is a further attempt at improvement. I shall keep on working at this till I get the proofs and hope gradually to get it ship-shape. Un abrazo.
>
> Yours ever,
> Roy

PS. I may have left out a verse or two in this as I've mislaid the original.

The 'ship-shape' often became a further beautiful gloss over of Lorca's text, rarely an effort to keep closer to the original.

As time passed, further complications pointed to the inevitable crisis. Roy's pride, individuality and outspokenness did not help to open doors in many literary circles and he suffered in silence hardships at a moment of growing family needs. Tambi was aware of this and helped him by paying for translations he knew perfectly well would never be published. Finally, after much hesitation, duty to Lorca's mother and loyalty to Lorca's work compelled me to break the contract. My letter to Tambi, with a copy to Roy, ended: 'However, you could and probably should publish Roy's final version under the title *Roy Campbell's Variations on Lorca's Themes*. Not as translations.'

Tambi's reaction: I am sorry but I quite understand the situation. Silence from Roy.

Three years later I met Roy at 1 p.m. in a crowded Fleet Street. He threw down his hat and walking-stick, took up his boxing stance and shouted at me, 'Come on Rafael, fight!'

I looked at his eyes smiling. 'Roy, don't be silly.'

And laughing, we both entered Ye Olde Cheshire Cheese.

I always remember with gratitude and joy these two great characters, in appearance so different. Roy Campbell, a wild force of nature: zest for life, defiance of death. Tambimuttu, an oriental aristocrat, sometimes penniless, always a giver.

Victor Musgrave

Bacon Rind, Poetry and the Sublime

I knew Tambi for the best part of forty years. I never really understood him; he seemed like a vague but pleasant breeze that one might unexpectedly encounter on turning the corner of a street.

In the latter half of the forties we were the only males in London whose hair was shoulder-length. Perhaps this was one of the reasons it always seemed reassuring to meet him, but it was more likely to be because he was totally unaggressive and undemanding. The first time I met him was the only occasion he ever asked me for anything and that was for half a crown to give in a pub to the marvellous writer Paul Potts, who spent it on beer.

He was the soul of friendliness, yet in a way there was a hint of something impersonal about him as if he were the instrument of the ceaseless literary projects he generated rather than their actual progenitor.

The second time I met him was soon after I arrived in London from Cairo with Ida Kar and we had installed ourselves in a small flat. There was a terrible storm outside when the doorbell rang. It was Tambi with two women novelists, all dripping wet. They had to take their clothes off and dry out.

I never saw Tambi angry, disconcerted or cast down. He was exactly the same to the penniless as he was to the wealthy and made not the slightest distinction in his behaviour between the completely unknown and the famous.

I saw him in the down periods of his life as well as the good times, but he never complained. I visited him when he was dreadfully ill in small rooms where every inch of floor, table, wash-basin and even the crumpled bed would be covered with books and manuscripts. He would be in extreme pain and barely able to move, a condition he seemed to ignore, referring to it in the most matter-of-fact way while trying to drag out his latest publications to show me. Often he could not even find them among the welter of print. It did not seem important, they were leaves left by the breeze. The essence of his being seemed to encompass health as well as adversity and whatever else came along with the same amiable equanimity.

We knew who he was and where he came from, but *what* he was will for me remain a mystery. He was like a benign spirit who descended from Ceylon upon London and New York and attracted to him like a magnet the literary giants and the unknowns, especially in the years when his office was the Hog in the Pound public house. As with his 'office', he never seemed to have a proper home, living in other people's houses or temporary accommodation. Perhaps the nearest he came to a real place of his own was when the October Gallery offered him a work-place and living-room.

Now, like a breeze, he has gone and never again shall I roam with him 'the endless terraces of Oxford Street'. Strange things stick in the mind – he was the only person I knew who, when he was young, ate not only the rind of the bacon but the bones of the chicken as well.

John Lehmann

For Tambimuttu

One day in the middle of the war Tambi arrived at my flat in London bearing a copy of his anthology *Poems from the Forces*. I asked him if he would sign it for me, and he sat down on my sofa, and, to my surprise, immediately began to write a poem. This was done with great frowning and lip-pursing; but when it was finished he transcribed it into the flyleaf of the book. This was, I thought, very characteristic of Tambi and his love of poetry, and needless to say I was delighted. I still have the book.

Tom Scott

From 'A View from Sixty-five'

London was also Tambi, who published me first,
and I lost no hour in knocking on his door.
It was opened by a man near my own height,
brown-skinned, skinny, with an eager, intelligent face
surrounded by a mane of lank, black hair,
with long, spidery, double jointed fingers
which seemed to harp the air as he talked.
He was full of childlike mischief, his laugh gurgling from
                          a mouthful of perfect teeth.

I was too intense even for him,
obsessively talking of poetry (I was starved)
which, unlike me, Tambi was surfeited on.
It was all very different from arguments with George
and others in Perth, the context utterly different.
Sophisticated London seemed too blasé
to find anything exciting. London was spoiled. I was
                              the 'provincial' boy.

But Tambi and I had many things in common,
not least that we were both aliens here,
he a Ceylonese Tamil, I a Scot,
and I was the more alien of the two,
a class-conscious, proletarian Scot.
He was upper caste and cosmopolitan,
educated, socially self-confident where I was
                              ill at ease.

He and his wife Jackie, a big-breasted blonde,
felt I was too intense and humourless,
and this brought out the mischievous Puck in him,
like the night he made me an Indian meal
that made me sweat torrents, too polite
and dour to admit defeat, while Tambi gurgled
and cackled, and danced arabesques with his spidery fingers
                              as I boiled in battledress.

Another night, concerned for my lack of sex-life,
he laid on a horsy woman twice my age
who tried to rape me on his floor, strong
as a man, and it took all I had to master her
without using my fists. As we rolled on the floor,
my spare ripped open, Tambi writhed with delight
and cheered us on. A tithe of that with Jackie in private . . .
                              he never risked it.

All good fun, but much as I liked him, and
good as he was to me, I had more need
of the kind of argument I'd known with George:
I couldn't whet such claws as I have on Tambi
and really needed intellectual stretching
much as a boxer needs a sparring partner.

I never found it all the time I spent in London,
                    and withered for it.

My fault? Maybe – or just bad luck.
But Tambi had another night laid on
a very different woman, an Oxford don,
whom I saw in a taxi back to her hotel,
and her advances really roused response:
such uninhibited female lust to me
was a thing unknown, it was another world, and I
                            was grateful for it.

On one of our evenings, I remember Tambi
asked me to recite 'Sea Dirge', which I did
in my normal voice. But when I finished
he protested NO – SEA DURGE!
and recited it himself in a Scots voice
grotesquely exaggerated, but with such passion
I myself could only sit back and wonder at it.

HYMENAIA:

A POSIE OF VERSE.

Collected from *Far & Wide*

To the honour of JOHN CONRAN IRWIN, *Asst. Keeper of the Indian Section, Victoria and Albert Museum, and* HELEN HERMIONE SCOTT *one of the members of the House of* Poetry London.

WITH AN APPENDIX

LONDON
Printed by *Eversholt Printing Works* for *Tambimuttu*
and to be sold at one penny.   1947.

Celebratory leaflet, handset by Tambimuttu, printed on an Albion press, and published in honour of the wedding of Helen Scott and John Irwin, 1947 ('Tambi and the Hog in the Pound Press', page 106).

Robin Waterfield

Tambi and the Hog in the Pound Press

In 1946 Tambi, being temporarily homeless, came to stay with us at 40 Crawford Street, off Baker Street. The house was a tall, early Georgian building with two rooms on every floor, but what attracted Tambi most were the two large dark cellars.

Somehow he heard that Douglas Cleverdon, the great printer and former apprentice of Eric Gill, and later BBC producer who had produced the first broadcast of Dylan Thomas's *Under Milk Wood*, had an old Albion hand press that he wanted to dispose of. The same press, we were told, on which Eric Gill had proofed his early trials of Gill Sans and Perpetua types in Bristol. The price agreed on, if I remember rightly, was £100, and we were to bear the cost of transporting it from Great College Street about a mile away. No ordinary removal firm would handle it; Albion presses are made of solid cast-iron and are no light objects. Eventually we found a specialist firm who would take the job on and they did very well, having only to remove the banisters round the stairs to the cellar, which made our narrow hall rather dangerous in the dark.

However, installed it eventually was, and Tambi began very skilfully to set the type for our first production, a wedding present for John and Helen Irwin to be called *Hymenaeia* and consisting of poems by friends, including one by George Watling, the landlord of the Hog in the Pound in nearby Oxford Street, where Tambi's friends were accustomed to gather, hence the name of the 'Press'.

Unfortunately, when it came to printing the work, we found the press had no platen, so a few copies, about forty or fifty, were printed off elsewhere in time for the wedding. The finished product reveals clearly Tambi's instinctive eye for layout and typographical elegance which he had cultivated since early childhood when he set up and printed his own poems on his grandfather's printing press in Ceylon.

The subsequent history of the press is somewhat mysterious. After Tambi moved on, the basement was occupied by a jobbing printer who found a platen and used the Albion. When we left London, he was still in possession. Some years later, Anthony Rota wrote to me in Iran, where I then was, to inquire about the press, and I told him all I knew. Inquiries at 40 Crawford Street were met by a fearsome lady with blonde marcelled hair, who said that she knew nothing about printing presses in her basement, which was then occupied by her poodle-clipping parlour!

If anyone knows the present whereabouts of the Albion, I should be glad to hear from them – this particular press has several claims to fame!

George Barker

Elegiac Sonnet for Tambi

Drink. Drugs. Women. Death.
Four best things to be desired.
Four small foibles that we shared
as the archangels of faith.
'Let us', we said, 'just for a joke
experiment with experience.'
And when the abused spirit broke
under this savaging of sense
we heard the voices of these four
evangelists start whistling like
frying lark tongues on a fire
till the booze and the dope and the women and death
sang up like children along the shore
and the bone and the poppy kissed for breath.

Elizabeth Smart

Extract from
'Dig a Grave and Let Us Bury Our Mother'

(from William Blake's 'Tiriel')

Mexico, a new country. For my eyes new distractions. Worlds of other beauty. My eyes have grown as large as dishes, but they overflow still. My eyes are large and strenuous. My voice is silent, left behind like the backward moss. Speak, fool! Tell the marvellous your eyes have seen, but that flows so fast off its slippery surface, round, fickle, rolling. If only eyes could hug and store, but like the stomach they can hold only so much. They devour, swell, drop away again.

The listening evening dissolves the sluggishness. Arise, slug! Over the strange desert, over the mountains, roams the revelation. Make me a prophet, then, to father the quick gold meaning. Darker, darker the mystery closing down until the blind mind looks within, is joggled will-lessly and floats in a pool of contemplation, takes shelter from the night. *Is afraid of revelation*.

These blind protective mists are terrible. They confiscate every sense. They annul all antennae.

Should I make a list, a resolution of will-power? Would a list rouse a slug?

Tack-a-tack! Tack-a-tack! A sound in the dusk. Voices, skulking dogs, geraniums breathing, the smell of wood-smoke.

Expand, expand, into the homogeneous mystery.

I can't.

What is poetry? Do not inquire. The secret dies by prying. How does the heart beat? I fainted when I saw it on the screen, opening and closing like a flower, though I had said I wanted to see it. That was my life out there, frail, fluttering. No wonder we insulate ourselves from wonders. Poetry is like this, it is life moving, terrible, vivid. Look the other way when you write, or you might faint.

The dark cactus shapes emanate in the gentle night, the bananas in paper bags wait like petitioners.

What was it you wanted to ask me, rejected lover? I turned away from the answer. You too avoided. The answer is too frightening. It is escaping on all sides in terror. You might as well grab evanescence here as there. Are your hands webs? In the libraries of dust, maybe. But it would be pain indeed to have no fingers in the night for love. Here! Here! the panting part cries, and only a webbed wing floats over the flesh dying for a touch.

My mother – this mystery that pursues me – I know only I tremble and do violence in my dreams. Or she turns to a little child and I give her pleasure for her own good. Or I fight her great soft body.

Insulator, rejected lover, now I find the world cold. But I suppose I had a reason for thinking it would do me good to cross this desert alone.

These violent dreams! This confusion! When will the water be clear? I cry for a lover. Or I cry for a hermit's rod. Or I clothe myself in buffer mists.

I sleep alone, the night rears in and possesses me with fierce fearful dreams. I remembered and weakened towards the sleeping companion whose presence made a nest of rose clouds that remade the unravelled day.

Yesterday I entered my face in a rose. Be a rose, woman! I said. And fell to plotting ways.

And do you know the rose never washes? Dew and rain wait upon her so dutifully. She breathes luxuriantly. Woman, did you hear? Perfume to make the senses rock!

Under the feathery-leaved tree, with the mountains on all sides, the pale dried maize-fields rustling all around, the cactus swords in rows between clouds, the valley in a haze, I begin to feel the idiosyncratic earth of this unknown land. I begin to sing its tune. The small yellow butterfly or the escaping lizard have the same rhythm. I am at last again a continuation of the ground I walk on. The dust, even, is part of it. My feet have a union of harmony, and the rocks I jump from hug, then render up in passing, their essence.

Elizabeth Smart

'What Is Art?' Said Doubting Tim

It's *not* leaving your mark,
Your scratch on the bark,
No, not at all
'Mozart was here' on the ruined wall.
It soars over the park
Leaving legions of young soldiers
Where they fall.

Dido cried, like a million others.
But it isn't her tears
That sear the years,
Or pity for girls with married lovers
That light up the crying I
With the flash that's poetry:
It's the passion one word has for another.

It's shape, art, it's order, Tim,
For the amorphous pain;
And it's a hymn,
And it's something that tears you limb from limb,
Sometimes even a dithyramb;
A leap from gravity,
That feels, in the chaos of space, like sanity.

The maker makes
Something that seems to explain
Fears, delirious sunsets, pain.
What does the rainbow say?
Nothing. But a calming balm comes
From Form – a missile that lasts
At least until tomorrow
Or the next day.

Peter Owen

I met Tambimuttu in the late forties, soon after I left school and was looking for a job. He was running *Poetry London*. There was no editorial job, but he suggested that I might sell the books in the London suburbs. Naïvely I agreed, unaware how difficult it was to sell anything literary outside central London. It was my first experience of major authors such as Nabokov and Henry Miller.

Tambi was delighted, as I *did* produce some orders, which apparently no one had previously done. But as I was on 'commission' (never received), it was impossible for me to carry on after my first trip. I kept the samples in lieu of commission. Tambi was committed to good books, unusual then, when the shortage of reading material after the war and the guaranteed sale of almost anything spawned illiterates who became temporary 'publishers'. This was the most fruitful period of his career when he launched many new writers who later became famous – Kathleen Raine, Elizabeth Smart, George Barker, Anaïs Nin, Nabokov and others.

Next time I met Tambi was in New York in the fifties, when I had become a publisher, doing much the same thing. He was relatively affluent with financial backing for a revival of the *Poetry London* imprint, called *Poetry London–New York*. His office was run by enthusiastic volunteers. We spent several evenings in the White Horse Tavern in Greenwich Village, made famous by the patronage of Dylan Thomas. It was my first introduction to the New York Bohemian milieu.

When we returned to London I met him occasionally – sometimes at the launch of yet another publishing venture. He continued to be enthusiastic, but publishing had become very professional and there was no longer a place for an eager unbusinesslike impresario who cared about good books but did not know how to market them.

Since then an even more sinister trend has emerged: editors looking almost exclusively for the big illiterate block-buster to feed their book factories. An indictment of contemporary cultural values, quite opposed to Tambi's.

David Gascoyne

PL Editions and Graham Sutherland

Before the end of the 1939–45 war Geoffrey Grigson had inaugurated with *The Poet's Eye* a series of anthologies with unifying themes illustrated by contemporary artists; and after the war, Faber's *Ariel* series of pamphlets containing a single poem appropriately illustrated continued to appear. Tambimuttu, however, probably deserves to be credited with having been the first editor since Harold Monro of the Poetry Bookshop to promote collaboration between poets and artists. In 1943 he was responsible for the publication of collections by Kathleen Raine, Nicholas Moore and myself, illustrated by Barbara Hepworth, Lucian Freud and Graham Sutherland respectively.

When, after accepting my *Poems 1937–1942* for publication by PL Editions (Nicholson and Watson), Tambi asked me if there were any particular modern artist I should like to have the book illustrated by, I immediately thought of Graham Sutherland. Not only had I seen the two paintings he had contributed to the International Surrealist Exhibition of 1936, I had more recently had several times occasion to look at *Entrance to a Lane*, a work of his that had been acquired early in the war by my friend Peter Watson, then installed in an apartment in Kensington which contained part of his collection. I asked Peter with some diffidence whether he thought Sutherland might find my poetry of sufficient interest to make him consent to illustrating it. Peter then sent a typescript of my poems to Sutherland at the White House in Trottiscliffe, Kent, which long continued to be his English address. Before long we learnt that he would indeed be willing to provide a certain number of illustrations for my book.

During the months that Graham Sutherland spent preparing his designs at intervals between his regular output of paintings, I went down to Trottiscliffe to meet him and his wife Kathy. They were reassuringly kind and understanding, and we made friends at once. I found Graham a quiet man, both warm and reserved, obviously possessed of a faith which found an affinity with something expressed in my poetry, though he seemed unwilling to discuss this explicitly. In fact, I think the kind of understanding we came to regarding the nature of the illustrations must have been essentially non-verbal.

In the end, eight designs by Sutherland were used for the book which Tambi first published in his PL Editions series in 1943. The front cover shows four peaks transpierced by a stylus or pen against a fiery background; while the back cover design represents three large moths against a lunar circle, evidently inspired by one of the five poems 'From the French of Pierre Jean Jouve' contained in the second section, a version of Jouve's 'Les papillons' (from *Matière céleste*, 1936). It is unlikely that Graham was familiar with the original French text, and I did not explain to him that I had taken a certain liberty in entitling my translation 'The Moths': though moths may sometimes be referred to as *papillons de nuit*, the proper term for them is *phalènes*. But because it is widely supposed that moths have a strong sexual connotation for the unconscious, especially in the female mind, and the imagery and content of the poem are of so unmistakably sexual a nature, I felt that moths were more likely to be the subject of the poem rather than butterflies, traditionally associated with Psyche and the disincarnate soul. The third design is for the title-page, which is handwritten in black on three white insets against a soot-black ground. My name is written in what appears to be a tidied-up version of my actual signature, though without the Greek ε I picked up in youth from an admired schoolmaster. My handwriting had by that time become unnaturally florid, under the influence an increasing use of Benzedrine was beginning to exert over me. Whether the Sutherlands ever suspected that I was daily using an amphetamine, still at that time a perfectly legal and easily obtainable substance, I never knew, but it would not surprise me to learn that they did surmise something of the kind.

The remaining five designs correspond to the five main groups into which the collection is divided. The first comprises the sequence of eight poems entitled *Miserere*, and Sutherland wrote this word across a blank space at the foot of an otherwise black, red and whitish composition suggestive of an imaginary landscape as it might have appeared at the moment of the rending of the veil of the temple, over which floats a celestial orb with a sorrowful eye and streaming three trails reminiscent of those of the comet in the Bayeux tapestry, which may have been inspired by the 'stricken sun' incapable of regeneration referred to in 'Tenebrae', with which the sequence opens, or the 'netherworld's/Dead sun' in 'Ex Nihilo'. It is forty-five years since I saw the originals of Graham's illustrations, but from my copy of the 1948 reprint of the book it is clear that coloured chalk as well as gouache and inks were used in their execution. The title illustration of the second section, designated *Metaphysical* (a term I had at one time thought of changing to *Metapsychological*), is to me the most mysterious of the set. It obviously represents a being, and just as obviously one of a supernatural order. There is nothing about it to suggest a phantom. It has no wings and so is unlikely to belong to the host of angels, though in a poem entitled 'The Descent' belonging to that part of the book there is an allusion to 'that Angel's eye'. On the right side of the page the figure's arm is swathed in broad, cape-like drapery, the white tinge of which merges into descending folds of grey, balanced on the left by a small greyish cone that looks as though it might be a cuff. But the most cryptic thing about it is that its head has no face or features, but resembles a visor without perforations for the eyes, surmounted by what at first sight appear to be four plumes. The breast or chest below the head tapers to an impossibly slender waist. If one knows that Graham Sutherland was a Roman Catholic, prolonged contemplation leads to the irresistible conclusion that the image might have derived from the Sacred Heart of popular pietist iconography, for the plumes could well be transmuted flames, appearing against a pink-tinged patch of sky. I have always found this quasi-surrealist apparition deeply impressive, and at least in its inscrutability appropriate to the subliminal depths the poems it precedes were intended to invoke.

The third and central section of the collection is occupied by a five-part poem originally written in English soon after the death of Alban Berg in 1935, then entirely rewritten in French during the summer of 1939, after my return earlier that year from Paris, where I had been living since 1937. Three of the subtitles of *Strophes elégiaques à la mémoire d'Alban Berg* are borrowed from movements of the composer's *Lyric Suite* for String Quartet; and two lines in the third part, 'Intermezzo', are borrowed from a poem in Baudelaire's *Le Vin* sequence, set by Berg in Stefan George's translation as an aria with orchestral accompaniment. Sutherland's illustration portrays, in the lowest third of the page, a shrouded reclining figure, 'watchful in the grave of time....' Above him are placed two apparently fractured stones, the one on the left inscribed with the word ELEGIAC. Above them float a number of curved black and grey forms that cannot be specifically identified but are clearly related to the horned or thorny configurations which form a recurring part of Sutherland's pictorial repertory from 1937/8 until the end of his life.

A striking amalgamation of horns and thorns with an amorphous human figure with arm raised as in quest furnishes the motif of the subtitle page headed 'Personal'. This image prefigures Sutherland's exploration of emblems and the emblematic undertaken immediately after he had completed illustrating my poems. It may be understood as a visual metaphor representing the labyrinthine path of one both on the horns of a dilemma and preoccupied with a thorn in the flesh. If thorns are a theme anticipating numerous future works, the standing forms of the twin monoliths which are the subject of the plate illustrating the concluding section, *Time and Place*, are to be found in various forms in a great many later works, and also look back to certain early records of neolithic monuments. These seemingly rock-hewn forms each taper to a narrow base; their wider tops are pierced by crescent-shaped holes through which are to be seen, like eyes, to the left the moon in its last quarter, to the right the sun, shown once more in a 'stricken' aspect. Between them, lower down, appears a curious small form that can scarcely be described even as anthropomorphic, though it seems to have twisted arms and legs. The poems of this last section reflect civilian experience of the early years of the war. A certain affinity may be discerned in the last of Sutherland's illustrations to *Poems 1937–1942* with some of the wartime paintings of Paul Nash: the chalky quality of a dead moon, the desolation of Nash's dead sea of crashed planes.

In the collection of the Graham and Kathleen Sutherland Foundation at Picton Castle, Dyfed, there are a number of illustrations to *Poems 1937–1942* that were not used in the book as it was eventually published. Three of them are reproduced (in black and white) in Roberto Sanesi's 1979 study, *Graham Sutherland*,* all described as illustrations to 'Poems' by David Gascoyne, 1942, and as being 17 x 13 cm in dimension; but one of these is mistakenly identified, as it contains a number of words quoted from a seventeenth-century metaphysical text I am unable exactly to identify, and the other two are evidently abandoned *ébauches*. One of these has 'Metaphysical II' written on the top right-hand corner, though it has no resemblance to the enigmatic supernatural figure referred to earlier, but appears to be a faceless standing form culminating in an enormous mouth uttering what may be flames being breathed out towards a dim winged creature. The other bears simply the date 1942 and consists of a black

*Centro d'Arte/Zarathustra (Italy), 45 pp. Italian text with English translation, 199 illustrations, 22 colour plates.

lower band surmounted by a disorganized mineralogical landscape of unfinished, contrastingly dark and light shapes, above which appear a faint indication of a disc and what may be a preliminary version of a moth.

In the previous paragraph I alluded to Sutherland's period of interest in emblems and the emblematic. At this period of my life I had become an avid collector of a variety of types of second-hand books. In the small shop of a refugee art-book dealer in Cecil Court next to Watkins, I one day came across and immediately acquired a number of remarkable plates from a dismembered seventeenth-century emblem book, probably Dutch. This led me on to form a small collection of examples of the genre, in which poems are printed facing often quite elaborate emblematic designs, sometimes by curiously gifted graphic artists. The best-known English poet to have had his poems, loosely to be characterized as 'devotional', illustrated in this way is Francis Quarles. At the time immediately after the publication of my *Poems*, the idea of illustrated anthologies began to appeal to certain publishers, despite wartime printing difficulties. I succeeded in compiling an anthology to be called *Emblems and Allegories*, and the work of Quarles was naturally prominent among the numerous poets I drew on for examples in my assembly. Originally I think my idea was principally to demonstrate that – though there was never in England a school of symbolist poetry as significant as that of late nineteenth-century France, or that could accurately be described as such – one could show how symbolism of the emblematic and allegorical type had played a considerable role in the development of English poetry. On one of my visits to Trottiscliffe, I took the typescript of this anthology and a copy of Quarles's Emblems with me to show to Graham. He at once became keenly interested in the field, and before long produced a number of illustrations, particularly of Quarles, not many of which I actually saw at the time. Some of them have occasionally been published in catalogues and reviews, particularly in one issue of Tambi's *Poetry London* magazine.

During the period when I got to know Graham and Kathy Sutherland, being unfit for military service I managed to obtain employment as a professional actor, adopting the pseudonym David Emery after my mother's maiden stage-family name, and for a year toured the country with the Coventry Repertory Company, playing in farce for ENSA. One week we found ourselves quartered in Tunbridge Wells. While there we had a day or two off for some reason, and while roaming the town I came across a fishmonger's offering a large, rare and delicious fish, probably rainbow trout, at what seemed a bargain price, and impulsively bought it. At a loss to know what to do with the delicacy, but knowing that Trottiscliffe was within easy distance and that Kathy Sutherland was a most excellent cook, I rang up Graham and announced that I should be arriving at the White House before long with a surprise. On reaching the Sutherlands', however, I found that my piscine present was not welcomed with the degree of enthusiasm that I had imagined the era of strict rationing might have induced. Kathy Sutherland was a very organized housekeeper who did not, I think, care to have her schedule unexpectedly altered. Both she and Graham were otherwise, however, as kindly welcoming as usual, and I think enjoyed the fish as much as I did in the end. The incident was no doubt mainly the result of my having become by that time largely dependent on Methedrine, one of whose effects on me was to stimulate the indulgence of unpredictable whims. Soon after the war I had a brief meeting with the Sutherlands in a Knightsbridge flat, during which Kathy, recalling this episode, confirmed my impression that, though tolerant of eccentricity, she did not really care for it beyond the point at which it becomes downright abnormality.

The last occasion of meeting the Sutherlands that I clearly remember took place in 1950 in Venice. I spent a couple of months there that summer, having received a generous travelling grant from the writer known as Bryher, daughter of a shipping magnate millionaire. At the end of my stay I found myself the guest for a week of Peggy Guggenheim, with whom I had a friend or two in common, at her Canal Grande truncated palazzo. During my stay there, Graham and Kathy Sutherland were visiting one of his dealers in a pleasant, less palatial apartment on the opposite side of the Canal, and Peggy asked me to accompany her when she was invited there one evening to dinner. Though our host may have wondered how I had managed to inveigle my way into high café society, the Sutherlands betrayed to me no sign of such speculation, albeit I was then still inclined to be paranoid on account of the after-effects of abusing amphetamines (which by now had fortunately become much more difficult to obtain). Graham's picture dealer, by the way, came later to a sadly unfortunate end.

From the mid-fifties till the mid-sixties I became increasingly incapable of producing a single satisfactory line of poetry; even postcards to my family required considerable effort, let alone letters even to close friends. I was extremely fortunate at this time to become the house guest at Aix-en-Provence and in Paris of a painter, widow of a painter, to pay tribute to whom this would be an inappropriate place. During these years I was still suffering from the after-effects on the central nervous system of prolonged dependence on amphetamines, and continuing to use a mild compound known as Maxiton, then still freely available in French pharmacies. But even more than this I was suffering from guilt at not having written enough to justify my thinking of myself to be specially gifted, and from a badly damaged self-esteem. Though my hostess had a Peugeot and enjoyed driving about Provence with me, and though I am sure the Sutherlands would have enjoyed meeting her as well as been welcoming to me had I ever suggested that we should drive over to see them at their Riviera studio and home, it never seriously occurred to me to make any effort to bring this about. I regret this all the more now that I know that Graham's regard for my poetry cannot have evaporated, as I thought it must have done, over the years, since proof to the contrary is provided by the fact that he continued to produce designs in illustration of them, such as the 'Inferno' with the text in his own hand, reproduced on a folding sheet in *Poetry London/Apple Magazine*, Vol. I, No. 1 (Autumn 1979). By that date I was beginning to recover from the last of the three serious mental breakdowns that had resulted from the long, apparently hopeless period of my non-productivity; but even then my reaction to this extraordinarily fascinating pictorial comment (dated 1978) on the experience of inner emptiness, so widespread nowadays, seems to me today to have been incredibly numb. Now that Jane Williams has brought to light still further proof, with the design found among the many papers and manuscripts Tambimuttu left behind when he died, which appears to have been intended to illustrate such a poem of mine as 'Mountains' (belonging to the *Metaphysical* section of my *Poems 1937–1942*) and which is reproduced in illustration of this article (opposite p. 76), I intensely regret that neither Graham nor Tambi are here any longer to receive from me some living sign of my gratitude for their continued faith in me and my work, now that I have fully recovered a normal degree of self-confidence.

David Gascoyne

Mountains

Pure peaks thrust upward out of mines of energy
To scar the sky with symbols of ascent,
Out of an innermost catastrophe –
Schismatic shock and rupture of earth's core –
Were grimly born.
      O elemental statuary
And rock-hewn monuments, whose shadow we
Lie low and wasting in, a prey to inner void:
Preach to us with great avalanches, tell
How new worlds surge from chaos to the light;
And starbound snowfields, fortify
With the stern silence of your white
Our weak hearts dulled by the intolerably loud
Commotion of this tragic century.

Diana Menuhin

Tambimuttu

The disappearance of Tambi from the literary scene is as though a
brightly coloured thread had been withdrawn from the tapestry,
leaving a gap in the warp that may never be harmoniously closed.

 In our peripatetic lives our meetings became ever more seldom and

119

by the same token in ever more varied and unlikely places. From my first meeting with him at the Hog in the Pound, brought about by Lawrence Durrell, when I set eyes on his gentle brown face, heard his soft, self-deprecating voice and recognized every quality of which Larry had told me, through collisions in India, New York and again London, one realized that his was the rare gift of remaining constant to himself and to those he loved.

When he rang up to tell me he would be going to Brown University in the States, I immediately advised him to rid himself of the English undergraduate's baggy tweed jacket and baggier trousers and put on the whole elegance of his native costume, high-necked jacket, jodhpurs and all. 'Even,' I added as he demurred with bewilderment, 'even if you will, drill a hole in your nostril and stick a ruby in.' Later in New York we met again: 'Diana, you were quite right, it made a great difference' (this with a flick of his long black hair that fell perpetually over one eye). 'Thanks to your advice I was once accused of being a 'pansy nigger' in a café on Third Avenue and beaten up by three drunken Irishmen.' With which he smiled, showing a large gap where some front teeth had been. Dear Tambi!

T.S. Eliot, discussing the onerous task of reading through piles of poetry manuscripts, told us that whereas he himself would find his judgement totally exhausted after a dozen or more, Tambi could wade through a mountain and produce at the end of the session a young unknown aspirant called Dylan Thomas. . . .

It was, I imagine, his complete devotion to poetry, coupled with his own generous, humble nature, that fed this extraordinary instinct.

We shall miss him – as he will be missed by so many – very much indeed.

Jag Mohan

Remembrance of Tambi in Colombo
(1950–1953)

When I met Tambimuttu for the first time in late 1950 in the office of *The Times of Ceylon*, he was no stranger to me. In fact, he was a familiar figure. I had heard enough about Tambi, poet and maker of poets, anthologist and publisher, friend of great and lesser known writers and connoisseur of wine and food, from two London-based friends of mine – the late V.S. Sastry and David Pinto. They had wined and dined with him in his favourite pub, the Hog in the Pound, and they had been to his office at 26 Manchester Square. Besides, I was quite familiar with his *alter ego*, his journal *Poetry London*, a few copies of which I had in my modest library, jostling with copies of John Lehmann's *Penguin New Writing* and issues of Cyril Connolly's *Horizon*.

That particular morning when he materialized before me, I was typing my weekly contribution to the Ceylon daily. Being an Indian, I was on a visitor's visa but with official permission to work as a freelancer for *The Times of Ceylon*, as an art critic and commentator on Indo-Ceylonese relations.

Tambi walked in, followed by a young boy carrying what looked like a suitcase. The image of Tambi zeroed in with the description of Tambi written by the English poet G.S. Fraser, thus: 'Tambi may seem extravagant and fantastic – his long hair, his triangular face, his shabby sports jacket, which alternates with a beautiful long, grey silk Indian coat, his strong expressive hands. . . .'

'Hello, Tambi. I hope I am correct,' I must have said.

'You know me. But I haven't met you, have I?' Tambi said extending his 'expressive' right hand.

I announced my name and mentioned the names of our two common friends. We shook hands and with that established a pact between the two of us in the same manner and style scores of others must have done with him.

Tambi turned round to the boy behind him and asked him to leave the suitcase near the editor's room. He paid him off and asked him to go.

121

'Have you just arrived?' I asked.

'No. This is my scrapbook. I will show it you. I have come to meet Victor Lewis,' he said. (Victor Lewis was the last of the English editors of *The Times of Ceylon*, and he was in his room.) Quickly I announced Tambi and ushered him in.

About an hour later, he came out carrying his heavy scrapbook. By then I had finished my article. We went out together and hired a quickshaw (as the Ceylonese taxis used to be called) and I took him out for beer and lunch at my favourite Chinese restaurant.

Thus began our friendship.

The next day, I had nothing particular to do and so I fixed an appointment with Tambi. I went along to the place he was staying – on the fringe of the Cinnamon Gardens, the élitist area of Colombo. He was staying with one of his cousins. Thoughtfully I had brought a bottle of the best brand of Ceylon arrack (country liquor) and a tin of cheese. I was most curious to see Tambi's scrapbook inside the custom-made leather and calico case complete with handle. When Tambi opened the beautifully bound scrapbook, it was a revelation, a veritable feast for the eyes and stimulus to the mind. Carefully and artistically pasted on the pages were letters from Ezra Pound and Augustus John, Ramon Gomez de la Serna (the Spanish poet now forgotten) and Pablo Neruda (then breaking ground through English translations), Anne Ridler and Kathleen Raine, Alun Lewis and Keith Douglas (both were killed in the Second World War), Henry Miller and Lawrence Durrell, among many others. Handwritten manuscripts of poems by various hands – Herbert Read, Henry Treece, George Barker, D.S. Savage, Ruthven Todd – were there, as also the original drawings that had adorned the covers of *PL* and the books of Editions Poetry London, in which Ronald Bottrall, Ronald Duncan and Richard March were collaborators with Tambi. And, of course, photographs galore, in which Tambi was seen with the high and the mighty in the world of letters, and the not so well known as well, Tambi exuding conviviality and camaraderie.

What was more interesting to me was Tambi's draft of the 'First Letter' published in the inaugural number of *PL*, which he had subtitled oddly enough as 'An Enquiry into Modern Verse'. I was unlucky not to have seen it before. I quickly copied down a fragment from this 'Letter'. Here it is:

Every man has poetry within him. Poetry is the awareness of the mind to the universe. It embraces everything in the world. Of poetry are born religions, philosophies, the sense of good and evil, the desire to fight diseases and ignorance and the desire to better living conditions for humanity. Poetry is the connection between matter and mind. Poetry is universal. Poetry is not individual. It exists as a whole in the universal mind. No man is small enough to be neglected as a poet. Every healthy man is a full vessel, though vessels are of different sizes. In a poetry magazine, we can only take account of those sizes of vessels, which represent humanity as a whole.

Meaningful words. High thoughts. Rich sentiments. These words should be engraved on his tombstone. (And I do not know whether Tambi was buried or cremated!)

As I neared the end of the scrapbook, I found two neatly typed sheets containing quotations from two books, which I asked Tambi to give to me. One was from Francis Scarfe's *Auden and After*. It reads: 'It can be stated definitely that there has not been a review [like *Poetry London*] since the Great War, which has gathered so many poets into its pages. Almost all the poets mentioned in this book have appeared in it....' This was like a certificate to Tambi. So was the other, which was from across the Atlantic, from the American poet Kenneth Rexroth, who in the introduction to his anthology, *New English Poets*, had written thus: 'Strictly within the field of poetry, the magazine that has moved the most mountains has been Tambimuttu's *Poetry London*.... For all the years of the war, he published the best verse and the newest verse in England.'

And Tambi chuckled and said at the end of that session, 'Jag, can you imagine that I started *PL* with the capital of just ten pounds and nothing more? And in wartime London.'

Then I left him and returned home, all along the way wondering how Tambi, a Tamil from Jaffna in the north of Ceylon – now the epicentre of the militant seccessionist movement in Sri Lanka – came to influence the English literary scene. Probably he is the only non-English person who has contributed something substantial to the mainstream of English letters in the twentieth century. The only other person I can think of is James Laughlin, who through his New Directions anthologies and other publications has contributed much to contemporary English letters. But he is an American and heir of a wealthy family.

Then followed days and months together. Whenever Tambi was not running off to tourist spots like Anuradhapura and Polonarruwa to 'recall memories' or to the Tamil-speaking areas where his numerous friends and relatives lived to re-establish relations, we spent a lot of time together.

Tambi was for some time treated like a whizz-kid or a wonder boy by the Colombo élite – both the Sinhalese and the Tamils. Every door opened to him and people welcomed him. But only for a while. The Ceylonese at that time – as even now – were modelled after the Victorian and Edwardian values of social interaction. The men were staid and the women were prim within drawing-rooms, maintaining etiquette. And Tambi was a Bohemian, careless about his dress and appearance. In his talk, the dreaded four-letter words now and again dropped out of his mouth, much to the discomfiture of his hosts. Only a very few families became fond of the native who had returned home and did not mind his waywardness.

Besides, Tambi was running short of money. The pounds and dollars he had brought were frittered away over mugs of cask-beer, of which he was very fond.

So for a beginning he started writing articles for the Lakehouse paper, *The Ceylon Observer*, on such subjects as 'Tambimuttu at the Races', 'Tambimuttu at Low Dives', 'Tambimuttu on Wines' and so on. Then he switched over to *The Times of Ceylon*. Victor Lewis persuaded him to write a daily poem on a topical subject *à la* Sagittarius of *The New Statesman and Nation*. Tambi had a great gift for rewriting nursery rhymes to suit the topics of the day. And he was paid handsomely.

Tambi and I became great friends. He was warm, affectionate and effusive. For hours on end we would sit in some bar or the other and talk about 'Criterion' of Eliot and 'Transition' of Eugene Jolas, in comparison to or contrast with *PL*. Or about Mulk Raj Anand, Raja Rao and the Ceylonese writer Alagu Subramaniam. Or about the anthologies and compilations he edited, like *Poetry in Wartime*, published by Faber and Faber (at a time when 'lights of reason and passion were being extinguished' in the European continent), *Selected Writing* in collaboration with Reginald Moore and T.S. Eliot (a tributary volume edited with Richard March). Our conversations would be permeated with scores of names, anecdotes, jokes, snide remarks and even gossip. Tambi had a great talent for occasional pauses and explosive laughter, grins and grimaces. Expletives in Tamil flavoured our talk, since I happened to know the language, though I was not a Tamil. And while I had my own mannerisms, gestures and way of talking, our styles blended very well.

Over the weeks and months I spent in his company I learnt that though he started off as a genuine poet, he was not much of a consistently creative poet. For him poetry was not an end in itself. It was a means towards several ends. But he was a man truly and trebly blessed by the legendary Indian goddess *Vagdevi*, who symbolized *vagartha* (compounded from *Vak* [word] and *Artha* [meaning]). She may be considered the Indian counterpart of the White Goddess of Robert Graves. That was why Tambi acted sometimes as the midwife for the emergence of poets and at other times as the catalyst for the birth of poems. Tambi had the unique gift of transforming pedantic and literal translations of poems from Indian and other languages into gems of transcreation. He belonged to the world of poetry, pulsating with rhythm and permeated with all poetic devices.

In late 1952 the crunch came. Tambi became almost an outcast in most of the homes where he had enjoyed hospitality. He had exhausted his sources of credit. He had to move into sleazy joints frequented by all sorts of characters. He ran short even of clothes. (For a month and more he wore a pair of trousers, whose bottoms had worn off, but it was cleverly hidden by the long Indian coat or *achkan*.)

It was then that he decided to cross the Palk Strait and try his luck in India. Besides, he had a great love of India and Indians. It was at this stage that I could be of some help. I wrote an article about him and got it published in the *Sunday Standard* of Bombay where I had worked for some time before I left India. This was a publicity gimmick and it worked out well. Not that people in India did not know Tambi, but my article helped to announce his arrival in Bombay.

I gave half a dozen letters of introduction to people whom I knew could be depended upon for helping Tambi. Among them one was to a hotel manager, who I suggested should make use of Tambi's liquor permit. Those were days of tight prohibition in Bombay and the liquor permits of foreign visitors sold for big sums of money. Tambi benefited from it. Another letter was to a lesbian friend of mine, who was a great lover of poetry. She sometimes used to recite verses from Baudelaire on the phone when I was in Bombay. She introduced Tambi to many people, who in turn introduced him to others. One of them was Safia Tyabjee, a granddaughter (or great-granddaughter) of

Badruddin Tyabjee, an early President of the Indian National Congress. Safia was an heiress as well. She fell for the charms of Tambimuttu and married him soon after.

Suddenly, one day in 1953, I got a letter from Tambi saying he was coming to Ceylon on a honeymoon trip along with Safia, whom I had never met. I was all agog and mightily happy with the turn of events in Tambi's life. A few days later I met both of them at the GOH Hotel in Colombo. Lo and behold, Tambi was unbelievably transformed. He was wearing a shirt with buttons and cuff-links bedecked with precious stones. He stood me a grand lunch and stuffed a small wad of notes in my pocket, by way of returning some small loans I had given him before he left Ceylon.

After their honeymoon tour of Ceylon, I saw them off.

Subsequently I lost touch with Tambi. I was, in fact, angry with him, for, when he was running *Poetry London–New York* and the Lyrebird Press, I had sent him the only manuscript copy of my selected poems and he had lost it. But Safia I did meet now and again. On one such occasion she said that she was divorced from Tambi and that he was now remarried to an American. She pointed to the tiny woollen socks she was knitting and said, 'This is for Shakuntala, Tambi's daughter.'

Safia Tambimuttu

My Life with Tambi

It was at three in the morning of 22 June 1983 that Chilly Hawes of the October Gallery, London, rang me in Bombay to inform me that Tambi was no more. So ended for me an association that had lasted over thirty years – years of marriage, divorce, separation, distance, time. So much to remember, so much to forget. Ours was a relationship which continued after the break-up of our marriage and we exchanged letters right up to the end. In fact, Tambi was planning a visit to India in connection with his literary projects when he died. I felt him near me during all those long years and it was his encouragement and affection that sustained me, and I think it was the same for him. It is consoling to remember his words that the years he spent with me were the happiest of his life.

I first encountered the name Tambimuttu in an article which he wrote on the Qutub Minar in Delhi in 1951. It was a very interesting article, and I wondered who the author was with the unusual name. It was on 26 June 1951 that I first met Tambi. Mrs Marjorie de Mel of Colombo, Ceylon, was the catalyst who was unknowingly responsible for this. She had asked Tambi to meet my cousin Muhsin Tyabjee when Tambi visited Bombay, as she had been impressed by my family, the Tyabjee clan. Mrs de Mel met various members of the family at Kihim, situated near Bombay. Kihim is a lovely place where family members have houses right on the beach, surrounded by tall casuarina and coconut trees. It is an idyllic village, quiet except for the swish of the trees, the murmur of the sea and the call of the birds. Tambi later wrote a musical skit on the family when we were in Kihim in 1952, in which we all took part. It caused a lot of amusement and comment among other family members.

Tambi wrote an amusing song, 'Another Little Tyabjee', set to the tune of 'The Geisha Girl', which I sang. It runs like this:

> I'm delicious as a catalyst of verse
> When I arch my brows she scintillates and flows
> Though I likes my bread and butter
> I prefer my Tambimuttur
> Take me to a Broadway flutter drenched in furs
> I'm as noisy as Amina *bahan*'s [sister's] brat
> Tell me folks how can a *Nishat* girl help that
> I'm curvaceous, svelte and slinky
> Though extrav'gant o' so ritzy
> And when I talk I lay down *Rahat* flat

Nishat, meaning happiness, is the name of our house in Kihim.

To go back to my meeting with Tambi, Muhsin invited him for dinner and also invited me among others to meet him. I had just recovered from flu and was feeling gay at going out again. Since

Tambi was staying at the Astoria Hotel, near Churchgate, a stone's throw from my parents' flat at 1 Ravindra Mansion, Muhsin collected us both in his car to take us to his flat for dinner. So I first saw Tambi sitting quietly in the car wearing a black *sherwani* (long coat), and was formally introduced to him. The only other Ceylonese I had met was Victor Dhanapalla, who settled in London. Tambi knew Victor well and told me the most fantastic stories about him which sounded like the *Arabian Nights*. Sitting in the drawing-room at Muhsin's, Tambi talked chiefly to me and said that I looked like him, the shape of the face being similar. 'You also look like Miriam de Saram, Brita de Maré and Buffie Johnson.' To find in one person three is what must have made my charms irresistible to him! I was unusually animated and full of spirits that evening and quite fascinated by Tambi's brilliant and racy conversation. I was wearing a white georgette sari with a velvet red border and matching *choli* (short blouse). Tambi looked very handsome and distinctive in his dark *sherwani* and almost shoulder-length hair, which was unusual in those days.

After this encounter we met every day till our marriage on 15 July 1951, eighteen days after our first meeting. Tambi took me to various restaurants and swore that it was the Tandoori chicken that won me over! We honeymooned in Delhi, Rampur, Nainital and Srinagar, staying away nearly two months. During our visit to Delhi we met the Prime Minister, Pandit Jawaharlal Nehru. This was a great event for us. Tambi had an interview with him and I went along. He waved to Tambi like a schoolboy when he saw him and said, 'Come in, come in.' He signed two photographs for us and Tambi gave him two poems which he had written on him for *The Times of Ceylon*, which seemed to please him.

We met Pandit Nehru later in Kashmir at different functions, including a dinner-party at the famous Shalimar Gardens. The garden was lit up, the fountains were playing and looked like fairyland – an evening to remember. Pandit Nehru waved his hand to Tambi and it made his day. Pandit Nehru looked aloof and withdrawn at the parties in his honour. He told Tambi that Kashmir would be the safest place to stay in case of war, which seemed a rather strange statement to us.

In Kashmir, we were the guests of the Government, so we met many interesting people. Among our friends was Gerald Hanley, the novelist, with whom Tambi drank beer at the Srinagar Club most evenings. Gerry told me that marrying an artist like Tambi was a tough undertaking, as all artists, including himself, were impossible creatures, that I should look on him as a brother and seek his help if I needed it any time.

We were taken round in a Jeep by the official escort, Captain Sharma, whom Tambi met again in Delhi in 1982. We stayed in a luxurious houseboat on the Dal lake. Tambi took many photographs of the surroundings and of me at this time. Dr Karan Singh, whose father had been the Maharaja of Kashmir, invited Tambi for tea at his palace on the lake to discuss poetry while I waited nearby in a *shikara* (canopied row-boat) on the lake in very picturesque surroundings. Tambi came back full of spirits and with poems which Dr Karan Singh had written.

On our return to Bombay we stayed for a year with my parents, Hadi and Ateka Tyabjee. We led a quiet life visiting relations and friends. Home life suited Tambi and he grew very attached to my parents, especially my mother, whom he adored. Tambi composed poems, wrote articles for various papers and magazines, gave radio talks, collected material for an Indian anthology of verse and also started learning Sanskrit. Mrs Rao, who taught him, gave lessons while she was exercising on Marine Drive in her tennis shorts. Tambi sometimes had to run to keep pace with her. It was a hilarious sight. She used to tell him, 'You are a barbarian, you cannot pronounce the simplest words.'

During this time I met Yehudi and Diana Menuhin, whom Tambi had known in London. At the concert in Bombay, Diana said loudly when she saw us, 'Tambi, what marvellous clothes you are wearing.' He was wearing a wine-coloured *saya* (long cloak) over his black *sherwani* with Kashmiri embroidery of the same colour, and my father's diamond buttons. He looked most elegant. Diana was wearing the same coloured outfit, but Tambi's was better.

We visited Ceylon before our departure for New York in 1952. I met Tambi's family and relations, who welcomed me warmly. They also said that Tambi and I looked alike and could pass for brother and sister. This was said by many people and by Tambi's friends too. Visiting Ceylon was a wonderful experience. The beautiful emerald isle and its people and their hospitality remain an unforgettable memory.

Then it was time to leave behind the beloved shelter of home and my parents and depart for New York. Tambi wanted to establish himself as a writer there, Bombay not being suitable for his talents. We were going to one of the toughest cities in the world, without jobs, where jobs were restricted for visitors, and with only six hundred dollars, without return tickets in case we failed in our endeavour. It needed great courage for Tambi to attempt this. He was not alone and had a wife to look after. I had led a very safe and sheltered life, was in poor health and had never been abroad before. So Tambi faced tremendous odds, and our life in New York was a series of ups and downs dependent on whether an article sold or not.

Our first stopover was London, where we were welcomed by Stewart Scott, his wife Jackie, Tony Dickins, Laurence Clark, Kathleen Raine and many others. We stayed four days and went to many parties and met people. T.S. Eliot invited us for tea. He urged me to encourage Tambi to keep on writing poetry and then said that I would hate the diesel fumes of New York. London was very hectic – so many friends of Tambi's, and so many parties at which I couldn't breathe, with the windows closed and hemmed in by tall people towering over me, the room full of liquor and cigarette-smoke! One of Tambi's friends presented me with a posy of violents and a glass of water, which cheered me up.

We sailed for New York on the *Queen Elizabeth*, the fastest and most luxurious liner of the time. Because the purser from the Cunard Line had given a letter recommending us to the ship's purser, we were treated like VIPs, though we travelled tourist class. The ship's officers went out of their way to do things for us. The stewards came often and offered us ice-cream and breakfast in bed, and the dining-room steward wanted to have special chicken curry made for us. Tambi revelled in all this attention, and we had a marvellous trip.

We reached New York in November 1952 during a dock strike. While going through Customs we were surprised to hear 'Tambi, what the devil are you doing here?' It was Rex Nichols, an English friend of his who had emigrated after the war. It was nice to meet a friend. One great advantage of being with Tambi was that he knew so many people everywhere that one never felt alone.

On our first day in New York we walked into a tavern on Third Avenue where the television set was on. After a drink or two, Tambi asked me whether I wanted to watch TV, as I had never watched it before. On hearing this, the proprietor came to our table and said that I could watch it for as long as I liked. After some talk, he said, 'You are strangers here and this is your first day in New York. Today is Thanksgiving Day and I would like both of you to eat your turkey here as my guests.' We protested, but he insisted, and gave us chicken soup, roast turkey with all its trimmings, and served us himself. As we left after thanking him, he said, 'I wanted you to have a happy recollection of your first day in the city, and please come here whenever you like. I shall be delighted to help you in any way I can. It's thirty years since I myself came here as a stranger.' I always think of the proprietor with gratitude. Our first day in New York will always remain fresh with me because of the hospitality of this American Hatim Tai.

We were loaned an apartment by Tambi's friend Mitch and Denise Goodman at 7 St Mark's Place, where we first started housekeeping. I had to learn cooking, shopping, and so on, and Tambi helped. He wrote to my parents: 'The breakfast she cooked and which we have just eaten is excellent. Percolated coffee, marmalade, eggs, and some meat. I made the bed tea this morning and shall do so every morning. You will be surprised to hear that since I left Bombay I have been getting up at six to seven. The weather is exhilarating and there is so much to do.'

After a fortnight we shifted to Stella Erskine's as paying guests. Stella was very kind and we were on very friendly terms with her. Some months later we moved to a large railroad apartment on 338 East 87th Street where we stayed till my departure for Bombay in 1958. Tambi wrote from Stella's:

Yesterday we went to the Poetry Center where I am due to lecture. I feel in good company at this Center since the others billed to appear are W.H. Auden, Mary McCarthy, Edith and Sir Osbert Sitwell, Elizabeth Bowen, Louis MacNeice, Aldous Huxley, Charles Laughton and Dylan Thomas. My future in America largely depends on this first lecture and am thinking up something good. My literary agent has been very busy and fixed up various writing and lecturing assignments, of which more later. Stella loves looking after people and the weekly rate of 25 dollars she charges us for board and lodging is unique, but all the same we want a place of our own.

New York was strange and bewildering. I did not like the city or think it beautiful till I was taken round by Jack Barker, an old friend of Tambi's, to Staten Island and other interesting places, and got the feel of the city. The city looked stark and forbidding, and the people tense and keyed up though hospitable and kind. I found the Americans somewhat aggressive and assertive. On the other hand, I admired them for their zest for living, their capacity for enjoyment, and hard work, their enterprising spirit, their warmth and friendliness and their direct approach to people. Most of the food came in paper containers or tins. My first cooking attempts were with a letter propped up in front of me with recipes from home. When we had guests for dinner, they often found us in the kitchen busy cooking. The guests occasionally lent a hand and helped with the washing-up. Americans are generally good cooks and enjoy new dishes, so that our Indian food was a terrific success with them. In fact, the necessities of life cost so much that there was little left over for luxuries, which were comparatively cheap. Americans accepted us without any reservations, and I found being an Indian was an advantage, as everybody made so much of Indians. My saris and Tambi's *sherwanis*, which he habitually wore in preference to Western clothes, were everywhere commented on and admired.

We were lucky to have a delightful English couple, Claude and Luki Miéville, and their two children, Claudia and Dominic, as our neighbours. It was through them that we got the apartment at 338 East 87th Street. It happened this way. When Tambi rang up the number given to inquire about the apartment and gave his name, Claude at the other end immediately said, 'What, are you Tambimuttu of *Poetry London*? Why, I have two of your magazines here. Come straight away.' When Tambi delayed going, Luki rang up and said, 'Hurry, the whisky is boiling over.' With such a beginning it did not take long for us to become friends, and soon we were running in and out of each other's apartments and spending a lot of time together. Luki used to bring Claudia and Dominic, aged five and two, to our place in the mornings and Claudia used to tell Tambi: 'I've brought you your tribute, Tambi. You won't boil me in oil now, will you?' She used to bring all sorts of gifts for Tambi, which we returned when she was not looking. This was a ritual that both enjoyed very much, and it amused us all. Rosy-cheeked little Dominic was very attached to Tambi and liked to follow him about with his bright, dark eyes. Luki introduced me to the Grand Union on 86th Street, an enormous food shop with branches all over the city. Claude and Tambi got on very well. They were terrific at parties, each stimulating the other. For me, Claude and Luki were like members of my family, and it was wonderful to have them next door. They left New York in 1953, which was a great loss for us.

Soon after our arrival Frances Stellof of the Gotham Bookmart threw a party for Tambi, to which about one hundred and fifty people were invited. Arthur Lall, Rajeshwar Dayal, among the Indians, my cousin Akbar Tyabjee, his dynamic mother Maryam and wife

Suraiyya, from the Pakistan Embassy, as well as prominent American writers, poets and critics. On 19 February 1953, Tambi gave a lecture at the Poetry Center on 'Contemporary English Verse', a tape of which is kept at Mt Allison University, Canada, and on 24 February at New York University on 'Modern Trends in English Verse'.

We settled down to life on 338 East 87th Street in Manhattan, where we had a large, rambling apartment, each room leading to the other without any corridors, and with a back and front door. The front room was our sitting-room, with divans and cushions in the Indian style and colourful, mirrored hangings on the walls. It looked very unusual and attractive, and was the venue of many a party or gathering where laughter and brilliant conversation dominated. The front room led to a smaller one with a bed and bookshelves, and a wall cupboard. This led to another room with another bed, chests with drawers, followed by one room furnished as a dining-room leading to a tiny room with closets, and finally to a big, airy kitchen where Tambi often used to do his writing.

Tambi worked hard but we also went out a lot, sometimes spending weekends with various friends and meeting innumerable people. It was not unusual to have visitors from England and other parts of the States dropping in to see Tambi, which resulted in many animated and interesting discussions over glasses of beer or whisky.

Tambi had friends like Robert Payne, Buffie Johnson Sykes, Jack Barker, Willard Roosevelt, Julius and Lois Horowitz, Elsa du Brun, Patric Farrell, Amy and Maurice Green, Sushila and Rajeshwar Dayal, Peg Rorison, Elizabeth Sherman Stamos, Bob Price, Arthur Gregor, Yehudi and Diana Menuhin, among many others. Rohini Coomara-swamy, the cellist, daughter of Ananda Coomaraswamy, was a particular friend. Tambi called her his American cousin, since he was related to her father. My cousin Akbar and Suraiyya Tyabjee and my Aunt Maryam were in New York, and we often spent weekends with them. Apart from these people, we had a large circle of acquaintances who invited us to various functions and for weekends. Many people who had heard of Tambi contacted us and asked us over. Tambi had the knack of making friends quickly and keeping them, although there were some who did not take to him. I managed to keep on good terms with such people so that we remained friendly with all. His colourful and dynamic personality blended well with my own *joie de vivre*. We made a good team and were generally liked as a couple.

I had been rather apprehensive about how I would fit in with

Tambi's friends, since I had no literary pretensions, but all his friends went out of their way to be nice to me. I soon looked on them as my friends as well.

Tambi was a genius, which means that at times he was difficult to live with! On the other hand, he was without guile and had the innocence of a child, altogether lovable as a person. I found it very stimulating to deal with a mind as alert and brilliant as his. But he was very impractical, and unable to cope with the realities of life. He had no money sense whatsoever, but fortunately he let me take charge of the finances and we managed to survive. We led a precarious existence depending on Tambi's earnings as a writer. From 1953 I had a part-time job with the Indian Delegation to the UN, and this helped to tide us over. Sometimes I had to pawn my jewellery to pay the rent or buy food, but as soon as Tambi sold an article, my jewellery was redeemed and returned to me.

For some strange reason we did not call each other by our given names. My family had a pet name for me, but Tambi seldom used it. He called me 'Monkey' and I called him 'Gundu'. Gundu means rascal. He used to sign Gundu on most of his letters to me.

Tambi was not a journalist but a creative writer, so it was more difficult for him to find the right publisher. Creative writing needs a certain amount of security and it was difficult for Tambi to function in his hand-to-mouth existence. I was completely unused to it. My role was to be the sheet-anchor and keep the ship afloat. He was very protective towards me and looked after me as well as he could. Often when we went to a cocktail-party or dinner and the hosts urged us to stay till late, Tambi would embarrass me by telling them: 'We will stay if you will give Safia something to eat at twelve or so, as otherwise she will wilt away.'

We sometimes spent weekends with Winthrop and Carlton Sprage Smith in their lovely house at East Hampton with a cascading tiny waterfall, surrounded by tulips and other flowers. Sloping green lawns led to a private quay. Winthrop delighted in throwing large musical parties on the green lawns, followed by dinner. At the India House receptions and dinners we met many leading personalities. On one occasion Dr Sarvapalli Radhakrishnan, the philosopher-President of India, sang Tamil lullabies to Tambi while holding his hand, and Krishna Menon extolled the charms of his native Malayalam. We were guests of honour at a Japanese reception in Los Angeles, where we were asked for autographs, and once at a ball called 'Song of India', given by a Negro association in New York, where *Ebony* and *Jet* magazines photographed us. We met Paul Robeson, and it was amusing to see Tambi dancing with Mrs Joe Louis who was a head taller than he was.

A very lively reception in Washington at Ceylon House in honour of their Prime Minister, Sir John Kotelawala, where Tambi was persuaded to sing his *baya* (calypso song) and 'Varsity Girl' songs, was a most enjoyable affair and quite different from other embassy receptions. Our own parties at 338 East 87th Street were very popular, and one Christmas party went on till seven in the morning.

I recall a most extraordinary incident which happened to one of our friends. She had been taken out by an acquaintance, a most respectable person, for dinner and then to coffee at his place. After coffee, he took out a whip and asked her to beat him with it. When she refused, he said, 'In that case, what about some plain vanilla sex!' When she related this incident to us, we could not stop laughing and the term 'vanilla sex' became a standing joke with us.

When we went to the Immigration Department to renew our visas, the clerk there said, 'Excuse me for being personal, but you both appear so different from the people who come here, and look so happy together, that it is a real pleasure for us to deal with you.' This kind of incident was not uncommon, and in spite of Tambi's vivid personality, we were accepted as a team and not merely as two separate persons.

Tambi enjoyed cooking and especially loved cooking at parties. During my Aunt Maryam's visit to New York she wanted to meet Greta Garbo. Tambi arranged a dinner-party, to which Greta Garbo agreed to come, provided the food was Indian. However, she didn't turn up at the party, but later Tambi managed to get her to see my aunt, though we didn't meet her ourselves! Aunt Maryam and Greta Garbo became very pally and spent a lot of time together.

In May 1956, *Time* magazine published an article on Tambi with photographs of us both. They took about sixty photographs and printed one. When I was in Paris soon after this, I was startled and thrilled when I went to an eating-place frequented by Americans, to be stopped and asked, 'Didn't your picture appear in *Time* magazine?' Such is fame!

In 1957 Tambi and I travelled to Los Angeles, Hollywood, San Francisco, Martha's Vineyard, the Grand Canyon and other places on a grant from the Asia Foundation. In Hollywood we were taken round the Metro Goldwyn-Mayer studios for four hours by George Murphy, MGM's public relations chief, and photographed with Leslie Caron and Knopf, who was directing *Gaby*. We lunched there. Otto

Preminger also took us round and we had lunch at his house – one of the best I've eaten. He had us photographed and said that I was very photogenic.

During Dylan Thomas's visit to New York, we were invited to his hotel. We were shown to his room, but he had not got up from bed. As there were clothes strewn all around, I moved some from a chair and sat down, to be told by him: 'Would you mind passing me my trousers?' Evidently I had been sitting on them! Later, we went to a pub and, at Tambi's request, Dylan wrote a verse for me. But when Tambi asked him, 'Are you sure it's not obscene?' Dylan retorted that he wrote nothing else, whereupon Tambi tore up what he had written. I picked up the pieces and put them in my overcoat pocket, but they fell out and I never saw them again. Dylan and Tambi made up, and Tambi invited him to our apartment for dinner on Dylan's birthday. Alas, by that time Dylan was in a coma and died a few days later. We went to the memorial service and I met the beautiful and fiery Caitlin, his widow. When Caitlin saw me she exclaimed to Tambi, 'Is she dumb? She must be, otherwise she would not be so beautiful.' I didn't know where to look. She then pulled Tambi's hair hard, and said, 'You know, I feel quite tempted by your wife', and we all laughed.

The years 1953 to 1956 were when Tambi did most of his writing. The *Reporter* magazine published the following articles and short stories: 'Uncle Sivam and the British' (1953), 'Elizam' (1954), 'The Tree-Climber' (1955) and 'Great Grandfather and the Demons'. 'The Pomegranate Tree' was published in *The New Yorker* in December 1954. All the short stories were based in Atchuvely, Ceylon, around Tambi's childhood years. Houghton Mifflin were going to publish these short stories, entitled *A Handful of Red Earth*, as a book for Book-of-the-Month Club, but alas, Tambi stopped writing short stories in 1957 when he restarted publishing *Poetry London–New York*, and the book never came out.

Tambi's short stories were very evocative and poetical. I feel it a great tragedy that he gave up writing and re-entered the publishing world, where he had to find sponsors to put up the money for each issue of his magazine. This letter from Tambi to my parents shows how seriously he took his short stories:

This is to let you know the good news that my collection of short stories – I have only five for the moment and must produce seven more – will be bought next week by Houghton Mifflin. They are among the oldest established publishers and are really distinguished. The editor who came to see me was full of emotion over my short stories and called them great. When I protested that I was only a beginner and pointed out the flaws in all the five stories – that they lacked good characterization, that 'Pomegranate Tree' was too slick, 'The Tree-Climber' a bit out of focus, that in fact they yet lacked the literary quality I so admired in, for instance, Eudora Welty, she burst out my stories were twice as good, and they all had a point, whereas Eudora Welty's last long story for *The New Yorker* called 'The Ponder Heart' had not. Of course, I don't agree. I think Eudora Welty a really master story teller and to write like her will take me some more time. I hope the other seven stories I write for the book will show a definite advance over the five I have now finally retained for the first collection, which, incidentally, is called *A Handful of Red Earth* – after the red earth of my village in Ceylon – and that when I have finished the book I shall at last have learnt how to control my medium to better purpose.

It was during this time that Peter and Edna Bellinson of Peter Pauper Press published *India Love Poems*, edited and translated in part by Tambi. The book is very popular in India and has been reprinted several times. Tambi had had *India Love Poems* published in London in a very lush edition with illustrations by John Piper. Tambi ghost wrote a book on yoga and was guest editor of the poetry section of the Indian edition of *Poetry Chicago*, and also of the India Supplement brought out by *Atlantic Monthly*.

In 1955, Professor R. Archibald of Brown University wrote an account of Tambi in his *Bulletin*. Professor Archibald and Tambi had corresponded frequently, and after the *Bulletin* was published Professor Archibald invited us on behalf of Brown University to stay at Gardner House – a very exclusive and historic mansion where very select guests are invited to stay. Our visit to Brown University was instructive and pleasurable. Professor Archibald was a rare person, a noted mathematician and a lover of modern poetry, and yet so simple and modest in his demeanour. He impressed us both as one of the finest persons we had met. He expressed a desire that Tambi should start publishing again, and oddly enough, on our return to New York, Tambi was consulted by a student from Columbia University who told us that his professor had said that Tambi knew more about modern poetry than anybody else and he too hoped Tambi would recommence publishing. This reawoke Tambi's desire to start a new poetry magazine in New York. Many people encouraged him in this venture. I was against it, as I foresaw the difficulties it would create, but Tambi went ahead with the scheme.

Starting a new magazine meant not only that Tambi had to start from scratch but that he had to find sponsors to finance the magazine. It was a thankless task. Each number of the magazine needed a sponsor to put up the money and, apart from the editorial work, Tambi had to find such sponsors. All were not like Willard, who said over the phone, 'Don't insult me by telling me who you are. How much do you want?'

The tremendous strain this put on Tambi made him drink heavily, until gradually it prevented him from functioning effectively. *Poetry London–New York* No. 1 came out, followed by Nos 2, 3 and 4 at long intervals, and by this time Tambi had become an uncontrolled drinker. This labour of love broke his health and nearly killed him. Once he started publishing he would not give it up, no matter the odds, until he could not carry on any longer. This was something I could not cope with at all.

In 1956 I returned to Bombay to spend some time with my aged parents and went back to New York later in the year. By this time Tambi was in a bad way and I joined the Al Anon Group, which helped me somewhat. This was a terrible time for both of us, and there seemed no way out of the nightmare.

In 1957 my health broke down and, after an operation and treatment at New York Hospital, I left New York for India in May 1958. Tambi could not cope with the responsibilities of marriage and wished to be free, so, six months after I returned to Bombay, we got divorced.

On my return to India I led a quiet but interesting life. On my father's death in 1961, Tambi wrote a most moving letter to my mother which I am quoting in full to illustrate his concern and feeling, in spite of being in far-off New York. This letter was written some months after his marriage to Esta, who became the mother of their daughter, Shakuntala.

150 Clinton Street, Brooklyn 1, N.Y., NY
8 January 1962

My dearest Amma,*

I was grieved to receive Safia's letter. There were so many things I wished to do for dear, patient and noble Bapoota† and so many bits of communication I wished to establish with him as soon as possible, but, alas, the opportunity was not afforded me. I have been labouring under a cloud (who isn't?) and although he has been in my daily thoughts and the desire strong to reach to that slender, purposeful and gentle figure always working at his desk (when I wasn't), I am afraid I have missed the cue and scrambled all the words and lines, and I feel bad about it. My days at Ravindra Mansion are a bright mark in a waste of drabness and his dear memory will always live with me.

I wonder whether you remember how he and I once planted two trees at *Nishat*. Knowing what the *malis*** are like, they are probably no longer there, but it has been a recurrent thought with me in this concrete landscape. I feel damned angry too since I had hoped to make a lot of money in New York and send him some to plant several more. I never even sent him the California dates.

It comforts me to know that he now lies in a peaceful spot with trees. Where is it? As soon as I am on my feet, and I can manage it with import permit from India etc. I would like to send some special medium growing datelike palms to shade his grave, if you think this is appropriate. Perhaps Safia would have better ideas from what she knows of the flora of this country. He was Bapoota to me.

And you are the only mother I had since I lost my own.

As I wrote to Safia, I have been rather indisposed, and especially so for the past two months. But now I am up again and writing this note to you for the beginning.

Since Esta is expecting a child in three months' time, I would like your permission to name it (if boy) Krishna Hadi Tyabjee Tambimuttu. If it is a girl I'll name it (her) Shakuntala Safia Tyabjee Tambimuttu.

What Safia mentions has surely been always in my mind, as she knows, and I think of her home as mine and mine hers and surely my children will be hers as well and she will see a lot of them.

I am still trying to get a foothold in the writing market here and hope to be successful soon. Then I shall, as I always say, return to England and India.

---

*Amma = Mother.
† Bapoota = Father.
**malis = gardeners.

It is good of you to wish me to have some of Bapoota's clothes. I shall be most glad to have them. I have stubbornly refused to wear European jackets here, not even Bapoota's linen hacking jacket.

Please let me know how you are both getting on – and in the meantime.

Love,
from Tambi

After twenty years I visited London and met Tambi again. He came to the airport and gave me a red rose that he had grown on his balcony. I was very moved. In the car he asked me to sing a song he remembered. He looked very ill. I was six months in London and saw a lot of him during this time.

After two years I invited Tambi to visit India, and he came with his daughter, Shakuntala Safia Tambimuttu, who was named Safia after me. I was her godmother and she treated me like a second mother. We both became very fond of each other. Tambi and Shakuntala did a lot of travelling in India and Tambi met a number of writers, poets and painters. He met the Prime Minister, Mrs Indira Gandhi, who encouraged him in his activities, and he was given a grant to establish an Arts Council of India and Ceylon to help promote cultural activities between the two countries and England. He was full of ideas when he returned to England and intended returning soon to start cultural movements on a big scale. He was in a very creative period of his life, but a few days before he could start for India, he fell down and fatally injured himself. His death followed soon after.

Tambi and I had fun and excitement and interesting times together. We were alike and different in so many ways. To share life with a creative person, with a stimulating personality, can be a tremendous adventure and very rewarding. So I found it. How can I forget those years? I was never so alive and so appreciated and loved by a wide circle of friends. No wonder those six years of my life seem so wonderful and meaningful. Of course there were hard times and difficult periods, but these we shared together as well as the happy times, and the memory of it will ever remain with me, vibrant and constant.

Above: Tambimuttu in the United States in the late 1950s. Copyright Bob Henriques. *Left*: Tambimuttu and Hsiao Ch'ien (formerly of the London School of Oriental Studies) on the BBC radio programme *Through Eastern Eyes*, 19 May 1942. Tambimuttu gave a talk on T.S. Eliot and Hsiao Ch'ien a talk on modern Chinese literature in the series *These Names Will Live*. (BBC copyright)

Photograph taken at the monthly radio magazine *Voice*, 1 December 1942. The magazine broadcast modern poetry to English-speakers in India, as part of the Eastern Service of the BBC. *Left to right, sitting*: Venu Chitale, BBC Indian Section; Tambimuttu; T.S. Eliot; Una Marson, organizer, BBC West Indian Programme; Mulk Raj Anand; Christopher Pemberton, a member of the BBC staff; Dr Narayana Menon, now Chairman of the National Academy of Music, Dance & Drama, New Delhi; *standing*: George Orwell, producer of the programme; Nancy Parratt, Orwell's secretary; William Empson. (BBC copyright)

Anthony Dickins with Tambimuttu in Tambi's first office in Craven House, Kingsway, London, probably in 1939 or 1940.

Tambimuttu and David Gascoyne in the early 1940s.

Elizabeth Smart in the mid-1940s, photographed by Tambimuttu.

Left to right: Nicholas Moore, John Craxton, Kathleen Raine and Tambimuttu in the Poetry London office at 26 Manchester Square in the mid-1940s. (Photograph Phil Boucas)

The wedding of George and Paddy Fraser, St Andrew's Church, Chelsea, 30 August 1946. *Left to right*: Tony Schooling; Tambimuttu; Harold Mussen; Gavin Ewart; Iain Fletcher; William Empson; Tom Scott; Helen Irwin; Nicholas Moore. (Photograph J.A.L. Pearce) *Below left*: George Murphy, head of public relations at MGM, and Safia, 1957. *Below right*: Tambimuttu and Safia in the early 1950s. (Photograph International News)

Claude Miéville

Times with Tambi in New York

The image of Tambi which I had formed when reading *Poetry London* during the war was clearly defined, but different in almost every respect from the real Tambi whom I first met in 1953. The former was something of an academic, certainly a scholar (his translations from the Sanskrit confirmed that), and must be hard-headed if, as I understood it, he had reported for *The Times of Ceylon*. In consequence I saw him in a well-cut, dark grey suit (probably with a discreet stripe), and very urbane, though somewhat cool and aloof; and very critical. The latter, the real Tambi, did not possess a well-cut suit let alone wear one, was warm, spontaneous, very humorous and kind. He was not at all aloof, but was urbane in that he knew his way around and could soon charm all but the most antagonistic, of which there proved to be many in New York (where, incidentally, he was once mugged), which was in many ways puritanical and parochial by our standards, and still is.

At the time I met Tambi, my wife Luki and I and our two children, Claudia and Dominic, lived in a railroad* apartment in an old brownstone house in Yorkville; which was, for the most part, a solid, German, lower-middle-class-cum-working-class area — artisans, foremen, supervisors and the like. Most were first- or second-generation immigrants who spoke German at home and in the streets, and tended to eschew anything non-Teutonic. We, English with a French name, had had our problems settling in. Into this neighbourhood Tambi and Safia fell, as from a clear blue sky. One evening in late 1952 or early 1953 a voice on the telephone told me that it was Tambimuttu, and did we know of an apartment which might be going begging (he had been told to try us), since they had recently arrived and were ill-suited. We did. The one above us was empty by good chance; and by equally good chance I had that day invested in a bottle of Scotch

*The term 'railroad' refers to those apartments, usually old, inexpensive and brownstone, without corridors, in which one room leads directly into the next and so forth. Ours and Tambi's had four rooms, of which two were minute, plus a bathroom and kitchen. One soon got used to the noise, and children got used to sleeping through it all. They had to!

(Guggenheim, American distilled, since we were not affluent).

Tambi and Safia arrived shortly afterwards; she in a sari, and he looking an absolute ruffian with hair abnormally long even for him, a chin which clearly had not seen a razor for some time, and wearing a dark, shaggy, baggy overcoat which further emphasized an image of intense hairiness. In the middle of all this the humorous, warm face which I came to know so well.

That first evening proved to be momentous, though not to be remembered clearly, since the three of us finished off the Guggenheim, Safia drinking little if anything at all; and we finally went our ways with loud hilarity and promises to repeat the treatment on the very next occasion. The upshot was that they moved in upstairs, and our lives changed.

The apartment above us, which they took ($100 under the table to the janitor who had had his suspicions about us all along, and was now firmly convinced that we were all nothing but a bunch of gypsies), was transformed into India overnight. Tambi and Safia had brought everything with them – bedding, cushions, exotic textiles and wall coverings from India and Ceylon, clothes of course and even a small granite slab ribbed like a washboard on which Safia ground her curry-powders from the nuts and herbs which she had brought as well. And of course hundreds of books. They must have travelled with many packing-cases, though I don't recall seeing any.

I was out all day earning my crust at Rockefeller Center, so Tambi and I went our different ways professionally and seldom saw much of each other during weekdays, although we would frequently meet in the evenings, drink, throw parties, dance, cook communal meals. Because of this, my memory of that memorable year takes the form of numerous individual, isolated events rather than of a continuous day in day out relationship such as might have been the case had I been working from home or been a writer. For instance, I remember one large party during which I walked into the kitchen to find Luki and Tambi on their knees on the floor, scooping up meatballs which had escaped from the pan and rolled God knows where – probably under the stove for the most part. They were then curried and fed to the many guests, who pronounced them delicious. After that I never ventured into the kitchen when the two of them were cooking. Better not!

I also remember the children (aged four and two) climbing the stairs every morning to the flat above, bearing tribute to King Tambi, as he had told them to call him – a cigarette, match, paper-clip or some such trifle. There were dire consequences if they failed to do so, and they took their mission seriously. Tambi loved children and used to read poetry to ours, which they adored.

Again, the four of us going to see a mildly erotic colour film which Robert Payne had made at the university where he was then teaching English. The actors were the girl students, and the *pièce de résistance*, a pillow-fight in a dormitory, shot in slow motion: pillows bursting open, the air thick with almost static feathers, young nubile girls bursting out everywhere, and this emphasized by the wide-angle lens which had been used. The sound was not synchronized, but that didn't seem to matter.

Then Dylan's death, and Tambi asking me to take photographs of him in his coffin where he lay, isolated and alone, somewhere near Columbus Circle. There was no one else there. In death he looked little different from when I had first seen him with Caitlin in Oxford in 1947 (?), when he delivered a diatribe at a Poetry Society meeting against young women who wrote poetry about love without knowing love, and poetry societies who published magazines with meaningless names ' . . . such as Trend, Era or Scrotum. . . .' Tambi then took us to Dylan's memorial service somewhere outside the city, after which and on the steps of the church Caitlin delivered her own diatribe against the America which she said had killed her husband.

Somewhere I have two tapes which remind me vividly of those happy New York days and their family style. One, Tambi's beautiful, sonorous voice reading Nicholas Moore's 'Come My December Lady' against a background of children's voices; and the other, all of us singing 'My Sister Lil' (a scurrilous song) while a fire-engine clanged its way up 87th Street, under the window.

When we left New York, Tambi presented me with *Claude's Own Book of Lovely Ladies* by Tambimuttu, Himself a Lover of Fair Ladies, published by the Guri Press, 338 East 87th Street, New York – the only book published by that press, I believe (Guri was Tambi's pet name for Safia). Tambi had typed and put together the book himself, and covered it with part of one of Safia's saris – under protest. The book, which is beautifully illustrated, is the forerunner of *India Love Poems*, later published by the Peter Pauper Press and elsewhere.

So we left, with letters of introduction from Tambi and Robert Payne jointly to friends in Paris and London. By luck we saw Safia again in Belgium and Italy, and Tambi in Suffolk and London, though not often, since I have been working mostly abroad. I wish we had seen more of him – a wish which anyone who knew him will share.

Fred Lewis

Meeting Tambi

It was the bar named the Ideal, generally known as the Ordeal, on Hudson Street between Perry and 11th in New York. A long, dark, dirty bar, low and narrow, diagonally across and taking what trade it had from the overflow and the expelled of the White Horse Tavern. It was late summer of 1959. The Angel was on the bar, enormous with tight skin the shade of drugstore counter marble drawn across the large frontal lumps of his forehead and irregular grey Bratwurst fingers with swollen knuckles that made me think of *National Geographic* cave formations.

I had been drinking for a while. I had just moved to the Village off a ruined marriage, and I was remarkably lonely. I got up, beer in hand, to play the juke-box near the door. A big man with a small blond walrus moustache, not tall but maybe 250 pounds, as he blustered into the bar with two taller men behind him, bumped my arm, deliberately as I saw it, spilling the beer. A clear and public insult. All my loneliness and bitterness seemed to rise up with my anger. I didn't think about odds or numbers or weight. I went at him.

Suddenly the Angel had vaulted over the bar and many people were around us. I was persuaded to return to my seat, the big man and the other two shooed to the street end of the bar.

I drank at my new beer. I am sure I made myself appear calm and hard, but my outrage and anger were fading fast to something like bravado when a soft voice to my right said, 'Don't hurt him. He's sick.'

'Yeh, he'll be a lot fucking sicker . . .'

'No, no, I know him. He really is sick.'

In the dark bar mirror I was aware of the figure at my right, tapping at his forehead. After a pause the figure said, 'What's your name?'

Surprised, relieved too I suppose at something so quiet and human in the gratuitously hostile setting, I looked at a short, thin, brown man with a very little smile at the corners of his mouth. He had a narrow, elevated forehead which didn't seem enough to, yet did, support his wide-set, soft, untroubled eyes. From his hair I knew he must be old – I was thirty-four – but I felt rather that I was looking into timeless boyishness. He had on a bedraggled chamois-type dark green shirt and khakis. I knew he was OK. I signalled the Angel to give us two beers. And I told the man my name.

'You are Welsh.'

At that I lighted up.

'My father was.'

'Then we are brothers, you see.'

'Oh?' I didn't see.

'Dravidian brothers.'

The Angel had given us our beer and busied himself at the street end of the bar. I stood and looked to the mirror over the bottles. So did Tambi. I was surprised: he was not short, but a good deal taller than I. I am summer brown, he much browner; my hair brown with an ashy summer gold in it, his black verging on grey. His face was lean and fine, mine chunky, blurred, not quite fat. Nevertheless, I saw that somehow it was the same face. We sat again.

'Do you really mean it?' I had been looking for a brother all my life.

'Of course I mean it.' For the first time he sounded a little Indian, an interesting didactic lilt to the voice. 'The Dravidians sailed the west coast of Britain three thousand years before Christ. Dravidian-Druid – same thing. My brother Singam studies all this. He has done for twenty years.' A little smile ran across his face. 'Writing a book about it.'

'I'd like to read it.' I chuckled. 'I guess it ought to be out soon.'

Tambi considered a moment. 'I don't think so. It's exhaustive, you see.'

'Where is he a professor?'

'Not a professor,' he said with faint distaste. 'He works by day – British Civil Service – and writes at night.'

I am very American, and everything he said seemed at the least implausible. But I believed it anyway.

'He sings gloriously,' Tambi went on, 'fantastic sincerity, delicacy.'

'Indian songs?'

'No, French love-songs. Only French love-songs.' His face erupted into a long giggle of glee. 'He is madly in love with my wife.'

'It's good you're not annoyed.'

'Good God, why should I be annoyed?'

'I think I'd be annoyed.'

'Good God, you Americans don't seem to understand anything. You have lost your bloody lyricism.'

There was actually nothing unkind in the tone of this observation, but it reminded me of a desolating disability I suffered: I was unable to look at anything easily, naturally, with the eyes of a boy. With love. I had to measure, compare, judge. In short, I never or almost never enjoyed anything.

'Maybe I have lost my lyricism,' I said after a moment, 'but I can sing like a bird. And sometimes like a bull.'

'Can you? Good. But then all Welsh can sing. Sing me a song.'

I looked to the street end of the bar. 'Not here,' I said. 'We'll go to my place. Right around the corner.'

So we did. To 396 Bleecker. One large room with bookshelves on three sides, over a garden. A perfect room for a scholar, as I told my therapist. But no scholar there. 'He is always at the bar.'

Tambi liked my voice a lot, and we sang to each other for several hours. About three in the morning he started talking about Wales. It seemed he just had to call the Brenterion Inn in Llanderfell. It seemed he had accompanied a friend – Robin Waterfield, I think – there as his best man some fifteen years before, had so to speak commandeered the place, persuading or maybe bullying them to keep it open continuously for three days, had danced on tables, had . . .

'Go ahead,' I said. 'It seems like a good idea.'

The person who took the call didn't know Tambi but the owner, whom he summoned, did. Tambi talked excitedly to three or four people for most of an hour.

'We must go there one day, Fred,' he said when he had hung up. 'You will adore it. Masses and masses of lovely people. Pots and pots of liquor.'

I had no money then. Tambi clearly didn't have any either. But I imagined climbing with Tambi toward it, high on a hillside, white with red shutters and great porches over the green happy hill.

Tambi left about dawn. We began to see a great deal of each other after that, and in 1963, at probably the lowest point of his stay in Angelica Amelica, he came to stay with me for nine months. They were bad times for both of us, and I drank a lot and did things for which I suppose I will always feel bad. I can't conceive Tambi feeling bad over anything he ever did. Whatever it is in Westerners and particularly Americans that makes them sick and uncomfortable with themselves was not in Tambi. So many other marvellous things were that there never would have been room for it.

I have never mourned anybody less, perhaps partly because so much of him has come over to me and remains. I think that is true of everyone who knew him well. My wife, Telo Reifel, wrote a play,

Swan, whose pivotal character was formed from her picture of Tambi. 'Happy Teaparty Cake' is a story my daughter has just completed celebrating him. He is very much with us, always. All of us grew up at least in part little, mean, envious, sullen, money-bound. His spirit that abided none of these things, that hardly honoured them with recognition, offered us a focus, a hope, a way West.

Tambi and I never did get to the Brenterion Inn. If ever I do, I will see him as I clamber up the green hillside, beckoning and calling from the wide porch, 'Hurry, Fred, all our friends are here. Hurry! It's the most magnificent *pahty*.'

Richard Eberhart

Tonal Depth

There was a tonal depth of mauve
When years were flickering on the lawn;
In the eloquence of antique air
I heard time's shiftings. Fate had gone

A moment backward where he was
Amid the orchards of the Spring, adream.
That was a goldenness and openness
When his other face was seen.

No depth was quite so deep as this;
No tone so rich; no lengthening shade
Compelled such vivid imagery.
As if one knew, but need not know.

Claire McAllister

A Song for Tambi

Turn your river-dark eyes to the fields of promise
Hear the once pipered fifes skirling under the hills.
Let the elms of the forest be the tall dead heroes
And your terrible longings be the mist as it sails.

Lay down the arrows; aside, now: pluck strings that are finer.
Say, say what the meadow-winds sang through your hair.
Pursuing the wild boars of dreams you run harder, O lover,
The dust-clouds blind. Now with song clear the air.

Put your heart like the bucket to the cut maple.
Let your life's blood drop sweet, gather deep the dream.
Let the moon throw its spear and the shaft of St Michael
Floodlight the ghost-cluttered passageways of the brain.

They are cluttered with conjured, O conjured sorrows.
Good for trapping the dust. Know love, nothing dies but the flesh
Let lost heroes secretly call and clear this forest
And song break forth from the love you thought dead.

If the thicket you thrash is your heart twisting, twisting.
See the lion stride by, grace itself, unalarmed.
Leave thorn fences to lackloves. Stretch your arms free this evening.
Time, striding by like the lion, is Time charmed.

Night closes the wood-lilies. Let it so close the eyelids.
From crown down to sole feel the fever, lo, falling.
O first and last tale learning over and over ever:
If dusk lead to dark then is dawning dawning.

Esta Busi

Let me set the scene. We are in a ground-floor apartment on Hudson Street in Greenwich Village, New York City. The year is 1959 or 1960. The apartment consists of one large room, a short hallway, a bathroom and a tiny kitchen. It is always dark there, as the two windows look out on to a dark courtyard or alley. The place is overwhelmingly cluttered with randomly placed boxes and piles of papers, notebooks, ledgers, magazines and books, with exotic items such as a coconut shredder used as a paperweight. Stacked in a corner by the door is the Poetry London–New York edition of poems by Michael Hamburger. The unsuspecting stranger stares bemused at the slim volume thrust into his hands with the bellowed greeting, 'Have a Hamburger!'

In the other corner of the same wall is a single bed next to a straight-backed chair used as a night-stand and dining-room table. Next to the chair, on the wall, is a payphone, another excuse for a laugh. When someone asks to use the phone, Tambi or someone else generously leads him to the phone and voices the hope that someone in the room has a dime. Tambi had the payphone installed to control his runaway impulses to phone friends all over the world. Almost anybody who knew him would have a telephone story or two to tell about Tambi.

The other furniture is quite simple: an imitation leather, up-holstered chair without arms, several straight-backed chairs gathered around the bed, and, in the hall, a cluttered chest of drawers. Each wooden piece is striped along its horizontal rims with cigarette burns. After the ashtray fills up, Tambi uses empty beer-cans and the edge of the nearest available surface. There are cooking implements and dishes and articles of clothing and linen, empty beer-cans and cigarette-ash mixed with and scattered among the books and papers. Tambi never did keep his personal and his professional life separate.

Sitting on the edge of the bed, hunched over his beer, holding a cigarette between his contorted and yellowing fingers, sits Tambi, the focus of attention. He is wearing a sarong around his middle which shows off his barrel chest with the hair beginning to go white, and his thin arms. I am sitting behind him, leaning against the wall with my feet up on the bed. There is the usual mixture of visitors – young men

149

who helped work on the last issue of *Poetry London–New York*, maybe a long-standing friend or two, and a few casual acquaintances picked up and brought home from the White Horse Tavern, just up the street. I say casual acquaintances, but no one was casual with Tambi. He had an uncanny ability to read people accurately, pierce their armour and touch them in a way that made them love him or hate him. Usually he was kind and loving to those whose hidden faults and fears he discovered so easily, but every now and then he would strike such a telling blow that I was surprised to see the victims again. And they did return.

Tambi would occasionally tell stories of his childhood in Ceylon and it is one of these that I should like to share with you. When Tambi was seven or eight years old (he was always vague about time so this is a wild guess), he and a brother or two were taken to visit an uncle. To commemorate their visit, and to ensure their return, the uncle had each boy plant a pomegranate tree near the house. The uncle told them that they would always have their own tree at his home to come to see when they were older.

When Tambi returned, years later, looking for his tree, he found that it had been chopped down. At maturity, all the trees planted that day produced the expected crop of fruit, but not Tambi's. His tree had only a single pomegranate, but what a magnificent one it was! It was the largest, the most gigantic pomegranate ever seen. All the neighbours came to see it and talked about it and eagerly waited to taste this wonderful fruit. It was sour. It was the worst-tasting pomegranate ever.

'Don't you see?' asked Tambi. 'It was so awful that no one could eat it.' He gestured grandly for emphasis. And then he giggled and repeated. 'So awful, so sour, no one could *eat* it' as he glanced sharply at me for my reaction. I was saddened by that terrible metaphor. But what did he see that was so funny?

Susanne English

Tambi in 11th Street

Back in the sixties there were two antic ginkgo trees in the middle of our block on West 11th Street in New York City. The trees were in full, designer green flutter long before the first gasp of ninety-degree heat hit the city; their leaves played with the sun, dappled the pocked, steaming pavement with cooling distraction for months. They gave a blessing of incongruous grace to the low tenement and town houses that distinguished our block and much of the surrounding skyscape of Greenwich Village from the rest of Manhattan. Later, by mid-June, the odd geranium, a spindly clutch of petunias or pansies would push out from the window-boxes that flanked the ginkgo trees, bidding collectively to define the season. Nobody who knew the soul of the block took the bids seriously. The flowers were mere and tardy acolytes; the ginkgos had ordained the summer. We rejoiced that some errant piece of fortune had brought them to our block. They were originals in New York, full of themselves, defiant of the official neglect that should have killed them decades earlier, lusty for each random rain, thriving.

Tambi's studio was four or five doors down from the easternmost of the trees. He shared a basement in the first of three six-storey walk-ups on the block with Chuck the carpenter, a kind Italian-American whose meticulous custom work adorned the kitchens of the rich people in the block, the town-house dwellers whose geraniums and petunias fought so hard to outshoot one another all summer long. Chuck's street-level bay window had a sign announcing his business. Tambi's corresponding window, which was always closed off by dark, louvered shutters, had no sign at all. It was a curiosity, this secret half-basement all shut up.

Then, in mid-July, a chaste white card appeared in his window: '*Poetry London–New York*, Voluntary Help Needed.' The door was ajar. *Poetry London–New York* was famous; the mystery of the louvered windows was solved. I stepped in, to find a slight, handsome fellow in a sheer overshirt and cool white trousers drowsing on the couch in the bay window, two empty cans of beer and a half-eaten jar of marinated olives and pimentos beside him. The publisher and editor himself. I'd seen his picture. A greying lock of chin-length hair bisected his left eye; his face, in the half-sleep, was troubled, innocent; his body seemed exhausted. I coughed; he opened one eye, rejected the sight, shifted and dozed off again. Above his head, lopsided from a nail, hung a signed photograph, a profile, unmistakably T.S. Eliot, whose friend this dozer had been. Surrounding him, masses of papers, boxes with mauve books spilling out, trash and dust defied what had clearly been a well-appointed space. Over his desk a picture of a voluptuous madonna draped in pink and contemplating a red rose dominated the faded brick wall.

Interesting. I coughed again, and said a tentative 'Hello'. He started, both eyes opened; he sat up. 'Yes. Hello.' In a second of scrutiny, as I backed off into shy grabs at the door-jamb, he made three decisions. This person is presentable. I think I can use this person. And, less certain, this person will not hurt me. Possibly. His politeness was so integrated, his defences were so set, I never, save once, saw his face that naked again.

Within ten minutes, the preliminaries done, I was shoehorned behind the books, Festschrifts for Eliot, balancing a cup of tea at the end of a rickety typewriter table and labouring ('Do you type?' 'I hunt and peck.') as he dictated a letter to Lawrence Durrell, thanking him for a piece, asking for another. Tambi paced slowly as he started the letter. As his thoughts gained momentum the pacing became more agitated. A cigarette extended the staccato gestures. Durrell must not simply contribute a new piece; Durrell must come to New York. The Reifels, they are Norman Mailer's friends, Larry dear, would love to meet him. They would have a party. There would be lots of parties, Larry, old chum. Lots of parties. The timbre of his voice deepened; the pace intensified. I saw it, while typing, because as he paced he would bump the eight cartons of books and thus me. The glances back were to make sure the topmost carton was not going to spill mauve books in my lap, jeopardize the full teacup.

Towards the end of the letter the gestures were messianic, both elbows out, forearms raised, fingers ending and contorting with expression. He painted a picture of welcome so seductive it could have exhumed Rimbaud, jollied him out of the grave to Orly and on the first jet to New York. Durrell never came; I'm not sure there was even enough postage money to get the letter mailed, but it was a grand introduction to Tambi, inert, winding and wound. And an introduction for him to me as well. I had just become the sole support of two little boys who outgrew their shoes bimonthly. I could not pull postage out of thin air, could not contribute the bags to mail out review copies of the mauve books, was not perhaps as usable as I had looked, there in the door-jamb. What splendid, aristocratic indifference he affected toward the small details of business. He had the faith of an unroofed abbot who, the day after the raid, sets up to say solemn high mass at his centre altar, in a gale, confident that someone will come along to take care of the little thing. A roof. Some stamps.

And of course somebody always did, those years in 11th Street. When I met him, Tambi had just pulled out of a disastrous, half-formed business partnership with an operator so transparently meretricious he made the skin on your spine pucker with distaste. When the partnership ended, so did Tambi's access to office space. John Gilman owned the lease on the studio, had used it as a photography workshop. His wife, Julie Streeter Gilman, was the pink madonna in the photograph over the desk. They gave the abbot his roof, and entertained him, for years. Panna Grady, a Hungarian heiress with an apartment in the Dakota, was a loyal friend, generous, then she moved to Brittany to live simply. Jim Burtle, an economist from Columbia University and a friend for decades, never said no. Some way, everyone was too polite to talk about how, some stamps and bags appeared. Review copies of the Eliot books got mailed. And someone was always around to pick up the tab for an evening at the Corner Bistro or the No Name Bar, and why not? The good humour alone was worth the tab, if you had the wherewithal to cover it.

Charlie Hoffman, an adept bill settler – you could never see how he'd done it, but proprietors beamed as they waved us out the door – had been a friend since the fifties, when he, Tambi and Safia had all lived in the same apartment building on the Upper East Side. Tambi was fascinated with Hoffman's pedigree. The family had started buying Manhattan real estate in the seventeenth century; at one point during the nineteenth each daughter, on her marriage, was given a block. He was more fascinated with Hoffman's father, with whom he'd spent a country weekend swapping erudition in upstate New York some years earlier. Hoffman's own feelings about his father were ambivalent; Tambi enjoyed a good-natured pick or two at those nerve endings.

'Charlie's father has eleven thousand books.' Tambi would start the banter.

'Books all over the dining-room,' Hoffman would add.

'Eleven thousand books. Think of it. He is a Velikovsky fan. An expert in Velikovsky.'

'Velikovsky, the weather, my life, you name it.'

'Charlie's father went to Oxford. The same college as the Duke of Windsor. Isn't it incredible?'

'And I skinny dipped with you, Tambi old friend.'

'Charlie's father was in the Lafayette Escadrille, isn't it fantastic, why did that wonderful man waste his life in real estate?'

'His father was authoritarian. He did what he was told.'

'A man of some sadness, it's true. I'd noticed.'

'Haven't we all some. He gave me a broom for Christmas.'

'Ah, a prudent man. Charlie's father is careful.'

'A year after my stepmother died, he married his housekeeper. A month later he bought the town she came from in Italy. He said it made him happy.'

'Then what is the secret? Marry the housekeeper. Charlie, old man, we must find ourselves some housekeepers immediately. Bartender, do you have any housekeepers here, please? We would like to look them over, if you don't mind.'

Former patrons would appear. Women who had known Tambi in his salad years as the publishing comet, the poet, the genius, the raconteur. Women who had been deeply moved, then, by his soulful reminiscences of Eden times in Sri Lanka; suffering times too. ('I lost my mother when I was sixteen. I have never got over it.') Women who had fallen in love with this hereditary prince whose Trincomalee ancestors were dragged through the streets, strapped and torn apart between horses whipped to opposite directions. Women fascinated with his final heritage, the legacy symbolized by his un-Tamil and detested baptismal names.

These patrons would appear. There would be more parties; later one of the women might be introduced, with dignity, cuddles and soft smiles, as 'my new business partner'. The pacing would start again as plans, numbers, issues, book ideas disgorged themselves from his released mind into the lighted atmosphere around him. But the new partner would ultimately have other commitments to attend. She would never leave; she would leave for a while. To tidy this up. Straighten that out. Back at home. For months, she was due in shortly.

I was simple minded in those days on 11th Street. I mourned with him over his hard luck, loathed the opportunists he told me had taken advantage of his artistic nature, cursed the benefactors who backed off, the venal friends, the poetry racketeers, the more adept finaglers, the postage problem, the dropped ginkgo leaves on which he'd slipped to a nasty fall one rainy September. I loved and still do the constant friends – Jim Burtle, Bill Tokeshi, John Gilman – who, if they deserted, left long after the drill had exhausted me. I was star-struck with the association, pleased to be included.

Tambi never did figure out quite where I fitted. I was too poor to be a benefactor, too absorbed with my own boys to want another, in any intimate way, no poet of note. I think I was decoration for the grand times, an admiring, credulous comfort for the low times. And welcomed, whatever the times, as if I were the Empress Zita von Habsburg, down for the day from her wearying exile in Tuxedo Park.

'Susie darling. So nice to see you. Have you met Fred? Goldie, George. Mary. Otto.'

A year or so after I stopped going regularly to the studio I was made an editor in a publishing house. I'd inherited some production duties on a book of poetry, the capturing of which had been a coup for the house. I didn't get the book because of any whiz talent in editing poetry; the poet needed coddling, and the new kid was freest to give it. The poet had won a prize. His book, once published, would grow feet, as is said when a book sells well, walks out of the bookstores. I coddled. The fact that this pampered fellow was one of the poetry racketeers Tambi so detested didn't intrude on the obsequies at all, except in the deepest part of my heart, the part that could, in a fugue or three, extract itself from the problems of shoes and schools and camps and warm winter coats, the part that wanted and wants to stay forever the *naïf*. One day I ran into Grover Amen, a Tambi poet who'd put in some time writing talk pieces and fiction for *The New Yorker* magazine. I knew John Gilman's lease was about to run out, that Tambi would need a new place. We caught up with one another. I told Amen about my job.

'Does Tambi know what you're doing?' Amen asked.

'Of course,' I said.

'Susie, I was down at the studio a week ago. Tambi thinks you're a secretary.'

Amen must have seen Tambi again; within three days the master was on the phone.

'Susie darling, you must come down to the studio this evening. You must. There is someone you must meet.'

He went on, exhuming Rimbaud, and I went to meet the new friend and benefactor. Timothy Leary. Leary was riding high then, sat in a corner affecting the clothes Tambi wore by right, projecting serenity, unless you looked too closely, stoned off his gourd.

'Susie dear, I am to be Tim's guru. Bill Hitchcock has given us a house. We will go to Millbrook and have a school. We will have a university. I will lecture on Tantric yoga and write poems to Rosemary (Leary's wife) – she is a goddess, a divinity, you must meet Rosemary. And Tim and I will write a book. Would you be interested in publishing the book, Susie dear?'

Of course we signed up the book; it went through several metamorphoses, I think it even got published, years after I'd gone to another publishing house, as Leary's book. There were invitations to Millbrook during Tambi's guru years, rather insistent ones, initially.

'Susie, you must get up here. I promise you that Tim himself will give you a trip. It will be as safe as bathing in a pool of fresh rainwater. It connects you to the most incredible things in your brain, centres you in the cosmos. . . .'

He sounded unchanged, manic, belied his own assurances. I had seen a teenager tripping on the street once, seen this child implode on himself, pass into inconceivably intense stress, seen a look of helpless terror that is still seared into my brain, as fresh a memory as last night's sunset. I was curious about Millbrook, wanted to see Tambi, tempted. But Millbrook was not the place for little boys. I didn't travel without mine, if I could help it, and so I told him no.

I don't remember how long it was after the Millbrook time that Tambi decided to return to London. He'd come back every year or so; there would be reunions at Jim Burtle's, at John and Julie Gilman's. At one, in Robert Payne's apartment, I found the poet Allen Ginsberg between two of Payne's priceless gold Indian statues. Ginsberg is warm-hearted, well connected in the world of grants and benefactors and tax deductible patronage. I told him Tambi was needy.

'We are all needy,' he said.

And that was incontestable. We are all in need, and there is precious little sating for the determinedly luckless, the guileless, for yesterday's comet, whose mother died when he was sixteen, who has never gotten over it.

Everything good that happened to me in my life for five years happened, directly or elliptically, because I stepped into Tambi's studio in 11th Street that summer day. Everything. I got married in the early seventies, moved to an apartment with a spare room on the Upper West Side. Tambi came to New York and I was happy to the point of joy to be able finally to offer him something. The spare room. He moved in. There were three good days, one interminable evening with a fellow from *Playboy* magazine and his friend, who had just flown in from Mexico, who left a package. Within forty-eight hours it was hopeless. I came home from work to find him on the couch, out cold, the couch in near-flame from the lit cigarette smouldering on the armrest. I came home from work to find him in the spare room with my boys, introducing them to the cigarette with the sweet odour, the cigarette he rolled himself. He was teaching them how to do it.

I made a few frantic phone calls, finally got Roxanne Chase, who had been our baby-sitter, had met and loved Tambi, had an apartment where someone was home all day, where there was not stuffed furniture. She and her husband, Tony Loder, called, invited him to come, to stay. We did not have to ask him to leave. Rox and Tony were young, romantic, star-struck, enthralled. Tambi had been cold; I gave him a winter coat, leaned over the dead geraniums in the window-box to watch him amble off down our new block, original, full of himself, still lusty, still thriving.

I've been back to 11th Street only once since then. The studio became a health-food store after Tambi left; my boys delivered packages for the store. I could never bear to go near it. When I went back it was shuttered, dark, awaiting a tenant. Chuck the carpenter's boy got badly hurt in Vietnam. Chuck was never the same after they brought his boy home; he closed up his shop too. The ginkgos are still there; the walk-ups we called home are now co-operative apartments highly coveted for the light, the air, their well-scaled proportions. They've been shined up with a lot of brass polish, a lot of window-boxes full of pansies. The ginkgos now look appropriate rather than miraculous. I like the street a lot less, now that the real-estate racketeers have beautified it so. Tambi wouldn't like it either. It lost its soul, and soul was one of his necessities, something he could spot and nourish and gratify. The talent couldn't pay the rent, but it's not the worst of talents to have.

Timothy Leary

Tambimuttu Shines On

In the twenty-three years since our first meeting, every time I think of Tambimuttu a light glows in my brain and I smile and feel a little better. And every time our paths intersected, the glow would increase and my smile would break into a happy laugh of welcome.

How can we describe this wondrous magnetism? Charisma? Nobility? Spiritual radiance? I am sure there are many jewelled words in Sanskrit to express more precisely this attractive power. Surely we can say that Tambimuttu was a transmitter of ancient wisdom and beauty. Perhaps he was not an entity of this time and place. Indeed, I always saw him as some timeless, precious vessel bringing us gifts from beyond. Yes, there was that mystery about Tambimuttu, that Merlin sense about him that transformed the ordinary situation into something a bit magical, raised us up a level or two on the splendour dial.

It was 1966 when he came to the mansion at Millbrook and covered his rooms with bookshelves crammed with his literary treasures and archives. I cherish the many hours I spent with him there, as he moved around the room like a graceful alchemist spinning out tales of cosmic mischief and poetic celebration. Some days we would drive the Land-Rover up the bumpy roads of the estate to a hilltop vista or to the hidden lake and watch the sun set and the swallows wheeling in the orange sky and he would chant his funny fables and we would laugh like Olympians. No matter what the social scene, no matter who was performing whatever soap opera, Tambimuttu always maintained his elegant dignity and benign aloofness, sometimes puzzled, no doubt, by the antics of mortals, but always chuckling with cheerful compassion. I felt some strange fraternal bond with this man. We had some wonderful heritage in common, some secret that we shared, some ancient connection. Over the thirteen years we never once lost this dear thread of mutual admiration. (Oh yes, I know he established this same tender, aristocratic bond with many others, but that was his special gift, wasn't it, isn't it, that he graced our lives with this sense of nobility?) Tambimuttu was a prince among us and being with him we shared the magnificence of his regal aura.

I am smiling now as I write these lines of love and high pleasure about this great presence that was with us and remains with us.

Grover Amen

My Last Meeting with Tambi

The last time I saw Tambi before he moved back to London was in 1970. The phone rang in the middle of the night. Tambi was in my neighbourhood. He had just received from the estate of Franz Kline a painting which he had 'commissioned' from the painter years before and which had been designed for some future issue of *Poetry London–New York*. I must come over immediately and have a look at the cover. I was feeling a little depressed because I had just lost my job at *The New Yorker*. I had been working on a long profile of 'Light' but had been unable to finish it and I owed them $20,000 in advances. However, Tambi promised to cheer me up, and I went over to the house of his friend, Anna.

The Franz Kline cover was marvellous. It had all the ramshackle energy of the large canvases but was more concentrated. The effect of a small Kline was strange, for I had always equated smaller versions of his work with reproductions. Perhaps the large scale was unnecessary after all. I remembered some critic saying that the preoccupation of the abstract expressionists with size revealed a latent homosexuality – one of the more cogent specimens of contemporary art criticism.

The arrival of the Kline cover had put Tambi in an expansive mood. He claimed that, despite his craziness, he was the only one who had the courage actually to live by pure faith and that no one else in America had the slightest notion of what it even meant. He said that he had always lived this way, that it was why he had so much energy and was never in a state of despair, no matter how bad things got. He said that when you lived purely by faith, you had no fear and it didn't matter how bad things got. He said that he always had a roof over his head and enough to eat and that everyone else in America did too, as opposed to Calcutta, but that, if he had to live on the street and beg, it would not bother him. He said the great modern fear was really of social indignity. He said that the whole point of trust was not to put faith to the test, that there was no test. Either you lived by it and accepted whatever came, or you didn't. It was useless wasting time trying to arrange your life. He admitted that such a way of life had its dangers, but he insisted they were nothing compared with common bourgeois misery.

Anna pointed out that he never ate anything anyway, living as he did on wine alone. Tambi ignored this thrust. He insisted that such matters as how one earned one's livelihood were ordained at birth, and there was nothing to be done about it. Anna said that Tambi's faith was suspect to outsiders because, in their eyes, it meant only that he was a bum and let other people support him. Tambi said this was perfectly true but the price he had to pay for the gift of his faith. He insisted it was all child's play, a mere bagatelle in comparison with the usual forms of household anxiety.

What Tambi said made sense, or would have if someone else had said it, but something about his extravagant claims to an enlightened spirituality irritated me.

'This is madness,' I said. 'You're not Thoreau. You're a crazy drunken con artist, and if you don't have enough to drink, you shake all over and get the DTs. I've heard you babbling about birds on your shoulder when you ran out of booze. You're sick as a dog. You can't function right in the world. You're a lost soul, a misfit. Come off it. Where do you get off giving us this spiritual boloney about living by trust and faith? You can't even piss straight after a few drinks.'

I got up to go, but Tambi came through with an interesting retort. It was the first time I had heard him communicate with me on such a quiet, personal level. He said without hostility: 'Listen, old boy. You're in a bad way. You're the prime example of what I'm talking about. You have absolutely no faith in your own powers, much less the powers of the universe. You're living in a veil of illusion, worshipping graven images and false idols. The Talk of the Town! And you talk about form and "making poems". You're completely out of touch with the primal rhythms of life. You hate what you're doing at *The New Yorker*. Get out! Get out!'

'But I'm not at *The New Yorker* any more,' I said.

'You might as well be,' he said. 'You're still carrying it around with you, *arranging* ironies, looking for the *bon mot*. Drop it, old fellow! Burn your bridges! Get on with it! Tum tiddy. Tum tiddy. Tum tiddy TUM!'

At this point Tambi jumped up and danced and stomped on the floor in a frenzied rhythm like the mad Dionysian Indian that he was. Soon he was in a state of ecstatic abandon, chanting an interminable medley of obscene limericks. 'The world's not your fault, old boy,' he told me. 'You still have a chance – pretty remote, I admit. Come on. Get up and dance. Oh, my fucking aunt, stop suffering!'

Geoffrey Elborn

Remembering Tambimuttu

The name of *Poetry London* was known to me long before that of its editor. When I was a librarian in Edinburgh, aged twenty, I remember hiding in the stack floors to gloat over these remarkable wartime volumes. The bumper volume 10, with a large illustration by Gerald Wilde, haunted me for some time, but it had scarcely occurred to me that its editor could even still be alive.

Some years later, in conversation with Kathleen Raine, I learnt that Tambimuttu had returned to found the Lyrebird Press, and indeed I saw in a bookshop in Newcastle a large prospectus with quotations from Edith Sitwell and others, praising the merits of the mysterious editor.

In those days I was trying to find a publisher for some poems of Sacheverell Sitwell, and wrote to Tambi asking if he would like to see the typescript. Eventually Tambi asked if I would come to London and meet him for lunch in a certain Italian restaurant in Frith Street, and rather nervously I arrived, uncertain what to expect.

A large Campari was ordered without any choice, as was the rest of the meal, but as I had almost no money and was surviving on a student grant, it was a relief not to have to worry about inadvertently choosing the most expensive item. I would not have dared to order the fresh salmon as a starter, and while we waited for it to arrive, I sat trying to form an impression of my host.

When I came to know Tambi later, I realized that he had several moods, but on this occasion he was extremely talkative and excited about the many projects in which he was involved. Memories of the forties and of those he had known such as T.S. Eliot, tumbled out, as I hurriedly gobbled my salmon. On looking up, I was embarrassed to find that Tambi, meticulously cutting his up into neat geometric squares, had hardly begun.

The alcohol slightly took over my recollections of that day, but as our taxi destined for Kensington arrived, Tambi signed the bill in a flourish as in a gentlemen's club, and was waved off the premises by, it seemed, the entire smiling and friendly restaurant staff.

The afternoon was filled with grand gestures, and nothing was done in a small way. A visit to a newsagent produced, it seemed, every magazine the shop had for sale, and these were paid for with a twenty-pound note plucked from a bundle of many stuffed carelessly in Tambi's heavy overcoat.

Laden with magazines and cartons of cigarettes, and pausing to wave to John Lehmann who was out for a walk, we went to Tambi's office, where we had coffee. During the conversation, Tambi discovered I had written some poetry, and I was struck by his faith, that without even seeing them, he said, 'I will publish them.'

All too soon, I had to catch my return train to Newcastle, but not without taking a small collection of books Tambi gave me, including the rare *Festschrift for Marianne Moore*. We promised to keep in touch, and I left in a mood of elation, almost taking away Tambi's overcoat, identical to mine, but identifiable by that bundle of twenty-pound notes.

The eventual running down of the Lyrebird Press meant no Sitwell book, and, fortunately for me, no poems of mine either, for glancing now at those that were published in a volume in Edinburgh, I would have been ashamed to have had them presented by Lyrebird.

Letters to Tambi remained unanswered. I heard vaguely that he was in New York, and it was not until I spotted the striking Piper design of a lyrebird on a magazine in a shop ten years later that I realized that Tambi had returned to England.

Efforts to track him down were made all the more difficult by the fact that his telephone number was ex-directory and he had not been into the October Gallery for some weeks. Someone there suggested that I should try a pub called The Harrington in South Kensington, and after several misses I spotted him entertaining friends over a table laden with glasses of beer.

When I had last met Tambi, he looked extremely prosperous, and I was now shocked at his lean and shabby appearance. Lean is an understatement; he looked starved and unwell. On that particular day, Tambi had received his unemployment benefit, and the pattern would often be repeated. Despite his being probably the poorest person there, he would insist on buying endless rounds of drinks until his money, supposed to last a fortnight, simply ran out. He spoke of his plans to bring out an Indian number of *PL* and I offered to help.

I was then living not far from the October Gallery and it was fairly easy for me to be there, as I hoped, on a daily basis. Often Tambi did not even have the fare from Kensington to Russell Square, but when he did arrive, always during opening hours, an afternoon drink was obligatory, and we always remained at the pub until it closed. At first we often went to one whose name I have forgotten, but which was renamed The Falklands after the war with the Argentine. Tambi used to enjoy the pub, partly because, as he said, 'It was there that Mr Eliot and I used to meet sometimes after he had finished working at Faber and Faber for the day. Of course he swore me to secrecy so that he would not be plagued by the curious.' After the pub was renamed, Tambi left it in disgust, preferring the Queen's Larder. It took me a long time to realize it was impossible to persuade Tambi to be punctual for anything, and to work without interruption. He had returned from a triumphant visit to India, where a whole culture and expression of society was quite the opposite to ours. It was pointless to attempt to impose a Western pattern of behaviour on Tambi, for his whole being was rooted in a civilization much wiser than ours.

I cannot say that I had any admiration for the October Gallery, beyond being pleased for his sake that Tambi had a room to work in, and a bed for the night there when he needed it. The completely impersonal behaviour of some of those who worked there, and their often patronizing attitude to Tambi, were not at all an encouraging atmosphere for him to work in. I was upset by the blank refusal of those I met to explain their philosophy to me, and I felt extremely uncomfortable knowing I, not of their party, was unwelcome there and suffered only for Tambi's sake. 'You ask too many questions,' he said to me one day, and doubtless he was right.

Nevertheless, the frequent quarrels Tambi had with those at the Gallery, many caused through genuine misunderstanding on both sides, created a difficult atmosphere and often meant that little was done to sift through the enormous pile of manuscripts that had been sent from India. Although often despondent about being misunderstood, Tambi was always optimistic, despite the insuperable problem of finding money to finance either the magazine or to provide enough to take him beyond the poverty level he was suffering. His endless vitality always made one feel ashamed at doubting anything productive would ever happen, and also made one forgive him the many moments of exasperation he created. I realized that if one was his friend, he expected total loyalty, no matter what that involved. Personal inconvenience was of no account, for Tambi took it as read that, if one was with him, he dictated the course of events. I remember one occasion when I had very little money, and even less after buying lunch with the added extra of two packets of cigarettes for Tambi. We were due to meet a friend of his who was working for the Indian High

Commission, and I had imagined we would take the tube, for which there was still plenty of time. But I had not reckoned on the pub visit, which could not be dispensed with, and as the time of the appointment drew dangerously near, a taxi was the only means of arriving punctually. Wearing the flimsiest of clothes, all of which were too large for him and which had been given him by a porter from the lost property department of a hotel, Tambi climbed out of the taxi and made his way towards the building of the High Commission in his worn carpet slippers as if he had arrived in full evening dress for a reception. He did not even glance around to consider the taxi-fare, and whether I could spare the cost was quite irrelevant. Tambi knew I had the money and that was enough. If Tambi had cash, he would have paid the fare, as he had always so generously done when he was able.

It seemed then that Tambi was battling against many odds: those with money did nothing to help either the project of the Indian Arts Council or to fund the issue of the Indian number of *PL*. But he was a very proud man and hated to ask those who could, such as Henry Moore, to help.

We seemed, after several months of hard work, to be achieving very little, and I began to wonder if I was the right person to help. Perhaps I said as much, but after bidding Tambi goodbye and thinking I would see him the following day, I was surprised to receive a telephone call from him later in the evening, asking if I would go over to change a typewriter ribbon in his Kensington flat. I hurried over on a rickety moped, and soon found that the ribbon problem did not exist but that Tambi simply wanted someone to talk to.

No one who ever visited the flat in Cornwall Gardens could ever forget the litter of papers and books, all mixed up with empty and full cans of beer, and Tambi somewhere amongst it all, oblivious of the chaos. Efforts to persuade him to eat would go unheeded, unless one dined with him, and that evening we ate delicious omelettes which, to my surprise, he expertly prepared.

I discovered then that the company which owned Tambi's flat was determined to evict him for rent arrears. They had successfully bought off the other tenants with a large cash payment, as they wished to redevelop the building. They had not tempted Tambi with their offer, and when he had ignored their demands for rent, it was impossible to avoid a summons to the county court. Jack Barker, an old and loyal friend whom Tambi used to tease about his love of litigation, found an extremely helpful woman from a law centre who offered to represent Tambi.

On the day of the hearing, it was pouring with rain, and by the time Tambi, Jack and I had trudged the long distance to the court, we were soaked through. Tambi, in his sodden slippers, squelched towards the stand, his appearance contrasting with the white starch of the unsmiling barristers acting for the housing company.

Tambi said very little, and Jack felt that he had perhaps not made Tambi understand the very real danger of eviction. However, the judge selected from several the one volume, I was told afterwards, which interpreted the Rent Act in the most liberal and generous way to the benefit of the tenant. After establishing that Tambi had no income beyond his unemployment benefit, the judge declared that Tambi would be allowed to remain in his flat on the condition that his rent was in future paid on time, and that he paid back the arrears at a certain rate. The weekly rate the judge fixed was very modest, and the four barristers, already furious that they had lost the case, leapt to their feet to protest that their clients would not be paid in full for another twenty years. The judge hesitated for a moment, and then said: 'Dear me, how right you are. I forgot that the defendant is a poor man. I rule that the arrears will be paid back at half the weekly rate I suggested.'

Simple arithmetic showed that Tambi would be well over a hundred before the company received the total arrears, and, leaving the court to find a sun-filled afternoon, we went to drink a few celebratory whiskies. Perhaps it need hardly be said that, of all of us, Tambi never doubted that he would win the case, although he did allow himself a smile of pleasure as we discussed the triumph over bureaucracy.

Not long afterwards I called one evening at the Queen's Larder, the pub near Queen's Square where Tambi could often be found. I was feeling dejected because my plans to write a certain book had come to nothing, and I longed to find someone who would lend a sympathetic ear. Tambi was there, but in a petulant mood, and after a quarrel over something quite trivial, I left the pub in a bad temper.

I dreaded seeing him again, wondering what I would say if we met, but by chance he came into a restaurant where I was sitting with friends, and joined us for a meal. We spoke of the old days of *PL* and Tambi suddenly remarked: 'You know I was in New York when my great friend Dylan died, and I took photographs of him, which are now in Wales. The trouble is, no one will bother much about me.'

Before I had a chance to reply he continued: 'Have you got a cigarette, old bean – now let's go to the pub.'

That was the last time we met, for the news a few days later was of his appalling accident. Yet despite the tragedy of his dying, it seemed that it was perhaps the right time for him to leave behind the many burdens which prevented him from carrying out his ideals, but knowing that he had started various projects which he could leave for others to complete.

Those who did not know Tambi, having heard of the many stories of his idiosyncratic personality, sometimes question if his place is in the files of eccentrics of English literature. When Tambi first arrived in London, he was referred to by Geoffrey Grigson as 'Tuttifrutti', and Grigson also ridiculed the contents of the war issues of *PL*, but an examination of the poets and artists Tambi promoted shows an extraordinary intuition in his choice. He understood very well the importance of imagination, and in a statement in the first issue of *PL* in 1939, he wrote: 'Every man has poetry within him. Poetry is the awareness of the mind to the universe. It embraces everything in the world.' This was directly opposed to Grigson's viewpoint in *New Verse*, something noted by Tambi in the third issue of *PL*, when he complained that: 'Geoffrey Grigson [persuaded us] ... that poetry in which objects replace emotions ... was the only poetry worth publishing....' Tambi, from the beginning of his editorial career to the end, never wavered in his belief in poetry of the imagination, and the work of those he encouraged, such as David Gascoyne and Kathleen Raine, remains as an indelible testimony in the history of literature to his own peculiar genius.

Tambi *was* eccentric, but eccentricity is perfectly valid if it is also the product of an original talent and not simply a performance displayed for public admiration or attention. Those of us who knew him will recall the eccentricities with a certain affection, but, in the end, the part that matters is his own impact on a particular age, and one which will outlast these memories.

Richard Burns

From 'The Manager'

Once, hearing music, I thought: A man or woman made this. And once there was a time before its pattern was. Before its form or harmonies had ever been conceived

Out of flesh and its travails. Out of the labour of hands. And before that, a time when not one single quaver of it had been the slenderest shadow. Less even than a shadow.

Lying dark in its maker. Until it was shaped, crafted and nourished into light. And he or she no angel but human to the core. Who made it for me, for you, that we

Might see clear through it, build our own work upon it, and by our willing love, also transform our world. That through us, matter be known, transparent and resplendent

As music. And with these thoughts, I rejoiced to be inside its history, to be alive in its time: my time now his and hers. And yours too, as you read this. Which is not the time its maker

Lay less than a pip in an apple, unformed, unborn, unnamed. Yet to you and me in our times that maker of music reached out. And me here, humanly touched, and moved to make this.

Roberto Sanesi

La bottega del vetraio

Vetri, spettri, cornici ... nel vano della porta
siede solennemente una figura, si piega, la notte
si gratta sotto la calza il piede della luna,
l'ombra rovescia il bravero del freddo: qualcuno
medita sulla morte, non vede altro che vita;
e forse allora lo stacco e nell'infrangersi
di quella pallida luce, che riflette e scheggia
le meraviglie del retrobottege

The Glassmaker's Shop

For Tambimuttu

Translated from the Italian by Richard Burns

Panes, spectres, frames ... in the hollow of the door
sits a solemn figure, leaning; night
beneath its stocking scratches the foot of the moon
and shadow turns up the collar of the cold: somebody
is brooding on death, but sees only life;
and perhaps the gap between them is in that pale
light's shattering, as it reflects and splinters
the wonders of the shop's back room.

Peter Riley

On Not Having Known Tambi

People become their names. And the name comes to mean the final quality of what the person did. So we are left with this strange oriental group of syllables which, if you get involved in British poetry and its recent history, you keep noticing here and there; and gradually you build up a picture of more or less what went on and what the name is beginning to mean. But it remains in some ways elusive: there is no *Collected Poems*, in fact hardly any poems at all; there was some editing and publishing which is almost all out of print, and quite a lot of talk; but really nothing in the way of monumentalia. Not, then, a *poetical hero*. Not one of those phonemes to be repeated like a gymnastic exercise in the halls of Sunday Supplement Culture and re-echoed down the corridors of Education until the motorway cafeterias of the land resound with the ecstatic incantations of the pop-poet cults. 'Hee-knee!' they cry, bending their knees in praise. 'El Yacht!' None of that hysteria. Just the continuance of a name which can't be forgotten. And these syllables – *tam-bi-mut-tu*, a maternal sound, like a prayer to a forgotten Indo-European mother goddess. You notice also the way they are spoken by different speakers; warmly by actual rememberers, sharply and twinklingly by those who like their poetry peppered with some signs of actual life, sneeringly by those who prefer their poetry entombed.

Because there was a person back there, a life force, of great vitality – that much at least is clear. It is also clear that there were a lot of terrible mistakes, a certain amount of sheer hustling, and a tendency not to pay bills. But the life force overrode these literary-bourgeois questions of propriety. Pound raised his half-crazed head deep in Italy and snarled about some whippersnapper who thinks he can be a new centre of poetry in London. The Cambridge pro-Leavisites screwed up their noses even harder than they were already and uttered stifled moans of 'Standards!' But the creative whirlpool in Soho was beyond these catcalls.

It says a lot for English poetry through to the 1940s that someone like Tambi could have become involved in it – precisely that poetry was the arena in which he chose to act, and was what he believed in. In spite of a persistent stress on refinement since the generation of 1914, poetry was still an active and unpredictable creative arena. It was somewhere where great risks could still be taken in the bid for the highest stakes – everything from surrealistic circus stunts to metaphysical contemplations. Through the 1950s poetry became, at least to the popular mind, something else; a kind of pedagogic tea-party, at which the quaint and typical behaviour of 'people' (including the even quainter 'self') was anecdoted by superannuated cartoonist professors in metrical patter. Tambi would have been the March Hare at such an event. Presumably had poetry been already like that in the 1940s he would have turned to something else instead: crime perhaps, show business, jazz, importing Bulgarian garden gnomes – who knows what? He was at home again, if disorientated, in the later 1960s when some sort of vision beyond the end of the corridor was again current in poetry. But as for recent years, well, what can a State-run arts programme on the one hand, or poetry seen as a kind of entertaining soap powder on the other, have to do with someone like Tambi?

And in spite of all the gossip, the rich gossip, there was a serious core to Tambi. I think poetry was his supreme field of action because it was the most individual act (the art forged from speech) in direct contact with cosmic realities, the spark uniting life and eternity without the mediating, disjunctive and etherealizing structures which are so distasteful to the Vedantic mind.

And if you believe in an art in this way (not even as your own art, but as something you promote and guide into the future), you will tend to rush in where angels fear to tread, and you will perhaps sometimes be taken in by false versions, but you will burn inwardly and you will never give up hope. And your name will remain.

I saw Tambi once, at the 1974 Cambridge Poetry Festival, where he turned up, a white-haired oriental gentleman supported by 'two young women dressed in cowboy suits' (I am told, but don't remember this detail) at the reading at Kettle's Yard given by Andrew Crozier, John James, Douglas Oliver and Rosmarie Waldrop. He was talent-spotting. And at that age (late sixties) he hit the nail right on the head, and turned up just where the heat was on, just where the future was poised.

Iris Murdoch

Poem and Egg

For Tambi

I would like to write a poem like a picture
Portraying something rather dark and big
In an atomic sea of pea-green hue,
Or else a sort of lumpy golden thing
In a dark sea of almost blackened blue
Suggesting I suppose the universe,
Not circular in fact but gently squashed,
Shaped like an orange or untapered egg,
A floating egg lonely as everything.

These ancient forms are really very simple,
And anything that sages have to say
Concerning what they symbolized or meant
Is likely to be rather commonplace.
They can be seen as images of God,
His bland unfeatured face,
Or of the great mama her lovely cunt,
Or lazy absolutes of any kind,
Or chaos pierced by mind,
Or simply seas of colour pierced by shape
Or colour swooning in its own embrace.

A poem cannot be like that, however,
Its ambiguity will tend to have a point
Which must be muffled, kept from being clever.
A poem can be never quite so plain,
So all-absorbing like an oval mouth.
It has to play a game to tell the truth,
It is more like a little flame,
Words soaked in petrol burning themselves up
Before the absolute, a pyre of sense
Asking forgiveness of the cosmic egg
For this impertinence.

171

Alan Brownjohn

One day he rang up. What about a poem for the new *Poetry London*? It was hard to believe, this being the voice of a legend, a legend connected with big, handsome, short-lived magazines, chaotic piles of manuscripts from famous names, lunch visits to friends which would turn into month-long residences. And 'He was an inspiration to us' had written G.S. Fraser, as if Tambi were an older master, not a contemporary. My poem was posted and forgotten; until the invitation to the magazine party, when copies were on the table, a freezing night, enormous crowds, Tambi a little overcome by the success and the affection. I took my copy, and read from it in the Orangery in Holland Park. Again the affection, and the respect, and the sense of being in a legendary presence who by rights should then have been twice his age; there were enough stories to fill that many years.

One day, a couple of years after that, I had a phone message, with a telephone number. Tambi had rung again. I rang back next day. 'Mr Tambimuttu?' Puzzlement. 'Ah, *Mr Tambimuttu*. He doesn't live here, but there was a party here last night, and a Mr Tambimuttu *was* doing some phoning. . . .' The legend was elusive, a sort of offstage inscrutability was part of his style.

About three months after that Eddie Linden rang to tell me he had died.

Shusha Guppy
(*with R. Apps and G. Moore*)

Natalia*

Weaver of words, who lives alone, with fear and sorrow
Where is the word, that sets you free, perhaps tomorrow?
Where is the earth, where is the sky, where is the light you long
for?
What hope have you, where you are now,
Natalia Gorbanevskaia?

Inside the ward, naked and cruel, where life is stolen,
From those who try, to stay alive, and still be human,
Where are the friends, where are the men, who among them can
defend you?
Where is the child, you never see,
Natalia Gorbanevskaia?

What is there left, behind the door, that never opens?
Are you insane, as they say you are, or just forsaken?
Are you still there, do you still care, or are you lost for ever?
I know this song, you'll never hear
Natalia Gorbanevskaia
Natalia Gorbanevskaia.

*Natalia Gorbanevskaia was arrested with other dissidents, Daniel and Siniavski, while taking part in a Christian demonstration against the invasion of Prague in 1968. She was put in a psychiactric prison and in 1974 some of her songs and poems were smuggled out of Russia. She was eventually released, largely as a result of pressure from Amnesty International, who had heard about her through Shusha's song, and now lives in Paris with her two children, where with Vladimir Bukovsky she edits a magazine called *Kontinent*, in Russian.

Audrey Beecham

New Needs

We want new idols, martyrs and new shrines
We want new intercessors and new saints
Not only looking up towards the Throne
But also down in pain towards the earth
They'd do, those Holy Beasts with many eyes.

When Lorca died his grave was buried too
That he was shot is known; not where he lies
So not to be a shrine. It's well believed
He asked to see a priest and was refused.

This aviator's fit and well: well nourished
Reared on the abattoir, of high morale.
No millstone round his neck: indeed below
That bully neck his decorations glow.
Too high above the world to see or know
What now he does, he lets the napalm go.

A child runs screaming. All her flesh is burnt
Her undernourished body starts to glow
She stumbles across the earth churning and riven
And is her howling heard by Hertsen in heaven?

My butterfly, soft bird, my captive lapwing
Flapping her wings against the tiger trap's
Four walls, her cage in Con Son Camp
In the Poula Condor Isles
My butterfly, soft bird
Let my birds go.
He of Assisi cannot help her now
We need new intercessors of a power
To make caged birds put heaven in a roar
O Blake where are you now
To help birds go?

We want new idols, martyrs and new shrines
We need new intercessors and new saints

Praying for power to shatter prison walls
Bind torturers and warders in a sleep
Bind up the tortured limbs, balm blistered skin
Burn bars, and lead all prisoners out in peace.

Bob Kingdom

'Oh, Bob!'

Memories of Tambi

The Harrington is a large, busy pub at the top end of Gloucester Road, London SW7, in the heart of bed-sit land. Tambi doesn't drink there any more, and I miss him. This is where we first met when he moved into his flat in Cornwall Gardens.

Very few people in the pub knew who Tambi was, what he did, or what he had done. 'That scruffy, long-haired Indian bloke was looking for you, earlier, Bob,' they would say. But why should they have known? This just happened to be Tambi's nearest pub, rather than the haunt of the South Ken literati; a short, slippered shuffle from his flat around the corner. The Fitzrovia pubs of his past, like those same Fitzrovia pubs today, had been replaced by a mindless free-for-all of crudely yacketing fruit machines and a juke-box, in favour of youth, which spared conversation little mercy.

I would usually find Tambi in the company of the more genteel locals from an earlier era, huddled at a corner table by the window in fear of their years and ears like social misfits: a retired Scottish naval commander and his wife who helped with proof-reading occasionally; an Irish peer who arrived either by bicycle or in a vintage Rolls-Royce, dressed in a bulky poncho affair and Russian fur hat, his OBE around his neck and lady-friend in pursuit; an actress wearing too much lipstick to look younger; and an assortment of imperious, watery-eyed couples that you never actually got around to being introduced to. On other occasions, Tambi would be sitting on his own in this corner, looking bitterly into his beer for having to make it last. At the sight of a friendly figure approaching, his lips would wave a smile and sink the remains of his beer all in one go. 'Ah, Bob' – cough, splutter – 'What will you have?' 'I'll get them, Tambi.'

Tambi's moods depended on the changing fortunes of his next editions of *Poetry London*. When the money ran out and production came to yet another temporary halt, he became empty and weary. These periods in the pub were rather like sitting beside someone in a hospital bed. But then, suddenly, Tambi's coughing chuckle would signify that the show was on the road again. The best times, obviously, were when we'd both had too much to drink, when our minds were racing irresponsibly from one silly fantasy to another. And when people other than the regulars would come into the pub: Jane Williams, Tambi's unofficial secretary and irreplaceable friend; an English writer on one of his occasional visits from France; the odd, aspiring poet in uninspiring anorak; the girls from the October Gallery, Chilli and Evans. On these occasions I would be expected to do my impressions. 'Oh, Bob, do your Dylan,' Tambi would say. 'Now do your funny one of Louis MacNeice. This is his daughter, by the way.'

Tambi would go for days on end without eating and then complain that he felt weak. I assumed he had some inner, mystical strength to compensate for this, but, when he vomited, it was all unmystical liquid. Once a week, Jack Barker, one of Tambi's oldest friends, would venture up from the country to force-feed him at a local restaurant, rather in the manner of a child being made to eat up all his greens, but not until closing-time had given him the Dutch courage to attempt such a mundane task.

In the last few years of Tambi's life, my relationship with him was mainly on a domestic level. He couldn't be bothered with the ordinary, everyday things. 'Oh, Bob, I have no toilet-rolls and no light bulbs. A long ladder I have to reach the sockets, but no bulbs to fix into them. At night I am plunged into darkness.' 'Tambi,' I said, 'we'll buy some toilet-rolls and we'll buy some light bulbs.' His eyes lit up at this inspired suggestion. 'We will take some cans back, also. I need Rothman's, too.'

Closing time magicked into lighting-up time at 14 Cornwall Gardens. 'Ah! I have light!' said Tambi, beaming up at the ceiling. I felt like the second person to invent the electric-light bulb. 'Now I will use my new toilet-rolls.'

As Tambi shuffled into the bathroom, chuckling gleefully, I surveyed his room for the umpteenth time. It was a place that couldn't make up its mind whether to be a flat or an office. There was a kitchen area behind a counter with last week's curried concoction (last year's, for all I knew) standing amongst a retrospective exhibition of other neglected pots and pans, piles of plates and 'take-away' containers. Office shelving of the metal, adjustable variety, slumped wearily in two corners under the weight of box-files, manuscripts, books, telephone directories, old gramophone records and faded potted plants at half-mast. A lamp standard near a black and white snow-stormed television always wore its shade at a jaunty, drunken angle and refused to shed light on a desk bearing a dusty portable typewriter and more books. At the side of Tambi's crumpled bed stood a hospital-type table on wheels, with one main supporting armed leg. This table contained bottles of pills, bills, letters, screwed-up tissues and a large, pub-strayed ashtray. The ashtray was always piled so high with cigarette ends it was impossible to be used as an ashtray any more. So the first thing was to empty it. The area beneath the table was littered with empty beer-cans, old newspapers, fallen blankets, shoes, more bills and letters, and the telephone. Whenever the telephone rang we would have to instigate a frantic search among all this debris, with only the source of the muffled ringing to guide us.

A last cough and a splutter and Tambi would emerge from the bathroom. 'You know, Bob, this is one of the finest apartments in London. From that balcony, Joan Sutherland sang.'

He would shuffle to the bed, pick up a robe and wrap it round him. Then, in a mysterious wriggle, he would unzip his trousers, allow them to fall round his ankles, lower himself slowly on to the bed, kick the trousers to one side, cough, and light a cigarette.

'Ugh, Bob. In my country and in India I am a celebrity. I have tea with Mrs Gandhi. I am interviewed on the television. They write articles about me. But here, I am living in this shit!' (Tambi had recently been to India with his daughter, Shakuntala, to discuss his dream project – the Indian Arts Council in London.)

I used to enjoy thumbing through Tambi's ancient address book which told you where people didn't live any more. Although battered, its dog-eared pages contained a fascinating memory of people and places in a unique way, because Tambi would always hand the book to people and get them to write down the information themselves.

Consequently, you saw alphabetically ordered entries of names like David Gascoyne, Augustus John, Louis MacNeice, Henry Moore, Henry Miller, John and Myfanwy Piper and Dylan Thomas in a variety of hands and steadiness of feet, a mixture of ink colours and nibs from long-lost fountain-pens, and faded pencil.

Tambi felt the cold, winter and summer, so his flat was always hot and stuffy. I remember meeting him in the pub during a particularly cold spell. 'Oh, Bob! I am so cold! I have nothing substantial to wear! Nothing!'

So, the next day, I popped into a second-hand shop in Fulham Road, which often acts as my own tailor, and bought the thickest overcoat I could find: a long, khaki, greatcoat with huge collar, deep pockets, bright brass buttons and a label inside that announced it was of French Army origin. This coat was so heavy it seemed to gain weight when rolled up, forced into a large Harrods' plastic bag and carried out of the shop. I arrived at Tambi's flat in a state of total exhaustion and presented him with this whole cloakroom of a garment.

That evening, a greatcoated Tambi staggered into the pub, beaming broadly, a twinkle in his eye, collar up, hands plunged deep into the pockets and looking a good two and a half inches shorter. It seemed as if the coat was wearing *him*. 'Oh, Bob! This is wonderful! I am French Army officer, and so warm!' He saluted with a coughing chuckle and then the coat walked him in the direction of the bar. When Tambi sat down with the drinks, his head almost completely disappearing inside the huge, upturned collar, we imagined all the adventures the coat had been involved in during its life. And thought of all the adventures to come.

A few months later, after Tambi's fall, his funeral service was as bizarre as his death had been spectacular. We all stood respectfully, packed into the small chapel of the crematorium; the family dressed in black; friends more colourfully so.

The voice of the anonymous priest broke the silence: 'We are here to mourn the passing of our dearly beloved Mary James in the certain hope....'

Eh? Confused faces frowned at each other. We heard the name again.

'... Mary James has left us in body, but not in spirit....'

'Meary James' Thurairajah Tambimuttu (1915–83); but the only name we expected, or wanted, to hear was 'Tambi'. I could hear Mary James's coughing chuckle. He'd have loved it.

Jean MacVean

Tambi – a Personal View

What can one say about Tambi? I can speak only personally. I had the greatest affection for him. I was very sad to hear of his death.

I remember the party for the first issue of *Poetry London/Apple Magazine*, with Tambi very handsome in a silver-embroidered tunic; his later dream of a book of poems and painting as a wedding present for Prince Charles; the dramatic days of Bruno Tolentino ('My grandmother has just given me an emerald mine') who was to have become a patron; the *Guardian* reporter, the girl photographer and the two exhausted Americans he brought to a party at my house. At another time he came to lunch with his daughter, Shakuntala, and a young cousin who never uttered a word.

I remember Tambi's poverty, the flat with the black beetle powder on the floor, the ashtrays almost hidden under stubs, the half-finished cans of beer; and parties at the October Gallery, Tambi's tiny office at the top of the perilous iron staircase; the launching of *PL/Apple* No. 2 in 1982, a magazine so alive with ideas it made others look colourless.

I admired Tambi's persistence, his refusal to be defeated by lack of money or ill health, his constant search for new ideas, new forms of expression, the fact that even in his last few hours in hospital he said to someone who visited him, 'I know we can work together.'

At the memorial concert held at the Bhavan Centre, one of his visions, the linking of East and West, began to come true. It was an evening of enchantment: Francis Scarfe's moving poem; Tambi's early songs; and the beautiful Indian dances with their stately, impersonal ritual; Shakuntala with so much of her father's charm; David Gascoyne reading some of his poems and one of Tambi's; the whole evening under the spell of the descendant of the kings of Jaffna.

With Tambi I was aware of a deep inner current flowing like some great Indian river towards distant, yet-to-be explored territory. The confusions, the dramas, all the surface of a life have fallen away and left his gifts and his last vision: the Indian Arts Council. He was a remarkable man. Of holy poverty.

Angela Kirby

The Impertinent Microscope

For Tambi

I pluck you from the air,
there is no help for you.
The space you leave,
the perforated sky,
is filled with birds,
with the black notes
of an old song.

Now I have you under glass,
spread-eagled, pinned
into shape. Beneath
the impertinent microscope
your body teems with life.
Cell, mite, sperm, phagocyte,
I chart the routes they take.

You are my geography.
With patience
I shall find and mark
your hidden places,
your valleys, streams, hills.
When your map is finished
I shall put you back in the sky.

Brian Patten

I last saw Tambi on two separate occasions: dressed immaculately and fit for a prince at a posh party; and looking down-at-heel and a bit lost in a pub in Gloucester Road. God knows how many people writing about him will say there were two of him – they might have known a different two. Perhaps there were more. The two I knew I miss, and here is a poem of mine both liked. Maybe they were both romantics.

The Bee's Last Journey to the Rose

I came first through the warm grass
Humming with spring,
And now swim through the evening's
Soft sunlight gone cold.
I'm old in this green ocean,
Going a final time to the rose.

North wind, until I reach it,
Keep your icy breath away
That changes pollen into dust.
Let me be drunk on this scent a final time,
Then blow if you must.

Bird Dance by Patrick Hayman (original in colour, medium, size and date n.k.).

Keshav Malik

Tambi in Delhi

When news got around that Tambimuttu was in Delhi, there was no little excitement – at least among the younger of the Indian poets. They had heard of this unusual Sri Lankan's exploits in wartime London. That, at a moment of utmost crisis, he had taken it upon himself to publish poetry, pick up some of the finest poets then writing in Britain, was deemed something of a marvel. The legend was still alive – that is, in 1982.

Since, at the time, I edited the National Academy of Letters bimonthly *Indian Literature*, I received a number of telephone calls from those of the poets in a hurry to discover Tambi's hide-out. But of this I had no clue whatever.

It was a good ten days later that I was to learn from my wife Usha that Tambi and his daughter, Shakuntala, were the guests of the Indian Council for Cultural Relations, where Usha happened to be working.

After a while Tambi and Shakuntala dropped in at my office – he was anxious to get the latest on who was doing what in Indian writing. This, in effect, meant supplying him with information on the twenty-two listed literary languages of the subcontinent – and that in the course of a mere afternoon. A tall enough order for any one person! At the end of the marathon session I suggested to Tambi he help himself to any of the volumes of verse on my shelf he fancied. The idea seemed to click; and, as far as I can now remember, he picked up about eighty volumes – including the recently issued 600-page poetry special of *Indian Literature*.

During that afternoon we had also decided to send out a hand-out eliciting poems for the Indian number of Tambi's own journal. By and by my in-tray was chockful of manuscripts. Of course, Tambi was sent many more of them by still other channels.

On one of the days following, Tambi read his, as well as some other poets' work at the India International Centre. If now I forget what it was Tambi read out, what is not forgotten is that the seminar room was packed to capacity, the evening memorable, and Tambi himself in great form.

Since at one moment or the other Tambi had broached the subject of contemporary Indian art, I thought it a good idea to chaperone him round some of Delhi's art galleries. A few such visits followed, of which the one to the art department of Triveni Kala Sangam – a premier institute of the three arts – proved by far the most fruitful. Here Tambi not only saw some fine work but met as well with certain of Delhi's noted artists, among them the director of Triveni's art department, Rameshwar Broota. Tambi, I recall, was particularly struck by Broota's powerful figurative compositions. Actually he found the whole ambience of the place appealing, and it seemed to set his mind ticking. For, there and then he had appealed to his newly made artist friends to do sketches, drawings and small oils to go with the proposed poetry issue of his journal. Small surprise that they all readily agreed, such was Tambi's magic! And I do know for certain that, putting aside their own work, about five of these artists did what was requested with dispatch.

But, alas, soon Tambi and Shakuntala left for their trip round India. Apparently it was during this time that he had decided to launch a body to project the arts of India in Great Britain. Some of his friends, like the late Srikant Verma or Mr Shamlal, may well have been in the know about this; I wasn't. At any rate, one morning, the newspapers announcing the formation of the Indian Arts Council (with me as one of the founders) was an utter surprise, but a pleasant one.

Returning to Delhi, Tambi put up at a hostel for government officers rather than any of the usual A-class hotels. But it seemed all the same to him, although, as it was the hottest part of the year, he took to the heat badly. Mercifully he was well supplied with crates of beer, with which his admirers had plied him. I had come to say goodbye; and now that we were such good friends, I could not resist reminding Tambi of our very first encounter in New York, at Mrs Dorothy Norman's, sometime at the end of 1952, or at the beginning of 1953. Yes, we had got into such a brush over one of India's endemic issues, much to the embarrassment of the hostess! – the occasion came back to Tambi with a bang, but he only chuckled and affectionately pressed my hand.

This affectionate touch was what remained after we had parted. Yes, there was Tambi's affection, but also his infectious enthusiasm. It would seem as though he knew how to revive a failing heart, bring a glow to the face.

Shock was not the word when, one morning, papers carried news about his death. I felt a kind of exasperation with the scheme of things: man proposing and God disposing, and so forth. But, after a while, a feeling of gratitude returned. Had not nature filled at least one of us with so much surplus spirit! At the condolence meeting in the library of the National Academy of Art each one of us who spoke had wondered how a sore loss was to be made good.

Keshav Malik

Vision, and After

I'm losing vision
but no longer pray for its return,
now only to live in the knowledge of the dark
places of the night.

Once was vision my trade –
it lured me into the farthest reaches
of space.

The X-rays I adored,
which turned the secrets inside-out –
the heart of ebony transparent
as bright day.

Then the pulse-rate rose,
eardrums reverberating
with what the eyes saw:

the world news,
all around a sensation of sparks.

Each second, an intimation of lightning
and with it
the heavenly drunkenness.

Intent on observing the great circumference
feet danced, failed
to walk straight;

such swell of ocean, miracle of fireworks,
nature – red-in-tooth – or – claw – or not –
a green queen,
and batons pounding on the heart: –
the world then of itself, generously gave.

Movement more movement,
the marrow-penetrating light of vision;
rain of meanings each moment –
the temples throbbing, body compliant –
a stage, in it a theatre in progress – no actors,
only a waxing star –
and I the solitary spectator.

Tremblings and shiverings
but still in ears the amazing ringing –
a thankfulness in the heart.

But the turn in the wheel
is all so sudden;
caught in its whirl,
empties out all vision;
then, only to live on
through the night in the mind alone –
and you may not look back or moan.

What new grace
of the darkness now comes?

Rakshat Puri

The Poet

Desolation
In a calculus of words:

Song in flight unwinged
Yet outreaching the grasp
Of time's hand
Far stretched but not
For ever.

Voices walk routine
Time hung and instinct wise.

Rooks and nightingales
Fuel the sky
With their calls distant
In the morning evening
And afternoon.

Metaphysical structures
Fall as words
In the lucid sound.

Beyond his anxious idiom
The poet is shaped and offered
On the altar before
His own time pursued
Icon of words.

Nissim Ezekiel

Afternoon Poem

Seized by memory or habit,
a force revives in them, creating
arabesques against a purple sky.
Fear of failure, loss of power
starts a tedious argument
in dissonance or harmony,
both beside the point.

High priests of personal opinion
or intermediaries between the absent gods
and their worshippers,
they scrape the barrel
for a spoonful of hope –
their receding foreheads
and advancing paunches
are very impressive.
I make a note of it
and carry on.
Half a life of heroic effort
brings us to arthritis or a suspect lung.
It is time for desperate measures
though in a perfectly natural way.
Do not mention
experience or age,
ideals and ideology,
year of marriage, number of children,
loves, infidelities, conversions to and from,
transactions with the great,
committees, speeches,
public appearances,
Honours real or imagined,
principles and values,
lessons learnt (or so you think).
All these are banal, burn them.

Do not go in for the middle style:
life without distress is stupefaction,
a glare of elegant insights
hiding meretricious fate,
drift towards a padded doom.

Floundering in the meaning
when most involved,
they glorify techniques of observation,
theatrical at last in the wings,
the riddle turning
sour on their tongues.

Miriam de Saram

Tambi

I knew Tambi briefly during various periods of his life. The first time I met him he was a youth of about nineteen. He just walked into my home (a very tight-laced one) and asked my assistance in the production of a play he had almost completed. I was taken aback by this unusual proposal from a complete stranger – and, moreover, had the greatest difficulty in driving him away before the arrival of my parents who, had they known, would not have taken to the venture with open arms.

He returned a day or two later threatening suicide (which I thought was a possibility) unless I agreed to help him – so I tried to – and that was my first encounter with this interesting, gifted and alarming personality.

He was bold – in those days we often travelled in rickshaws. He would think nothing of waylaying me and ordering the rickshaw to halt. I was to get down for a walk and talk about his play, his poetry and publications. He knew there could be serious repercussions had my parents had any intimation of these proceedings, but this aspect never seemed to register. I realized his latent gifts and wished I could help. He would seize a pencil and paper and write a few lines which would read like a poem. His third slim volume of verse, *Tone Patterns*, published in 1936, was dedicated 'To Miriam'.

Our next meeting a few years later in the mid-thirties was in London. Tambi had found his milieu, literary friends and conditions, where he could develop and be happy. I had married Robert and was in England to help my father, who was Ceylon's first Trade Commissioner. Tambi's many interesting letters of that period I lost when Europe was plunged in war, and we had to leave London in a scramble.

I did not see him after this period for a while, although he would send me the magazine, *Poetry London*, on and off as the spirit moved him.

Not until our son Rohan was eleven and we had decided on a possible musical career for him, did Tambi arrive in Ceylon – this time to give us an introduction to Kathleen Raine. It was through Kathleen that Rohan met Gaspar Cassando (the great cellist and pupil of Pablo Casals) at the home of Louis and Griseldol Kentner. Four months later, Rohan and his father were installed in Florence, at work with Cassado. Eight hours a day for the next four years.

It was at our home in Colombo that we met his absolutely charming Indian wife Safia (Tyabjee). I remember that evening well. There were a few friends and we sat in the garden philosophizing and drinking for several hours, till there was no more.

By 1956, Robert, who had chaperoned Rohan during his musical education in Europe, had returned to Ceylon (on his father's death) to help in their family firm of lawyers.

I now took over as guide. Once again we met, this time in New York. Rohan and I were on our way to Casals and Puerto Rico. Tambi, Safia and Rohini (musician daughter of Ananda Coomaraswamy) wafted us through a whirl of bright night-lit streets and skyscrapers, which was a new experience for us. From then on my preoccupation was Rohan and music, and we lost touch except for an occasional letter, full of enthusiasm and ideas for the establishment of a new world of poetry and his magazine *Poetry London–New York*.

The last meeting was in 1982 in Ceylon. He looked frailer, wiser. We talked more quietly than ever before. I was surprised. The word to describe the quality of this meeting could perhaps be 'Acceptance'. Shakuntala his daughter was unwell; we ended the evening with her.

I felt Tambi had started on a new quest. The quest of the 'Peace that passeth all understanding'.

Physically frail but wiry, Tambi had a mind of great determination and intensity. This intensity, however, could melt in a moment to a carefree smile or chuckle, and as rapidly regain its serious composure. He seemed to swing between polarities. Although he could be demanding and tiresome to a point nearing ruthlessness, he could also be thoughtful and kind. But his true genius lay in discovering genius. He had taste, unerring intuitive feel and a bundle of contradicting characteristics. Assertive one moment, completely helpless the next, he swayed others in a complementary fashion. They felt anger and then compassion for him, and often decided for compassion. At the core of him was this incompatible twin make-up, helplessness with a certain necessary ruthlessness to balance it – and genius as well, of course. He was driven by his inner daemon and seemed to act and react with a 'mindless mind'. He could not integrate these varying factors. Instead, the powerful ground elements of all matter (known to the Vedas as Apo, Thejo, Vayo, Pattavi) claimed mastery. With a high degree of realization but without the capacity to create the 'oneness' in himself (which would mean the integration of body, senses and every aspect of the mind), he needed always the support of another. To advance, he would have to turn inwards for his strength and hold his attention there. The inability to succeed here left him swinging between his inner and outer selves.

Had he been able to cultivate this inner spirit he might have ended up in the foothills of the Himalayas, but this would have required perfect detachment, equanimity, renunciation and an abiding oneness of purpose until that level of spiritual intuition was reached, and the field of Enlightenment glimpsed. The inner renunciation of sense objects would have been difficult, but I felt he was fast approaching this point when last I met him. He understood the paramiters (perfections), though he had yet to attain them.

Mulk Raj Anand
with Jane Williams

Talking of Tambi

The Dilemma of the Asian Intellectual

JW: When I first met Tambimuttu I was instantly impressed by his vision and purity of intent, which were, I recognized straight away, the accumulation of knowledge from his ancient cultural background. His gentle, polite gestures and his acceptance of me as I walked into the flat-cum-office in Cornwall Gardens, balanced perfectly with the force of his vision I felt so strongly, could not have failed to draw me to him at that time, as had been the case with so many others. It was this vision that was the moving force behind 'the great editor', 'the great literary entrepreneur', 'the catalyst'. To him poetry was the 'Word'.

MRA: And the 'Word' was vibration. The vibration found artistic expression from the compulsion to find 'wholeness' – combining the poet's pen with the artist's brush, and with music, too, because all these forms of expression combine to evoke imperceptible feelings.

JW: Tambi came from a very gifted family with a long tradition in the arts, especially in literature and poetry.

MRA: So he said. But he didn't mature until much later. He had a perception in the beginning. But he began to feel deeply later.

JW: He was misunderstood by many people.

MRA: That was his fault. He had hardly any will. I think the fundamental thing about Tambimuttu was that he came from a background which was obsessively traditionalist. Nothing shocked him out of the awareness inherited by most Asians, including myself, of transcending the ordinary world. I've taken a long time to get over it – the sense of destiny which is in most Orientals. You know, Man's fate is determined in the East by the conviction, asserted again and again by the sages in the ideas of the Upanishads downwards, that God, the transcendent spirit, has already decided the destiny of the whole universe – that the Creation is an accomplished fact.

Now since the Renaissance in Europe, in the European mind –

apart from Christianity, which also shares with the Eastern religions the determinist view – there is the conviction, among the majority of the intelligentsia, that Man makes himself. This has resulted in the frequent extroversion of the Will of Man. And apart from the Catholics who tended to believe in miracles, the conquest of the world by the West has been an important part of Man's willed effort to make himself. Not only was conquest a question of gain. Gain was a way of life. Living is a question of sharing, but the Westerners often didn't share. They absorbed everything to themselves, and they became more and more greedy. So Western civilization has advanced from the point of view of development, but ended up today in the crisis of overdevelopment, which is the crisis of development of weapons to dominate the world, and to gain more share of the world's wealth for themselves.

This attitude was not present in the minds of Asia. There, the world being determined by God, you had to share the produce in it, you had to share the fruits of the soil and you had to live together. The family was important. The group was important, because you live not only for yourself as individual man – as Mephistopheles teaches Faust to do – but you live in terms of other people. Others are important. *I* am only *I* because *you* are! That is the Asiatic view. That is called the 'Being'. *Being* can only *be* by sharing everything, including feelings, thoughts, moods and worlds, etc.

JW: This was very much Tambi's view.

MRA: Unfortunately, the Western initiatives were for individual gain, as I said, as in the prototype Faust, who is cut off from other people, who is egocentric and who wishes to develop his own consciousness to the highest point of awareness and doesn't care what happens to other people. He gets the Devil into him, because the intellect becomes very important, by which one manoeuvres everything to one's own advantage. The idea that it is possible to have some intuition of other things beyond oneself, and beyond one's gains, made the European personality prone to selfishness: the care to preserve one's area against other people's space because other people are encroaching on your area, your space, mental and physical. Tambi entered this society and had to subscribe to its ways.

JW: The difficulty in uniting one's sense of one's own personality and one's own particular progression, or 'karma', with a sense of universal destiny is something I understand very well, as I have experienced it personally. I tried to talk with Tambi about this but he was very difficult to draw on such matters.

MRA: As I have explained, the 'Word' to us is 'vibration'. The vibration is necessary to communicate. So from the earliest times Asian poetry has been 'communicable vibrations'. And those vibrations are not only to report what you feel about the outside world, but they are stirrings which are vague because they are inner experience of a kind which doesn't always come into prose – it comes in impressions, or rather insights. Insights are embodied in our culture, say in the Vedas, in two-line Sutras – only two lines, not more than two lines. Because the Indian poet – the Indian sage – knew that if you prolong your inspiration technically further than the inspiration, you make it go beyond inspiration. You then utter prose. Poetry is the extroversion of the inspiration at any given moment, which is only inside one symbolical experience, complete in itself. Therefore, you find in the Japanese haiku poems three lines only. In a poetry festival called *Mushairah* in India, the poets are given one line and they have to add other verses. This is a very good exercise in coining words, in verbiage, but it is often not poetry. I suspect that Tambi inherited the attitude of the early sages, but he was not able to get this across to the West.

JW: No, that's true. He expressed this view in his editorials, but I don't think it was ever really understood by most people. I hope that now people will try to understand what he was saying.

MRA: The reason may have been that he had to deal with people who were in 'bits and pieces'. Virginia Woolf did in prose what the poets of the generation just before her had done in imagist poetry. But few people were really aware of the predicament of being 'bits and pieces'. Only a man like D.H. Lawrence. In Lawrence's impetuous images in poetry, and in Laura Riding, there are glimpses of impression beyond impressions. Lawrence is able to see into nature and show that he is aware of the whole of nature.

JW: A very important aspect of Tambi's philosophy was always 'wholeness' – 'wholephrasing' in poetry and the 'collective voice' – and in fact when he was in America he laid plans to establish what he called an 'Institute of Holophrasis' – a Greek word meaning *holis*, whole/*phrasis*, phrase, the expression of a complex of ideas by a single word – which, in Tambi's extended sense, gives poetry its form and substance. He described this fully in his longest and most discursive editorial in *Poetry London–New York* No. 4.

MRA: Unfortunately, his presence in London in the years I knew him was among people who were mostly 'bits and pieces' – half-men, quarter-men or decimated. There had been the breakdown of the economy of America in 1932, and the poets were not wanted. Now when you disinherit people, the disinherited cannot speak completely. They speak only in bits and pieces, because they have been deprived by society, the kind of society in which we live, of all the awareness which could come from the fact that they are participating in the world. Then each individual has to discover his own bits and pieces, in impressions, not in totality. The poet is lost in the wastelands. So Tambi felt his main job was to try to see if he could collect enough people who had some awareness. That is why I think he came very early under the influence of Eliot, because Eliot was aware of the fact that Tambi meant to *see* and not *look*, was aware of things by inheritance, which were beyond the average young poet who is writing calf-love poetry at the age of nineteen. And he succeeded, to some extent, in bringing people together, in the war especially. The poets on the front had no platform and he gave them a platform. That was a tremendous achievement on his part. Because he was able, then, in the face of death, to rescue creativeness. All these poets during the war were facing death. Their creativeness was an attitude, an inspiration, to conquer death.

Now when you are facing death, and you're creative, you feel you want to defy death, and then you naturally use words, because those words are going to go to someone to whom you want to communicate your love. Always in the best poetry there is this inspiration of love against death – to conquer death by love. Essentially, then, Tambi was aware, much more aware than most, of this. That is why he published so many war poets. They were facing a crisis which made them aware of their own creativeness. Many of the poets, either consciously or unconsciously, became creative, because they were up against it.

One important thing which he missed, and his generation missed, was what the earlier poets had grasped about the disinherited. Day-Lewis, Spender, MacNeice and Auden had glimpsed the need to participate in the struggle of people to evolve a sharing society. They had the realization, beyond individualism of the middle classes, that they would have to begin to share, politically and economically, the gains of knowledge and experience and the fruits of the earth. Unfortunately, however, they couldn't get over their middle-class upbringing. Now this is something which I am afraid the Western poets have never understood. When the great French Revolution happened and the idea of liberty, fraternity and equality became a living reality, there was a tremendous emphasis on being as sharing.

After all, revolution was made by people whose food was being gorged by Louis.

Now in the Russian Revolution something more important happened, which the poets in the West have seldom understood. That revolution brought into bloom a new spring for mankind, where sharing was to become possible as if almost in a Utopia. But Utopia is not possible in the same world where you had greed and individualism of the extreme kind, as in the West. The poets in the thirties did have some awareness of what the Russian Revolution meant. But the war of those who wanted more *lebensraum* – living space – came on. And while the poets were certainly wanting to survive against death by creativeness, they never got to understand that fascism was the culmination of the greed of imperialism – it was the attempt to conquer the whole world for new would-be imperialists.

In the tremendous battle of wills, inspired by the highest individualism and utmost greed, millions of people on all sides died. The gain was loss on all sides. They all lost their empires. I'm not talking politics, I'm talking of civilization! Civilization ruined itself, killed itself through greed. What we have now is a very misguided effort to recover the mood of Empire again by taking the gains of the Antarctic. This kind of thing means that the Western civilization still goes on burrowing into the need to have more and more. They do not realize that unless they share with the Third World some of the gains they have already made, they will lose their markets in the ex-colonies.

Tambi was not quite aware of all this. I began writing earlier than he and in prose. My novels *are* about the poor and disinherited of Asia. Naturally I was abused and misunderstood, except in the Third World, and the world of the poor of Europe. But the literati thought that I was a communist stooge. I am saying this because one important lapse on Tambi's part was not to remember that he came from the disinherited society.

JW: That is partly true, because I think when he arrived in London he was confronted with the effects on himself of his own upbringing, where the English dominated Ceylonese culture so much. He was taught in a Jesuit school and England was presented as the superior culture. When he came to London and mixed with the artistic Bohemian cultural atmosphere of Fitzrovia, many of his friends being Cambridge or Oxford graduates, I think he felt the dilemma of his own cultural heritage and the impressions embedded in him through his English-dominated upbringing.

MRA: The middle section took him up. He took no part, for

instance, in the freedom struggle of Sri Lanka that was going on. Nor did his friend Subramaniam. These poets were mainly concerned to become brown Englishmen. Tambi was already one. I think why he was not aware of the slavery in the Empire was because his own people were fairly well off. They themselves had been used to having slaves. And they faced the dilemma of the patriarchal order, as Coomaraswamy, who was another Ceylon man. They could not forget their high status in feudal society. So they clung to the cliché of Eastern thought in terms of God determining fate. The tragedy of the Asiatic intellectual has been, and is now, that he is torn between the Eastern idea of Man's fate being determined by God, and the Western idea that Man has to develop. Both extremes end up in a cul de sac.

JW: Yes, they do, and I have found that in my own thinking. I am very conscious of a sense of karma – Tambi sometimes used to say to me, 'You're transgressing karma' – and also of a sense, a very strong sense, that life is cyclic, as though it has been predetermined.

MRA: This is very important. I asked Tambi several times, 'Why don't you write a hundred-page autobiography?' He never got down to it, because he couldn't face this situation between himself as the inheritor of tradition and what he wanted to become. In our later talks, when he came to India, and married Safia Tyabjee, I found that he had become aware of the need to be honest and say all this and by that time he had read the three volumes of my autobiographical novel. I began writing a confession in 1925. Before any of my novels were published I wrote a confession about my failures. This arose from the answer to the questions in *Brihadaranyaka Upanishad* 'Who am I?' 'Where have I come from?' and 'Where am I going?' It is a classic question posed 2,300 years ago. I think every poet must answer that before he writes poetry.

JW: In fact everyone must ask that.

MRA: Now this question was being posed for me, fortunately, by the poet Mohammad Iqbal, who was my mentor in my youth. Iqbal wrote a book called *Asrare-e-Khudi* – 'Secrets of Self'. This was the only book I brought with me when I came to London. It is a very important document of our time, at least for the Asians. I tried to interest Tambi in it, but he never got to it, because the kind of Persian language in which the search for self was couched was outside his awareness. He had not read Rumi or Hafiz or Saadi. He had read mainly the Vedic poets. Now Iqbal suggests that you cannot be a 'self' of any kind. You have to choose to be. You can direct yourself into selfhood. But you have to exorcize, by ruthless self-analysis, all the falsities, the vanities, the superficial impressionism and all those things which stand between you and wholeness.

JW: That's true, because I think part of Tambi's dilemma was also that in himself he knew who he was and what he wished to do, but in the West he also wanted recognition, as an individual.

MRA: In my case what I did was that I went through the painful experience of trying to be myself by writing my confession. Then in one of Virginia Woolf's 'at homes', Edward Sackville-West said there can be no tragic writing about the poor. You can only laugh at them. At that time I was writing the story of an untouchable boy. But I was so shocked by this dictum that I left my studies and went back to Gandhi's Ashram, to learn to be myself.

Well, fortunately for me, Gandhi disrobed me of my corduroy suits and necktie and suede shoes. He said to me, 'Why are you wearing these clothes? Won't you get hot?' I said, 'They are the only clothes I have.' He said, 'You look like a monkey.' I said, 'You also looked like a monkey once in your frock-coat.' So he said, 'Now, you go and change.'

After I came back in wearing his secretary's *kurta pyjama* he asked, 'What do you want from me?' I said, 'I want to show you my novel.' 'A boy and girl affair?' he said. I said, 'No, it's about love – your kind of love.' ' What's my kind of love?' I said, 'It's about an untouchable.' He said, 'You mean Harijan, son of God. Well, I'm reassured that having lived in Europe you've still got enough sympathy left to want to do this.' So I said, 'I have come here merely because I have found myself censored for even thinking about the people.'

Anyhow, I settled down and he said, 'There are three vows before you can live in the Ashram. The first vow is that you mustn't look at women with desire.' I said, 'Bapu, I'm sorry, my girl-friend paid my fare, and I will be dreaming of her at night if I don't think of her during daytime.' So he said, 'Well, you can dream of her at night, but don't think of her during daytime.' Now the next thing he said was: 'You are not to drink here.' So I said, 'I'm sorry I have been pub-crawling all the time in London. We write out of pub talk.' He said, 'Well, you can do that in London but not here.' And then he said, 'You must clean the latrines once a week.' So I said, 'I will do that.'

I showed him my novel. He cut a hundred and fifty pages out of the two hundred of my stream-of-consciousness prose *à la* Joyce. So I had to rewrite the whole novel again. He said, 'You know an untouchable boy wouldn't talk in those long sentences. He wouldn't talk at all – he has no mouth.'

I learnt sincerity and truthfulness from Gandhi. It was a turning-point in my life. Gandhi had found his truth by combining his idea of the ancient heritage with Ruskin and Morris, and his love for others included love for the vast poor. I began gaol-going – my second conversion was to gaol-going. I brought the novel back. It was turned down by nineteen publishers. Edward Sackville-West was right from the Western point of view. The poor were not in it. They were disinherited. And you could only laugh at them. Not weep for them.

Ultimately my confessional novel proved to be a very intense approach to myself. I have published four books in this series.... I would never use the European novel form. I have broken it up.... This breaking of the novel form has become integral to my confession, and this kind of autobiographical narrative is the kind of creativeness from which I have had to make myself into some kind of wholeness. That is why I often told Tambi it would be a good idea to attempt not a long autobiography, but to confess his experience as a poet coming from Ceylon and settling here and trying to 'be'.

JW: Tambi was always reluctant to say anything about himself, and I think he always felt that if he elaborated too much in philosophy or self-examination for other people it would be meaningless or misleading, that what he was trying to say could best be expressed by his own work and writings and that these should speak for themselves. I remember when I first met him I recognized instantly his ancient wisdom. I was only in my twenties and quite naïve at the time, and I tried to draw him out on the spiritual level, but all he said was 'I am the quiet stream – I leave my works along the wayside like flowers for other people to find.'

MRA: My own feeling is that while that may be a very sincere point of view, I don't think he faced himself, even in the European manner. I had to face my European self – shift the emphasis from the karmic experience as a determining point of departure to the point that one 'makes oneself'. Bits of poems can't do that.

JW: Well, Tambi did suffer inner torment. And during the ten years I was close to him I saw the torment of the duality within him. A part of him was strongly individualistic, but the other aspect was completely without ego and impersonal, and he could never draw together these two sides of himself.

MRA: You are quite right. I put it this way: he retained his sense of the destiny of man, while at the same time he wanted to be an individual, and he could be neither – he had glimpses of both.

JW: Yes, and this was his very painful dilemma. I have often tried to understand why, when he didn't have the resources to do his work, he used to sink into the most terrible self-destructive depression. It was almost as though he were punishing himself, tormenting himself in a kind of way and he would not eat, and would get very sick. Part of this was perhaps his upbringing, in that as a child he was very close to his mother and he was fussed over by her so much that there was one part of him that was the child that physically always wanted to be looked after.

MRA: He wanted every woman he met to be mother. I had to get over this by facing the woman directly. One woman said to me, 'I am not your mother or sister, I'm your sweetheart.' Now this experience he never faced. The important thing is that it would be a very good idea to bring out his conflict in terms of, say, Rimbaud. Rimbaud couldn't get over his conflicts either. Same predicament.... I feel the success of Tambi is in his failure.

JW: Yes, that is very profound, because in a strange kind of way that is what he wanted. A part of him wanted proper recognition of the meaning of his work, which he could never get in the West, but on the other hand he knew that in this fact lay the purity of the meaning of his work. I think people will now begin to analyse far more what he was trying to do.

MRA: I don't think so, because Western man has now gone over into the kind of attitude of non-participation which is compelled in him by the threat of nuclear war. There is no time now. I find now that most of the poetry I have read is again in bits and pieces. I feel that Western civilization is not facing itself again for the third time in our century. They are moving towards a third world war out of sheer greed – the greed which started the First World War and the Second World War. It seems to me this time the villains are in America – the richest part of Western civilization. It is symbolic that they don't want knowledge. They have left UNESCO. The whole situation of the world is now more tragic than in Tambi's time. Here again the Asian intellectuals have to make up their minds.

JW: It's also a crisis time, isn't it? Because although it seems as though the situation is very negative, at the same time – and this is natural law and a part of Indian philosophy is it not? – as well as the negative forces there is a very powerful current towards enlightenment and realization.

MRA: Yes, Nehru among the Indians tried to achieve some balance. In our small wars of chieftains there was slavery of people going to fight. Murder and sacrifice, blood sacrifice of people, for the sake of the king. That era is gone. In the threatened war there will be no survival of any kind. In those previous wars, people survived. Now chemical warfare is not part of the rules of the game and the neutron bomb is the cancellation of all humans – it's an aggression against all men. We are in a far more terrible period than before the Second World War.

JW: Although I can't help feeling that everything Tambi did was very significant in terms of his timing.

MRA: He didn't live to face the new situation. Now there is the holding back. I was reading a Kenyan poet who was four years in gaol for confronting the Government and saying that you have brought the same kind of colonialism that we destroyed when we became free. The novelists of West Africa are saying the same thing. The point is that people who are not saying these things are people out of date. Today, if the intelligentsia of the West and East don't participate in the kind of rally which happened on 2nd October last year [1983] in Hyde Park, I am afraid we will be betraying our functions as creative people, because creation itself is being stopped. So poetry has no meaning in the world. Poetry is after all the re-creation of life itself. It is the smouldering fire that makes life possible. Without the opportunity to create, then with nuclear death overtaking the whole of mankind, and the whole planet being destroyed, there is a final crisis of mankind. I am afraid those who do not ask questions now will say the same thing as they did after the Second World War – we didn't think it could happen here.

JW: I am convinced though that Tambi's reluctance to talk about himself and enter into this kind of discussion was deliberate. I think he felt, rightly or wrongly, that that wasn't his function.

MRA: In my opinion it was a weakness on his part. He pandered to the neutrality of people like Eliot. I must tell you we were able to draw Tambimuttu into a *Voice* magazine programme with George Orwell at the BBC later, but he came reluctantly. Eliot had to give up his near pro-fascism. He said that what he had said about *Action Française* was all wrong and in the *Voice* magazine he joined us. But I feel the most courageous man of that time in England was George Orwell. Not only did he write afterwards *1984*, but he anticipated many things that were going to happen after the war in his book *Animal Farm*. Now the fact that Tambi never could accept Orwell, but accepted Cyril Connolly, was due to a sense of inferiority to the European middle-class intellectual.

JW: Yes, but Tambi was always rather cynical about intellectualization. I think he wanted his work to demonstrate silently what he was trying to say.

MRA: His work couldn't come through. We are talking of the need for poetry, the importance of poetry. The reason it becomes necessary to utter the Word at all is because we fear death. The Word has to come in answer to the predicament we face. Malraux and Sartres and Camus were not people devoid of spirituality. But they were people who asked fundamental questions, because they saw the threat to creativeness and the poetry of life in the forces which were making for war. Eliot faced the crisis in *The Waste Land*, but in *The Four Quartets* he surrendered to transcendence. I suppose Tambi might have wanted to do the same, but I feel that Eliot was forced, after writing those poems, to face himself again during the war. And his greatness lies in the fact that he acknowledged he was wrong about the *Action Française* – and he deplored the fact that Ezra Pound had joined the fascists.

JW: You have illuminated for me Tambi's predicament.

MRA: But I must tell you with all this that I think Tambi had inherited sweetness and generosity of heart from his family. He was very charming and generous and there was a dignity in his weakness, the beauty of innocence as in a child.

JW: I wonder whether you could perhaps briefly return to some reminiscences of Tambi when you met him and the times you had.

MRA: I met him soon after he came to London. He was then living in Marchmont Street. I was living in Woburn Buildings. Always every second evening we adjourned to my room to have tea – three, four or five of us. There was Subramaniam, Iqbal Singh, and Dr Shelvankara. Then we occasionally addressed envelopes for the India League, because we were working as volunteers in the fight for freedom. Tambi went to the pub, where we joined him. We spent many evenings pub-crawling together. In our personal contacts I remember Tambi as a very loyal friend. If we were not meeting for a little while, he would come and seek me out. And when he came to India he made a point to write to me before, and came to see me. We shared a silent love because we had both inherited loving from our ancestors.

Sunil Janah

Tambimuttu – a Brief Encounter

Early in 1983 I had a letter inviting me to a meeting to discuss the formation of an Indian Arts Council in Britain. It was signed by Tambimuttu as the convener. I had heard about him and had known that he was associated with the poetry magazine and was himself a writer and a poet. But beyond that I knew nothing about him and had not the vaguest notion of the kind of person he was. The South Indian name brought back visions of immaculately clad, very proper gentlemen – cultural or some other attachés to the Indian embassies all over Europe, with whom my encounters had not always been very pleasurable. I am sure that they knew a great deal about our classical music and religious lore, but their most noticeable traits had been their enormous capacity for citing rules to obstruct whatever I wanted done and their total disinterest in the photographs of our country and our people which I had been invited to exhibit.

I could not attend that meeting but was curious about this distinguished man who happened to have invited me to a meeting, no doubt dedicated to a high purpose. In our commercial world this purpose eventually descends to raising money and getting grants. It seemed safer to telephone him after the meeting was over, although I was in such a negative frame of mind. The friendly, civilized voice at the other end made me feel glad that I had decide to call. I was asked to join him at lunch at the October Gallery. I had some difficulty in locating it in Old Gloucester Street but when I found it I found him too, waiting at the door – a frail, bright-eyed man with a mop of unkempt white hair. I was touched by this gesture and was almost embarrassed by the warmth of his welcome to a total stranger. He led me through the exhibition halls to the courtyard and up an iron stairway to his den. A den it was, with rows of bookshelves and books and papers scattered and piled up all over the place along with typewriters, tape recorders, word processors and such other gear which even a harmless writer needs around him now. I couldn't imagine how he could ever find anything in the midst of such disorder unless he had an extraordinary system in his head backed by an equally extraordinary memory. I remembered dear friends I had in India whose orderly minds cheerfully allowed far worse. No one can perhaps survive in India unless he acquires the capacity not only to tolerate but to take some positive delight in the confusion around him. It made me feel at home in surroundings so very familiar.

It was not, however, a shared disregard for external tidiness that made me feel at ease in his company, nor had it anything to do with our coming from similar cultural backgrounds. I found in him a delightfully interesting and interested person who could draw one out of the protective shells we acquire. Many others learn to acquire the technique of doing so but one recognizes instantly what rings true and knows that he has found a friend. It is difficult to put the reasons into words but we trust such feelings. I may only presume that they were mutual, for we talked and walked about within the premises for a long time and seemed reluctant to part. I had taken with me a few prints of my photographs of the Indian people, mostly of rural and tribal life. These seemed to fascinate him. He looked absorbed and wanted to see more. 'We should put them up in our gallery,' he said while we were lunching at the canteen on the fish he recommended. I knew, of course, that it was not my artistry, but the timeless quality of life in India, which I happened to have recorded, which he was admiring.

His interest gave me an excuse to invite him to dinner with us. He accepted readily. On the day when he was expected, I thought that I should call to let him know how best to find his way to our house. But I had no reply from his number. Then I tried the number of the gallery. 'He died yesterday morning,' I was told by a grieving woman's voice. I literally shook in my shoes. I was about to find a new friend who could bring back so many of my old remembered ones back to life again. Sadly, he had to die before I could even really know him.

Lawrence Durrell

Poets under the Bed

The poetry publishing world is going to suffer deeply at the passing of J.T. Tambimuttu, who, for some forty years, has occupied a curiously commanding position in the London world of letters, as friend, guide and publisher of so many poets of the first rank. We all know what quarrelsome and unstable people artists are, yet their affection for and trust in Tambi and his doings were unbounded, even among those who might have had most to criticize about his work. They spoke of him always with a loving and humorous concern, through which shone affection and admiration.

I am thinking of Eliot, who spoke of him in a wondering whisper, and described him as the most courageous of the younger publishers. And even those he might exasperate by one of his manoeuvres never for a moment lost their basic affection for him. We need this sort of living reminder in a philistine and positivistic civilization, and if Tambi could claim anything it would be that he won the affection of souls so different as, say, Henry Moore, Graham Sutherland, David Gascoyne, Henry Miller, Anaïs Nin, and scores of others.

He could also be careless and irritating. Our moments of exasperation with him were real ones, but it was always a loving and concerned exasperation, and I do not think he lost a friend ever, despite divergencies of policy or practice.

My own memories of him go back to before the war and before he had made his mark on the London scene. Some of the sites from which he elected to operate were fairly bizarre – like the steam-room of the Russell Square public baths, which he adopted as a head office for a brief period. Indeed, if he finally left the baths it was with reluctance, and because of the deleterious effect of the steam on his manuscripts.

My very first meeting with him was at a rendezvous off Tottenham Court Road, where he had rented a room in a cheap boarding-house, and lay in bed late of a morning, going over his plans to bring poetry to the public at large. It was my first interview with him and I saw with amusement that the entire contents of his first number reposed under his bed in an enormous Victorian chamber-pot. It was into this

Left: Kathleen Raine with Tambimuttu's third wife Esta and their daughter Shakuntala, to whom Kathleen Raine is godmother, in 1963.
Below: Katharine Falley Bennett, Tambimuttu and Kathleen Raine at the launching of the Lyrebird Press, 21 June 1972. (Photograph Tom Hanley)

Francis Scarfe, Iris Murdoch and Tambimuttu at the launching of *Poetry London/Apple Magazine* in October 1979. (Photograph Keystone Press Agency Ltd)

Above: Tambimuttu and Allen Ginsberg at the launching party of *Poetry London/Apple Magazine* in October 1979. (Photograph Keystone Press Agency Ltd)
Left: Tambimuttu in the French Pub (the York Minster) in Dean Street, Soho, in 1972. (Photograph Times Newspapers Ltd)

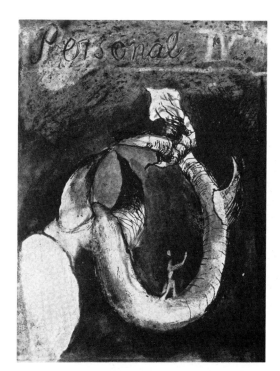

Illustrations by Graham Sutherland to David Gascoyne's *Poems 1937–1942*, Editions Poetry London, 1943. (Reproduced by permission of Kathleen Sutherland). *Above*: Inset flytitle, Personal IV. *Below*: Inset flytitle, Time & Place V.

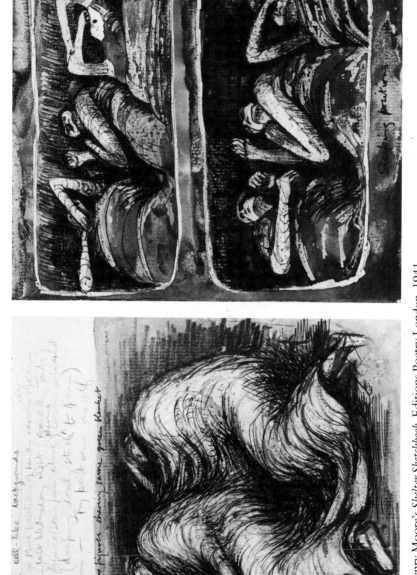

Two pages from Henry Moore's *Shelter Sketchbook*, Editions Poetry London, 1941.
Left: page 80, 'Two figures sharing the same green blanket'; *right*: page 56, 'Sleeping positions'; both in pencil, wax crayon, watercolour, pen and ink. (The originals are in the collection of the Henry Moore Foundation. © Henry Moore Foundation 1949, reproduced by permission of the Henry Moore Foundation.)

that he dipped for his authors.

Of course there were later and more affluent times and more up-to-date offices, but like a true lover of art and literature Tambi had a great affection for the seedier side of his adored London. Many a pub taproom earned his allegiance as a boardroom, and for a while he could not be prised away from the Hog in the Pound in Oxford Street, a most uncomfortable venue in which to discuss literature.

He leaves the general state of poetry publishing much improved for his presence and happy activity, and he himself felt that he had scored a praiseworthy success in his efforts to found and organize an Indian Arts Council in London which might arrange exhibitions of Indian treasures already in our collections but which never see the light of day. It is to be hoped that this activity will continue after he has gone; it would be his most effective memorial.

Sebastian Barker

O Holy Air of at Last Peaceful Ecstasy

Dedicated to the Memory of Tambimuttu

O holy air of at last peaceful ecstasy
Trouble no spirit, nor in the nightmares of children
Place the inappropriate, but, as prayers beseech you,
Console in the uttermost. Moisten cracked lips
With jellied oils, temper the moribund with swifts,
Throw a hazy mantle on the hills, a humour in the nose
Smelling the rotten blossom. Deepen interest in tavern music,
Make more profound the shabby attitudes of reproductionists,
Sponge down the dusty iris thrown away at the party's end,
Keel-haul the metaphysics of well-fed literati,

Shave the windows of too-long dormant nuns,
Cook the asparagus of the spherical foodman
Constantly in brandy. Hasten the actual. Make war on the
                                        intransigent,
Topple the untoppable. Befriend the insect;
But do your duty to the pestilent mosquito.
Tarry not with voluptuaries; eschew the attentions
Of butter-tongued dignitaries; seduce the saint;
Murder the apothecary: pestle him tenderly
Righteous or not. Instruct your gardeners,
Make them merry, who order your ordainments.
Trample the aesthete, make him cunning, fashion him
A bicycle to ride below the patterns of your shoes.
Ignore the holy, comb them with compassion
Unseeable in senses. Make sense of reason
Purblind with passion: arm-in-arm it
Over the ocean death dies floating on
(An incident melting in the greater fact). Consider
The slander of species. Hail the salesman
Mystic to humility. Greet the unfabulous.
Sorrow with others who have not yet your latitude,
And laze with the great that for one day they may be happy.
Scowl at miracles, that brightness shall be forthcoming.
Draw out the toad, tender him truthful arguments.
Lean on the unwary, befriend them with coincidence.
Try not to trouble the shark, but feed him with money.
Isolate the incendiary, placate him in his own conflagration.
Stupendify the ignorant, that tongues shall rattle.
Make curious the antique, that stars shall gossip a mighty device.
Dignify strangers. Give the unloved a better chance.
Castigate bankers with pretty daughters: teach them responsiveness.
Open the stone, disclose the crystal, rearrange the engineering of
                                        hypermatter.
Dislodge certainty, unhinge credulity, screw to the black gem the
                                        brazen angel.
Kiss fortitude. Be strong in courage. Mimic the indecipherable
And give it a better name. Sustain humour,
May it last a thousand years in the casual moment,
And turn up, like serendipity, in the auctions of speech.
Glorify aggression, that even as it reaches its mark
It turns into water, more dangerous by far. Heave

The stones off flesh, regain for it, nor time,
The breathing of beatitude bikinis seek to conceal.
Flirt with the elderly. Make fun with infants
That giggling may be more widespread. Toast
The transitory bishop in his everlasting assumption.
Squeeze the infinite, make it a little smaller.
Torture the inscrutable, cause it to reveal its bathos.
Tease the inevitable, teach it the manners of the newly-wed.
Draw distinctions with doctors, that knowledge may proliferate.
Adore the pace of the snail, reason with the slow motion of the
                                                                    acrobat.
Chastise the unoffending prince, may he learn from you alone.
Molten the unexampled rose, unkempt in the city garden,
That Who observes What may not be an issue any more.
And may the dragons of your turnpiked atmosphere,
And the somersaulting lions of your very dangerous presence,
Draw back like staggered diplomats, when, strolling from afar,
The flying flesh abandoning, his spirit draws to a close.

Indian figure in Chinese calligraphic style by
Chou Shiuh Lin, 37 × 25.5 cm, ink on paper.
Painted specially for this volume.

Michael Horovitz

After Tambi's Funeral

For M. J. Tambimuttu – body cremated: 30 June 1983,
spirit entered heaven: every day – RIP

What's left
of a life –
old bones
underground

or burned away
to a lingering scent
brief embers
of ashes, turned

to faint shadows –
smoke bruising
then leaving
the afternoon air

– What's left?

The blank
blue page
of your passing

and we who mourn
awakening
to finer
awareness –

of life lost,
swift final
dissolution
of the compost
of many seasons

with a few scraps
of newsprint, assorted

rumours and memoirs
and garbled phone quotes.

After reaching
'a certain age'
those considered
important enough
get officially
obituarized

and the measured
assessments
are filed –
pre-sentimental
postscripts on tap
(to be 'in
at the death' –
though the person
who's pre-
meditated   the valediction
may turn out to go
before the subject –
who may in turn
have obituarized
his or her, unbeknown
assessor . . .)

What's left is the removal

the ground beneath
our feet, arrested
in their tracks

at each new bruited
news of someone's death
that pause: the diminishment
the inevitable
reminder, prospect
of one's own

and all the other
buds and branches lopped,
trees of life

felled to dust
before their best
potential seeds
can take root

yet –
'cast a cold eye'
let the body
die   as it listeth
and the spirit   fly –
see there . . . free at last
of these mortal coils,
palsied toils

. . . free to win
the infinite spoils
of sky, topless high
beyond reason and rhyme
'that sweet golden clime
where the traveller's
journey   is done'

– Rest in peace
brother spirit,
homing bard.

London's lyrebirds
sing on
though your flashing
eye and tongue
be gone –

your vision
lives on.

Bhavani Torpy

Another Buddha

Towards the closing weeks of his life Tambimuttu was to make one last discovery. The poet was Sri Chinmoy Kumar Ghose, a Bengali poet writing in English. Tambi had no doubt at all he had found a poet of world stature who had truly penetrated and transcended 'Appearance and Existence'. In his inimicable way he quickly digested a few volumes of Sri Chinmoy's poetry and said he knew at once he had found another Buddha. 'I truly believe Sri Chinmoy to be an avatar,' he told an audience at the Bharatiya Vidya Bhavan, after watching a performance of Sri Chinmoy's play *The Son*, about the life of Christ. He saw the play a week or so before he died so tragically. For Tambi it was a cosmic experience which brought together many of the varied strands of his life, particularly the Christian and the Hindu. 'It was so sensitively and movingly performed and the theme so universal and dear to my heart that it moved me extraordinarily.' In the play, the words 'Thy will be done' from the Lord's Prayer are paralleled with the central message of the Gita, *Nimitta Matram bhava savyasachin* – 'Be thou a mere instrument'. The play features a scene in India in which Jesus and a *rishi* converse and recite some verses from the Gita in Sanskrit.

> Weapons cannot cleave the soul.
> Fire cannot burn the soul.
> Water cannot drench the soul.
> Wind cannot dry the soul.

Sri Chinmoy offers in the play a unique interpretation of the significance of Jesus' life, seen from the perspective of India's highest spiritual vision. For Tambi it had got to the nub of it, the universal consciousness. His plans to take the play to India were to remain only a dream, but he was greatly uplifted by the play.

Sri Chinmoy's mantric poetry near perfectly expressed Tambi's 'ideal' of poetry. He very much liked Sri Chinmoy's poem 'The Absolute', which he likened to the poetry of the great seer poets of India – the Vedas, the Upanishads and the Gita. In Sri Chinmoy's shorter poems he saw the folded bud, the miniature galaxy, the macrocosm in the microcosm.

> I see a garden in your face.
> I see a rose in your heart.
> I see celestial beauty in your eyes.

In the simple, childlike words and images he saw drops of pure nectar.

When I first met Tambi it was as a result of reading about the forming of an Indian Arts Council in the UK in a daily newspaper. He told me of his recent progress through India, of his talks with Indira Gandhi, of his great plans to open a window to Eastern culture through the Indian Arts Council, and it was at this time that I introduced him to Sri Chinmoy's poetry. He said several times in his last days how astounded he was to come across 'the gift of Sri Chinmoy'. He placed him with Rama, Krishna and Buddha and others in the transmitting of eternal wisdom across the centuries. His perception of his stature was instant and uncompromising. He saw in him the poetic process, so beautifully described in the *Poetry London–New York* No. 4 Preface, at work to change the face and fate of humanity. He had found his avatar, his seer-poet, but was not to meet him or to publish his poetry. This contact with Sri Chinmoy, however brief, was a source of great joy and consolation to Tambimuttu as he moved closer to his own source.

Sri Chinmoy

The Absolute

No mind, no form, I only exist;
　　Now ceased all will and thought.
The final end of Nature's dance,
　　I am It whom I have sought.

A realm of Bliss bare, ultimate;
　　Beyond both knower and known;
A rest immense I enjoy at last;
　　I face the One alone.

I have crossed the secret ways of life,
　　I have become the Goal.
The Truth immutable is revealed;
　　I am the way, the God-Soul.

My spirit aware of all the heights,
　　I am mute in the core of the Sun.
I barter nothing with time and deeds;
　　My cosmic play is done.

Ananda K. Coomaraswamy

The Coming to Birth of the Spirit

You cannot dip your feet twice into the same waters,
because fresh waters are ever flowing in upon you.

Heraclitus

The present article embodies a part of the material which I have
assembled during recent years towards a critical analysis of the Indian,
and incidentally Neoplatonic and other doctrines of 'reincarnation',
regeneration, and transmigration, as these terms are defined below.
These doctrines, often treated as one, appear to have been more
profoundly misunderstood, if that is possible, than any other aspect of
Indian metaphysics. The theses which will be proposed are that the
Indian doctrine of palingenesis is correctly expressed by the Buddhist
statement that in 'reincarnation' *nothing* passes over from one
embodiment to another, the continuity being only such as can be seen
when one lamp is lighted from another: that the terms employed for
'rebirth' (e.g. *punar janma, punar bhava, punar apādana*) are used in at
least three easily distinguishable senses: (1) with respect to the
transmission of physical and psychic characteristics from father to son,
i.e. with respect to palingenesis in a biological sense, defined by
Webster as 'The reproduction of ancestral characters without change',
(2) with respect to a transition from one to another plane of
consciousness effected in one and the same individual and generally
one and the same life, viz. that kind of rebirth which is implied in the
saying 'Except ye be born again' and of which the ultimate term is
deification, and (3) with respect to the motion or peregrination of the
Spirit from one body-and-soul to another, which 'motion' necessarily
takes place whenever one such a compound vehicle dies or another is
generated, just as water might be poured out of one vessel into the sea,
and dipped out by another, being always 'water', but never, except in
so far as the vessel seems to impose a temporary identity and shape on
its contents, properly 'a water'; and thirdly, that no other doctrines of
rebirth are taught in the Upanishads and *Bhagavadgita* than are
already explicit and implicit in the Rig-Veda.

214

'Spirit' we employ in the present introduction with reference to *ātman*, *brahman*, *mrtyu*, *purusa*, etc., alike, but in the body of the article only as a rendering of *ātman*, assuming as usual a derivation from a root *an* or *va*, meaning to breathe or blow. But because the Spirit is really the whole of Being in all beings, which have no private essence but only a becoming, *ātman* is also used reflexively to mean the man himself as he conceives 'himself' (whether as body, or body-and-soul, or body-soul-and-spirit, or finally and properly only as Spirit), and in such contexts we render *ātman* by 'self', or sometimes 'self, or spirit'. Capitals are employed whenever there seems to be a possibility of confusing the very Man or immanent God with the man 'himself'; but it must always be remembered that the distinction of spirit from Spirit and person from Person is 'only logical and not real' – in other words a distinction without difference (*bhedābheda*). A sort of image of what may be implied by such a distinction (which is analogous to that of the Persons as envisaged in the Christian Trinity) can be formed if we remember that the Perfected are spoken of as 'rays' of the Supernal Sun, which rays are manifestly distinct if considered in their extension, but no less evidently indistinct if considered in their intension, i.e. at their source.

The Upanishads and *Bhagavadgita* are primarily concerned to bring about in the disciple a transference of self-reference, the feeling that 'I am', from oneself to the Spirit within us: and this with the purely practical purpose in view of pointing out a Way (*mārga*, Buddhist *magga*) that can be followed from darkness to light and from liability to pain and death to a state of deathless and timeless beatitude, attainable even here and now. In the Upanishads and early Buddhism it is clear that what had been an initiatory teaching transmitted in pupillary succession was now being openly published and in some measure adapted to the understanding of 'royal' and not merely 'sacerdotal' types of mentality, for example in the *Bhagavadgita*. On the other hand, it is equally clear that there existed widespread popular misunderstandings, based either on an ignorance of the traditional doctrines or on too literal interpretation of what had been heard of them. The internal evidence of the texts themselves, with their questions and answers, definitions and refutations, is amply sufficient to show this. Hence, then, the necessity of those innumerable dialogues in which, alike in the Upanishads, *Bhagavadgita* and Buddhism, that which in 'us' is, and that which is not, the Spirit are sharply distinguished and contrasted; the Spirit being that which 'remains over' when all other factors of the composite personality 'identity-and-appearance', or 'soul-and-body' have been eliminated. And furthermore, because 'That One that breathes yet does not breathe' (*Rig-Veda Samhita*, X, 129. 2) is not any what as opposed to any other what, It or He is described simultaneously by means of affirmations and denials, *per modum excellentiae et remotionis*. The following analysis of the Supreme Identity (*tad ekam*), restricted to words derived from *an*, to 'breathe' or *vā* to 'blow', may contribute to a better understanding of the texts:

Despirated Godhead   *avātam, nirātmā, anātmya nirvāna*, Pali *nibbāna*. Only negative definitions are possible.

Spirit, God, Sun,
    'Knower of the
    field': King   *ātman*, Pali *attā*. In motion, *vāyu, vāta* 'Gale of the Spirit'; and *prāna*, 'Spiration', the 'Breath of Life' as imparted, not the breath empirically, but the 'ghost' that is given up when living creatures die. Being 'One and many', transcendent and immanent, although without any interstice or discontinuity, the Spirit, whether as *ātman* or as *prāna* can be considered in the plural (*ātmanah, prānah*), though only 'as if'. Form, as distinguished from substance: Intellect.

What-is-not-Spirit;
    Moon; the Field,
    World, Earth: the King's domain   *anātman*, Pali *anattā*. The hylomorphic, physical and psychic, or lower-mental, vehicle of the Spirit, seemingly differentiated by its envelopes. Mortal substance as distinguished from its informing Forms.

These are not 'philosophical' categories, but categories of experience from our point of view, *sub rationem dicendi sive intelligendi*, rather than *secundum rem*.

We can scarcely argue here in detail what was really meant by the palingenesis, metempsychosis, or metasomatosis of the Neoplatonic tradition. We shall only remark that in such texts as Plotinus, *Enneads* III, 4. 2 (Mackenna's version), where it is said that 'Those (i.e. of 'us') that have maintained the human level are men once more. Those that have lived wholly to sense become animals ... the spirit of the previous life pays the penalty', it must be realized that it is a metempsychosis and metasomatosis (and not a transmigration of the real person) that is in question; it is a matter, in other words, of the direct or indirect inheritance of the psycho-physical characteristics of the deceased, which he does not take with him at death and which are not a part of his veritable essence, but only its temporary and most external vehicle. It is only in so far as we mistakenly identify 'ourselves' with these accidental garments of the transcendent personality, the mere properties of terrestrial human existence, that it can be said that 'we' are reincorporated in men or animals: it is not the 'spirit' that pays the penalty, but the animal or sensitive soul with which the disembodied spirit has no further concern. The doctrine merely accounts for the reappearance of psycho-physical characteristics in the mortal sphere of temporal succession. The intention of the teaching is always that a man should have recognized 'himself' in the spirit, and not in the sensitive soul, before death, failing which 'he' can only be thought of as in a measure 'lost', or at any rate disintegrated. When, on the other hand, it is said that the 'Soul' is 'self-distributed' (cf. *ātmānam vibhajya, Maitri Upanishad*, VI, 26) and 'always the same thing present entire' (ibid., III, 4.6), and that this '"Soul passes through the entire heavens in forms varying with the variety of place" – the sensitive form, the reasoning form, even the vegetative form' (ibid., III, 4.2) it is evident that it is only as it were that there is any question of 'several Souls', and that what is described is not the translation of a private personality from one body to another, but much rather the peregrination of the Spirit (*ātman*) repeatedly described in the Upanishads as omnimodal, and omnipresent, and therefore as occupying or rather animating body after body, which or rather bodies and sensitive souls, follow one another in causally determinated series.

All this is surely, too, what Eckhart (in whom the Neoplatonic tradition persists) must mean when he says 'Aught is suspended from the divine essence; its progression (i.e. vehicle) is matter, wherein the soul puts on new forms and puts off her old ones ... the one she doffs she dies to, and the one she dons she lives in' (Evans ed., I, 379), almost identical with *Bhagavadgita*, II, 22 'As a man casting off worn-out garments, taketh other new ones, so the Body-dweller (*dehin* = *śarīra ātman*), casting off worn-out bodies, enters into new ones'; cf. *Brhadaranyaka Upanishad*, IV, 4.4 'Just so this Spirit, striking down the body and driving off its nescience, makes for itself some other new and fairer form.'

The three sections of Upanishads translated below begin with the question, 'What is most the Spirit?' That is to say, 'What is this "Self" that is not "myself"? What is this "Spirit" in "me", that is not "*my*" spirit?' It is the distinction that Philo is making in *Quaestiones ... ad Genesis*, II, 59 and *De Cherubim*, 113 ff. (as cited by Goodenough, *By Light, Light*, pp. 374–5) when he distinguishes 'us' from that in us which existed before 'our' birth and will still exist when 'we, who in our junction with our bodies, are mixtures (σύνκριτοι) and have qualities, shall not exist, but shall be brought into the rebirth, by which, becoming joined to immaterial things, we shall become unmixed (ἀσύνκριτοι) and without qualities'. The 'rebirth' (παλιγγενεσία) is here certainly not an 'aggregation' or palingenesis in the biological sense, but a 'regeneration' (palingenesis as a being born again of and as the Spirit of Light), cf. Goodenough, p. 376, note 35.

'What is most the Self', or 'most the Spirit'? As the late C.E. Rolt has said in another context (*Dionysius the Areopagite on the Divine Names and Mystical Theology*, 1920, p. 35), 'Pascal has a clear-cut answer: "Il n'y a que l'Etre universel qui soit tel ... Le Bien Universal est en nous, est nous-mêmes et n'est pas nous." This is exactly the Dionysian doctrine. Each must enter into himself and so find Something that is his true Self and yet is not his particular self.... Something other than his individuality which (other) is within his soul and yet outside of him.'

'If any man come to me ... and hate not his own soul (ἑαυτοῦ ψυχήν, Vulgate *animam suam*) he cannot be my disciple' (Luke 14: 26). The English versions shrink from such a rendering, and have 'hate not his own life'. It is evidently, however, not merely 'life' that is meant, since those who are at the same time required to 'hate' their own relatives, if, on the contrary they love them, may be willing to sacrifice even life for their sake: what is evidently meant is the lower soul, as regularly distinguished in the Neoplatonic tradition from the higher power of the soul which is that of the Spirit and not really a property of the soul but its royal guest. It is again, then, precisely from this point of view that St Paul says with a voice of thunder, 'For the word of God is quick and powerful, and sharper than any two-edged sword, piercing even to the dividing asunder of soul and spirit' (Heb. 4: 12), and consistently with this that 'Whoever is joined unto the Lord is One Spirit' (I Cor. 6: 17; cf.12: 4–13).

With this may be compared, on the one hand, *Bhagavadgita*, VI, 6 'The Spirit is verily the foeman of and at war with what-is-not-the-Spirit' (*anātmanas tu śatrutve vartetātmaiva śatruvat*), where *anātman* = Buddhist *anattā*, all that, body-and-soul, of which one says *na me so attā*, 'This is not my spirit'; and on the other, with Eckhart's 'Yet the soul must relinquish her existence' (Evans ed., I, 274), and, in the anonymous *Cloud of Unknowing*, ch. XLIV, 'All men have matter of sorrow: but most specially he feeleth sorrow, that feeleth and wotteth that he is', and with Blake's 'I will go down unto Annihilation and Eternal Death, lest the Last Judgment come and find me unannihilate, and I be seiz'd and giv'n into the hands of my own Selfhood'. All scripture, and even all wisdom, truly, 'cries aloud for freedom from self'.

But if 'he feeleth sorrow that feeleth and wotteth that he is', he who is no longer anyone, and sees, not himself, but as our texts express it, only the Spirit, one and the same in immanence and transcendence, being what he sees, *geworden was er ist*, he feels no sorrow, he is beatified – 'One ruler, inward Spirit of all beings, who maketh manifold a single form! Men contemplative, seeing Him whose station is within you, and seeing with Him – eternal happiness is theirs, none others' (*Katha Upanishad*, V, 12).

An 'actual experience of Unknowing and of the Negative Path that leads to it' (Rolt, op. cit.) is not easy to be had, unless for those who are perfectly mature, and like ripe fruits, about to fall from their branch. There are men still 'living', at least in India, for whom the funeral rites have been performed, as if to seal them 'dead and buried in the Godhead'. 'It is hard for us to forsake the familiar things around, and turn back to the old home whence we came' (Hermes, *Lib.*, IV, 9). But it can be said, even of those who are still self-conscious, and cannot bear the strongest meat, that he specially, if not yet most specially, 'feeleth joy', whose will has already fully consented to, though it may not yet have realized, an annihilation of the whole idea of any private property in being, and has thus, so to speak, foreseen and foretasted an ultimate renunciation of all his great possessions, whether physical or psychic. *Mors janua vitae.*

Francis Scarfe

An Elegy for M.J. Tambimuttu

I

In the fading of my days
Let me to the end be true,
At the parting of our ways
Humbly I must speak for you,
    Despising praise
  That gilds a fallen prince:
I bow to the holy man
For his gift of pure intent;
I forgive the wayward saint
  His necessary sins.

II

In poverty he lived and died
Preaching the poem.

Begging across continents
He touched leprous gold
Cruel silver flowed
Like blood from his pauper's hands
As he preached the poem:

A madman filling the bowl
For the holy monument
In poverty he lived and died
And ten times sold his soul
As he preached the poem:

I say to the mean minds
The meaning of his life was prayer
The poem is where
The lives of all men meet
The poem is everywhere:

220

Wash the words
Scour the words
Till East and West
Meet in the globe of the poem
Where all are one:

In poverty he lived and died
As he preached the poem.

III

Laughing through sadness
In permanent exile
His homeless mission:

A man at home
In his frail beauty
The poem's body:

In a thousand loves
Seeking the music
Of his lost homeland:

Grasping through darkness
The essential light
Of the fleeting soul:

The holy voice
Of the martyred prophet
In our homeless world

No death can silence
But will be heard
Across time's distance:

I pray in reverence
To the deathless dead
Who welcome him

In the house of love
Where the Creators
Kiss his luminous hands

Wash him with spices
Crown him with tears
Bless him with wine:

Oh friend that we loved
Be there to receive us
When the dark is over.

'In Memoriam Tambi', music by Rohan de Saram.

Tambimuttu

Fitzrovia

On the third day after my arrival in London in January 1938, in a Japanese ship, the Nippon Yushen Kaisha's *Kashima Maru*, which had been built in Victorian England and boasted the service and cuisines of two cultures, and not in a sailing-boat as reported by J. Maclaren-Ross in his highly coloured book of misrepresentations and fairy-tales titled *Memoirs of the Forties*, I had already discovered Fitzrovia, and settled down at 45 Howland Street, maybe in the same house where Verlaine and Rimbaud had once conducted their stormy love affair.

I have a nose for cities and had instinctively set forth the previous night from the now vanished Melbourne House Hotel, in Gower Street, in the general direction of Fitzrovia, and discovered the Harem, a night-club by the Wheatsheaf Tavern in Rathbone Place, and as I was sipping my beer at my table, who should materialize through the Harem Hollywoodized bead-chain curtain but the fabulous Greta Garbo! She was accompanied by a tall, most distinguished-looking individual with reddish hair and beard and piercing eyes. His aquiline features and bearing were arresting, and as he hesitated by the entrance with roving eyes, which were like radar probes, I shot up from my seat impulsively. Would they care to join me for a drink? He was delighted. He was an errand-boy (by which he was referring to his nomadic, picaresque style of existence), and a poet to boot. 'And so am I,' I said, truthfully, having published three slender collections in Ceylon. Could I have a look at some of his poems? 'Most certainly,' said Charles Haddon Redvers Gray, producing his walking-stick with a flourish. His house keys were attached to its crook with a bootlace and a sheaf of poems neatly wrapped round the stem and held together with rubber bands. I recognized at a glance

223

that the 'poems' were 'occasional' schoolboy scribblings, jottings in a schoolboy script, flagrantly romantic and almost illiterate.

'What is that?' I asked, pointing to strips of red cloth he had wired into the lapel of his rust-red overcoat which, balanced incongruously on top of a rusty bicycle, was a well-known feature of Fitzrovia in those days. 'It's the flaming torch I am carrying around the world.' Below the 'torch' he sported a nut and bolt secured right through the coat's fabric. 'It's the right nut screwed in the right way,' Redvers explained. I was most surprised to hear that this first-ever English Bohemian I had met, my introduction to Fitzrovia, was also a qualified solicitor who had inherited his father's law practice in the City. 'You must leave your hotel at once and I'll find you a room in the Howland Street house where I live. And I'll introduce you to Philip O'Connor tomorrow. He is a *real* poet, you know. See you at noon at Madame Buhler's. She is Swiss, and her son, Robert Buhler, is an up-and-coming painter of these parts.'

I never met the lady I had mistaken for Garbo again or discovered who she was. In all probability she was the midnight stripper in the Blue Angel night-club I had heard of; and Redvers seldom missed that ecstatic moment when, according to reports, 'everything came off'.

The Post Office Tower has today erased the houses of Howland Street; and Madame Buhler's, where writers, editors and artists met over aromatic cups of continental coffee, has similarly vanished.

I dropped in at Madame Buhler's the next day for my appointment with Redvers and Philip O'Connor, and noticed a hunched-up, sandalled, and long-haired figure with intense eyes and pursed lips, his high cheek-bones rotating on his tense cobra neck, who surveyed the place like a vinegary monarch, took one peppery look around, and then walked out as casually as he had sailed in. I correctly guessed it was the figure of Philip O'Connor, whose explosive and poetic images, tinged by what Indians call *rasa* or poetic taste (literally, taste in the mouth), were already familiar to me in the literary periodicals of the time.

Redvers was sorry he was late, and suggested I called at 4 Fitzroy Street, where, he said, Philip often holed up. It was the flat's sole occupant, Peter Murray, with an aureole of blond, curly hair (currently a psychiatrist), who answered the bell. Girls thought of him as the most handsome chap in Fitzrovia in those days, Stephen Spender running a close second. 'Do come in, I am Philip's brother,' he said, and some months later confessed to me in 'the Country Pub' in Rathbone Street that as I crouched by his gas fire on a brown pouffe he thought I was either the Devil or Someone Else.

Peter sat in his chair with clasped hands, smiling and nodding his Apollonian head as he always does, and the conversation was sunny and bright, with sudden rapier-sharp innuendoes meant to be portentous statements which I suspected at later meetings he had picked up from Philip O'Connor, who was an idol of and model for our circle. The O'Connorish, surreal, revolutionary or simply witty remarks and mind-blowing insights were exciting to hear and drew the right vibrations into a room (we were the *jeunesse dorée*, the hippies of our time), but, particularly in Phil's case, they were anti-social and self-destructive, since their superficial glitter had no real ocean of thought underneath. Anyway, before our meeting ended Peter had already asked me to my first literary party in England.

The first friendships in a new environment have a special quality and meaning and it was at Peter's party that I first ran across Anthony Dickins, Gavin Ewart, Stephen Spender and Laurence Clark, whose poems I have consistently printed in *Poetry London* although he was too J.C. Squire-ish and Georgian for most editors. With his towering fur cap, heavy motoring gloves, gnome-like face, humorous eyes behind large horn-rimmed glasses and his shock of fuzzy brown hair which stood on end like a distress signal, his 'motor' always at hand for our escapades, his plane of First World War vintage with folded wings rolled into his garage, he was an enchanting and whimsical character, a true English eccentric.

Gavin Ewart, who wrote the famous quatrain,

> Miss Twye was soaping her breasts in the bath
> When she heard behind her a meaning laugh
> Then to her amazement she discovered
> A wicked man in the bathroom cupboard.

was a shy, reserved and eternally well-turned-out figure with a disarming smile and charming manners whom one could never possibly suspect of writing poems like the one on Miss Twye or a similar one I printed in *Poetry London – New York*:

> Ah! Love is sadly limited,
> A monstrous heart, a tiny head!

Gavin was, like Laurence Clark, a detached observer of Fitzrovia, never a denizen, but they were both seen around often, since many of their friends lived there, and when they attended the sessions in the pub after the war, which was not often, they appeared to be losers in the game of life, though they did not seem to think so. Laurence seemed to peek at life from behind a tree, as he actually did once peek from behind a chimney-pot, and wrote a poem about it which is included in his mimeographed collection of poems.

Stephen Spender has never changed throughout all the years I have known him. Sensitive and diffident, he dominated Peter's room that evening with his great height and handsome face, large, open eyes and curly hair. His head might have come straight out of a Greek sculptor's studio. He slouched and swayed as he talked and it seemed the words were being wrung out of him, which is the same experience I had with his young friend Lucian Freud, whom I met soon afterwards. With both I think it was due to their basic shyness. I had much admired this sensitive's poems in *The Faber Book of Modern Verse*. The images were 'new', like Dylan Thomas's, and this first impression persists and guides me today to read any new poem Stephen produces with a Spenderesque eye, searching for a Spenderesque turn of vision, a Spenderesque turn of phrase, and I am seldom disappointed however slight the poem may be.

I was very fortunate to meet Anthony Dickins at this party within a few days after my arrival in London. He had just come down from Corpus Christi, Cambridge, where, as the Organ Scholar, he had Marlowe's room, with a grand piano, on top of which sat a bust of Aleister Crowley's Black Mass woman, Betty May, by Hugh Sykes Davies, a don at St John's who was Kathleen Raine's husband until Charles Madge of Mass Observation, the poet from South Africa, drove up to one of their parties, carried Kathleen into his tiny sports car and drove off. Later he did the same to Stephen's wife, the amazingly tiny and petite Inez, much to 'the sensitive's' great grief.

Betty May had been barred from Cambridge. One night I picked her up in the Fitzroy Tavern, the heart of Fitzrovia before the start of the war, after she had pulled up her skirts in public to show her thighs – 'Look! I've still got beautiful legs.' It was Betty's revelations about Aleister in *Tiger Woman* that brought this interesting poet into disgrace. 'The Beast 666' and his patron Lady Frieda Harris were both wicked and entertaining, and, because Aleister had sunk into neglect and his poems deserved recognition, I arranged to have them reviewed in *Poetry London*.

Tony, who was studying conducting under Sir Henry Wood at the Royal College of Music, was thoroughly impressed with my early poems (dedicated to Noëmi) and, strangely enough, by my songs, which I had composed from the age of sixteen for a couple of years. Within the next few days we called on the music publishers in Shaftesbury Avenue, where I was presented with six or eight discs of the old Eclipse record with my very first song on it, which had been sold in Woolworth's and managed to sell another, 'The Hindu Love Song', to Day & Co.; which, however, never appeared, probably due to my indifference. In England I was shedding part of what England had given me in Ceylon.

We went to Stephen Spender's *Trial of a Judge* at the Group Theatre which had also performed Auden's and Isherwood's *Ascent of F6* and submitted some of my poems to a couple of magazines. We found a house, 114 Whitfield Street, where the jolly landlady who was immensely fat, Mrs Schouterden, married to a Belgian, living at 64 Grafton Way, W1 (the address for the first two issues of *Poetry London*), supplied us with lunch and dinner for 30*s.* a week or rooms only for 12*s.* 6*d.* Redvers Gray would arrive each morning on his rusty bicycle and play his flute in the street. He would then climb the stairs, squat in the *padmasana* or lotus position on the floor, and with palms outstretched on either side, eyes pointing to the ceiling and the tip of his neatly trimmed beard cocked at my head, 'Alms for the love of Allah, alms for the love of Allah,' he would chant. 'And what would my Lord and Master have for breakfast this morning?'

Breakfast was served in bed from Pop's Café next door, for a commission of 6*d.* a week. It was one of many Redversian plans to get rich by serving as many Fitzrovians as possible in this manner.

No. 114 was bombed during the war and a crowded one-storey self-service Indian restaurant occupies the spot; which I patronize nowadays. The old fish-and-chip shop right opposite, which still stands there, deserted, sold us 4*d.* or 6*d.* worth of fish and chips, or cod's roe, of which I was very fond, born as I was by the seaside of Atchuvely in the northern Jaffna peninsula. The 'fisherwoman' brought the fruits of the sea straight from the catch for our delighted inspection and she haggled over prices with Elizam our cook in the courtyard of Grandfather of Stone House (the other being Grandfather with the Beard), descendant of Pararajasekharan VI, the last King of Jaffna (from whom Grandfather with the Beard is also descended), the poet, editor and philanthropist, S. Tambimuttu Pillai of Atchuvely. The Portuguese invaded us in 1505 ... and then came the Dutch ... and then the British. The Old Bombay Emporium (today the canners of the popular curry and other spices) still stands in its original modest state in Grafton Way and Indian restaurants flauntingly display their exotic names in Whitfield Street and Grafton Way.... The eternal migration and intermingling of cultures – and I feel I was the pioneer of all this hustle and bustle, this little Indian colony.

Almost overnight No. 114 got filled with our friends. The American Adam Zion Margoshes, friend of Philip O'Connor and, during the war, founder of the famous Phoenix Bookshop in Greenwich Village (Fitzrovia had worked its magic on him), was one of them. He was also founder of *The Village Voice* along with my friend Norman Mailer. Charles Blackburn, who designed the logo and the second lyrebird for the cover of *Poetry London* (the first was designed by Lucian Freud) and who was working for the Metal Box Company, was another. He was always nattily turned out, in perfect taste. He was a serious artist as well. At No. 114, since he lived on the top floor, he was our watchdog for the moment the girl in the building opposite his room took off all her clothes and paraded up and down with perfect unconcern, although she knew we were all watching.

Mary Hunt, whom I later introduced to Ralph Kean, who married her, lived in this house when she was sixteen. I had rescued her from Lucian Freud at Boris Watson's Coffee An' (it stood for 'Coffee An' What') one night. Bunny Kean ran the documentary Crown Film Unit with Donald Taylor and Basil Wright, maker of the classic documentary *The Song of Ceylon*, which I was pleased commissioned scripts from the impoverished Dylan Thomas. When I was impoverished myself, in New York, I sold a letter from Dylan to the House of Books, New York, which read: 'Dear Tambi, Please let me have the guinea you owe me for my last poem. Yours, Dylan.' I suppose it rests in state now in the University of Texas.

Mary's beauty was stunning. 'She is the most beautiful English girl I ever saw,' the poet Ruthven Todd told me when he saw her sunning herself on a deck-chair on the roof half-way up to my room. The fashion of my introduction of Mary to Bunny was stunning too. I had taken her to my nightly haunt, the Caribbean night-club in Denman Street, scene of some of my best-known exploits (Anne Valaoritis beware!), where nice black hefty Rudi from Martinique, the proprietor, always sang Jean Sablon's 'J'attendrai' for me, his moon-face glowing in the half-dark, when she suddenly announced that she would very much like to sing a song through the mike. Mind you, she was only sixteen and I was probably breaking the law taking her there in the first place. Anyway it was wartime and the streets were dark, and everything was happening around me, so with Rudi's permission I led her to the stage and sat back to watch her beautiful face and lovely body, whereupon she started crooning to the mike as if it were a baby and, dammit, took her blouse and bra off as if to feed it. The audience loved her singing and swaying after that, especially Bunny in his dark corner, dark, handsome wolf, who demanded to be introduced, and so the deed was done.

Augustus John and Matthew Smith both fell for her. A book of drawings by Augustus has her face on its cover and Matthew left her £2,000 a year, together with all his paintings and drawings, which were strewn all over the place in her duplex in Cornwall Gardens when I visited her on my return from New York in 1968. Matthew once told me of his secret remedy for sleeplessness. He sprinkled cold water over his naked body and lay on the floor. He was so miserable and cold after that, that soon he was glad to be back in bed again.

Word of our parties soon got around Fitzrovia, since they could smell 'em all the way down Grafton Way and Whitfield Street because of the incense sticks from Mysore we used.

Another beautiful girl of our circle was the tall and buxom but most perfectly proportioned Hetta Crouse from South Africa who graced our parties with fellow South African sculptor René Graetz. But we soon lost her to unambiguous William Empson. She invited me to do some gardening with her and dutifully I went down to Bill's garden. When we were in the drawing-room I said, 'Come and sit on my lap, Hetta.' 'That is not your style, Tambi dear,' she said. 'I hear you have been gardening with Hetta,' Bill told me the next day. That's how close we were those days in Fitzrovia, even before the magazine had appeared and everybody knew everybody else. It was exactly the same in Paris before the war. In no time I had run across Zadkine, Brancusi, Tristan Tzara, Henry Miller, Brassai, Giacometti, etc. It seemed to me Paris was just like London.

By the end of February 1939, when the first number of *Poetry London* had been in the bookstalls for a month, with the special souvenir cover drawn by Hector Whistler, nephew of James McNeill Whistler, who came to our chiefly Sibelius musicals at 3 or 4 a.m. in the morning with a steaming pot of hot coffee in his hand (his cousin Rex Whistler had a studio in Charlotte Street while Hector lived in Bloomsbury), our humble dwelling in Whitfield Street had been

visited by many celebrities of today. We had a pre-publication visit
from Larry Durrell and his brother Gerald, who at that time was only
fourteen.

A few doors away in Whitfield Street stood Dr Marie Stopes's
Family Planning Clinic. She wrote constant letters to me with
enclosures of her poems. She and our present-day Sir John Waller,
collateral descendant of Edmund Waller, the Cavalier poet who wrote
'Go, lovely rose!', had founded a company which published a
magazine called *Kingdom Come*, which I had unkindly nicknamed
Condom King although they had very kindly published some of my
poems. As everybody knows, Sir John needs no advice on birth
control and when I've asked him, 'Why this liaison, Johnny?' he's told
me: 'It's normal, isn't it? Marriage is unreal.'

Anaïs Nin and her husband Ian Hugo also surprised me with a call
quite early one morning after we had had a magnificent evening
together in Larry's Campden Hill Road house, which Anaïs had lent
to him and his first wife Nancy, who was a tall, blonde and beautiful
girl, a painter. Larry sang the Corpus Christi carol from the Old
English, strumming his guitar:

> Lullay, lullay, lullay, lullay,
> the falcon hath borne my make away.

He had written to Anaïs in Paris enclosing the first copy of *PL* and
asking her to come straight away to London to meet me, 'since you
both have similar handwriting', just as he had written that very same
month to Dylan Thomas to tell him that his 'crabbed, botchy script'
resembled Emily Brontë's.

Anaïs had caught the night train that very day, she told me later on
in New York, and as I left that party Hugo stood by the bedroom
door by the stairs holding the coffee-table edition of *The House of
Incest* in both hands like a white Cellophane-wrapped tea-tray or an
oriental gift. When I got back to Whitfield Street, I read through the
book in half an hour and got so excited and curious over the identity
of the author that I rang up Larry at once, late as it was. 'Is Anaïs Nin
a man or a woman?' 'My dear chap, you've been talking to her all
evening' was his surprised reply.

Rumours spread quickly in Fitzrovia and we didn't even have to
bother hunting for a printer. One day a gentleman with a bowler-hat
and rolled umbrella turned up at 114 on behalf of the Women's
Printing Society of Brick Street, Piccadilly, with an offer to print the

first number of *PL*. He had heard of the project from the poet and novelist Rayner Heppenstall. The nice lady printers and Hector Whistler made us postpone the publication day from January 1939 to one in February. One unfortunate lady compositor had pied up a whole galley of type by dropping it on the floor, and several of our large size pages had to be hand-set all over again. It was damned unfair since George Barker himself had helped with the typography.

When the magazine appeared, the pioneers of TV were naturally there to collect Tony and me at Broadcasting House in their big bus to appear in their *Picture Page* from the famous Crystal Palace, which seemed hellishly miles out of London and beloved Soho. The big board said 1. RHUBARB with girl appearing on the stage carrying the plentiful rhubarb in a basket and then 2. POETRY (I'm not joking) for Tony and me. We were so good they asked us to stay on for the evening show. They had made up Tony with dark paint but not me and it was damned hot under the arc lamps, and the next day two girls rushed up to us in a coffee place in Tottenham Court Road – 'We saw you on TEEVEEE!'

Some of those I have mentioned so far were true Fitzrovians in the sense of Bohemians, and of Byron's a-roving at night, of which Redvers Gray was the paragon. But there is one chief person I would like to add, with whom I had many a midnight chat in James McNeill Whistler's old studio in Fitzroy Street. Paul Potts, 'The hick poet from the Canadian prairies', as he called himself, would prop his feet up on a chair and, puffing away at his corn-cob pipe, recite some of his poems (which he now quite wrongly calls non-poems – he has been brainwashed by the critics during my absence in America). Even the sentences he constructed in his sonorous Canadian voice had the structure of music and poetry. He was a pure poet, a poet of the future, with a Whitmanesque sweep and ring, who spoke of ordinary things in simple and unaffected language: 'But listen people/ Anywhere punching time;/If you're walking to the moon/I've got clean sox for you.' And: 'But I have tried/To leave for ever in your ears/The noise that men make/When they break their chains.' One felt at home with Paul and his open, naked face with the long aquiline nose and domed forehead wreathed with corn-cob smoke; his humorous and restless disillusioned eyes which stubbornly clung to his dream and the few people he loved.

It was from the nests of Whitfield Street, Howland Street and Fitzroy Street, with the Fitzroy Tavern for our home run, that the idea of Fitzrovianism in the verbal sense was first born. It was Redvers

Gray's influence and his love of William J. Locke's *The Beloved Vagabond* which gave me the idea of our group as vagabonds and *sadhakas* or seekers, as the Buddha was at the start.

I had turned up in London only to surprise the girl I was going to marry with my unexpected presence. I had written to tell her I had fallen madly in love with a girl called Noëmi – a name I had fished out of Guy de Maupassant – and would she look after her when she arrived in England. She wrote back 'Hurrah! Of course'. In the meantime my novel *Noëmi*, which was herself, was on its way to her by sea, with me to follow a couple of weeks later – a couple of weeks too late. She did give me the chance of having her back when she called on Tony and me when we shared a room on top of the arch opposite Great Ormond Street Hospital. Tony played the piano for her at five in the morning and I took her for coffee at the all-night café right beside Russell Square tube station. She had wandered all night all over Fitzrovia from one address to another and it was a miracle she had found me at all.

She was pregnant, should she have the baby? Being a noble man I said, of course, and she left at once.

It left me with a sense of the eternal loneliness of men and women despite all our words and stances. When we die we die alone, to be recycled in the Supreme Energy of Brahman. And thus it was that I became a true Fitzrovian like my friends Augustus John, Roy Campbell, Gavin Maxwell, Elizabeth Smart and Kathleen Raine, all of whom used to visit Fitzrovia with me. But I had had it in my soul a very long time ago. When I was fourteen I was living in Forbes Road, Colombo, and my cousin Anton Gardiner and I called ourselves the Vagabond Pair after Dumas's *The Three Musketeers*; I mean the book and not the film (I went to the cinema almost daily, sometimes two theatres a day, which was easy, since my uncle, Sir Chittampalam Gardiner, owned nearly all the cinemas in the island). I even composed a song 'The Vagabond Pair' for us to sing (and that was after the film), which my younger brother Thuraisingham roars out in his great baritone in London today. Anton and I accompanied each other home, those one hundred yards between our houses, every night, chattering often until four or five in the morning. And one day Anton produced a poem he had written:

> So we'll go no more a-roving
> So late into the night,
> Though the heart be still as loving

And the moon be still as bright.
For the sword outwears its sheath,
And the soul wears out the breast,
And the heart must pause to breathe,
And love itself have rest.
Though the night was made for loving,
And the day returns too soon,
Yet we'll go no more a-roving
By the light of the moon.

Deeply moved, I put my arm round him and said 'Anton, you are a much better poet than I.' It took me a couple of years before I discovered that Byron had written it, probably basing it on a Scots original. Anton had turned the tables on me, and I couldn't charge him with deception since it was I, G.K. Chesterton, founder of the Chestertonian Coffee Club at my college, who had made him Byron in my club.

Tony replaced Anton for me in London and thus it was that I used to exhort Tony and others to come with me to Fitzrovia, a-roving in Redversian fashion.

The fact that the name I gave, Fitzrovia, persists, does not surprise me, because of the unity of spirit and atmosphere which made it unique in the London of those days. Even Julius Horwitz, the American GI as we called him, has perfectly captured the spirit of the place with great clarity and truthfulness in *Can I Get There by Candlelight?* It is one of the best books to come out of the last war.

I had another surprising experience of the survival of a second term I had used during the war to describe a pub in Rathbone Street. I had just returned from my honeymoon with Jacqueline Stanley, from Elizabeth Fairclough's place, in Chipping Campden, where Stephen and Inez Spender had honeymooned the previous fortnight. It was in Chipping Campden that I had discovered my first 'country pub' in Jackie's company.... After a certain hour in the evening, the Wheatsheaf, the Fitzroy and the Black Horse had an overload of people and it was time for us to move on. I did so to this pub in Rathbone Street, which is the continuation of Rathbone Place after it curves around the Marquis of Granby towards the Duke of York. It was a 'beer only' one-room bar on the left side of the street, almost denuded of people except for a few workmen and their friends, and it reminded me of the country pubs of the Cotswolds. Retreating there became a regular habit with us and, since the pub-crawl was a well-timed affair, we all got to know where we could find each other at any time of the day, or evening, even before and after pub hours, since night-clubs, restaurants and cafés were beads in the smoky necklace of the pub-crawl.

Years after the end of the war I was walking down Rathbone Place one evening towards the Wheatsheaf and in front of me there were a young couple. And I heard the young man tell his girl-friend, 'Come on, Mary, let's go to the Country Pub for a drink.' It was a circle round the inner circle I had drawn some years earlier. Truly life is cyclic.

My pub-crawl varied from period to period, but the most romantic was the one which included Margot Fonteyn, Moira Shearer, Bobby Helpmann and Constance Lambert at the New Theatre right opposite 8 New Row, my address at the time. The night they performed my friend Edith Sitwell's *Façade* (she once threw one of her famous Sesame Club tea-parties for me) I pretended to be an Indian ignoramus, and in loud tones in the bar, so everybody could hear, kept on repeating to Stewart Scott, my buddy of the time, shaking my head, 'My, Stew, I loved that fuckade', while keeping them all in view hitched to the corners of my sewing-machine eyes.

I hope it is understood from this article that Fitzrovia had no topographical or geographical boundaries. Stewart Scott used to turn up by taxi every day from Hampstead, Highgate, or Julian Trevelyan's studio in Hammersmith, wherever he happened to be, for breakfast with us in a café in Charing Cross Road.

Subra was 'the Ceylonese William Saroyan', admired by E.M. Forster as well as Harold Acton, with his wine-red scarf and Buddha face, dream man of our pretty girls, and men, a barrister from Lincoln's Inn who cruised into the harbour of every pub like a velvet pussy-cat luxury liner with all her lights on, regular as clockwork round the pub-crawl, by which habit he was trapped by me, since he did not keep his appointments with P. Saravanamuttu, Tea Commissioner of Ceylon, his father's emissary; the father writing to me please send my son home, your grandfather was my friend, his doctor fiancée arriving with her doctor husband and crying right in front of my eyes, I sleeping across the door of the bedroom where he spent his last night with the utterly beautiful Katharine from Scotland with auburn hair, seeing him into the cousin's car to his doom in Ceylon before I left for my office. Subra dashing down from Jaffna to Colombo on my arrival in 1950, 'You sent me down here, now please take me back'. Subra of the Beautiful Face with your raven looks and Buddha's eyes, gentle manners, drinking yourself to death in the Arizona Bar in Jaffna on poison arrack, which also killed my elder brother in New York. At least I brought you a bottle of whisky to atone, and my uncle Ratna couldn't ever find you with his bottle, until I told him about the Arizona Bar; I know now why my letters from America were ignored by your relatives.

Redvers was the shine and Subra the substance of Fitzrovia. We were all together at that time like one name in the Fitzrovia of my mind. To quote from Paul Potts:

> To break new ground
> To take small weak dark seeds
> Out from unfertile sand
> Then to throw them proudly at the sun. . . .
> To sing on
> Until the world is Blackpool
> In August in the afternoon.

It was only an attitude of mind that comes to each generation in every country, and in different ways, but for me it happened in lovely Fitzrovia.

The wedding of Julia Shaw-Lawrence, spring 1968, Palace Gate, Kensington, London. *Left to right*: Muriel Shaw-Lawrence, Tambimuttu, Jane Henderson. Susan Payne is in the background. Words and lyrebird drawing by Bettina Shaw-Lawrence. 25 × 20 cm, pen and watercolour over photographic print, 1986.

POETRY LONDON - NEW YORK

People want not stars or poets, but false prophets.

Editor: THURAIRAJAH TAMBIMUTTU

Published by the Poetry Institute Inc.
with the assistance of Eliot Glassheim and Terry Frederick
Production: Philippe Chaurize

VOL. 1, No. 4   SUMMER, 1960

Fourth Letter

The New Moderns

Poetic compression of the highest order is only possible within a culture which expresses the total man, and is universally understood. To cite the supreme example of my literary experience: I do believe now, and the impression stretches back to my childhood in Ceylon, that the Indian epics, the *Mahabharata* (which contains the *Bhagavad-Gita*, a 'popular' account of an infinitesimal part of the philosophy of Action[1]) and the *Ramayana*, or Kalidasa's play in Sanskrit, *Shakuntala*, express fully the involvement of the human spirit in a culture and take into account palace, market place, law-court, cottage; cities, villages and the hills and plains; heaven and earth and all the places in between, which are their realistic subject matter.[2] These works transcend others with restricted commitments in poetry such as scientific objectivity, revolution and anarchy, or the inverted passion of the 'sensitive', committed to little else besides itself.

Shakuntala presents a view of reality which is rationally convincing, scientifically accurate and spiritually satisfying. It is the epitome of poetic experience in the theatre, unique in literature. It describes in compressed terms how ideas melt one into the other to make the universal state. Identities and opposites— Gods, heaven and earth, the vines, creepers and animals, the moon and the flowers— are united, and are its equally real protagonists. They are concretions of the same universal electrical energy (*prana*) and atom (*anu*) disposed and patterned differently to create Matter, its Appear-

[1] Ananda K. Coomaraswamy, in his *Hinduism and Buddhism*, naming it "the focus" of Indian thought and Aldous Huxley (accepting this statement) "one of the clearest and most comprehensive summaries of the Perennial Philosophy ever to have been made" were not understanding it in this way. This understanding of it, like that of certain modern Vedantists' is 'lapidary'. To make the point clearer I shall return to it later on in the conclusion of this letter in PLNY No. 5.

[2] The action in the air in Indra's car and in the heavenly hermitage as well as the poetic symbols are acceptable to the Indian mind which thinks of all forms and states as being continuously manifested and absorbed back into the primal flux of energy which is continuously active. Thus Indian culture not only accepts the existentialist state of life as uneasiness and movement but satisfies the demands of modern scientific interpretation.

237

ance and its Actions. Words and categories are only islands in the sea of ever existing vitality, are leaves of grass, best realised and transmitted through poetry. In poetry, words must grow into a "form of life" embedded in a large linguistic context to describe the reality beyond specialised commitments. Words and ideas *are* limitations which may only be expanded through poetic perception based, as in this play, on a universal culture. The process is demonstrated clearly in *Shakuntala*. As Goethe wrote:

Would'st thou the young year's blossoms
  and the fruits of its decline
And all by which the soul is charmed,
  enraptured, feasted, fed,
Would'st thou the Earth and Heaven itself
  in one sole Name combine
I name thee, O Shakuntala! and all at once
  is said.
              Translated by RABINDRANATH TAGORE

Shakuntala is the merging of Heaven with Earth. Her mother was a nymph and her father a hermit. Her birth in a forest hermitage was the consequence of Restraint becoming Passion, Law transforming itself into Nature from which it was first abstracted. She is an immortal human, sister to the trees, vines, beasts, birds and bees which, as significant life-forms as herself, contribute to the dramatic action. In the expansion or destruction of categories, whichever way we look at it, here is telling poetic compression, the pure essence (be it Indian *prana,* Shavian life-force or Lawrence's "blood") and an inclusive cosmography. The poetic word— what Fahr-el-Nissa Zeid paints on her pebbles or what Jackson Pollock could have done with a boulder. Shakuntala's simplicity is not naivete but character, which guards her love through the bitterest betrayal of confidence. The impul-

siveness and innocence of her youthful *Gandharva* marriage (voluntary union) are the obverse side of her womanly maturity and devotion in the heavenly hermitage: the physical beauty of the union of Nature's children combines with the moral beauty of a higher union after parting and suffering; the everyday household with the forest hermitage, Restraint with Freedom.

This is not the place nor the occasion for an exegesis of the culture and the binding of the human spirit with it that produced *Shakuntala, Ramayana* and the *Mahabharata.* My present purpose is to simply state that we lack such a culture today—a universal culture which might enlarge the private sensibility of the poet and thus ease his task of communication.[3]

In this quandary the poets have sought refuge in an objective world of their own invention, in revolution and anarchy, or mere "inscape" and passion: the Objective Rhetoricians whom we have had in plenty since 1914 when Ezra Pound inspired the publication of the "imagist" anthologies based on the non-poetic ideas of T. E. Hulme; the Anarchists, with Sir Herbert Read for a spokesman, who threw their bombs during the early 'Thirties; and the supreme poet of "inscape" and passion, Dylan Thomas, "the most masculine of our poets (whose) style and . . . rhythm lay in the strongest stress of all our literature on the naked thew and sinew of the English language . . . [4] These volitions of the fragmented human spirit had their own interest and antidotal effects. When Pound

---

[3] As with Pound's *Cantos,* it needs much learning to understand *Shakuntala,* except that, with the 5th Century play, the learning was part of a 'universal' culture—the use of High and Low (vernacular) Sanskrit was only incidental and I am not speaking of Sanskrit literature *per se.*
[4] Gerard Manley Hopkins on John Dryden.

nd Eliot in England attempted to make language technical and "precise", Auden an away with it; Thomas enriched it. And it is by the degree of emphasis placed on such human volitions, as objectivity, anarchy or "inscape" and passion, that we were aware of the 'timbre' of poets.

But the poetry of the partially engaged spirit, of artificial and conceptually limited attachments, could not long involve Man with his need for total engagement. It is for this reason that "Modern Poetry" has become the apparition at which few people will look today.

"Modern Poetry" became lifeless soon after the composition of that "objective" and yet vague and impressionistic[5] poem *The Waste Land*, though it was given occasional vitality by the established poets who understood the mysteries of the manufacture' of "Modern Poetry" and were able to move us in one or two much anthologized poems; by those who were always 'dependable', and they are in most of the anthologies; and especially by "The New Moderns" like Kathleen Raine, George Barker, Dylan Thomas, David Gascoyne, the early Lawrence Durrell and Spender and latest Edith Sitwell: those poets of wholephrasing* who we remember promised us the bottle with the wine once more. I may as well include Walter de la Mare and Roy Campbell who were excluded from Michael Roberts' taste-forming "Faber Book of Modern Verse" because they had not felt "compelled to make any notable development of poetic technique,"—emphasis on the bottle,

not its contents. I do not use the term "New Moderns" as an advertising label for a new Movement, without much merit, strongly evidenced by work already produced. It is rather a descriptive term, just as Imagism was, to conveniently describe a process that has already taken place and which, I think, will be increasingly operative in the future. After Eliot's chief decade of poetic influence (roughly 1917 to 1927—the decline began with *Ash Wednesday*) and the doldrums that followed, it was these poets who showed a green element of development for the future. Along with the children of T. E. Hulme's Imagism, such as Wallace Stevens and Marianne Moore, who wrote a clear, concrete poetry which recorded impressions by visual images, and poets in the main English tradition like Robert Graves, Edwin Muir or Yeats, they provided us with a total image among the wry, hollow fruit of the desert. In combination with their predecessors and their limited commitments, "The New Moderns" began to express the involvement of the human spirit in a newly emerging culture, and, somehow, to the maker of a passional and lectionary of the human spirit, created that multifoliate tree which is the true poetry. Their collective voice made a *Mahabharata,* an epic of the age, when an imported French culture fragmented daily into various "Movements": Impressionism, Imagism, Surrealism, etc., poetry of dissociation from total experience at a period when there was not a single poet writing in English, except Yeats, who could have been said to have an unfragmented and major poetic sensibility. This is the reason *Poetry London* was made into a sounding board for many schools of writers.

The chief concern of *Poetry London*

[5] Although Impressionism is based on the scientific fact of the dispersion of light and was therefore thought to be a 'concrete' method, I am using the word in T. E. Hulme's sense in *More Speculations* since it does actually describe the net result of the use of an analytical language full of sharp visual images.

* Holophrasis. See p. 9 and Section 3.

was necessarily with "The New Moderns" who had brought back to 'objective' words their suggestive and sensuous elements. It was only they (of whom Dylan Thomas, with his increased density of words, warring images and compression, was the most vital spark) who seemed to promise a sharpening of meaning and impact to a less cynical and 'analytical', and thus more fully reacting audience. Besides those I have already mentioned there were others like Keith Douglas (killed in action in World War II), or W. S. Graham and Philip O'Connor, who introduced a healthier aspect to modern poetry. Their poems were faithful and small, rather than ambitious, sprawling and pontifically commentating. Though in a minor key, the poetic core was intact. Norman Nicholson was another. A Cumberlander, like Wordsworth, he wrote Nature poetry which I found more appealing. Wordsworth with his rustic pretensions, his scientific monomania for the plain and ordinary word, his artificiality and specialised commitment, never thought of looking for the most expressive word. Since Auden's telegraphese could produce moving poems, *Poetry London* did publish some verse which represented "Modern Poetry's" aftermath of Objective Reporting with its clinical approach and matter-of-factness. But much of it still required "analysis"—understanding the poem through footnotes, questions and evidence pieced together — rather than osmosis through mind-feeling.

This analytical hostility to a poem, which has been a feature of American criticism since I. A. Richards began "explicating" poems in 1924 in *The Principles of Literary Criticism*, was catered to increasingly by Eliot and Pound by wilful extension of the complex passages in European writing. (Their early poems and those of the European poets who influenced them were not 'difficult'.) The simplest themes of many other poets were developed on planned lines of 'inorganic' complexity. It was the age of obscurity and a-vitality. Such writing bred not sympathy and love, but greater hostility or, at best, an arid, intellectual titillation. There is a great deal of difference between complex experience expressed in the simplest terms possible and wilful obscurity which is really annoying obfuscation.

The situation had its parallel in Analytical Philosophy. In the words of the American philosopher William Earle, which are applicable to "Modern Poetry": "Our entire attitude toward sentences is *hostile* . . . This analytical hostility is obviously incompatible with love, with serenity and with any comprehension of those meanings and subtleties which presuppose sympathy and love for their very sense."[6] To which I should add that the stimulation to spasmodic mental effort by a work of art is not the same as giving *immediate pleasure*. Whatever the hidden depths that are plumbed in repeated readings, there should be an initial contact with a poem through its auditory rhetoric, its flow, collisions and breeding of images, and fusion of ideas and feelings. The poetry of ratiocination like Eliot's *Four Quartets*, of literary "angles" and borrowings, a critic's poetry, which is not felt deeply, can never touch us in this way—it loses in direct proportion to the amount of purely intellectual comment. It is interesting that several critics, including Pound, seek to prove Eliot capable of emotional impact by reference to a single poem. "It is complained that Eliot

[6] Noonday Review No. 1.

is lacking in emotion. 'La Figlia che Piange' is an adequate confutation."[7] Drawing an analogy from painting, Pound compared Eliot's emotional value to the "cold gray-green tones" of Velasquez in the detail of *Las Meninas*. Skillful though it is, it is still the poetry of the partial commitment and intellectual comment wherein an attractive girl becomes an abstraction of the mind.

It must be stated that although I praise what I have called "New Modernism"[8] I don't necessarily mean that its poets are much better than those in the body of "Modern Poetry". Such a comparison is not intended, though Dylan Thomas possessed the only major potential among the poets of the period and would have outstripped them all in his winter tales. Rather that the "New Moderns", within the mainstream of Anglo-American poetry and more keenly aware of wholephrasing, were 'getting through', when "Modern Poetry" had reduced the public to a state of apathy with its loss of incantatory magic and emotional depth, its analytical hostility, and its finicky, self-conscious attitudes. "The New Moderns" had felt that the 'Thirties needed the return of lost virtues.

To begin with, they avoided the dry and brittle language of detachment because it was not poetic but scientific. They were conscious of the full resonance of words whether they were of everyday usage,

consciously 'literary', or merely invented. Whereas their predecessors strived for clarity with the language of symbolic logic, which had been made barren by the Imagists and Analytical Philosophers (who start with marks which have no meaning and give them meaning with other marks which are their definitions), they straddled several levels of suggestion using words in their full density with understanding of their overtones. Each word was embedded in a large linguistic context that swelled into "a form of life" as Dylan Thomas dramatically proved.

Though they were very much at home in the use of the "free-verse" used by Matthew Arnold, for instance, and newly discovered by Hulme in the *vers-libre* defined by Khan in 1880, they showed a preference for well-defined rhythms and metres and the showing of unfashionable clothes in a new light.

They did not believe that poetry, originating as it does in intuitive perception, needed to be completely 'explicated', as modern critics would have us believe. The poem itself in its immediacy was the experience. Jabberwocky or pobble-who-has-no-toes was also poetry.

They felt as Milton did that poetry should be simple, sensuous and passionate, but were aware that the first epithet was a relative term. Consequently they found Dylan Thomas "easy" and Eliot sterile and difficult in *Four Quartets* or *Ash Wednesday*.

Along with the Rationalist Philosophers, the Modern Poets had distrusted their emotions and, drawing inspiration from Impressionist painting, had cultivated an oblique "tentative half-shy manner of looking at things, . . . no longer concerned that stanzas (were) shaped and polished like gems, but rather that

---

[7] *Literary Essays of Ezra Pound.*

[8] At school it was Poetry, and in Great Britain Modern Poetry. Although I never discovered who had first given formulation to the idea, it was an inescapable fact. This being so, in view of the holophrasis which is the central fact about poetry (see Section 3 of this Letter.), it was inevitable that there should be New Modern Poetry—a true agglutinative process just like the title of this magazine. And since we do have New Criticism, why not New Modern Criticism, or better still, New Modern Interpretation?

ьome vague mood (was) communicated."[9] Strange to relate, and though it seems a contradiction in terms, their extreme cerebrations without conviction or sincerity had resulted in vagueness. They, therefore, made excessive demands on the reader's patience and inventiveness to supply the links that were lacking in the narrative. "The New Moderns" on the other hand arrested the immediate attention of the reader by their full look at the subject on hand, their incantatory style, and their acceptance of the emotional and passionate nature of man. They created the conditions for an increase of communication to the degree that they possessed what Wordsworth called *organic* poetic sensibility. They were aware that the greatest complexities were transmissible if the surface of a poem—its form, sound and imagery—was arresting and attractive enough. One may float on the surface of a subject and still be aware of its depths. On the other hand, the "tentative half-shy manner of looking at things," the attempt to communicate a "vague", sophisticated and edifying view in a string of visual images was a wilful limitation of poetry. As Wordsworth wrote, "Poems to which any value can be attached were never produced . . . but by a man who, being possessed of more than usual organic sensibility, had also thought long and deeply." Poetry of the impressionistic type like most of Pound's *Cantos* does not spring from sustained "organic sensibility".[10] Though the poems may be systematic and methodical, they are not systemic or "of the bodily system as a whole, not confined to a particular part." [11] Because these poems are deficient in the "organically" felt sense — the element which strikes the reader immediately, they do not communicate themselves *directly* at all levels of communication, but only after much 'thought'.

The wholephrasing "New Moderns", however, brought "organic sensibility" back to the verse of passing sensations and ideas about consciousness, the vague, impressionistic, unsynthesised raw materials of poetry. They were aware that writers such as Pound in his *Cantos*, Eliot in *The Waste Land,* and James Joyce in *Finnegans Wake* (which is a refractory jungle of poetic imagery to the degree that it is not wary of—as Dylan Thomas was in his *Adventures, kunstwissenschaft* —the scientific and mosaic artist's approach to art) were unable to make a synthesis—a sensory equivalent to experience, not its methodical interpretation— from dissociated perceptions and/or sensations. *Synthesis, not analysis, is the highest poetic utterance.*

Poets detach one of the aspects of poetry (like sound or purely concrete images) only when they are experimenting, that is, playing from the sidelines— just as the mystic or 'lover' dissociates an object for contemplation, like a material figure, or, in the East, an element like sound in the Method of *Laya* which has an intimate bearing on the incantatory element in the wholephrasing which is poetry. The analogy is appropriate since the great poet's ecstasy is similar to the mystic's when he is one with his object by awakening of senses through concentration on his object or element. (That which is really our own we are one with Hence the human act of love is taken

---

[9] T. E. Hulme in *More Speculations.*

[10] It is time that the admirers of Ezra Pound who certainly include myself confess that his ambitious *Cantos,* for all their fragmentary brilliance, fail in this way.

[11] *Concise Oxford Dictionary*

s the symbol of mystical experience, passionate striving to become one.) In his way the poet and the 'lover' open their conscious selves to universals.

The poets of dissociation and analysis in "Modern Poetry", on the other hand, were mostly concerned with the immedicies of consciousness and not with passing through them towards the universal, and this precluded the writing of great poetry. If they had succeeded in dealing with universals and reached a synthesis of experience, which is what I meant by culture at the start, their writing would have had greater significance. But no such synthesis was forthcoming except *The Waste Land* (1922) which none of my friends will admit to having really understood, and *Four Quartets* which was writing about writing and thinking about thinking, very hesitant and "half-shy", what George Orwell called "gloomy mumlings" in his review in *Poetry London No. 7*. Orwell found little in Eliot's later work which had made any deep impression on him.

I had occasion to write of Eliot in April 1939: "There are great possibilities in modern verse, but as long as there is no sane paper to publish *new* work, modern poetry may never emerge from the Laforgue infection of T. S. Eliot, which has had a disintegrative effect on the minds of many poets", while three months before I had already spoken of Dylan Thomas as a "great poet". In what other way may we describe a poet who has evoked reactions in us which seem to be universally true?

2

We all believe in PANDEMONIUM. At least some of the time.

For me it is a one-word poem.

The most vivid way of knowing is through poetic words which in one unified movement attach the greatest number of facts—like the loom which with one stroke binds a thousand threads. The poetic word (it is more than the visible idol of the Imagists—the 'image', being sound and shape and movement in the time-span and the type of time-span dealt with within the poem, modifying, itself changing, growing) condenses a world of ideas and phenomena into a reality that we can grasp and feel. It differs from the scientific word, which is as unlike *pandemonium* as possible! It transmits, in an instant, what would otherwise need many sentences of prose. The word "orange" in the following lines by Grover Amen in this issue, stands for the whole of Reality. Within the 'unified field' or field of consciousness of the poem it is a model of the universe:

> Even a casual orange,
> Inessential and exact,
> Can acquire the unexpected
> And original color of fact.

The name of Sivam (Shiva) in the Hindu Pantheon for the force of Creation, Preservation and Dissolution (which is Wordsworth's 'Nature' in modern scientific terms) is also a poetic word, different from the same word in journalese. It is the Word (Veda) for the rhythmic character of the universal process. Sivam of the thousand and eight names, as the Beginning, the Middle and End, God of Sacrifice and Joy and Sorrow, is confusing multiplicity in movement (*pandemonium*) expressed in the synthesis of the poetic word. *Pandemonium* has that resonance. (pan-banging, Wallace Stevens' HARMONIUM), movement, chaos and multiplicity, as well as the order and unity of the universe in the idea of the harmonium and shape of the single word.[12] Furthermore it is related to the facts of our existence and thinking which we must order constantly both in their general application and from situation to situation, which is the central idea of Indian thought—the existentialist attitude. In its suggestion of a unified place of uproar or movement with several figures in it (and a poem with its images is just that) it proposes the pure poet's intuitive knowledge, direct and timeless, of the similarity of all states and objects in the universal flux of energy which Wallace Stevens states conceptually and diagrammatically and not in purely poetic terms in *The Glass of Water*:

That the glass would melt in heat,
That the water would freeze in cold,
Shows that this object is merely a state,
One of many, between two poles. So,
In the metaphysical, there are these poles.
Here in the centre stands the glass. Light
Is the lion that comes down to drink. There
And in that state, the glass is a pool.
Ruddy are his eyes and ruddy are his claws
When light comes down to wet his
    frothy jaws.
And in the water winding weeds move round.
And there and in another state—
    the refractions,
The **metaphysica**, the plastic parts of poems
Crash in the mind . . . [13]

In the terms of a painter, probably Picasso or Braque, Stevens says that all states and images are manifestations of light and tensions of opposites unified or in movement in the body of the poem. Time is conceived here as endless. The same idea is expressed in purely poetic terms by

Claire McAllister in her *Mystery*[14]. A images are united in a sheet of brightness the thin ice-sheet: or the braincell pressed, staining all sight inside:

Let pressed be the braincells,
    staining all sight inside,
Pressed, until body be but a goatskin
    hold much heady wine,
Till Time like the ice-sheet begin,
    melt thin . . .

or cubistically and mathematically b Rorimer Dushkin, in the last section o her *The Walls* which begins:

Risen suddenly as sound the building thrust
From turbines, cubic walls of glass and ligh
Into space and cleanliness and freedom
And the sealed flight of airplanes . . .

Delmore Schwartz states simply "Fo Poetry is light and it is light" in his lates collection[15] which St. John Perse posits i a synthesis of all-inclusive differentiated ness which is undifferentiated or Unit (Blake's vision, Whitman's *Leaves o Grass*)—the characteristic of the pur poet's knowledge; with sense of the indi viduality of the parts and the whole of th poem existing simultaneously, the hall mark of great poetry:

We shall not dwell forever in these
yellow lands, our pleasance . . .
The Summer vaster than the Empire hangs over the tables of space several terraces of climate. The earth huge on its surface over-flowing its pale embers under the ashes—Sulphur colour, honey colour, colour of immortal things, the whole grassy earth taking light from the straw of last winter—and from the green sponge of a lonely tree the sky draws its violet juices.

---

[12] It is interesting that Stevens at first thought of calling his *Collected Poems* "The Whole of Harmonium" which confirms my interpretation of his word.

[13] *Collected Poems* (Knopf)

[14] Appearing in *Botteghe Oscure*, No. XXV.

[15] *Summer Knowledge, New and Selected Poem* (Doubleday).

A place of stone and quartz! Not a
pure grain in the wind's beard. And light
like oil.—From the crack of my eye to
the level of the hills I join myself, I know
the stones gillstained, the swarms of
silence in the hives of light; and my heart
gives heed to the family of crickets. . . .

Anabasis: Tr. by T. S. ELIOT[16]

In its basic simplicity, synthesis is the
nity of opposites — the dialectic of
olarities. With elaboration in a poem,
lay or painting, it is the marriage of
ational categories, aspects and objects
nto an absolute unity, and thus presents a
vorking model — a unified view of
Tature. Binary in movement at its
implest (the half-in-green-leaf and half-
n-flame tree of the Celtic *Mabinogion*),
t becomes more complex movement in
Dylan Thomas, resembling a ticking watch
—since it is *made* like a poem—, a folded
ud or a miniature solar system like our
ymbol of the atom and electrons, in what
shall term the holophrastic process
holophrasis : Gk. holis—whole, phrasis—
hrase, "the expression of a complex of
deas by a single word"—Webster) which,
n my extended sense, gives poetry its
orm and substance. It is the extent of
olophrasis (synthesis) of sense, rhythm,
ound and form elements which determines the varying degrees of difference
etween a line of poetry and a line of
rose. The process itself is explained by
Thomas in *I, in My Intricate Image* :

Beginning with doom in the bulb,
   the spring unravels,
Bright as her spinning-wheels,
   her colic season
Worked on a world of petals;

She threads off the sap and needles,
   blood and bubble
Casts to the pine roots, raising man
   like a mountain
Out of the naked entrail.

16 Harcourt, Brace and Co.

Beginning with doom in the ghost,
   and the springing marvels,
Image of images, my metal phantom
Forcing through the harebell,
My man of leaves and the bronze root,
   mortal, unmortal,
I, in my fusion of rose and male
   motion,
Create this twin miracle.

Opposites and 'perfect' identities are
unified or related to each other in movement in one holophrastic thrust. Poetic
perception unites the things known with
the knower, who is also the universe of
the poem. Poetic synthesis happens in a
flash because the poet has *become* the
objects of the phenomenal world of matter
and individualized consciousness. He has
achieved the unitive knowledge of super-
rational intuition, direct and timeless. This
unitive knowledge results in 'pure' poetry
(Dunlop's poem in this issue is a good
example . . . I am, of course, using the
word in a different sense from A. E.
Housman's or Robert Penn Warren's)
and all other types of poetry are con-
tingent on this basic process; also, it is
the extent of holophrasis and unitive
knowledge that decides to what extent it
is poetry rather than prose, and determines
its category, or its degree of being sensory
equivalent to experience.

Such synthesis is the basis of poetic
language and it is a misuse of terms when
Wordsworth speaks of the language of
common speech, and William Carlos
Williams of the "common" rhythm and
the "common" word to describe poetic
language.[17] The possibilities of rhythm and

17 Wordsworth's *Preface* is psychologically sound
revelation—of certain facts. However, the rough
notation missed the manner by which poetry is
made in the polysynthesism I have described—
polysynthesism being the exact description, the
uniting of many parts into one, into a high degree
of synthesis.

the word are infinite—as many as there are good poems. Their realism and vividness reside within the poem itself. The Imagists' "exact word", a type of commitment which has restricted Anglo-American poetry through Eliot and Auden, and W.C.W.'s "common" word interpreted in various ways by the "Beat Generation" are only examples of the imprecision of words in expository prose.

Ideally, poetry (a) is a synthesis of all facts and angles of commitment within one word, or more practically, one poem. (b) includes movement and counter-movement of all kinds, including rhythm, tone and ideas, shades and pitch of speech, and process of looking. Poetic clarity thus does not depend on the language of common speech, but on the vividness of the thing said. The most highly charged line is the most poetic and *natural* in the sense that is best approximates the condition in 'Nature', not as interpretation, but as a sensory equivalent for it. (Abstract painting and non-objective painting are 'natural' regardless of their language). To stress my point by extension to its logical conclusion, the *ideal* poem should contain, in one word, the stuff of *Kosmos*—the greatest holophrasis possible. If we grasp this idea we shall be able to notice and define more clearly how, within the poem, the word of Pound differs from that of Richard Eberhart's or Louise Bogan's or again from Roethke's or Jean Garrigue's. We should even be able to weigh them in a quantum-ic balance of a great many dimensions as specific materials.

In the Thomas lines I have quoted, the only diagrammatic, 'lapidary' image is "worked on a world of petals" which is a good image for the 'flat' landscape of most "Modern Poetry", or that of a 'flat'

painter, like de Chirico, in his understanding of live space full of movement and energy. With de Chirico or Wallace Stevens, space is regressus ad infinitum, whereas it should be free and unbounded, *expanding* as in Thomas, with the full depth or resonance of Nature. To clarify what I mean, the 'lapidary' or stone image has boundary and definition to it. It has movement in one direction only as in narrative verse of the Jack and Jill sort, finally vanishing to a point:

The brown waves of fog toss up to me
Twisted faces from the bottom of the street,
And tear from a passer-by with muddy skirts
An aimless smile that hovers in the air
And vanishes along the level of the roofs.
Morning at the Window: T. S. ELIOT

The symbol for the 'lapidary' is the stone figure of the Pharoah's daughter who carries in her womb a baby in whose womb is another, thus repeated to infinity. Whereas the poetic word with several outflexions of sound and meaning has no bounding edge to it but is, instead, as G. S. Fraser wrote in a poem, a "round word plopping open out in rings," or as Gail Belaief puts it in this issue "the infinite edge of a moon"—the sort of image that wouldn't appeal to the prosaic engravers on glass of "Modern Poetry". The symbol for this is not the lapidary figure of the princess, or the recession in two parallel mirrors, but the more kinetic one Shri Krishna's foster mother once saw. Noticing the child trying to eat a clod of earth she opened his mouth and was amazed to see a miniature universe in the background and in the foreground the picture of the Gokulam-district, no bounding edges to it—where they were living and in that Gokulam the picture of a little child opening his mouth to his mother. This immense holophrase is a "womb of war"—Dylan Thomas' description of the natural growth of images in his poems[18]—or what to the philosophy of the Vaishesika is the Void when matter takes its own form by simple aggregation as a poem does. It is not only one of recessus ad infinitum but of an expanding universe and there is movement and countermovement in and out of the complex image with the natural tension which exists in a tissue of plant cells or in "the timeless story of that slow combustion which ever consumes and sustains itself in the interior of the spinning atom ... " as Joseph Campbell and Henry Morton Robinson state it well in their skeleton key to *Finnegans Wake*. Dylan Thomas' images and the larger image of the poem have this life-tension. The roughest description of this 'pure' poetic process *which is the primary one from which the other types are derived* would be a cylinder filled with a mixture of gases, the molecules being the words of the poem, and the mass of enclosed gas its apparent body, what some people mistake to be the technique and others its images. The molecules which are elastic and in ceaseless motion collide with each other and off the walls of the containing vessel. They are speeded up or slowed down and tension exists between them. If the gaseous matter were of several kinds with countless fusions, new polarities and manifestations of new forms (through the passing of energy through it) it would approximate to the basic phenomenon of the poem. Even this simple American version of a *haiku* by Elizabeth Gilbert I was handed the other day has the tension and movement of the pure poetic process because of polarities and fusions which create a large meaningful whole:

Cool and moist as ice,
The summer's wide red laughter—
Watermelon slice.

So that we may not be stuffy, learned and precious about poetry I may as well add that our youngest contributor also knows that polarities and identities and fusion into a whole, a "story", make up the poem or Reality:

---

[18]"A poem by me needs a host of images. I make one image—though make is not the word; I let, perhaps, an image be 'made' emotionally in me and then apply to it what intellectual and critical forces I possess; let it breed another, let that image contradict the first; make of the third image, bred out of the two together, a fourth contradictory image, and let them all, within my imposed formal limits, conflict. Each image holds within it the seed of its own destruction, and my dialectical method, as I understand it, is a constant building up and breaking down of the images which come out of the central seed, which is itself destructive and constructive at the same time . . . The life in any poem of mine cannot move concentrically round a central image, the life must come out of the centre; an image must be born and die in another; and any sequence of my images must be a sequence of creations, recreations, destructions, contradictions. . . . Out of the inevitable conflict of images—inevitable, because of the creative, recreative, destructive and contradictory nature of the motivating centre, the womb of war—I try to make that momentary peace which is a poem."—Thomas in a letter to Henry Treece. Thomas has been accused of a preoccupation with death and sex. A less 'discursive' reading of his poetry will show an immense, overwhelming preoccupation with Birth and Life rather than with death—a rereading of his famous "death" poem "Do not go gentle into that good night" will show that every phrase, every line, is concerned with Life and not death:
Do not go gentle into that good night,
Old age should burn and rave at close of day;
Rage, rage against the dying of the light.
"Good night" means 'good', not death; "Rage, rage against the dying of the light" is an affirmation of life.
Wild men who caught and sang the sun in flight,
And learn, too late, they grieved it on its way .
"Grieved" is what they should *not* have done. He speaks of men "who see with blinding sight", always of the Positive, living rage denying there is a death. And there is no sex *per se* in Thomas' poetry, any more than there is 'wine' in Khayyam's quatrains.

There is a mouth
That we can see
There is a nose
That we can have
There is a pair of glasses
Lying in a deck chair
And that is the end of the story.

SARAH SYMONS (Age 6)

To carry on with the analogy, the more highly organized poetic process would be to have each molecule, or at least some of them, a complex Sarah story. This is the reason that the most highly worked and polished poems—what I called Poetry in a Grey Flannel Suit in PLNY No. 2, the poetry of English tea and muffins germane to the *Ladies' Home Journal,* are not necessarily of much interest as poetry. In Thomas' lines, however, the polarities, tensions and resolutions as in our symbol of the spinning atom have a much greater resonance in Nature.

3.

Holophrasis or wholephrasing of sense (and we must bear in mind that the opposite process is also happening) occurs naturally in poetry between specific words, phrases and narrative lines. In the Thomas lines I have quoted, the life of the bulb is holophrased with "doom", unravelling spring, "bright as her spinning wheels" with "colic" etc. The bulb and spring are no longer just that. Similarly whole phrases are telescoped into a single idea— "beginning with doom in the bulb", with "My man of leaves and bronze root", for instance—and since it happens throughout the lines, all of them become one idea. As for the opposite process, there are new polarities created and preserved in lifelike tension—for example the spring unravelling the springing marvels creates the

new image of the child's toy, which later develops into "the metal phantom".

Such fusions of narrative lines are of brief duration, any number of them maculating the poem, or long, running through the entire body of the poem. Fusion of two or more lines of narrative to the poem's close occurs in many poems, one example, a purely interlinear one, being e.e. cummings' poem No. XIV in Part One of *is 5.*

this man is o so
Waiter
this;woman is
please shut that
the pout And affectionate leer . . .[19]

There is the *Dvisandhana* style in Sanskrit which may relate the tale of the *Ramayana* along with the life-story of the poet's patron or the linguistic holophrasis of Pound in the epic *Cantos*—to describe it as Pound meant it, the poem as one word—which is paralleled by poems which may be read in either Sanskrit or Kannada. Then there is the 'purely' poetic holophrasis of the three levels of meaning (at least) in Dante's epic *Commedia*: the narrative of the journey itself, the spiritual autobiography and the larger allegory of the Christian's life in this world. In Sanskrit, the Saptasandhana style has, I am told, seven narratives of the lives of as many great men. Though extreme, it also is an example of the many kinds of unions poetic language carries, which the language of science cannot. I cannot think offhand of a poem with several lines of narrative, so I quote an early poem of my own. Telegraphesing it in wartime London, I was conscious of five locales: a fire-torn street, the beach

---

[19] *Collected Poems,* (Harcourt, Brace).

at Hastings, a London bedroom, a maternity hospital and a South Indian village with cottages, roots, the monsoon, and a temple image of Lakshmi sprung in her beauty from the froth of the ocean holding the thousand-petalled kamala (lotos) and later born out of the *kamala* and as Sita in the *Ramayana* "by her own will, the mistress of the worlds, in a beautiful field opened up by the plough," Chanchala or Lola, the fickle—the existentialist state. Loka-matha—"mother of the world", Indira and Jaladhi-jha "Ocean-born" (out of the flux) :

INVOCATION TO LAKSHMI[20]

Where the Woman droops by the catastrophe
The sun hangs beads and the traffic flows
On. She is melting.

She, the mother of us all, the golden
Six-handed mother is melting
Flowing into the sand.

Hold us in your liquid tears
And let us grow like the bulrush
Speared to the sky—

The vast tent. Hung with stars
Dust, jewels, the splendid gape
Of the disrobing morning.

    The statues on the beach are flesh and
      blood
    Nerved to their sex
    And changing hours.

    Weep big eye into the round
    Of the hollow day.

The rains will come with the stinging thorn
And the ninth month wave
Hurled to the heart

Of the mud-house. Wet, dry, round
We shall be washed
With the morning

And cockburst. Weep Mother into the lake
Into the pool, the sound, the flowers
The chaos of hours.

Bind us in the pool of tears
With the splendid rose
Of the morning.

    Mixed to the roots, the fire, the rain:
    The falling dust;

    Heavy with your proffered tears
    O make us grow.

The use of the 'exact' words for making poetry is, in a way, my theme, though ideally (and this may distort intention and the type of experience to be conveyed) my 'exact' words will initially be large agglutinative masses of significance—like Dylan Thomas' or Hopkins' or the Big Word of the backdrop in the theatre—to make the most meaningful poem possible that is consonant with direct communication and poetic clarity. To take the idea to its logical conclusion, the most 'exact' word would be the complete image of the poem or finished work itself. This would give meaning to the 'collective voice' on any subject—the anthologist's method— affording us the circular view. Dylan Thomas' or Hopkins' words are, of course, very specially their own and a reading of them would illustrate my point. To illustrate it from another type of poet, here are some lines from the Persian *Rubaiyat* of Omar Khayyam which John Yohannan points to as the best known poem of recent times in his *Treasury of Asian Literature*.[21] I should add that I think of Khayyam as (in "at its simplest binary" terms) Sufi Adorer of the Adored (in 'lapidary' words —Lover or Poet) in the same tradition as Rumi and Hafiz, the latter compared to Shakespeare by Ralph Waldo Emerson as a "pure poet", and by John Payne, his translator, to Dante and Shakespeare ; and

---

[20] *The Penguin Anthology of Religious Verse,* ed. by Norman Nicholson.

[21] Mentor Books.

that a re-reading of Khayyam's quatrains, in view of what I have described to be the pure poetic process, reveals that his "wine" has little resemblance to the actual substance since it is equated with what I have termed the universal flux of energy: to him God and Life-Force. This is as it should be since in Sufi thought, love, wine and rose-petals like those of the lotos and soma in India—*madhu* in Sanskrit, mead in English) are symbols of the spirit of man one with everything around him, aware of their unity and interdependence — desire, stillness, passion, appearance, disappearance, Creation, destruction, past, present and future—up to the Re-entry and Return from the Creative Principle or Energy (in the Joycean, Viconian and Indian cycles) of which scientists, more than "modern" poets, have brought us some reports, peripheral though they are:

Here with a Loaf of Bread beneath the Bough
A Flask of Wine, a Book of Verse[22]—and Thou
　　Beside me singing in the Wilderness—
And wilderness is Paradise enow.

And lately, by the Tavern Door agape,
Came stealing through the Dusk an Angel Shape
　　Bearing a Vessel on his Shoulder; and
He bid me taste of it; and 'twas the Grape!

It will be seen that the words which breathe and live in the clear air of eternal snows or Lawrence of Arabia's "desert", Vaihesika philosophy's the Void, Whitman's *Leaves of Grass* or in lapidary language My Love for Her (in women Him) are large agglutinative masses of significance, as they are throughout the poem, which gives it its imperishable form —which we cannot find in the trivia of "Modern" poets. "Bread" conjures up

───────────
22 Whitman's *Leaves of Grass*.

infinities, wheatfields, life etc.; "Bough", as in Chinese brushwork, suggests the whole landscape up to the horizon and Refuge, Abode, Dwelling within the Beloved etc. . . . , holophrasis of a high poetic order. The *Rubaiyat* is also a suitable example for the poem itself as the best poetic image. As in the ghazals (two-line verses) of India, each quatrain is a complete poem, a complete image, dancing in the enormous room of the *Rubaiyat* as a greater wholephrasing and sensory equivalent to experience and not its discursive interpretation. (The systematization and methodicity of the verses were imposed on them by Fitzgerald so that it is only by scrambling them again that we get near to the original. But even in translation, the shape is more mouvemente, more dramatic and vigorous than the lapidary form of "Modern Poetry", the difference between the Elgin marbles and Jacques Lipchitz or Alexander Calder). The images are not 'lapidary' but what I have termed "expanding" with full resonance in Nature as if they are quanta of energy, integrated, related and in movement in the larger energy unit of our symbol of the atom or miniature solar system and therefore life-like and vivid as in the Herbert Morris poem in this issue—the differentiation of undifferentiatedness (though the literary figures are large materials), the electronic picture as in the music of Louis and Bebe Barron—Whitman's *Leaves of Grass* or Yehudi Menuhin's multi-dimensional image for Indian music—that of the thatched cottages of India rising out of the earth and then returning to it in natural flux. That is the pure poetic process, the very purpose of poetic language as opposed to the prosaic. The "expanding" image is what Western scholars of Persian metres have

alled that "certain pleasing ambiguity at
he very base of . . . poetry". In these life-
ke characteristics and vividness of quanta
f energy in balance and movement I think
es the universal appeal and permanency
f appeal of both Khayyam and Thomas,
r Kalidasa's *Shakuntala*, the drama of
he Fatal Ring.

To refer to the Grover Amen lines once
gain, it is noteworthy that while the
American poet discovers the general,
Nature's pandemoniac flux and multiplicity, in the particular of the "orange",
Rajendra Shah finds it in the particular
of the "earthenware" which promises
him the general once more on the last day
of Creation—which fact should prove
satisfactory to Jaspers' *Existenzphilosophie* uncertain of firm ground beneath
us after the dissolution of Existenz or
Creation. We saw that poets are aware
that all objects and states are interchangeable and unified in the general flux of
energy—as it is only possible in a synthesis of modern sciences, the syncretist
sciences of India (examples: Nobel Prize
winner J. C. Bose's plant physiology, the
ars amatoria) or *within the poem*—which
therefore makes it more Reality than
Illusion—a different concept of the poem
from the historical materialism of "Modern
Poetry" and its best available interpretation, Caudwell's *Illusion and Reality*. In
the Rajendra Shah poem however—as in
Finnegans Wake where the book teeters
at the dissolution on "A way a lone a last
a long the" and after the active silence
begins the time cycle once again with the
first sentence of the book "riverrun,
past Eve and Adam's . . . "—Creation
itself is a state which changes! Within
the 'unified field' of the poem, the
"earthenware pot" (thus in the original)
is the poetic word for all the dissolving

phenomena of Creation which as in the
continuous change of water to vapour
and back to water again, will appear once
again:

LAST DAY[23]

In the house which was full of din,
  in the dusty courtyard
I kept the small baggage of the last age
And then the misty sad sun's
First ray shone in the sky; and that direction
  awoke in tremor.

The neighbouring big ones living asked my
  welfare,
The housewives looked at me and got talking,
Out of curiosity children encircled me,
The dog barked for a minute and then
  smelt my feet.

Locks were unlocked, the doors made a moan,
Their bodies were close-bound, in a motionless
  condition.
Then the stale air from within, finding way,
Ran out. As if a dead soul rose unfettered.

I went in the house and the darkness
  covered me for a moment.
Then as if lit in a pencil of light I saw
  the old earthenware.

    Tr. from the *Gujerati* by P. MACHWE

As to how these alchemies of "orange"
and "earthenware" are possible, only the
poems may explain convincingly. Any
amount of 'explication' will not give us
the same sensory effects. What may be
done, however, is to find other sensory
equivalents for the poems. This last statement is not extraordinary since, as I have
already hinted and as will become abund-
antly clear as we proceed, the poem, like
'Nature' herself, is an energy unit as
Stevens suggested in *The Glass of Water*.
It is the microcosmic unit of energy of
the macrocosmic unit of energy which is
ENERGY and THAT is endless. Or to
express it in a less 'lapidary' manner,

---

[23] Indian Number of *Poetry: A Magazine of
Verse.* Jan. 1959. Guest Editor: Tambimuttu.

poetry is the interpenetration of several macrocosmic units with the microcosmic, as in Indian mythology. So, in spite of all the discursive explications possible to explain the poem's chemistry, the most direct way of understanding it, as we do *actually* understand it, is to think of each word as a quantum of energy (which it is on a soundtrack) or a particle (as in the Quantum theory) with a kind of periodic wave under particular conditions, including those necessary for *continuity*, and then we sense that "orange" becomes transferred to the greater Energy again in the poem's 'hyperspace' of many dimensions—'hyperspace' being the term used in an extension of the Quantum Theory where the poem breathes and has a life of its own and where its rasa or taste (literally) resides. In the case of "earthenware" it effects two changes, first into the greater Energy and then into the particular energies of 'Nature'. Because this is the character of the pure poetic process —aggregation of energy units into a large organic whole—it will be a simple matter to take a particular poem and replace most of the words in it with other words and arrive at another poem with the same cohesive wholeness and perhaps a different meaning. Since it will only be an academic exercise I shall refrain at present from actual illustration.

After this description of the pure poet's method, it will be seen that although men of the physical sciences and *Existenzphilosophie* and painters of Abstract Expressionism in America like Kline, Okada, Stamos, Still, Rothko or de Kooning have begun to think in cosmic or universal terms, the mostly sterile poets of "Modern Poetry" and their interpreters have not. It seems that Ovid in his Metamorphoses was nearer to the bone of poetry than the

syllable-counting and common-speech rendering poets of today:

Now I shall tell you of things that change
  new being
Out of old: since you, O Gods, created
Mutable arts and gifts, give me the voice
To tell the shifting story . . .[24]

The translator, Horace Gregory, comments on this with regard to painting in this issue:

The landscape shimmered, yet in the
  foreground—Look!
A rose sprang at his side, flushed
  drunken-red,
Stared at him with an almost human head
Swayed closer, stirred its lips as if to speak

The rose was cultivated as himself;
Above them rode the sun and shrill bird-calls
The painter threw his brushes to the ground
And to the rose he shouted, "False,
  false false!"

and it is worth noting that Arthur Gregory in his poem in this issue is also aware of the metamorphoses that along with whole phrasing is the fabric of poetry, though I cannot agree with his modern Christian concept of being "humble" with life since it is truly with pride that a poet sings of metamorphoses including his identity with the Supreme Energy which he realizes is within his own breast, for, as in Hindu marriage, the idea of superior and inferior does not enter, but rather identity not equality: *the Self becoming the Self* which generates what is termed aesthetic emotion in art:

How good to know there is no loss,
That life is beyond harm in those
who are humble before it, who honor it . . .

That self and divine revelation which Dante described in his *Vita Nuova*:

---

[24] The Beginning of *The Metamorphoses* (**Viking Press**).

. . . at the beginning of her ninth year, the Glorious Lady of my mind, who was called Beatrice by many who knew not what to call her, appeared to me, and I near the end of my ninth year saw her. She appeared to me clothed in a most noble color, a modest and becoming crimson, and she was girt and adorned in such wise as befitted her very youthful age. At that instant I say truly that the spirit of life, which dwells in the most secret chamber of the heart, began to tremble with such violence that it appeared fearfully in the least pulses, and trembling, said these words: "Behold a god stronger than I, who coming shall rule over me!

4.

Imagism began as a private joke, as I suspect the Beat Generation did, to judge from Kenneth Rexroth's articles in *Evergreen Review No. 2* and *New World Writing No. 11*: "Social disengagement . . voluntary poverty—these are powerful virtues and may pull them through, but they are not the virtues we tried to inculcate—rather they are the opposite . . . " The Imagist manifesto itself, published in 1915, was not even new in ideas. In 1800 Wordsworth had treated its six points at greater length and with greater psychological insight in his Preface to the *Lyrical Ballads*: the use of everyday speech, free-verse ("some of the most interesting parts of the best poems will be found to be strictly the language of prose when prose is well-written") the exact word, particulars, freedom in the choice of subject and concentration. Imagism with its narrow commitment was redundant, since poets like F. S. Flint, G. Fletcher and D. H. Lawrence had already reacted to the changed environment from Victorian times and expressed themselves in the accepted manner. Con-

rad Aiken and Edith Sitwell came temporarily under its influence but soon abandoned it. Pound too disowned it soon after its inception, prescribing the Bay State Hymn Book and 'Amygism'[25] among other things for a remedy. But no critic, as far as I am aware, has made sufficiently clear the radical changes Imagism (the clear evocation of a material thing through the image, as distinct from Symbolism, the use of symbols which stir subconscious associations) brought to the art of poetry. The entire body of "Modern Poetry" (of "perfect" objectivity with its natural consequence of a lack of poetic focus) practised the thin, dry 'edifying' evolvement of Imagism so noticeable in Eliot for its characteristic "Modern" look. It is only when one has nothing truly poetic to say that the manner, the "way of putting it", becomes an overly critical concern. Gautama Buddha put it rather well to the Brahmin who was concerned with the prescribed form, the outward technique, of the Burnt-offering:

> I pile no wood for altars;
> I kindle a flame within me, . . .
> My heart the hearth, the flame
> the dompted self.[26]

What "The New Moderns" did was to abandon most such constricting viewpoints. Trustful of their own intuitions and spontaneous convictions, they did not construct poems which the prevailing literary theory dictated as being most appropriate. They were unafraid of the telling adjective, of impulses, of 'feeling' and even love which the modern dehumanization of art had made unfashion-

---

[25] Amy Lowell is meant, and the *Massachusetts Bay Psalm Book*, first book printed in North America (1640).

[26] Tr. by Ananda K. Coomaraswamy in his *Hinduism and Buddhism*.

able. Risking the stigma of naivete, it took the editorial courage of a Walter De la Mare to compile anthologies of love poems. The words of Edgar Lee Masters are pertinent to the poetry of analysis as well as the younger poets of today:

What is this I hear of sorrow and weariness,
Anger, discontent and drooping hopes? . . .
Life is too strong for you—
It takes life to love Life.

To put it another way, we need the absence of the type of analytical hostility William Earle speaks of to know genuine poetic commitment.

Love poems, especially, and there were very few of them, were bound to look ridiculous in the new language. It was only Auden, the arch rationalist romantic, the link between "Modern Poetry" and "The New Moderns", who could dash off a love poem and write with feeling:

> Lay your sleeping head, my love,
> Human on my faithless arm;
> Time and fevers burn away
> Individual beauty from
> Thoughtful children, and the grave
> Proves the child ephemeral;
> But in my arms till break of day
> Let the living creature lie,
> Mortal, guilty, but to me
> The entirely beautiful.

In the age of analysis and the material thing clearly evoked (Auden's lines show the virtues) love was squeamish and forbidden subject matter through the lack of definition for an amorphous word in a developing language. In the groping towards a poetic language for precise statement of subtlest perceptions and resolutions, but botched with Modern Man's *raison*, the word did not have the prestige of an ancient tradition which invested this word with the highest sensibility, the tenderest emotion, most devoted attachment and supreme revelation, where the word would have its exact meaning in philosophic concepts, becoming the exact material image, and exact symbol. Had this view been as clear to the "Modern" poets, they might have touched universals, and therefore greatness. Furthermore, the word with the sentiments attached to it, would not have appeared an amorphous one unsuitable for modern poetic use, but would have had the authority of a known scientific fact. In the dehumanization of poetry, the Modern Poets had lost the meaning of love and along with it their audience. Known exactly to Eastern thought and to William Blake, it was not revealed to Modern Poetry even through faith, much less through knowledge, and those statements to fill the lack, like John Betjeman and Geoffrey Taylor's *English Love Poems*, missed the meaning of love . . . of the entire process.

Poetry as love is the most exact statement. Even hate and "disaffiliation" (the "Beat Generation's") are also attachment. Love describes the merging of the poet into the absolute of poetry, where the contradictions and multiplicities do not exist. It represents commitment to direction, objects, phenomena: reason for the poem's very substance and meaning. To describe the love poem: it is attachment to the slightest gesture and physical sensation, the loftiest spiritual goal, every tiny detail: the hour and the season, the trees outside:

> This fruit has fire within it,
>   Pomona, Pomona
> No glass is clearer than are the globes
>   of this flame
> What sea is clearer than the pomegranate
>   body holding the flame?
>   Pomona, Pomona[27]
>   LXXIV, *The Pisan Cantos*: EZRA POUND

---

[27] Old Italian goddess of fruit trees.

. . . the texture of these usual days

                        . . . hands
that have held earth and leaves
and opened doors into the common
    house . . .

a girl
woken into herself
And simply now,
stroking the cat or lifting
from the black oven
simples of meat or bread . . .
                    Robin Skelton

Betjeman and Taylor, however, not understanding that the interpenetration of matter and spirit, the sacred and profane, *is
love*, said: "We have not included in our
definition of love poetry poems expressing
the love of man for God, nor have we
included impassioned expressions of the
lusts of the flesh," which omissions cancel
forthwith the possible description and
meaning of love. To abstract the purely
physical and the purely spiritual from a
third kind of love (we do not know what,
if anything, is meant) is a fallacy.[28] The
difficulty here is the imprecision of language. While the Technical Philosophers
of today delimit the meaning of words
in five-hundred-word articles on the bald
or closely-shaved meaning of a word, what
is really needed is the *expansion* of the
meanings of words through poetry to

proved by the anthology itself:

THE BACHELOR'S SONG

How happy a thing were a wedding
  And a bedding,
If a man might purchase a wife
  For twelvemonth and a day;
But to live with her all a man's life,
  For ever and for ay,
Till she grow as gray as a cat,
  Good faith, Mr. Parson, I thank you for that.
      Thomas Flatman (1637-1688)

make language descriptive of what we
really think and feel, to create a modern
biological style: a wholephrasing of our
total consciousness and needs: the centripetal (and centrifugal) symbol for which
is the poet Rumi's founding of the colorful
order of whirling dervishes who placed
themselves at the perfect centre of the
divine order of things, through the holophrasis of dance and song. This is precisely the task which was beyond the
limited and a-poetic use of language by
the Imagists and the "Modern Poets".

"The New Moderns", however, preferred the poetic word to the 'exact'
scientific word, the word of analytic hostility, and thus evolved a revealing biological style—they were Objective as well
as Subjective, using language poetically,
and not merely for journalistic exposition.
It is true that science and philosophy also
reveal. It is equally true that unless these
processes preserve the same holophrastic
method as great poetry (which is organically sound), they describe partial truths
only.

As a result of such compression by
"The New Moderns" the poetry of the
day, of the chiefly rational and objective,
became warm and evocative, imaginative
and incantatory. Poetry became once more
the revealing synthesis of experience and
not its specialised analysis. The rarefied
atmosphere of Eliot's "Let us go then, you
and I,/When the evening is spread out
against the sky" gave place to Thomas'
"The force that through the green fuse
drives the flower". The emasculation of
poetic vitality and spontaneity gave way
to writing in 'depth', with instincts, feeling
and thinking marshalled behind it. They
were not, of course, absent from "Modern
Poetry". The difference was one of
balance.

It was for the restoration of a proper balance to "Modern Poetry" at a period when it had deteriorated into journalese and superficial 'exactness' that surrealism, with its emphasis on subconcious impulses and spontaneity, itself a limited commitment, seemed important to the twentieth century. Likewise uninhibited and little sifted recording of the passing states of consciousness in an anarchist framework seems vitally important to those who have been called the "beat" generation. While awaiting the arrival of a "beat" poet of stature, and few of them are even worthy of print, it is sufficient to say that, irrespective of achievement (in poetry, changes in "attitude" precede those of actual poetic achievement), the general direction is on the lines of a further 'breakthrough' in modern poetry as practiced by "The New Moderns", supported by this magazine in the *Poetry London Yearbooks of Jazz* (1946 and 1947), and the sponsoring of books by Hugues Panassié. Whatever the poetic value of the combination of poetry and jazz (the pure form in which each finds wholephrasing is hampered by the other and a combination changes the medium—to jazzetry, as in the poetry in the anthologies) it was a possible step towards giving poets a paying trade in our times in the theatre. Another aid was 'poster poetry' in the *Poetry London* Ballad Books (some of it set to music and issued on records) which is being currently revived in England.

With great vitality and spontaneity, qualities which made it seem important to the age of analysis and petrified forms, jazz describes existential attitudes filled with urgency and passion, opposing the creative act to a subterranean state of existence born of anxiety. The world of jazzmen and 'beat' poets is identical. In a world of insecurity and fear the creative moment without attachment to the past or future has an immediate value to both performers and audience. Shiftless within the social context of creative urge and repression, they must question all concepts of good and 'bad' just as the religious mystics and the poets do. These include 'middle class' attitudes (in the English sense meaning 'middling' as opposed to the aristocratic or 'full' and the "rustic" in Wordsworth's sense[29]) as well as the basic puritanism of modern ideas which results in the moving but finical and overworked 'lapidary' art of the best known "Modern" poets which, in its analytical, commentating and expository style, resembles the form and substance of prose. Marianne Moore puts it rather well in her well-known poem *Poetry*:

I too dislike it: there are things that are important beyond all this fiddle . . .
    . . . One must make a distinction
however: when dragged into prominence
  by half poets, the result is not poetry,
nor till the poets among us can be
'literalists of
the imagination'—above
  insolence and triviality and can present
for inspection, imaginary gardens with
  real toads in them, shall we have it.

These "Modern" poets' art is different from the English poet Kathleen Raine's whose lines, irrespective of contemporary myths about 'poetic stature', have that undefinable quality called by the Indians

---

29 "Accordingly, such a (rustic) language, arising out of repeated experience and regular feelings, is a more permanent, and a far more philosophical language, than that which is frequently substituted for it by Poets, who think that they are conferring honour upon themselves and their art in proportion as they separate themselves from the sympathies of men, and indulge in arbitrary and capricious habits of expression, in order to furnish food for fickle tastes and fickle appetites of their own creation." Preface to *Lyrical Ballads*.

rasa[30], 'the essence of poetry' which is not forced(for which alone they read it instead of tracts on the nature of man and society) :

THE HYACINTH[31]

Time opens in a flower of bells
the mysteries of its hidden bed,
the altar of the ageless cells
whose generations never have been dead.

So flower angels from the holy head,
so on the wand of darkness bright
    worlds hang.
Love laid the elements at the vital root,
unhindered out of love these flowers
    spring.

The breath of life shapes darkness into
    leaves,
each new born cell
drinks from the star-filled well
the dark milk of the sky's peace.

The hyacinth springs on a dark star—
I see eternity give place to love.
It is the world unfolding into flower
the rose of life, the lily and the dove.

The 'middle class' attitude and the basic puritanism in modern ideas I have referred to accounts for the sophomoric use of certain unprintable words, which is after all a matter of tone, context and point of view. Through the path of 'sin' or the unpuritanical in Western terms, Eastern mystics like Krishna, or more recently Ramakrishna, showed the way of full realisation of man's potential. In

sound, the jazzmen extoll the physical aspects of sex, pleasure, ecstasy, just as Shri Jayadeva's 12th Century poem the *Gita Govinda,* the chronicle of love of Radha and Shri Krishna, does, symbolsing the quest of the soul for the divine. To quote from the poetess Muddu Palani (c. 1765) :

With beads of perspiration on her cheeks
    that shone like mirrors,
With the musk-mark on her forehead
    melted and streaming down;
With the bracelets adorning her wrists
    tinkling time,
And from her eyes' fountains a great
    radiance pouring;
Under the burden of her breasts,
    her slender waist swaying,
Stormy like ocean, her bosom, with
    infinite love and her waist-knot every
    now and then becoming undone.
Her shoulder blades shining, and plaited
    hair dancing by her hips.
Her every sigh like the breeze, rising up
    to high heaven,
Did Radha with oil pressed from champak
    flowers massage her Krishna
To her heart's content.

From *Radhika Santhwanam.*
Tr. from the Telugu by TAMBIMUTTU
and R. APPALASWAMY.[32]

In the same way, Jazz is the affirmation of life-force, though it does not possess the high spiritual or intellectual orchestration which invests the physical with the enduring qualities of the spiritual in *Gita Govinda,* or in the guidebooks to the transcending of oneself through sex and pleasure, such as *Kamasutra* or *Kokoka Shastram.* Even so, the utterance of jazz has seemed important to some young poets like Allen Ginsberg, and older painters—Stuart Davis in *Something on the Eight Ball* or *The Paris Bit*—Mondrian in *Broadway Boogie-Woogie.* It

---

[30]4.xi.59 Tonight Robert Frost speaking at the Twenty-Fifth Anniversary Dinner of the American Academy of Poets explained in his homely language that poetry was "the quintessence of all sciences" (an expression once read somewhere which still haunted him) and "the phrase of angels". I think he meant *rasa,* without English equivalent—termed "sentiment" by Western scholart and "emotions" by G. H. Ranade in his *Hindusthani Music.* I think it is nearer to taste, meant quite gastronomically—not exactly "food for the mind" but for the entire man.

[31] *Stone and Flower* (Editions Poetry London).

[32] *India Love Poems* (Peter Pauper Press).

pointed to the physical and primitive needs hidden behind social and cultural conventions. It pointed to the reality of vital values as opposed to the culturalist, which has been my recurrent theme and which Ortega has treated at length in *The Theme of Our Time;* to the imagination and creative subconscious promptings shaped into living forms. In the orgiastic and orgasmic it extolled movement and vitality, which, at the creative moment, are the qualities most admired by jazzmen and the 'hipster', the beatific of non-commitment, 'cool' with his own flask in his hip pocket.

It may be that 'beat' philosophy is simply the Bohemian in every American businessman gone out of hand, a bourgeois fantasy confined to the coffee-house a bawdy joke against conformity. However, it is certainly within "The New Moderns" in several respects, including the emphasis on vitality and spontaneity. To quote from what I have previously written about "The New Moderns": "The mission of living poets is . . . the demonstration that culture, reason, art are biological functions also, and as such cannot be solely directed by objective laws or laws independent of life, but subject to the laws of life.

"We should find that objective standards of beauty are not enough and that these should conform to vitality, localised within the biological scheme, and surrendered to spontaneity":

FESTINA LENTE.
(Hasten Slowly)

Qnhat? gif Art bee slowe: swetelie let yt growe

Als wexeth tendre Gress neath Goddys smalë Raine;

Bot of cryegg, strybyg, roryg, godyg, drybyg,

Wexeth nocht saif Dust y-laft upõ ye Plaine . . .

                    H. LE SCOT, *Canticŭ ffiliorŭ* BESELEEL.

                              [*circa* MCCCC.

We toil, we beg, migrate across the seas,
We worship, rule, make music, erect our songs;
All this to this wretched body of ours,
Which tortures us for a measure of rice.[33]

From the Tamil of poetess Avveyiar (1st Century A.D. according to the British scholars, but immemorial according to Tamil chronicles).

---

[33] The Greeks, who were the greatest intermediaries in the trade of India with Europe, borrowed many Tamil names, which have found their way into most of the European languages. Among these are the Greek words *oryza* from the Tamil *arisi*, rice; *karpion* from *karuva*, cinnamon; *ziggiberos* from *injiver*, ginger; *peperi* from *pippali*, pepper; *beryllos* from *vaidurya*, beryl and so on." —H. A. Popley in his *The Sacred Kural* (The Tamil Veda) quoting from Vincent Smith's *The Oxford History of India*. The word iron is derived from *ir*, "dark". The Tamils worked the D. Mushet process patented in 1800, used in Ceylon in 4th Century B.C. (Sir Robert Hadfield).

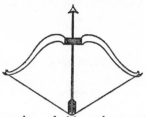

Grasping the bow the great engine of things known by hearing (*shruti*)
Fix in it the constantly concentered arrow of well hammered together Reflection
Drawing it with the concentered mind filled with THAT
Pierce (keep moving) Beautiful Young (becoming) Life the Imperishing as
        the Mark (Love).
The triple lettered (infinite charactered) word Aum YES[26] is the bow

The arc (horn-Tamil kombu)   of the U in the middle the engine
Let fly the arrow which is the self
The infinite poem (ENERGY) is said to be the mark
With attachment (Desire) is it to be penetrated;
Become one with IT as arrow in the mark

                Mundaka Upanishad ii, 3, 4, in Now-Is or Now-ese
                (To be concluded in PLNY No. 5.)

7.xii.59   TAMBIMUTTU

---

[34] As Max Muller correctly pointed out in *The Vedanta Philosophy* (Susil Gupta, Calcutta) the derivation of Brahman (Word or Supreme Energy) and *Om* (YES, in Tamil) are only possible from prae-Sanscrit or Tamil since they are meaningless terms in Sanskrit. "Much, for instance, that is said in the Upanishads about the sacred syllable *Om*, seems to my mind mere twaddle at least in its present form. I cannot bring myself to give specimens, but you have only to read the beginning of the *Chhandogya Upanishad*, and you will see what I mean. It is quite possible that originally there was some sense in the all the nonsense that we find in the Upanishads about the sacred syllable *Om*. This *Om* may originally have had a meaning, it may be a contraction of a former *avam* and this *avam* (which we have in Tamil, see Gnana Prakaser, *An Etymological and Comparative Lexicon of the Tamil Language*) may have been a prehistoric pronominal stem, pointing to distant objects, while *ayam* pointed to nearer objects. In that case, *avam* may have become the affirmative particle *Om*, just as the French *oui* arose from hoc illud. And thus we read in the *Chhandogya Upanishad* 'That syllable is a syllable of permission, for whenever we permit anything we say *Om*, yes.' If, then, *Om* meant originally that, like *Amen*, it may have assumed a more general meaning, something like *tat sat*, and that it may have been used as representing all that human language can express. Thus in the *Maintrayna Upanishad*, after it had been said there was one Brahman without words, and a second, a Word-Brahman, we are told that the word is the syllable *Om*. This sounds absurd, unless we admit that this *Om* was meant at first as a symbol of all speech, even as a preacher might say that all language was *Amen, Amen.*" Compare *Amen* to Arabic *Amin*. Now my point is that in Tamil *Om* does actually mean YES. As Gnana Prakaser has pointed out in his Lexicon it is extremely difficult in a mainly inflexional or transformed language such as Sanskrit to discover the earliest form of the word—*tad* or *tat*, 'that' becomes *tesam, han* 'to strike' becomes *jaghana*, whereas it is easy enough with a language that is mainly agglutinative or terminational like Tamil where the root-word does not change.

Most Indian scholars are now agreed that three-fourths of Indian culture is non-Aryan and predominantly Dravidian or Tamil (see *Race Movement* and *Prehistoric Culture* by S. K. Chatterjee of the University of Calcutta). Whether the Tamils colonised Sumer or the Sumerians colonised the Tamil land of India is for the historians to decide. What I want to disprove is the *divide et impera* of the Viceroys of India translated into actual living conditions in many parts of the modern world. I also want to prove the unity of human experience and of mankind. As the Sumerian cities had a separate god for each one of them, the Tamils had their regional deities according to natural division of land—hill country, forest, pasturage and tillage. *Mayon*, the dark-coloured (Vishnu) and *Seyon*, the red-coloured (Sivam) are indigenous while Indra and Varuna were probably the Vedic ones of the Aryans.

Like the Indo-Aryans and Chinese, the Tamils believed their Veda or Word (scriptures) were 'heard'—*shruti*, i.e. traditional. (Compare Gospel according to St. John, the antiphonal which begins "In the beginning was the Word And the Word was with God). That God is Sivam (Shiva) In all languages, God and Good are synonymous. Sivam means goodness, purity, greatness, love and auspiciousness. Many Indian scholars claim this word to be pure Tamil and Sir Grierson confirms this.

It is interesting that Herodotus says the Tamils (Termilai) came from Crete to civilize Greece and were known as the ancient Lycians, I, 173 (See S. K. Chatterjee, *Modern Review*, Calcutta, Dec. 1924.

Tambimuttu

For Katharine (*Kamala*) Bennett and All True *Sadhakas**

I

The space within the pitcher, filled with sound like
    the whorled chank,
Is the concentered speech of *sattva*,† your words opening
    out in bright rings
In the immeasurable ocean, which is timeless and shoreless.

And did you once merge with that? What was it like,
Was it hot and fiery like your inward-looking eyes? Was it
Beginningless and endless like Shiva's pillar of fire

Interpenetrating the Absolute, the Zero, the Supreme?
Exfoliating, folding, like a water-lily, it is sacrifice lifts us
    up in smoke and flame
We are the instruments, or victims, of the cosmic sacrifice.

Living is action. We can't be without breathing, thinking
    and dreaming,
And actions may have no moral value. But those of *yajnas*,
    the rituals of sacrifice,
Lead us to paramount states, the deities, the most important
    functions of man.

Through your gentle and voluntary acceptance of the
    ritual of sacrifice
You have taken your place in the cosmic symphony,
    as an equal;
The only purpose of your existence is the performance of
    this ritual.

---

*Sadhakas = seekers
† *sattva*: the centripetal tendency towards a centre, towards more cohesion, more concentration, more existence, more reality – towards light, perfection, illumination or divine reality.

260

You are the hearthstone, and your words are the fire,
Your breath is the smoke and your tongue the flame,
Your eyes are the fuel and your ears the sparks:
In this eternal fire we offered ourselves
And you were born.

And was it like that, in the family home, the daily fire,
    of Sarasvati Devi, your mother?
Finally, was it a gong, the cooing of the kokila, the tinkling
    of bells, a flute, a lute, or a bee?
And when the mind was stilled, did you hear the hair-raising
    inner sound?

You grew giddy, but ignoring the inner sound which
    engulfed you
Did you merge with *shadba* – the Principle of the Word,
    and hear the sound
Never before heard, which rises in the heart, pervading all?

You could have told me, but you didn't.

The goddess is the hearth, and Shiva the fire,
Courtship is smoke, and yoni the flame;
The penetration is the fuel, pleasure the sparks:
In this fire the gods sacrifice semen
And the child is born.

II

The space within the pitcher is not separate from the
    space outside:
It was not distinct before the pitcher was made:
It will not be distinct once the pitcher is broken

And is not, therefore, distinct while the pitcher exists.
Tat tvam asi – Thou art That – the extraordinary
    phenomenon
Of the continually expanding form, which sweetly grows

Into the undifferentiated continuum of the Supreme Spirit,
Limitless, undifferentiated, indivisible
The division of space between you and me is only appearance.

You must tell me, when we meet again.

III

I met you briefly, between stops, between this point
  and another,
Before the curtain fell, the scenery was rolled away, and
  the music stilled.
The big drums of the eyes throbbed and nearly broke
  in our ashram

And your answering voice had Manhattan Island trembling:
The buildings collapsed and the boiling streets shot avenues
  into the Hudson
And hot drops fell from the bent lamp-posts that had once
  enshrined you.

You were the crescent of the infant moon, for me,
  on the white-as-milk brow of Shiva.
Return, return, so we may all drink of its *amrita*, when its
  cup is full
In this ashram and future ashrams, the brilliant jewels
  of your steps.

> *We offer fire to fire, fuel to fuel,*
> *Smoke to smoke and flame to flame,*
> *Matter to matter and sparks to sparks:*
> *Into fire do the gods offer you;*
> *And from this searing burning we have seen your person*
> *With the colour of light.*

Note: Anthropomorphic images of Shiva show him with the fifth-day crescent moon on his brow. Its cup is full of *soma*, the sacrificial offering, the power of procreation coexistent with that of dissolution. It is the chalice of semen, the Energy of sublimated Eros, in the fire of sacrifice. *Soma* is also *amrita*, the beverage of the gods, of immortality. Semen in the sacrificial fire (alternative to human sacrifices) itself becomes fire. 'The acts of devouring and being devoured are successive states of everything.' – Giridhara Sharma Chaturvedi in *Shiva Mahima*

The 'Gita Sarasvati' by Tambimuttu

It is believed that Tambimuttu wrote the 'Gita Sarasvati' during the late 1960s while he was living in Cambridge, Massachusetts. One of the earliest drafts is headed 'A Film Script for "Shiva of the Thousand and One Names". Part One: "Creation and Dissolution"'. Another draft exists of a different part of the film script entitled 'Shiva of the Thousand and One Faces' and it appears that only a quarter of the intended complete film script, which was to take the form of an epic dance-drama in the traditional Indian style, may have been written. However, this particular piece, which Tambimuttu later named the 'Gita Sarasvati' after his favourite goddess, Sarasvati, goddess of the arts and of knowledge and learning (a picture of whom riding the 'gander', printed on Indian cloth, hung above Tambimuttu's desk, which many a visitor to his home in Cornwall Gardens, South Kensington, will remember), formed Tambimuttu's credo. It meant a great deal to him, but there were few who knew of its existence. He made several recordings of himself reciting it to different background music, and there were several versions of the typescript. We cannot be absolutely sure what was the final version, but careful comparison has been made of the various texts and the version that appears here is as close, it is believed, as possible to the final version. The following note was found attached to what appears to be one of the earliest drafts:

Before beginning this recording I must state that this is a first draft, and that parts of it are to be elaborated on in the second. This is particularly true about *satchitananda* and the monosyllabic mantra Óm, for the proper understanding of which by the general public a background of Indian metaphysics is needed. As for the form of unity of structure of the narrative, I must add that the ending of the first part of the film has not yet been written.

J.W.

Tambimuttu

Gita Sarasvati
A Theology for Modern Science
The Creation and Dissolution of *Kosmos*

In the beginning was God (*Prajapātir vai idaṁ āsīt*);
And with him was the Word (*Tasya vāg dvitiya āsīt*);
And the Word is God (*Vāg vai paramaṁ Brahma*).

With the cracking glacier sound, with thunder of Time's hooves on
    the mountain
The great horse of the sacrifice is in the mountain.
The timeless sound of the conch-shell is in the intricate ear,

With the roaring sound, *haṁ*, so speaks the Word, the Veda,
The multifoliate tree of Shiva's Energy, which is woman, *Sarasvati*,
Whose every branch, bough and spray is the ancient vernation of our
    knowledge;

Green and quivering on the mountain top
Half in green leaf and half in flame
Like the Celtic tree of the *Mabinogion* –

The Welsh Word by the broad river of Time
Pulsing and bright as a shaft of light to the Void, Shiva –
The poetic word, with several overlays of meaning
Not closely cropped and shaved for discursive or journalistic use
Colliding with another in the sentence of poetry,
Colliding, sounding, detonating, with several outflexions of meaning
Which criss-cross and outflex again, creating new words
Which repeat the process to infinity, to create the poem.

The poetic word should contain large, agglutinative masses of
    meaning.
Ideally, it would be the whole poem, dancing with other poems to
    make a sentence.
The Word, the Word, Veda, Veda . . . the immense word

In which are telescoped all sounds, meanings, forms;
In the minuscule, the great word of the backdrop in the theatre, the
    mountain, the prairie,
The great Word of the poem and epic, and, then, the immense Word
    of the Universe

Leaves of grass sum of the books and learning in libraries,
The seed-word (*bīja*), the semen of Shiva (*bījavan*), in Sarasvati,
Is the creator of the Kosmos. . . .

The Word works the turning cog-wheels of the Kosmos,
The spheres in the heavens
And the revolving, bright spheres in our minds.

In the beginning was the Word
And the Word was with God
And the Word was God
Was the chanking echo from Kosmos.

The Word is said and the Thing appears.
It said, in Hebrew, 'Let there be Light (*Aur*)' and there was Light
    (*Aur*).
The Word creates: the thought moulds matter

And the worlds come tumbling in with the tongue of jazz . . .

Weaving the Mediterranean Logos of Heraclitus,
Plato, and the Alexandrian, Philo, who showed the way
To the deliverer of the Fourth Gospel.

The Word (*Vak*) was made flesh; but there is a difference in ideas
Between the 'perennial philosophy' (*sanāntana dharma*), the remnant
Of a universal store of knowledge, the possession once of all mankind

And Christianity. To *dharma* (Eternal Law) God is the material cause
    of the world. Its matter.
To the dualism of the Christian Logos it is not. To *dharma*, the Word
    is not incarnated in
One historical person, but in all matter and men.

The Word was made flesh, not in one historical place,
On one particular date, in one particular person.
It appeared from THAT, which is Shiva, and now appears in the flesh
    and other forms of matter

Of all individual living beings, or *Jivas*, limited as they are,

Each of whom, through Veda, the Word, the multifoliate, flowing
    tree of the Scriptures
May directly become Shiva, whose Sarasvati, the female energy,
    is the Word: *Vak*:

The Christ figure, alone, walked the earth as God in human form,
With the remnant of the universal store of knowledge, a crown of
    thorns, a harsh rosary in his hands,
And the voice of bombed London, the Congo and Vietnam, sent to
    the stakes

Cried with expanding, Kosmos-sized words, 'What about me?'

The Christ, alone, was God in human form,
Others were not, are not,
And will never be.

But *Vak*, the Word, manifests herself in every man
And is known and knowable as Sarasvati is in herself
That is Shiva, in that spiritual experience which is the Veda,
    or the Word.

In the beginning was God (*Prajapātir vai idaṁ āsīt*);
    And with him was the Word (*Tasya vāg dvitiya āsīt*);
    And the Word is God (*Vāg vai paramaṁ Brahma*);

So that the sentient rose of flesh, the fiery boulder and mountain,
All forms of matter, atomic beings (*Jivas*) 'spotted through' with Life,
May through the Word become IT, Shiva himself, whose creative
    energy is Sarasvati, caressing the vina,

The talking, human lute,
Capable of conversation, of producing all sounds; Who wears the
    brilliant garland of light round her slender neck
Which is the Letters, the Syllables, the Words and Sentences of Speech
    (*Vak*),

Sarasvati rides the Wild Goose, the Gander, *haṁsa*, that abstract bird
    of light,
Whose very name is the mystic embryo symbol of all breathing things:
The natural name of the vital breath, manifested as the inhaling (*haṁ*),
    and the exhaling (*sah*), of all breathing creatures —

Linked as they are to the pulsation of the Cosmic Gander, the
    universe, expanding and contracting,
Breathing in and out, as plants do, though on different time scales;
And inert matter breathes also, ringing in the book of changes.

Sarasvati rides the vital breath, the Swan, the Wild Goose, the *haṁsa*,
Which swims on the surface of the water, but is not bound to it.
Flying through space, it migrates, north and south, following the
    seasons.

O Divine Essence, *Haṁsa*, free wanderer between the celestial and
    earthly spheres,
Descending upon the waters of the earth, taking wing again to the
    utmost on high
You are the divine substance which is embodied in us, and yet
    unconcerned with us.

We are earth-bound, limited in life strength, in virtues and
    consciousness,
But as a spark of the divine, which is unlimited, immortal, virtually
    omniscient and all-powerful,
We are wanderers of the two spheres, like the wild gander.

The macrocosmic gander (*haṁsa*), the Supreme Self in the body of the
    Universe,
Whose song of inhaling (*haṁ*) and exhaling (*sah*) is the sound the yogi
    hears when he controls the rhythm of his breath (*prāṇāyāma*)
Is said to be a manifestation of the 'inner gander' which is within us.

Thus, by constantly humming its own name, *haṁsa, haṁsa*, in our
    breath
The inner presence reveals itself to the yogi-initiate . . .
The song of the 'inner gander' has a final secret to disclose:

Haṁsa, haṁsa it sings, but at the same time, with the syllables
    reversed,
'So-ham, so-ham,' it insists; and since *sa* means 'this', and *haṁ* 'I',
The lesson is this: 'This I am, This I am', throbbing in the music of the
    breath.

The individual 'I' of the limited faculties, sodden with delusion,
Tight and four-square, hooped like a barrel in the *Mā* bond of Illusion
    of World-Appearance, *Māyā*,
Am actually This, He, Self (*Ātman*), the Highest Self,

Of unlimited consciousness and existence.
'I am He (*Paramātman*), who is free and divine.'

Every moment of inhalation and exhalation asserts the Supreme Void
　　in whom breath abides, 'And,' sings the glorious bird,
'*When the sun and moon have disappeared, I float and swim with slow
　　movements on*
The boundless expanse of the waters. I am the Lord, and I am the Gander.'

Sarasvati rides the *haṁsa*, the breath-spark of Kosmos.
Without her there is no Creation. And she proceeds from the
Nothingness, the Void that is Shiva. But how can that be?

'How can Being be produced from non-Being?' the Indians
　　questioned;
In the beginning there *must* have been pure Being, One, and without a
　　second.
Through yoga, through introspection, they had become conscious

Of an ultimate void within themselves, 'Of a stage beyond thought
　　and dream,
Beyond knowledge, motionless, indescribable, unbounded by space
　　and time', omnipresent.
Was this the causal principle? Was there a motionless substratum for
　　matter

And a substratum for time, as there seemed to be one for thought?
Were these different substrata, the forms of a still more subtle one, the
　　indescribable Shiva?
The Indian philosophers thought deeply before they built a model for
　　the universe.

When we try to find the root of any aspect of the created world
We begin to imagine there must exist beyond its form
Some sort of causal state, some indifferentiated continuum

Of which that particular form is a seeming development.
The first of the continua underlying all perceptible forms appears to be
　　space.
Absolute empty space is conceived as a limitless, undifferentiated,
　　indivisible continuum
In which reside the imaginary divisions of space. The seeming
　　localization
Of heavenly bodies, and their movements, creates the illusion of a
　　division of space.

Similarly, time is indivisible. Absolute time is an ever-present eternity, which seems inseparable from space.

Relative time results from the apparent division of space by the rhythm of the heavenly bodies.
The third continuum known to us is thought. Everything exists with a form within a co-ordinated system.
It seems to be the realization of a plan, the materialization of an organized dream.

Hence the visible universe was conceived as the form of the thought of its creator.
Whenever we go to the root of anything, we find no longer a substance, but a mere form, a concept,
Whose nature can be identified with that of thought.

And since the Kosmos is a creative process, the manifestation of a conscious power,
We are led to search for an active, or conscious, substratum for each of the perceptible phenomena,
Which proceed from the goddess Sarasvati from whom is Nature born (*Prakriti*), whose substratum is Shiva, whose creative energy she is.

The substratum of space is existence (*sat*);
The substratum of time is experience or enjoyment (*ānanda*);
The substratum of thought is consciousness (*Cit*).

And so *sat-cit-ānanda*. The Goddess appears at the root of the three aspects (*guna-s*) of existence
As Reality, Consciousness and Experience – in all *satchitānanda*.
As Reality, she is the power of co-ordination, the centripetal 'holding' tendency visible in the sun.

As Experience, or joy, or pleasure,
She is the power of the centrifugal disintegrating tendency, visible in fire.
As consciousness, she is the power of understanding, the revolving tendency visible in the moon.
Creation arises from this triple form of power, of which Shiva's trident is the symbol.

She is Sarasvati, the goddess of speech, of music and poetry, she is 'creation by the Word'.
The Word or Sound (*Sabda*) brings meaning or object (*Artha*) and

Pratyaya (Mental Comprehension) to us;
But to normal men, Shiva, in his transcendent, quiescent state
Is soundless (*ashabda*), is not a meaning or an object (*nirvishaya*), and
　　is beyond our comprehension (*pratyaya*).

In the transcendental Shiva, therefore, there is
Neither name (*nāma*) nor form (*rūpa*).
In this Infinite Calm of It (Shiva) there arises now a metaphysical
　　Point of Stress or Bindu

Which stirs forth (*prasarati*), as the multiple forces of the Universe.
It is through this Bindu, the point limit, where the universal being and
　　the individual being unite
The Universe is manifested and then withdrawn again at the
　　dissolution.

This movement is Shiva, through Desire, or Love (*Kāma*), through
　　the stress of the One wishing to be Many,
The movement through his Lady Sarasvati, *Saras*, or the flowing one,
　　is Creation
The universe is the result of the Divine Desire (*Kāma*) or Will (*Icchā*).

In the physical world, the Divine Desire (*Kāma*) is, among other
　　things, sexual desire.
In the transcendent, it is the first creative impulse of the One wishing
　　to be many.
It begets Itself as Man, beings, things, the weathers, moods and
　　constellations.

Transcendent Love constantly works through individual sex-impulse
　　for the continued
Creation of the universe. The Divine Sarasvati in Shiva (She as
　　abstract as himself) is eternal and the beginning of all things.
And thus spoke Parmenides of another century: 'He divided Eros the
　　first of all the Gods.'

'Flow' or 'Motion' (*Saras*) is the accent of her lovely name: Sarasvati
White are her garments and transparent whiteness is the colour of
　　Ether (*Ākāsa*) and the Cosmic Intellect (*Buddhi*).
The flowing One is 'She who goes pure from the mountain to the sea.'

Sacred river, now called the Sarsuti, that falls from the high Himalayas
　　into our chaliced minds and bodies,
'Watery and elegant' the Sarasvati river, is your name: flood of fertility
　　your hips like ripe fruits curved like the sandbanks,

You flow in and around the static Ether which materialized at the
    Creation

With the roaring sound *haṁ*, and then stood rigid.
As the still sea of ether on which the whole universe opens and flows
As the World-experience, with its dualism of subject and object.

This dual play of Sarasvati, of subject and object, takes place in the
    Ether of Consciousness (*Cidākāsa*)
In such away that Consciousness (*cit*) is neither effaced nor affected,
When transcendence of the false duality and Immanence with the
    Primal Cause

Is achieved through the yogic, psychedelic, the saintly, or poetic
    ecstasy.
This is creation (*Srsti*) or, more properly, seeming development
    (*Parināma*),
Since the English word 'Creation' involves an absolutely first
    appearance, and does not truly describe the process.

It excludes the notion that God is the *material cause*.
Christian 'creation' being neither out of pre-existing matter
Nor out of God's own substance.

To clearly state the process, Shiva Itself, in the form of Its Power
    (Sarasvati) goes forth (*Prasarati*)
To create the illusory world-play (*Māyā*) of subject and object, which
    is transcended by yogis, the psychedelics, saints, and poets.
This creation (*Srsti*) endures for a while (*Sthiti*) – that is, One Day of
    Shiva, which is billions of years.

Then it is engulfed in complete dissolution (*Mahapralaya*) for One
    Night of Shiva, of equal duration.
Sarasvati, his Sakti, or Energy, has re-entered Shiva
And in *Mahapralaya*, a new creation is potentially contained, in the
    undifferentiated, unmanifest, Shiva-Sarasvati.

The Supreme Sound (*Sabda-brahman*) as a coming forth (*Ullāsa*) of
    Shiva has subsided into the eternally existing Calm
Just as the rising wave breaks and sinks upon the ocean; or a fountain
    into the waters that feed it;
Only to rise again when the Divine Desire stirs.

This awareness of the creation and dissolution of the Universe
    experienced in the yogic or other (psychedelic) expansion of the
    self

In which the cosmic body reveals itself as the throbbing mirror of IT,
in vibrant shapes and patternings in motion of extraordinary
colour,
Is the thunderous OM, yes, of modern cosmology. The burning
prelude was a single searing sun, a dense 'primeval atom'

Which exploded and sent all matter rushing outward in the pristine
sheer symphony.
The speeding galaxies are the gossamer strings and frets and fluted
belly of her vina, and of the big explosion . . .
The roaring sound *ham* which proceeded from OM, which is Shiva,
pervading space, time and forms.

The roaring sound of the cosmic flash of light, of the burning
beginning,
Is still with us, transformed to radio waves, first caught on a New
Jersey hilltop.
Light and radio waves are forms of electromagnetic radiation of
different frequencies,

The latter, the slowed down whimper of light. Was it like OM? the
first manifestation of articulate language, the music of the
spheres, the hum in the sea shell
Of the one eternal syllable of which all that exists is but the
development?

The past, the present, and the future are all included in the sound OM
And Shiva, who exists beyond the three forms of time, is also implied
in it.
OM is the one indestructible sound, the Immensity beyond, which is
said to contain all rushing language and meaning

Including the first sound of creation. Some think the galaxies will go
on flying forever,
Asserting the principle of the expanding universe. The greater number
Believe in the pulsating model, the yogi's, the model of the heart.

They know mutual pull of gravitation will slow and stop the galaxies
And they'll fall down to coalesce again
Like a round of pebbles thrown up to the Void.

This Universe, extruded from Shiva, our astronomers say,
Is about ten billion years old, and will expand
For another thirty billion years – the Day of Shiva.

Then it will stop and plunge for another forty billion years, the Night
of Shiva, into an incredibly dense mass
Destroying all galaxies, stars, planets and the life clinging to them, in
an endlessly self-immolating holocaust.

Congealing once more, pressures will rise, temperatures soar to
billions of degrees
The entire mass explode again. And as flaming matter flies outward,
Galaxies, stars and planets will coalesce into the delicate lace of
creation,

Bright discs and globes hang on the infinite wand of darkness,
Non-living atoms and molecules stumble on to the key to self-
reproduction,
And life begin a new cycle, as though it never existed before.

And that is what through introspection and *samadhi*, the trance state,
the Indian yogis, become sages, perceived and taught.

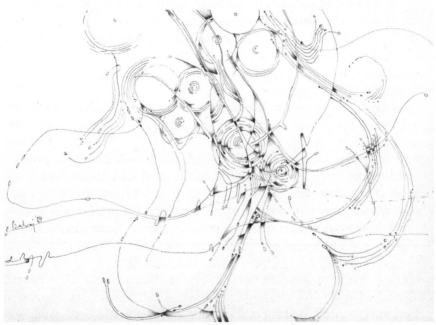

The Bride by Balraj Khanna. 21 × 29.5 cm, ink on paper, 1983.

Tambimuttu

21 March 1970

In this book-lined cave of Shakespeare and Company, facing the Seine and Notre-Dame, the leaves of my life are faded, the letters faint, the type chiselled archaic but, as in psychedelically ballooning, bursting and colouring dreams they pulse like neon lights, like the Cosmos, like the muscles, like the traffic. The Seine flows on like Goddess Ganges from Shiva's bright hair on these words from my typewriter. Flow. The energy of matter. The energy of my body.

I have loved the letters of the alphabet, the garland, the goddess of learning – of science, of literature, of music, of art – wears round her splendid neck. Sarasvati, *saras* or the flowing one. She plays the *veena* or the many-stringed lute, making the music of our awareness. I have heard it in the music of Ravi Shankar or Ali Akbar Khan, the ordered music of nature behind the veil of appearance: discovery of scientists, the knowledge of the ancients. The unfettered, flowing, metamorphosing, ordered music of *Kosmos*. Freedom, Growth, Flowering, Return to Supreme Energy, or Shiva ... Sivam, the pure one with a thousand and one names.

Since I have lived the life of flow and motion I have no records. Whatever poets' letters, manuscripts and the drawings I had were swallowed up by the dealers in New York to the tune of nearly $30,000. The contracts I signed with authors and artists, worth a small fortune, have vanished. The offices of British Eagle Airways in New York shut up the very day a parcel of my most valuable possessions (correspondence, my collection of unpublished poems, short stories and other manuscripts, my father's unpublished Ganga Vamsa, the history of my family, the story of the Race of Goddess Gange (Ganges) from Orissa under the Himalayas, the books I had bought from various authors – Henry Miller, James T. Farrell, Timothy Leary – for establishing myself as a publisher, once again, in London), was delivered to their office, in the Empire State Building, and they went bankrupt. I visited the guard of the Empire State, lawyers for the liquidation, estate agents, the Sheriff, in hot pursuit. ...

POETRY
LONDON

1939-1951

ALAN SMITH

Originally published in
ABMR (Antiquarian Book
Monthly Review),
April/May 1979.

POETRY LONDON
1939~1951
PART 1

After the statutory period of
oblivion the publications of the
1940s are now starting to attract
attention. The decade is
particularly rich in collectable
imprints, and in this two-part
article Alan Smith penetrates
the shrouding myths and
explores the lively world of
Poetry London

ALAN SMITH

'It is only in *Poetry London* that I can consistently
expect to find new poets who matter' — T. S. Eliot

'The axis which runs through *Poetry London* is that
all poems are poems and equally worth printing. The
only axis is to have no axis, beyond that faith in
muddle and contradiction which has made *Poetry
London* the most foolish (if representative)
periodical of its time' — Geoffrey Grigson

In wartime England the writers, editors
and critics were indulging in their own
dog-fights, and in an environment of
factions, cliques and movements one
man had the effrontery to write

'every man has poetry within him . . .
no man is small enough to be
neglected as a poet . . . each poet is
a leaf, a significant leaf of Poetry
the multifoliate tree . . . the critic
is not our concern. Let him get
squashed under his
own
microscope.

Meary James Thurairajah Tambimuttu (universally known as Tambi) had founded the magazine *Poetry London* in 1939, and so pungent and provocative were his editorials that it was almost impossible to plead neutrality. For almost a decade the literary world enjoyed the knockabout fun as torrents of lavish praise and vitriolic abuse streamed from the pens of the supporters of the rival camps. Hostilities were resumed in 1971 when Frank Cass published a reprint of all the issues of the magazine. The *T.L.S.* reviewer bemoaned the 'vatic posturings of charlatans and mediocrities' and the reader is left with the impression that the good verse to be found 'here and there in the quagmire' was merely the result of the law of averages holding up in the face of impossible conditions. The collector is likely to find that the roll-call of illustrious contributors acts as an effective antidote to such critical venom.

The magazine was only one part of the total publishing venture that is collectively known as Poetry London (or PL). From 1943 to 1947 the publishing house of Nicholson and Watson produced a separate list of books (Editions Poetry London) devoted to poetry and poetic prose, and in effect this list was a subsidiary imprint directed by Tambi. Following the withdrawal of support by Nicholson and Watson the venture was backed by Richard March and the imprint continued until 1951. The seventy or so books and pamphlets that were produced by Poetry London constitute an interesting and important slice of the literary cake of the 1940s.

Many of the books still exude an individual excellence — be it of writer, artist, typographer or printer. Some of the books are easy to find and a confident start can be made; some of the books are scarce but not so scarce that the collector has to make unalterable compromises. But the intending collector must not delay — after almost thirty years in the doldrums the artistic achievements of the decade are now beginning to receive well-merited attention.

As yet, the chronicles of Poetry London are scrappy. In those days Tambi was a colourful bohemian, and colour is a soft option when it comes to literary reminiscences. The most famous account of the PL story was told by Julian MacLaren-Ross in his posthumous book **Memoirs of the Forties**. Indeed many other accounts have cribbed unashamedly from this source. Tambi has written that it is 'a book of misrepresentations and fairy-tales' but in terms of period flavour it is probably good value. In terms of facts, however, MacLaren-Ross is unreliable — there is over-much dependence on hearsay, the chronology is wild and truth is manipulated for effect. This article attempts to set the bibliographical record straight and to provide the foundation for a more detailed historical study.

Tambi was born in Ceylon in 1915 and belongs to the minority community of Jaffna Tamils. His claim that 'I am a Prince in my own country' stems from the fact that his family line can be traced back to the last King of Jaffna. He arrived in England in 1938 having already published three collections of poetry in Ceylon. Within a matter of days he had joined up with an assortment of poets, artists and bohemians who were to be regularly found in 'Fitzrovia' — the name given by Tambi to that

Richard March.

SELECTED
WRITING

edited by · · REGINALD MOORE
poetry selected by TAMBIMUTTU

NICHOLSON & WATSON
NUMBER ONE, CRAVEN HOUSE, KINGSWAY, LONDON, W.C.1

Tambimuttu's introduction to Nicholson and Watson.

part of London around the line between Fitzroy Square and Soho Square. One of the first of his new-found friends was Anthony Dickins, a student musician recently returned from a spell of work in India. Dickins became an enthusiastic advocate of Tambi's talents (both literary and musical) and for his part in helping to get the magazine under way he was given the title of General Editor in the early issues.

Late in 1938 Tambi and Dickins had scraped up enough money to print and distribute a prospectus for 'Poetry – the only poetry monthly in Britain'. At that time Geoffrey Grigson's *New Verse* and Julian Symons' *Twentieth Century Verse* were the established outlets for modern poetry, and their dismissal on a wildly optimistic technicality was typical of the fresh and cheeky style that was to become the hallmark of *Poetry London*. Sufficient subscriptions came in to allow the venture to get off the ground, and *Poetry* appeared in Feb and April 1939. The qualifying word 'London' was not in regular use at this time and did not appear on the covers.

The costs of the first two issues exhausted all the available funds and the magazine went into limbo for eighteen months. A gift of £100 from James Dobie brought the magazine back to life for four issues, and the more modest promise of bi-monthly publication was honoured. The cover of issue 3 was notable for the first appearance of the lyrebird motif – on this occasion drawn by Lucian Freud – a motif that was to persist throughout all future manifestations of Poetry London,

and a bird that still flies today at the masthead of Th Lyrebird Press.

It was Nicholas Moore who had the original idea for series of poetry pamphlets. In the guise of Epsilon Pres he had already published his own collection **A Book fo Priscilla** and had plans for further pamphlets. I discussion with Tambi it was mutually agreed tha publication should be under the banner of Poetr London. The four pamphlets are undated – and th British Library did not obtain copies until 1948 – bu they can be confidently placed in the period May-De 1941.

Issue 6 – which appeared in June 1941 – gave th impression that *Poetry London* was a confiden flourishing enterprise. Called, for some obscure reason 'First Anniversary Number' the issue was enlarged to 5 pages and produced in an edition of 2200 copies. But, i reality, the money had run out and this was to be th last issue in what can be regarded as the first phase in th history of Poetry London. Tambi entered into a perio of intense poverty and frustration which culminated in nervous breakdown. The prime agent in the process o rehabilitation was T. S. Eliot.

Almost from the beginning Eliot had been an admire of Tambi's ability and editorial flair, and he ha commissioned Tambi to edit an annual anthology o contemporary poetry for the Faber list. The first (an only) **Poetry in Wartime** appeared in Aug 1942. Elio also made personal contributions to help Tambi throug this period and was a source of influential suppor

---

Left: The cover of the first issue of **Poetry** *designed by Hector Whistler.* **Right:** *The second number of the magazine.*

POETRY

LITERARY EDITOR · TAMBIMUTTU   GENERAL EDITOR · ANTHONY DICKINS

APRIL 1939

STEPHEN SPENDER • LOUIS MACNEICE • DYLAN THOMAS • CHARLES MADGE
GEORGE BARKER • DAVID GASCOYNE • LAURENCE WHISTLER • CLIFFORD DYMENT
RUTHVEN TODD • PAUL POTTS • IDRIS DAVIES • GLYN JONES • LYND NATHAN
DORIAN COOKE • MAURICE CARPENTER • LAWRENCE DURRELL • H. G. PORTEUS

Nº 2   ONE SHILLING

during Tambi's quest for an established position in the London literary scene.

After the uncertainties of the 'phoney-war' period conditions had settled down and publishing was to experience several boom years. Almost everything that was printed was eagerly snapped up. Poetry, essays and short stories were particularly favoured — partly because writers and readers had only short periods of time to spare from the business of war, and partly because such material allowed publishers to conform to (and sometimes circumvent) wartime restrictions on the supply and use of paper. One of the most persistent anthologists of this time was Reginald Moore, and he had asked Tambi to choose the poetry to be included in the first issue of *Selected Writing*, which was published by Nicholson and Watson in April 1942.

Nicholson and Watson (henceforth, for brevity, called NW) was 'under new management'. The eponymous owners had put the business into voluntary liquidation at the end of 1940 and it had been acquired by Duncan MacIntosh and his young protegé John Roberts. MacIntosh was the chairman of a long-established printing company — Love and Malcomson — and in a private capacity he had majority shareholdings in NW and Wells Gardner Darton who were to place much business in the way of Love and Malcomson. In 1942 Roberts was the new managing director of NW and he had inherited a valuable allocation of paper but little

or nothing in the way of literary assets. Roberts was searching for talent; Tambi was wanting an opportunity.

Selected Writing was the catalyst: Tambi was summoned to meet Roberts and MacIntosh. They were impressed with his *Poetry London* achievements, and with the range of his literary and artistic contacts — many of whom were not contractually tied to other publishers. Roberts proposed that NW should sponsor further issues of the magazine and that Tambi should be allowed to generate his own series of books for publication by NW. Under the terms of this offer Tambi would have his own office and staff and — subject to NW's over-riding financial control — would be allowed to manage and develop his 'imprint' in his own way. Tambi accepted the offer, and 'PL' and 'Editions Poetry London' were to become the distinctive identifiers of his contributions to the NW list.

The first output from the new order was a sumptuous issue of the magazine which went on sale in October 1942 in an edition of 10,000 copies. Henry Moore provided an interpretation of the lyrebird for the cover and two drawings from his 'Shelter' portfolio. The issue was dedicated to T. S. Eliot 'with respect and affection'. Issues 8 and 9 followed rapidly, and the latter contained three original lithographs by Graham Sutherland. 50 signed sets of the lithographs were offered at 10/6 per set.

In July 1943 the Editions Poetry London imprint got

The 1938 prospectus, and a miniature issue of the magazine that served as a prospectus in 1948.

POETRY

THE ONLY POETRY
MONTHLY IN BRITAIN

Edited by **TAMBIMUTTU** *and* **ANTHONY DICKINS**
at Sixty-four Grafton Way, London, W.1.

SIXPENCE

POETRY
LONDON

off to an auspicious start with **Stone and Flower** — a book of poems by Kathleen Raine with drawings by Barbara Hepworth. Amongst the handful of other titles published that year was another sensitive collaboration between poet and artist — David Gascoyne's **Poems 37-42** with illustrations by Graham Sutherland. This was certainly the most successful PL book, and in later years it reached the dizzy heights of a third impression.

1944 was not a good year: only two titles reached publication, and the foundations were laid for the notorious ever-growing list of 'forthcoming books'. Later in that year the PL organisation was strengthened (Nicholas Moore was one who joined the staff) and from early 1945 onwards Tambi presented Nicholson and Watson with an impressive array of books.

Throughout the period of book publishing the magazine had not put in an appearance, and in truth Tambi believed that it had served its primary purpose. But back in 1939 Tambi had promised a 'new poets' number and in 1945 he belatedly honoured this promise in a grand (some would say grandiose) manner — a 264-page large-format book that was stuffed with new poets (many of whom were his drinking companions) and which served as issue 10 of the magazine. **Poetry London X** (as it was called) also contained contributions from Tambi's regular sources, drawings by Mervyn Peake and three lithographs by Gerald Wilde. 75 signed sets of the lithographs were put on sale. The book was the epitome of the 'every man is a poet' philosophy, and was variously described by Tambi as 'a knock at the Establishment' and 'a load of dung spread on the starved fields of current literary life'. Needless to say the book was savaged by those critics who did not approve of such iconoclastic behaviour — the more so since such 'indifferent verse' was packaged in such luxury.

One lavish production of 1945 that was and is universally admired was Henry Moore's **Shelter Sketch Book**. Fine copies are uncommon because the flimsy hinges have difficulty in taking the strain of the heavy art paper in oblong format. The book is unusual in that it carries a facsimile signature and date (Oct 1940) on the front free end-paper, and the facsimile is good enough to have fooled experienced bookdealers and collectors.

The high rate of publication from 1945 onwards was achieved by a strong development into prose works. Tambi's approach was that if it was good of its kind then he was interested in having it in his list — for example, the two collections of jazz writing that were enthusiastically promoted by Nicholas Moore. Paris was

---

The manifesto printed in the 1938 prospectus.

POETRY

(*London*)

An Enquiry into Modern Verse

● New, entertaining, *alive*, this is the poetry periodical that youth has been waiting for.

● Our intention in this non-party paper is to print work that poets feel they *want* to write rather than what they *ought* to, in order to conform to the shibboleths of certain political and literary cliques.

● Mr Eliot has already observed that " In the present chaos of opinion and belief we may expect to find quite different literatures existing in the same language and the same country." We will make it possible for these different literatures to appear together, so that the public may have a clear and comprehensive idea of what is happening to poetry today.

● We are interested only in *achievement* in the mode of expression called poetry; we print all who merit attention, regardless of their opinions, especially young and unknown writers.

● Every form of *honest* thought will be given a clear voice on this poets' platform. With the results, we hope to be able to resolve the present-day muddle in poetry and criticism.

● A representative selection of modern poets has been invited to appear in the first few numbers:

GEORGE BARKER	H. B. MALLALIEU
ROY CAMPBELL	NIALL MONTGOMERY
*LAURENCE CLARK	NICHOLAS MOORE
DORIAN COOKE	*PHILIP O'CONNOR
WALTER DE LA MARE	GEOFFREY PARSONS
LAWRENCE DURREL	PAUL POTTS
T. S. ELIOT	FREDERIC PROKOSCH
*PATRICK EVANS	HERBERT READ
*GAVIN EWART	*KEIDRYCH RHYS
R. B. FULLER	*D. S. SAVAGE
DAVID GASCOYNE	*STEPHEN SPENDER
B. H. GUTTERIDGE	*JULIAN SYMONS
J. F. HENDRY	GEOFFREY TAYLOR
RAYNER HEPPENSTALL	DYLAN THOMAS
*JOHN LEHMANN	RUTHVEN TODD
*LOUIS MACNEICE	*LAURENCE WHISTLER
CHARLES MADGE	W. B. YEATS

* Appearing in the first number.

I enclose 6/6, subscription for one year's issue of POETRY.

Name ....

Address ....

....

Date ....

a fruitful source of material and Henry Miller, Anais Nin and Vladimir Nabokov were represented on the PL list, and would have had further representation if PL had had the financial muscle to defend obscenity actions.

At the end of 1946 NW had cause to review their investment in PL. The publishing climate had changed: the public now had more options for the disposal of leisure time and money; costs were escalating and profit margins were being eroded; supply and production conditions continued to be bad and much-needed working capital was tied up in stocks and work in progress. Some of the PL titles produced gross profits, but such profits were puny compared with the high overhead costs of Tambi's ménage. NW felt that they could no longer carry a prestigious but increasingly unprofitable operation such as PL and Tambi was told that he must start to look elsewhere for financial support. PL was not summarily dismissed, and NW continued to progress titles that were already in the production schedule.

Alternative financial backing was not immediately forthcoming. Some approaches were made by individuals who really wanted to use the imprint to promote their own literary talents, but Tambi was not prepared to compromise his reputation. In the middle of 1947 a chance introduction to Richard March was followed almost immediately by an offer to put £5000 into the business. Tambi accepted, and in September 1947 a new company was registered — Editions Poetry London Ltd

— with March and Tambi as directors, and Nicholson and Watson fade (almost) from the scene.

Herman George Richard March was born in 1905 and his family were long-time residents in Java. After leaving Oxford he had been a teacher of languages, journalist, occasional contributor to *Scrutiny*, and had been involved with experimental theatres as an actor and stage-manager. After the war he joined the B.B.C. European Service and wrote regularly for *The New English Weekly*.

The transition took place smoothly. The flow of books continued, and the magazine started to appear again at almost regular intervals — but shorn of the lavish accoutrements of earlier days. There was however a little confusion. Whilst almost all of the literary assets stayed with Editions Poetry London, three PL books eventually emerged from the Nicholson and Watson pipe-line and were published under their imprint. One of these was the long-overdue study of **Alfred Wallis** by Sven Berlin. Almost as an afterthought NW added the words 'Poetry London' at the foot of the title page, but in all other respects the book was presented and classified as a standard NW title. The other examples were Wyndham Lewis's **America and Cosmic Man**, and S. W. Hayter's monograph on **Jankel Adler**. In these latter books there was not even an afterthought, and PL collectors must decide for themselves as to what constitutes a complete PL collection.

Tambi realised that poetry and poetic prose could not

Berthold Wolpe's designs for the first two PL books.

STONE
AND
FLOWER

KATHLEEN RAINE

with drawings by

BARBARA HEPWORTH

PL

·POEMS
OF
HÖLDERLIN

Translated with an introduction by

MICHAEL HAMBURGER

PL

in themselves sustain a profitable business, and it was decided to diversify. Two subsidiary imprints were created — William Campion (not to be confused with The Campion Press) and Mandeville Publications. Campion was to be devoted to 'general fiction', and Mandeville to 'juvenile publications'.

The first Campion title was firmly geared to the objective. **Jan's Journal** was a collection of Ronald Duncan's highly popular articles selected from his regular column in the Evening Standard. But the development of Campion was overtaken by events and the remaining few titles would not have looked out of place in the Poetry London list and could not have been money-spinners. **The House without Windows** by Maurice Sandoz was an expensive production with jacket and illustrations by Dali, and the collector will find that the book is not easy to come by. The two titles by March himself can partly be accounted for by his desire to clear his desk before the business was wound up in 1951.

At first sight Mandeville was a bizarre diversification: Poetry London and Billy Bunter were not obvious bedfellows. Again this was an example of Tambi's interest in anything that was good of its kind and he had been an admirer of 'Frank Richards' for many years. He even went so far as to publish a piece of his doggerel in the magazine, but the fact that the comic character in the poem is called Grigson might have influenced his judgement!

It was not long before March began to have misgivings about his somewhat impetuous investment into Poetry London. The venture was consuming much more money than he had bargained for — in terms of shares and debentures his cumulative investment was of the order of £20,000. As always, Tambi's undoubted entrepreneurial talents were offset by an undisciplined and sometimes dilatory approach to matters of organisation and procedure. Perforce, March became more involved with the day-to-day activities, and Tambi found that his style was being cramped. Relations between the partners started to go sour.

When the company was formed March had asked for 51% of the shares and — to his eternal regret — Tambi had reluctantly acquiesced. Early in 1949 March exercised his latent power. At the Annual General Meeting he proposed that Tambi should step down from the Board of directors, and that henceforth he should be employed as editor-in-chief and technical adviser. Tambi stormed out of the meeting. Subsequently the Board (which, nominally, included Ronald Duncan, Nicholas Moore and Ronald Bottrall) terminated Tambi's services with the company and he was told never to attend the offices again.

Opinion was sharply divided. March's supporters believed that, on balance, Tambi was a liability and that March was justified in taking such action. Many of the Poetry London stalwarts felt that March had resolved his problem in a brutal fashion and, if there had to be a break, that March should have cut his losses and left Tambi to soldier on with his intensely personal creation. Anthony Dickins organised a protest and some long-standing contributors refused to have anything more to do with the magazine. March stood firm, and

late in 1949 Tambi returned to Ceylon to seek capital for a fresh start.

The most significant consequence of Tambi's departure was that many of the 'forthcoming books' were stopped dead in their tracks. A trade catalogue of published and forthcoming titles (issued in March 1948) contains a mouth-watering list of promises, most of which were to remain unfulfilled. March took over as editor of the magazine, and although some of the past contributors continued to appear there was a noticeable shift in the overall style, and increased coverage was given to aspects of German culture — a March speciality. The lyrebird disappeared from the cover. From the middle of 1949 onwards Mandeville made most of the running and PL and Campion titles were infrequent.

March suffered from ill-health and early in 1951 a form of cancer was diagnosed and he was told that he had at most a few years to live. He immediately started to make arrangements to put his affairs in the best order. Imminent and essential books were processed quickly and in September 1951 the final titles in the Editions Poetry London and William Campion imprints were published. The last book — The Collected Poems of Keith Douglas — had been long-awaited. In 1943 PL had negotiated a contract, and Tambi had worked closely with Douglas in the period immediately prior to the poets' death on the Normandy battlefield. A first selection had been included in Alamein to Zem Zem, and this should have been followed by Bête Noire, but Tambi's departure brought about an editorial hiatus. The collection was eventually assembled by John Waller and G. S. Fraser, and the book sparked-off textual controversy that has never been resolved to Tambi's satisfaction.

September 1951 also saw the last issue of the magazine. The final editorial echoed the 1950 death-rattle of *Horizon* — 'we are going into limbo for 12 months to see if the situation becomes more appropriate to the publication of a literary magazine'. However, as far as the magazine was concerned March wanted to keep his options open. March intended to continue with the Mandeville imprint — and indeed he published Billy Bunter and Tom Merry Annuals until his death in 1955 — and he gave protection to the magazine by transferring it to the Mandeville operation. In the event no further issues of the magazine were forthcoming and before his death March gave back the magazine to Tambi as a final reconciliatory gesture.

March sold the shell of the Editions Poetry London business as a vehicle for tax-avoidance. All that remains in the Public Records Office is a note to the effect that Editions Poetry London changed its name to The New Fiction Press — a publishing house that was to gain notoriety in 1954 when Lord Chief Justice Goddard sent the owners to prison for having the audacity to publish a handful of pulp-fiction titles by Hank Janson!

Tambi eventually settled in New York and in 1956 Alexander Calder's version of the lyrebird adorned the cover of the first of four issues of *Poetry London — New York*. The editorial fingerprints were unmistakeable. The prose was longer in wind than the famous clipped rhetoric of 1939, but the call-to-arms was identical — 'our aim is to ignore the poetical theorising and to get at the best poetry of our time'. Editions Poetry London —

New York also put in a brief appearance and several books were published. In collaboration with The Spoken Word Inc. PLNY (as it was called) produced two long-playing records of contemporary poets reading from their own works. But after a couple of years the financial resources were exhausted and Tambi took himself off to the wilder fringes of American academic life.

Tambi came back to London in 1968 and with the financial assistance of Katharine Falley Bennett he started The Lyrebird Press. The imprint has limped from crisis to crisis, but several of the published titles carry the subsidiary legend 'Editions Poetry London'. More recently Tambi has found a new backer — David Frost's company Paradine Developments — and at £450 a copy the PL collector can bring his collection right up to date with **India Love Lyrics** and get an original John Piper drawing into the bargain. What price those Graham Sutherland lithographs of 1943?

PART 2

A COMPLETE CHECKLIST OF THE IMPRINT

Prefatory notes

Each component part of the Poetry London operation is listed separately. For completeness, the Mandeville list is carried through to 1955.

Each section is in chronological order of publication (with alphabetic sequence of author surname used in the event of a tie). Exact publication dates have still to be identified, and for present purposes the dates that are given correspond to the entry dates in the 'Books of the Week' compilations in contemporary issues of The Bookseller.

Publication dates quoted on the imprint page are unreliable: there was often a considerable delay between printing and publication. As an extreme example, David Wright's **Poems** *are given as 1947 on the imprint page, 1948 on the jacket, and the book appeared in Jan. 1949.*

The interpolated remarks are intended to be no more than a personal selection of information snippets likely to be of interest to the collector.

Poetry London was notorious for the length of the elapsed time between the promise and the fulfilment. Many public promises were made — either through the medium of jackets or the trade catalogues (produced in Dec. 1946 and Mar. 1948) — which were not fulfilled. In most cases the rights had been secured and the books were somewhere in the production schedule at the time of Tambi's departure in April 1949. A few of the titles eventually surfaced elsewhere, but the remainder were stillborn — either because they were intimately associated with Tambi, or because resources were not available in the limited time remaining before the demise of PL in 1951. The list of 'unfulfilled promises' is included:

- *so that collectors do not waste their time.*

- *so that critics can (if they wish) take these titles into account in any assessment of the work of Tambi. Tambi's virtue was that he intended to publish these books; his vice was that he didn't.*

A scarce William Campion title.

Maurice Sandoz.
THE HOUSE WITHOUT WINDOWS
A Novel
Illustrated by Salvador Dali

Section A:
Poetry London Magazine

Vol. 1	No.	1	Feb. 1939
		2	Apr. 1939
		3	Nov. 1940
		4	Jan./Feb. 1941
		5	Mar./Apr. 1941
		6	May/Jun. 1941
Vol. 2		7	Oct./Nov. 1942
		8	Nov./Dec. 1942
		9	Undated (May 1943)
		X	Feb. 1945
Vol. 3		11	Sep./Oct. 1947
		12	Nov./Dec. 1947
Vol. 4		13	Jun./Jul. 1948
		14	Nov./Dec. 1948
		15	May 1949
		16	Sep. 1949
Vol. 5		17	Jan. 1950
		18	May 1950
		19	Aug. 1950
		20	Nov. 1950
		21	Feb. 1951
Vol. 6		22	Summer 1951
		23	Winter 1951

NOTE:

Tambimuttu was the editor for issues 1-14. Issue 15 was started by Tambi and completed by Richard March. Issues 16-23 were edited jointly by March and Nicholas Moore (the editorials were by March).

Anthony Dickins was variously described as General Editor or Associate Editor in issues 1-6, but in fact he was only intimately involved with the first two issues, and his role could more aptly be described as Business Manager. After issue 2 Dickins joined the army, and further contact with PL was irregular and fleeting.

Issue 10 (**Poetry London X**) is in book form, and will also be found as item 8 in Section C.

Section B: The P.L. Pamphlets

1 GEORGE SCURFIELD The song of a red turtle
May 1941
2 ANNE RIDLER A dream observed Jul. 1941
3 G. S. FRASER The fatal landscape Sep. 1941
4 NICHOLAS MOORE Buzzing around with a bee
Nov. 1941
5 FRANTISEK HALAS Old women Apr. 1948
6 TAMBIMUTTU Natarajah Sep. 1948

NOTE:

The first four pamphlets were produced by Tambimuttu and Nicholas Moore as a collaborative venture. It was intended that they should appear bi-monthly, starting in May 1941, and circumstantial evidence suggests that this schedule was achieved.

Pamphlet 5 is unusual in that it was produced from sheets printed in Prague.

The first two PL Pamphlets

Two of the early PL Pamphlets

Section C: Editions Poetry London

1 KATHLEEN RAINE Stone and flower Jul. 1943
Drawings by Barbara Hepworth. The first two books were designed by Berthold Wolpe, and he also designed the PL colophon, which, in modified form, is still in use today.

2 MICHAEL HAMBURGER Poems of Holderlin
Aug. 1943
This should have been the inaugural PL title, with publication on June 7 1943 to coincide with the centenary of Holderlin's death.

3 DAVID GASCOYNE Poems: 1937-1942 Dec. 1943
Jacket and drawings by Graham Sutherland.

4 ANNE RIDLER Cain Dec. 1943
The first of several jacket designs by Anthony Froshaug.

5 G. S. FRASER Home town elegy Oct. 1944

6 CHARLES WILLIAMS The region of the summer stars Oct. 1944

7 NICHOLAS MOORE The glass tower Jan. 1945
Jacket and drawings by Lucian Freud.

8 TAMBIMUTTU (ed) Poetry London X Feb. 1945
Jacket and lithographs by Gerald Wilde. Drawings
by Mervyn Peake.

9 PAUL POTTS Instead of a sonnet May 1945

0 RONALD BOTTRALL Farewell and welcome
May 1945

1 HERBERT CORBY Hampdens going over Jun. 1945

2 DAVID DAICHES Virginia Woolf Jun. 1945

3 M. CARPENTER/J. LINDSAY/H. ARUNDEL (eds)
New lyrical ballads Jun. 1945

4 L. DURRELL/B. SPENCER/R. FEDDEN (eds)
Personal landscape Jun. 1945

5 W. S. GRAHAM Second poems Aug. 1945

6 EDWIN HONIG Garcia Lorca Aug. 1945

7 HENRY MOORE Shelter sketch book Aug. 1945
Jacket by Henry Moore and, like many PL jacket
designs, it was based upon an idea by Tambimuttu.
'Henry Moore October 1940' is printed in facsimile
on the front free end-paper.

8 ELIZABETH SMART By Grand Central station I sat
down and wept Aug. 1945
Jacket by Gerald Wilde.

NABOKOV'S GREAT NOVEL

THE REAL LIFE OF

SEBASTIAN KNIGHT

*"God's rarest gift to humanity,
a deeply and truly original
gift . . . his English has a master's sensitiveness and power."*
—Evening Standard

PL

EDITIONS POETRY LONDON

*The second issue jacket designed by Tambimuttu in the
manner of Victor Gollancz*

*The first issue jacket designed by Tambimuttu in the
manner of Ben Nicholson*

19 HERBERT PALMER The dragon of Tingalam
Sep. 1945

20 BETTY SWANWICK The cross purposes Nov. 1945
Jacket and drawings by the author.

21 JACQUES MARITAIN Art and poetry Nov. 1945

22 HENRY MILLER The cosmological eye Feb. 1946

23 NICHOLAS MOORE (ed) The PL book of modern
American short stories Feb. 1946

24 VLADIMIR NABOKOV The real life of Sebastian
Knight Mar. 1946
The first-issue jacket was designed by Tambimuttu
in the style of Ben Nicholson. There were com-
plaints that the jacket did nothing to help sell the
book, and Tambimuttu designed a replacement
which aped the busy typographical jackets of
Victor Gollancz.

25 JOHN BANTING A blue book of conversation
Oct. 1946

26 DIANA GARDNER Halfway down the cliff
Oct. 1946

27 CONRAD AIKEN The soldier Oct. 1946
   Contains some material that is not to be found in
   the original American edition.

28 HENRY MILLER Sunday after the war Nov. 1946

29 PAUL GOODMAN The facts of life Nov. 1946

30 RONALD BOTTRALL Selected poems Dec. 1946
   Preface by Edith Sitwell.

31 JACQUES MARITAIN The dream of Descartes
   Dec. 1946

32 JOHN WALLER The merry ghosts Dec. 1946

33 KATHLEEN RAINE Living in time Jan. 1947
   Jacket woodcut by Eric Ravilious. The book was
   designed by Oliver Simon and printed on special
   paper by The Curwen Press.

34 WITTER BYNNER (tr) The way of life according to
   Laotzu Jan. 1947

35 MICHAEL HAMBURGER (tr) Twenty prose poems
   of Baudelaire Feb. 1947

36 BERNARD SPENCER Aegean islands Feb. 1947

37 KEITH DOUGLAS Alamein to Zem Zem Mar. 1947

38 ALBERT McCARTHY (ed) The PL yearbook of
   jazz 1946 Mar. 1947

The first issue jacket designed by Julian Trevelyan

*The intended second issue jacket, but it is thought that
this did not progress beyond the proof stage*

39 KATHLEEN NOTT Landscapes and departures
   May 1947

40 WILLIAM ABRAHAMS Interval in Carolina
   May 1947
   Jacket by Bettina Shaw-Lawrence.

41 STEPHEN COATES Second poems Aug. 1947

42 PIERRE SEGHERS (ed) Poesie 39-45 Nov. 1947
   Jacket by Tambimuttu.

43 GERMAN ARCINIEGAS (ed) The green continent
   Nov. 1947
   Jacket by Julian Trevelyan. Sales were disappoint-
   ing and a simpler typographical jacket was prepared
   but there are doubts as to whether this version was
   issued.

44 VLADIMIR NABOKOV Nikolai Gogol Nov. 1947

45 HENRY MILLER The wisdom of the heart Dec. 1947

46 LAWRENCE DURRELL Cefalu Jan. 1948
   Jacket by Vivian Ridler.

47 ANAIS NIN Under a glass bell Jan. 1948

48 ALBERT McCARTHY (ed) Jazzbook 1947
   Feb. 1948

49 RICHARD MARCH The mountain of the upas tree
   Apr. 1948
   Jacket by William Stobbs. The book was set in
   type by The Fortune Press but it was diverted to
   PL.

50 IAIN FLETCHER Orisons, picaresque and metaphysical Sep. 1948

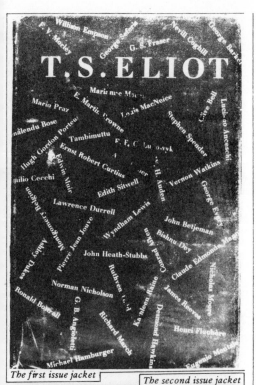

The first issue jacket | The second issue jacket

51 RICHARD MARCH/TAMBIMUTTU (eds)
    T. S. Eliot: a symposium Sep. 1948
    There are two issues of the jacket: the second issue
    was prepared when it was announced that Eliot
    was to receive the Nobel Prize.

52 G. S. FRASER The traveller has regrets Oct. 1948
    Published jointly by The Harvill Press and PL.

53 CLEANTH BROOKS Modern poetry and the tradi-
    tion Dec. 1948
    Not (as is implied) the first English edition.

54 DAVID WRIGHT Poems Jan. 1949

55 SVEN BERLIN Alfred Wallis Feb. 1949
    Published by Nicholson and Watson, but with a PL
    credit.

56 JAMES REEVES The imprisoned sea Mar. 1949

57 STEFAN THEMERSON Bayamus Oct. 1949
    Drawings by Franciszka Themerson.

58 RONALD BOTTRALL The palisades of fear
    Nov. 1949

59 NICHOLAS MOORE Recollections of the gala
    May 1950

60 GWYN WILLIAMS (ed) The rent that's due to love
    Oct. 1950

61 STEFAN THEMERSON The adventures of Peddy
    Bottom Dec. 1950
    Drawings by Franciszka Themerson.

62 J. WALLER/G. S. FRASER (eds) The collected
    poems of Keith Douglas Sep. 1951

NOTE:
Editions Poetry London Ltd. was formed in Sep. 1947 and so,
technically, items 1-41 were published by Nicholson and Watson
and items 42-62 by EPL Ltd. At the time of the change the
production pipe-line was simply diverted, and several of the EPL
titles carry Nicholson and Watson credits.

Section D: William Campion

1 RONALD DUNCAN Jan's journal Jun. 1949
    Jacket and drawings by Betty Swanwick.

2 ILIAS VENEZIS Aeolia Dec. 1949
    Preface by Lawrence Durrell.

3 MAURICE SANDOZ The house without windows
    Nov. 1950
    Jacket and drawings by Salvador Dali.

4 RICHARD MARCH The sentinel May 1951
    A playscript.

5 RICHARD MARCH The darkening meridian
    Sep. 1951
    A revised edition of a book first published by
    The Fortune Press in 1943.

NOTE:
William Campion (William – the son of Richard March; Campion
– the maiden name of Betty Jesse, one of the PL staff) was
created as a subsidiary imprint to be devoted to 'general fiction'.
After Tambi's departure March concentrated on Mandeville and
Campion became of minor relevance.

Section E: Mandeville Publications

1 MARTIN CLIFFORD **Tom Merry & Co. of St. Jims**
   May 1949

2 J. RADFORD-EVANS **The hoax of a lifetime**
   May 1949

3 MARTIN CLIFFORD **The secret of the study**
   Oct. 1949

4 FRANK RICHARDS **Tom Merry's Annual (No. 1)**
   Nov. 1949

5 J. RADFORD-EVANS **Girls will be girls** Dec. 1949

6 GEOFFREY WEBB **Prince of the furies** Jan. 1950

7 MARTIN CLIFFORD **Rallying around Gussy**
   May 1950

8 J. RADFORD-EVANS **Once upon an island**
   Jul. 1950

9 FRANK RICHARDS **Jack of all trades** Jul. 1950

10 J. RADFORD-EVANS **Brenda Dickson's Annual**
   Sep. 1950

11 FRANK RICHARDS **Tom Merry's own Annual**
   (No. 2) Sep. 1950

12 GEOFFREY WEBB **Prince has five aces** Oct. 1950

13 H. OHLSON **Scourge of the mountains** Nov. 1950

14 MARTIN CLIFFORD **The scapegrace of St. Jims**
   Jun. 1951

15 MARTIN CLIFFORD **Talbot's secret** Sep. 1951

16 OWEN CONQUEST **The rivals of Rookwood
   school** Sep. 1951

17 FRANK RICHARDS **Tom Merry's own Annual
   (No. 3)** Sep. 1951

18 FRANK RICHARDS **Tom Merry's own Annual
   (No. 4)** Sep. 1952

19 FRANK RICHARDS **Billy Bunter's own Annual
   (No. 1)** Sep. 1953

20 FRANK RICHARDS **Tom Merry's own Annual
   (No. 5)** Sep. 1953

21 FRANK RICHARDS **Billy Bunter's own Annual
   (No. 2)** Sep. 1954

22 FRANK RICHARDS **Tom Merry's own Annual
   (No. 6)** Sep. 1954

23 FRANK RICHARDS **Billy Bunter's own Annual
   (No. 3)** Oct. 1955

NOTE:

Mandeville (named after the hotel which was the venue of the monthly luncheon meetings of Tambi and T. S. Eliot) was created as a subsidiary imprint to be devoted to 'juvenile publications'. Many of the titles were by Charles Hamilton under his various pseudonyms — Frank Richards, Martin Clifford and Owen Conquest. After the departure of Tambi Mandeville became the dominant PL operation. Mandeville survived the demise of Editions Poetry London and continued until the death of Richard March.

Section F: Poetry London Apocrypha

When Editions Poetry London Ltd was formed in Sep 1947 the link with Nicholson and Watson was broken Three of Tambi's productions remained in the NW pipe-line and were eventually published by NW. Sven Berlin's **Alfred Wallis** (which languished for 5 years in type) has a reference to Poetry London on the title page and is therefore accorded a place in Section C. The other titles contain no reference to PL:

1 WYNDHAM LEWIS **America and cosmic man**
   Jul. 1948

2 S. W. HAYTER **Jankel Adler** Nov. 1948

Tambi spent £8000 on having the blocks made for a monograph on Ben Nicholson (text by Sir Herbert Read). Further finance was not available to progress the book, and in order to ensure that the book could be published Tambi sold the blocks to Lund Humphries The book was published in Nov. 1948 and it contains an acknowledgement of the conceptual role played by Tambi and Editions Poetry London.

In 1946 Tambi and Robin Waterfield purchased a printing press from Douglas Cleverdon and several modest publications and ephemeral items came off this press. Some of the items carry the imprint 'The Hog in the Pound Press' — a name that derived from the hostelry that was frequented by the PL staff. For further information reference should be made to the article by Selwyn Kittredge.

A Victoria and Albert Museum lecture programme, printed by Tambimuttu at The Hog in the Pound Press

The Indian Dance: a lecture & demonstration by RAM GOPAL

To mark the opening of an exhibition THE HUMAN FORM IN INDIAN ART at the INDIAN SECTION, VICTORIA AND ALBERT MUSEUM

Ram Gopal was born in 1918 at Bangalore, South India, and started dancing at the age of six. His father, a well known Sanskrit scholar, was a Rajput; his mother, Burmese. He specialises in the Tandava (masculine) style of the Barata Natya and Kathakali techniques, which he learnt under M.S.Pillai, Chandapanikar, Kunju Kurup, the greatest living dance masters of South India. Later he made a special study of Kathak, Manipuri and other northern schools of folk and classical tradition. He has toured in China, Japan, Java and the Philippines. In 1937 he toured the United States of America, and the following year visited Europe with his own company, performing in London, Paris and Berlin. This is his first post-war appearance in Europe.

PROGRAMME

Ram Gopal will begin with a talk on the traditional schools of Indian dancing. This will be followed by a demonstration of the following styles and techniques:

Bharata Natya, Kathak, Manipuri, Kathakali.

Printed by Tambimuttu at The Hog in the Pound Press, 40 Crawford Street W.1

ection G:Unfulfilled Promises

)Y CAMPBELL (tr) The complete works of Garcia
   Lorca

\URICE CARPENTER John Nameless and other
   ballads

ITH DOUGLAS Bete noire

:RRE EMMANUEL Tombeau d'Orphee

\UM GABO Art monograph

:NRY JAMES The turn of the screw
   Illustrations by Phillipe Julian.

JGUSTUS JOHN Drawings
   With essay by Lord David Cecil

:RRE JEAN JOUVE Defense et illustration

:RRE JEAN JOUVE Le Don Juan de Mozart

:RRE JEAN JOUVE Poems

VNDHAM LEWIS Absolutism and the writer

\ED MARNAU The collected poems

:NRY MILLER Hamlet: vols. 1 & 2

E. MOORE A defence of common sense and other
   essays

JGUES PANNASSIE The real jazz

JGUES PANNASSIE Twelve years of jazz

:RA POUND (tr) Confucius

\THLEEN RAINE Faces of day and night

*\ jacket by William Stobbs for one of the 'unfulfilled
romises'*

APPASSIONATA

POEMS 1936-1946

FRANCIS SCARFE

PL

KATHLEEN RAINE A place and a state
   Illustrations by Julian Trevelyan

ANGEL DEL RIO Federico Garcia Lorca

JAMINI ROY Art monograph

FRANCIS SCARFE Appassionata

MATTHEW SMITH Art monograph

GRAHAM SUTHERLAND Sketchbook 1936-42

BETTY SWANWICK The hoodwinked boy

JOHN TUNNARD Art monograph

JOSE GARCIA VILLA Poems

VIC VOLK A Canterbury tale

NOTE:

Several promises were deliberately omitted from the 'definitive'
trade catalogue of Mar. 1948. For interest these are appended.

DAVID GASCOYNE (ed) Allegories and emblems

FRANCIS SCARFE Ode to Christ

DYLAN THOMAS Adventures in the skin trade

DYLAN THOMAS Poems

POETRY LONDON:1939-1951
Published Source Material

1 D. J. ENRIGHT The significance of Poetry London
    The Critic No. 1 Mistley, Essex Spring 1947.

2 R. C. ARCHIBALD The Ceylon poet — Thurairajah
    Tambimuttu
    Mary Mellish Archibald Memorial Library Bulletin
    Vol. 5 No. 7 Mount Allison University, New
    Brunswick April 1955

3 J. MACLAREN-ROSS Memoirs of the forties
    Alan Ross London 1965

4 ANTHONY DICKINS Tambimuttu and Poetry
    London
    GAVIN EWART Tambi the great
    London Magazine Vol. 5 No. 9 London Dec. 1965
    Also Feb./May 1966 issues for letters from Ronald
    Bottrall and Robin Waterfield.

5 T.L.S. reviewer Interment of the intellectual
    Times Literary Supplement London 19 Feb. 1971
    Also 26 Mar. 1971 issue for letter from Nicholas
    Moore.

6 SELWYN KITTREDGE Mr Tambimuttu's birthday
    books
    Papers of the Bibliographical Society of America
    Vol. 67 Second Quarter 1973.

7 TAMBIMUTTU Fitzrovia
    Harpers and Queen London Feb. 1974.

8 JANE WILLIAMS Tambimuttu profiled
    New Style No. 5 London 1977.

ADDITIONS AND CORRECTIONS

Section E
The Mandeville check-list should also include:
11A LESLIE COMPTON (ed) **The Denis Compton
Annual** Oct. 1950.

Section F
The Hog in the Pound Press 'published' several modest
publications and ephemeral items, but the actual printing
press that had been transferred from Douglas Cleverdon's
premises in Bristol was incomplete and recourse had to
be made to jobbing printers. However, Tambi was
responsible for some of the type-setting (including the
V & A lecture programme).
E. E. Cummings' **1 x 1** had been printed and was in the
final stage of binding when the poet declared that there
were errors in the spacing of the text, and asked for the
type to be reset. Tambi took the view that the errors were
of minute proportions and inconsequential, and refused to
go to the expense of starting again. Cummings' response
was to offer the book to Cyril Connolly, and it was
eventually published by Horizon in October 1947.

Published Source Material
Tambi's article 'Fitzrovia' appeared in the February 1975
(not 1974) issue of *Harpers and Queen*.

Alan Smith
November 1979

ADDENDUM
Compiled by Jane Williams

LYREBIRD PRESS BOOKS: 1972–1982

General

RAMMURTI S. MISHRA **Fundamentals of yoga**
(HB) 1972.
RAMMURTI S. MISHRA **The textbook of yoga
psychology** (HB) 1972.
HUGH PRATHER **Notes to myself** (HB and PB)
1972.
GARY LIVINGSTON **Exile's end** (HB) 1973.
R.E.L. MASTERS **The hidden world of erotica**
(HB) 1973.
JOSEPH CHILTON PEARCE **The crack in the
cosmic egg** (HB) 1973.

Editions Poetry London Series

WITTER BYNNER (tr) **The way of life accord-
ing to Lao Tzu.** Illustrated by Frank Wren (HB and
PB) (PL 2) 1972 (First published 1944 by Editions
Poetry London).

PRITISH NANDY (tr) **Poems from Banglades**
the voice of a new nation. Selected by Tambimu
tu, illustrated by Feliks Topolski (HB and PB) (als
limited edition) (PL 1) 1972.
ANNE RIDLER **The jesse tree: a masque i**
verse. Illustrated by John Piper (HB and PB) (als
limited edition) (PL 3) 1972 (the limited edition w
the winner of the Silver Eagle at the Nice Inte
national Book Fair in May 1973).

Microdot Series

ROBERT SHURE **Twink.** Ilustrations by Ra
Zimmerman. (PB) (Microdot Book 2) 1972.
TAMBIMUTTU (ed) **Festschrift for KFB.** (H
and PB) (also limited edition of 100 plus :
presentation copies) (Microdot Book 1) 1972.
BENOY CHAKRABORTY **Watermarks.** Illu
trations by Frank Connelly. (HB and PB) (Microd
Book 3) 1973.

CALDER & BOYARS/LYREBIRD PRESS

RAFAEL MARTINEZ NADAL **Lorca's the pu**
lic: a study of his unfinished play *El Público* an
of love and death in the work of Federi
García Lorca. 1974.

OTHER PL BOOKS (not Lyrebird Press)

VICTORIA ROTHSCHILD **Bin ends.** Cov
illustration by Gerald Wilde. Editions Poetry Lo
don, 1980.
TAMBIMUTTU (tr) **India love poems.** Illu
trated by John Piper. De luxe edition published
Paradine 1977 (original edition published by Pet
Pauper Press in United States).
Theatre of all possibilities. Cover illustration
Zara Kriegstein, with lettering by Berthold Wolf
Editions Poetry London, 1980.

POETRY LONDON/APPLE MAGAZINE N
1. Edited by Tambimuttu. Cover illustration: Lyr
bird design by Graham Sutherland (also a limit
edition). Mather Brothers, Preston, 1979.
POETRY LONDON/APPLE MAGAZINE N
2. Edited by Tambimuttu. Cover illustration: Lyr
bird design by John Piper. London, 1982.

To Faith

Faith causeth Agni to burn
Faith giveth oblation:
Praise we faith, of happiness the highest.

Bless thou the giver, Faith,
Bless the would-be giver,
Bless the liberal worshippers,
Bless the song I raise.

As the new gods honour the old gods,
May my new worship honour the liberal worshippers,
Whom the wind-god Vayu shieldeth.

Faith maketh gods and men to kneel,
Faith maketh worship;
Yearning maketh faith, bringer of riches.

Faith maketh prayer,
Faith in the morning, faith at noontide,
Faith at the setting of the sun.

O Faith, give us faith.

Transcreated from the Sanskrit
by P. Lal
(Rig Veda : Mandala X Song 151)

The drawings on this and the following page are by Denton Welch; used as decorative tailpieces in *Poetry London*, Volume 2 Number 9, they are reproduced here slightly larger than in the original. © Poetry London [1943].

POETRY

LONDON

THE LYRE BIRD

Moore
42.

Nº ELEVEN

THREE-SHILLINGS & SIXPENCE

NICHOLSON & WATSON